PRAY
FOR THE DYING

Quintin
Jardine

PRAY
FOR THE DYING

headline

First published in 2013 by
HEADLINE PUBLISHING GROUP

1

Cataloguing in Publication Data is available from the British Library

978 0 7553 5698 0 (Hardback)
978 0 7553 5699 7 (Trade paperback)

Typeset in Electra by Avon DataSet Ltd, Bidford-on-Avon, Warwickshire

Printed in the UK by CPI Group (UK) Ltd, Croydon, CR0 4YY

Headline's policy is to use papers that are natural, renewable and
recyclable products and made from wood grown in sustainable forests.
The logging and manufacturing processes are expected to conform to the
environmental regulations of the country of origin.

HEADLINE PUBLISHING GROUP
An Hachette Livre UK Company
338 Euston Road
London NW1 3BH

www.headline.co.uk
www.hachette.co.uk

For Eileen, for ever, or as close to that as we can manage.

PreScript

From the *Saltire* newspaper, Sunday edition:

Strathclyde Chief Constable believed dead in Glasgow Concert Hall Shooting

By June Crampsey

Mystery still surrounds a shooting last night in Glasgow's Royal Concert Hall in which a woman was killed in a VIP seat at a charity concert, inches away from Scotland's First Minister, Clive Graham MSP. The identity of the victim has still to be confirmed officially, but it is believed that she was Antonia Field, the recently appointed Chief Constable of the Strathclyde Force, the second largest in the UK after London's Met.

The killing was carried out by two men, who were themselves shot dead as they tried to escape, after murdering a police officer and critically wounding another.

A security cordon was thrown round the hall immediately after the incident, but reporters could see what appeared to be three bodies outside in Killermont Street, one of them in police uniform. A fourth man, said to be a police officer, was taken

1

away by ambulance, and a spokesman for Glasgow Royal Infirmary confirmed later that he was undergoing emergency surgery for gunshot wounds.

Edinburgh Chief Constable Bob Skinner, husband of Scottish Labour leader Aileen de Marco who was a guest of the First Minister at the fund-raiser, took command at the scene. Briefing media in Glasgow City Chambers, he refused to name the victim, but did say that it was not his wife, nor was it the woman who had accompanied her to the concert, believed to be Edinburgh businesswoman Paula Viareggio, the partner of another senior police officer in the capital, Detective Chief Superintendent Mario McGuire.

Most of the eyewitnesses refused to speak to journalists as they were ushered away from the concert hall. Many seemed to be in shock. However, world-famous Scottish actor Joey Morocco, Master of Ceremonies for the evening, told the *Saltire* as he left, 'There was complete confusion in there.

'The conductor, Sir Leslie Fender, had just raised his baton and the house lights had dimmed when I heard three sounds that I know now were shots, one after the other. Then everything went completely dark, pitch black, and someone started screaming.

'Before that, though,' Mr Morocco continued, 'I was standing in the wings and I was facing the audience. In the second or two before the lights went out, as the shots were fired, I saw movement in the front row. There were three women on the First Minister's left.

'Aileen, she's a friend, by the way, she was sat furthest away from him, then her companion, Paula, and then the lady who'd arrived with Mr Graham. I don't know her name, but somebody

2

said she's the chief constable. I saw her jerk in her seat then start to fall forward. That's when the lights went out.

'The emergency lighting came on automatically, after a few seconds. It wasn't much good, but I could make out that the seat next to the First Minister was empty and that there was a shape on the floor.

'There was panic after that. I heard Mr Graham shouting for help, then I could just make out a policeman rushing forward. I think it was Mr Allan, the assistant chief constable. I tried to use the mike but it was useless with the power being out, so I jumped up on to the conductor's podium and yelled to everyone to stay in their seats and stay calm until the lighting was restored. But the people in the rows nearest the front, some of them realised what had happened and they started to panic.

'Mr Graham was brilliant. He stood up, called out to everyone to stay where they were, for their own safety. It was an incredibly brave thing to do,' Mr Morocco added. 'He might have been the target himself and the gunman might still have been there, but he put himself right in the line of fire, then he took off his jacket and put it over the woman on the floor. That's when I knew for sure that she was dead.

'Thing is,' he explained, 'she was wearing a red dress. Normally at a big public event Aileen wears red, her party colours, but last night, for some reason, she didn't. So I'm wondering if she was the intended target and whether the gunman just made a mistake.'

Addressing journalists in a hastily convened briefing in the Glasgow City Council Chambers, after being asked by the First Minister to take charge of the situation, Mr Skinner refused to comment on Mr Morocco's speculation.

'It's way too early to be making any assumptions,' he said firmly. 'We believe we know who the shooters were, but we're a long way from understanding their motives.'

Asked whether Al Qaeda might be involved, he replied, 'I'm not ruling that out, but the gunmen were not Muslim and the nationality of a third person involved in the plot makes that highly unlikely. However, I can tell you that this was a well-planned operation carried out by people with special skills.

'We've been able to establish already that the hall was blacked out by an explosion that took out the electricity substation serving the building. It was remotely detonated as soon as the shots had been fired. We're also sure that the two men gained entrance to the building dressed as police officers, and ditched their disguises before trying to escape.'

He refused to go into detail on how they had been killed, or by whom.

When I spoke to him later, by telephone, he explained that neither of the victims could be identified before their next of kin had been told. He added that the First Minister was under close protection at his home, and that his wife was also being guarded at a secret location.

One

'I put Paula in harm's way, Mario,' Bob Skinner murmured, as he gazed at his colleague, their faces pale in the glare of the freestanding spotlights that had been set up to illuminate the scene. 'I am desperately sorry.'

Never before had Detective Chief Superintendent McGuire seen his boss looking apprehensive, and yet he was, there could be no mistaking it.

'How exactly did you do that, sir?' he replied, stiffly. 'Your wife invited my wife to chum her to a charity concert. Given that Aileen is a former and possibly future First Minister of our country, most people would regard that as something of an honour.'

'Someone tried to kill her,' Skinner hissed. 'There was intelligence that a hit was being planned. You know that; I knew it. I was asleep at the fucking wheel, or I'd have considered that as a possibility.'

'Then it was Paula that saved her life, Bob,' McGuire pointed out, more gently. 'If she hadn't told Aileen that she was wearing a red outfit, on account of her being so pregnant it was the only thing that would fit, then Aileen would have worn her usual colour.'

The chief constable frowned. 'But Paula isn't wearing red.'

'No, she found something else. Thank your lucky stars again that she didn't think to tell Aileen about it. Stop beating yourself up, man.

Nobody's going to blame you for anything, least of all me. Paula's all right, she's off the scene, and that's an end of it.'

Skinner nodded towards the splayed body, a few yards away from where they stood, in front of the auditorium stage of Glasgow's splendid concert arena. 'She would blame me, if she could.' He put a hand to an ear. 'If I listen hard enough I reckon I'll hear her. Five minutes, that's all it would have taken. If we'd got to our informant five minutes earlier . . .'

'You'd probably have been caught in traffic,' his colleague countered, 'and got here no quicker. Okay, if the Strathclyde communications centre hadn't been on weekend mode, you might have got the word to ACC Allan and prevented the hit . . . but they were and you didn't.'

'Speaking of old Max,' Skinner murmured, 'how is he? I didn't have time to talk to him when he met us at the entrance. "She's dead," he said. That was all. I assumed it was Aileen. I didn't wait to hear any more. I just charged inside and left him there.'

'He's wasted; complete collapse. When I got there he was sitting on the steps in the foyer with his face in his hands. He had blood on them; it was all over his face, in his hair. He was a mess.' He paused. 'The guy you were with, the fellow who took Paula and Aileen away. I only caught a glimpse of him. Who is he?'

'His name's Clyde Houseman. Security Service; Glasgow regional office.'

'He's sound?'

'Oh yes.' Skinner's eyes flashed. 'Do you think for a minute I'd entrust our wives' safety to him if I wasn't sure of that? I told him to take them to the high security police station in Govan and to keep them there till he heard from me. And before you ask, there's a doctor on the way there to check Paula out, given that she's over eight months gone.'

'But she was fine, as far as you could see?' McGuire asked, anxiously.

'Yes, like I said. Obviously, she got a fright at the time . . . not even Paula's going to have the woman in the seat next to her shot through the head without batting an eyelid . . . but when I got to her she was calm and in control. Far more concerned about Toni Field than about herself.'

'Did she see . . .'

'Not much. Even when the emergency lighting came on, it wasn't far short of pitch dark, and Clive Graham got between her and the body, and made his protection officers rush her and Aileen out of there, into the anteroom where I found them. Aileen screamed bloody murder, of course.'

'Was she in shock?'

'Hell no. It wasn't from fright. She just didn't want to leave. I'm a cynic where politicians are concerned, and my wife's no different from any of them, maybe worse than most. She wanted to be seen here alongside Clive Graham, who appears to have been a complete fucking hero. He'll get the headlines and Aileen was livid that she'll be seen as a weak wee woman, hiding behind her husband. I wasn't fucking wearing that, mate. I told Houseman to get them out of there, regardless of what she wanted, and I sent Graham's people back to do their job.' He grunted. 'You know that actor guy, Joey Morocco? Didn't he turn up on the bloody scene while all this was going on, demanding to know that Aileen was all right!'

'Morocco? The movie star? What's his interest in Aileen?'

'The very question I put to him, but she said they were old friends. News to me, but they were all over each other. I might as well not have been here. He offered to take the girls to his place, but I told him that unless it was bomb-proof like the Govan nick, that wouldn't be a starter. Then I told him to clear out, with the rest of the civilians.'

'How long are you going to keep them there?'

The chief constable's eyebrows rose. 'Christ, Mario, I haven't thought that far ahead. I've been here for twenty-five minutes, that's all, trying to keep this crime scene secure till the forensic team arrive. Anyway, this isn't our patch. That's an operational decision for . . .'

'Indeed.'

Both police officers turned towards the newcomer. McGuire, irked by the interruption, frowned, but Skinner knew the voice well enough. 'Clive,' he murmured in greeting, as the First Minister stepped into the silver light, with his two personal protection officers no more than a yard behind him. He was tartan-clad, waistcoat and trousers, but no jacket. The chief constable guessed that garment was draped over the body of Toni Field.

The woman had been his arch-enemy. She had been a surprise choice as head of the Strathclyde force, a job for which he had declined to apply, in spite of the entreaties of his wife and of the retiring chief. Most Scots assumed, therefore, that she had been appointed by default, but Skinner recognised the quality of her CV, and even more important its breadth, with success in the Met and England's Serious Crimes Agency added to relevant experience as chief constable of the West Midlands.

She and Skinner had been on a collision course from their first meeting, when it had become clear that Field was in support of the unified Scottish police force advocated by Clive Graham's government, and that she expected to be appointed to lead it, regardless of his own ambitions.

As it happened, those no more included heading Graham's proposed force than they had inclined him towards Strathclyde. Skinner was firmly against the idea, on principle. He had shunned the

Glasgow job because he felt that a force that covered half of Scotland's land mass and most of its population was itself too large.

He had always believed that policing had to be as locally responsible as possible, and when he had discovered a few days earlier that his wife, the First Minister's chief political rival as leader of the Scottish Labour Party, intended to back unification and help rush it through the Holyrood parliament, their marriage had exploded. Aileen had moved back to her flat, ostensibly for a few days, but they knew, both of them, that it was for good.

'How are you?' he asked the First Minister. He had no personal issues with him. His position and that of his party had been clear from the start; his wife's, he was convinced, was based on political expediency, pure and simple.

'In need of another very stiff drink,' Graham replied. 'Yes, I've already had one, but I suspect I'm going to get the shakes pretty soon. What happened . . . it hasn't quite sunk in yet. Please brief me, on everything. I can't get any sense out of the locals, and my protection boys don't know any more than I do.'

Both Skinner and McGuire realised that he was making a determined effort not to look at the thing on the floor.

'Are the ladies safe?' he continued.

'Yes,' Skinner replied.

'The pregnant one? She's . . .'

'My wife,' McGuire whispered.

The First Minister stared at him.

'This is DCS McGuire,' Skinner explained. 'My head of CID. I had promised my kids some attention today, so Aileen invited Paula to use the other ticket.' Not a lie, not the whole truth. 'And yes, thank you. She's okay. Obviously Mario here will be keeping her in cotton wool from now on, but she'll be fine, I'm sure.'

'That's good to hear. Now, do you believe there's a continuing threat?'

'No, I don't, but we shouldn't take any chances.'

'What happened? None of us really knows, Bob. Who was it? Did they get away?'

'It was a professional hit team. Originally there were three, but one of them, the planner, died a few days ago, unexpectedly, of natural causes. The body was dumped in Edinburgh. The other two didn't think for a minute we'd identify him, but we did, and as soon as we knew who he was, we knew as well that something was up. We guessed the venue, but we got the target wrong. We thought they were after the pianist, the guy who was supposed to be playing at this thing.'

'Theo Fabrizzi?'

'Yes. For all his name, he's Lebanese, and he's a hate figure for the Israelis. We didn't find out any of this until the last minute. When we did, we got him out of here. You were probably told he'd been taken ill, but that was bollocks. The guy's a fanatic, a martyr with a piano; he wouldn't back off, so we arrested him and took him away, spitting feathers, but safe.'

'My God,' the First Minister exclaimed. 'Why wasn't I told this at the time?'

'We were too busy sorting the situation out,' Skinner shot back, irritably. 'Or so we thought. And there was another reason,' he added. 'I shouldn't have to tell you that your devolved powers do not include counter-terrorism. That's reserved for Westminster.

'As soon as we identified Cohen, the planner, MI5 got involved, with the Home Secretary pulling the strings. There had been intelligence that a hit was planned in the UK, but no details. With Cohen and his team in Scotland, assumptions were made, and we all bought into the piano player as the target. Then the Home Secretary got brave . . . God save us all from courageous politicians in fucking bunkers in Whitehall, Clive . . . and decided that she wanted her people to catch the rest of the team. She declared that it was a Five operation, and that the police shouldn't be alerted, in case of crossed wires.'

'So how did you get involved?'

'I was in play by that time, having asked them for help in identifying Cohen.'

Graham's face was creased into a frown that made him unrecognisable as the beaming man on the election posters. 'But if . . .' he growled.

Skinner nodded. 'There was someone else involved, the man who supplied the weapons. My MI5 colleague and I got to him,' he paused and checked his watch, 'less than ninety minutes ago. We interrogated him and he told us that from a remark by one of the shooters, when they collected the guns last night, the target was definitely female.

'Obviously that changed everything. At that point . . .' he paused, '. . . well, frankly, it was fuck the Home Secretary's orders. We headed straight through here. I tried to stop the event, but in all this mighty police force, Clive, I could not find anyone willing to take responsibility, until it was too late. You know what happened then.'

'What about the terrorists? Did they escape in all the confusion? Nobody can tell me, or will.'

'They're dead. They were making their escape when we arrived. They'd just shot the two cops manning the door.' He sighed, shuddered for a second, and shook his head. 'Fortunately my Five sidekick was armed or we'd have been in trouble. We didn't negotiate. Captain Houseman killed one. I took down the other one as he tried to run off. But don't be calling these guys terrorists, Clive. They weren't. No, they were . . .'

He broke off as his personal mobile phone . . . he carried two . . . sounded in his pocket. He took it out and peered at the screen, ready to reject the call if it was Aileen spoiling for a renewed fight, but it was someone else. 'Excuse me,' he told the First Minister. 'I have to take this.'

Graham nodded. 'Of course.'

He slid the arrow to accept, and put the phone to his ear, moving a few paces away from the group, skirting Toni Field's body as he did so.

'Hi, Sarah,' he murmured.

'Bob!' she exclaimed. Skinner's ex-wife was cool and not given to panic, but the anxiety in her voice was undeniable.

'Where are you? Are you okay? What's happened? I've just had a call from Mark. He told me he heard a news flash on radio about a shooting in Glasgow, at an event with the First Minister and Aileen. That's the event that she and Paula were going to this evening, isn't it? He says someone's dead and that your name was mentioned. Honey, what is it? Is it Aileen?'

'Shit,' he hissed. 'So soon. They're not saying that, are they, that it's Aileen?'

'I'm not sure what they said but Mark was left wondering if it might be. He's scared, Bob, and most of all he's scared for you.'

'In that case, love, please call him back and calm him down. Yes, I am at the scene, yes, there is a casualty here, and others outside, but none of them are Aileen or anyone else he knows. And it's certainly not Paula. They're both safe.'

'But how about you?' Her voice was strident.

'You can hear me, can't you? I'm okay too. I might not be in the morning, when it all sinks in, but I am fine now, and in control of myself.' As if to demonstrate, he paused then lowered his voice as he continued. 'Are you alone?' he asked. 'Are you at home?'

'Yes, of course, to both.'

'Good. In that case, I need you to do a couple of things. Call Trish,' their children had a full-time carer; their sons had reached an age at which they refused to allow her to be called a nanny, 'and have her take the kids to your place. As soon as you've done that, get hold of my grown-up daughter. I'm guessing she hasn't heard about this yet, or she'd have called me, but Alex being Alex, she's bound to find out soon. She may be at home; if not, try her mobile . . . do you have the number?'

'Yes.'

'Fine, if you can't raise her on either of those, try Andy's place. Tell her what I've told you. I don't have time to do it myself; the fan's pretty much clogged up with shit here.'

'Where will you be?'

'That remains to be seen, but I'll keep you in touch.'

'When will you be out of there?'

'Same answer.'

'When you are,' she told him, 'come here first. It's important that the kids see you as soon as they can.'

'Yes, sure.'

'What about Aileen?'

'What do you mean?' Bob asked.

'Will she be coming back with you?'

'No,' he replied, with a sound that might have been a chuckle or a grunt, 'not even in protective custody. I told you last night, she and I are done.'

He glanced to his right. The First Minister and McGuire had been joined by a youngish man, in a dark suit. Strained though it was, his face was familiar to Skinner, but he found himself unable to put a name to it. Graham caught his eye, and he realised that they were waiting for him to finish his call. 'Now, I must go,' he said.

'Take care,' Sarah murmured.

'Don't I always?'

'No.'

A brief smile flickered on his lips, but it was gone before he returned his phone to his pocket. He rejoined the group, and as he did so he remembered who the newcomer was. They had met at a reception hosted by his wife, during her time as Clive Graham's predecessor in office.

'Bob,' the First Minister began, 'this is . . .'

'I know: Councillor Dominic Hanlon, chair of Strathclyde Police Authority.' He extended his hand and they shook. 'I'm sorry for your loss.'

Hanlon whistled, softly. 'I could say something very inappropriate right now. It's an open secret that you and Toni didn't get on.'

'You've just said it, Mr Hanlon,' Skinner snapped. 'You're right; it's as far from appropriate as you can get. Are you implying I'm glad to see her dead?'

'No, no!' The man held his hands up, in a defensive gesture, but the chief constable seemed to ignore him.

'Colleagues don't always agree,' he went on, 'any more than politicians. Like you two for example; anywhere else you'd be at each other's ideological throats.' He felt his anger grow, make him take the councillor by the elbow. 'Come here,' he growled. He pulled him towards the body on the floor, knelt beside it and removed the covering jacket, carefully.

'This is what we're dealing with here, chum. Look, remember it.' The back of the head was caked red, and mangled where three bullets had torn into it. The right eye and a section of forehead above it were missing and there was brain tissue on the carpet.

Hanlon recoiled, with a howl that reminded the chief constable of a small animal in pain, as he replaced the makeshift cover.

'Poor Toni Field and I might have had different policing agendas,' he said, 'but we each of us devoted our careers to hunting down the sort of people who would do that sort of thing to another human being. You remember that next time you chair your fucking committee.'

'I'm sorry,' the younger man murmured.

'You want to know how I feel?' Skinner, not ready to let up, challenged. 'I feel angry, so walk carefully around me, chum.'

'Yes, of course,' Hanlon said, patting him on the sleeve as if to mollify him. 'Surely, the chances are it wasn't Toni they were after. Everybody outside is saying it's Aileen that's been shot . . . our Aileen, we call her in Glasgow. There's folk in tears out there.'

'I thought it was her myself until the First Minister told me otherwise. Only the people in the front row could possibly know what's really happened and I doubt if any of them do. They all think it's Aileen because that's the natural assumption. I think these people made a mistake, and shot the wrong woman.'

'For God's sake, man!' Graham barked, beside him. 'This is Aileen's husband, don't you realise that?'

'Yes, of course! Sorry.' The councillor seemed to collapse into his own confusion.

Skinner held up a hand. 'Stop!' he boomed. 'Enough. We'll get to that, and to Dominic's theory. First things first.' He turned to McGuire. 'Mario, did you come through here alone?'

'No, boss,' the massive DCS answered. 'Lowell Payne, DCI Payne, our Strathclyde secondee, he's with me. He's outside in the foyer; it was sheer chaos when we arrived, with no sign of anybody in command, so I told him to take control out there, calm people down as best he could, and move them out the other exit, so they wouldn't go past bodies outside.'

The chief nodded. 'Well done, mate. My priority was in here when

15

I arrived. With Max Allan not making any sense, all I could do was get hold of a uniformed inspector and tell him to contain the audience within the hall, until we could be sure that there was no further threat outside. Where is everyone?'

'Payne said he would gather them in the foyer and in the smaller theatre. There's enough back-up lighting for that to be managed safely.'

'Okay, that sounds fine. Now, you shouldn't really be here at all, but you charged through here like a red-taunted bull as soon as you heard your wife might be in danger. Whatever, your priority will always be her. Get yourself off to the Govan police station, pick her up from there and take her home.'

'What about Aileen?' McGuire asked.

'She stays there, till someone in authority says otherwise. Find Clyde Houseman and tell him from me that he takes no instructions from anyone below chief officer rank. On your way, now.'

He turned back to the politicians. 'Now. You two were working up to say something before Dominic here put his foot in it. What was it?'

'We've got a crisis, Bob,' Graham replied. 'Strathclyde is in trouble, and that's putting it mildly. The chief constable is dead, the deputy chief took early retirement a fortnight ago, Max Allan, the senior ACC, has just been taken away in an ambulance with severe chest pains, and the two other ACCs are far too new and inexperienced in post to move into the top job, even on a temporary basis . . . and even without the force facing one of the highest-profile murder investigations it's ever known, as this will become.'

Hanlon nodded, vigorously. 'As you've just pointed out to me, Mr Skinner, graphically, this is a major crime, and even if Toni's killers . . . and the killers of one, maybe two police officers . . . are lying dead in the street outside, the matter isn't closed.'

'Maybe three, maybe four,' Skinner murmured.

The Police Authority chairman blinked. 'Eh?'

'How did they get the uniforms? We don't know that. Did they bring them, or did they take them from two other cops we haven't found yet?'

'My God,' Hanlon gasped. 'I hadn't thought about that.'

'Bob,' the First Minister intervened. 'This investigation needs a leader. This whole force needs a leader and it needs him now. We don't have time for niceties here. I want to appoint you acting chief constable of Strathclyde, pending confirmation by an emergency meeting of Dominic's authority. That will take place tomorrow morning.'

'Me?' Skinner gasped. 'Strathclyde? The force whose very existence I've opposed for years? Is there nobody else? What about Andy Martin? He's head of the Serious Crime and Drug Enforcement Agency. He could do the job.'

Graham shook his head. 'He could, I agree, but everybody knows he's your protégé, not to mention him being your daughter's partner. He'd be seen as second choice, and I can't have that. I need the best man available, and that is you. Please, help me. Your deputy in Edinburgh is more than capable; she can stand in there. Please take the job; in the public interest, Bob, even if it does go against your own beliefs.'

Skinner stared at him. 'You've really boxed me in, man, haven't you?'

'It's not something I'd have chosen to do.'

'No, I believe you. That's the way it is, nonetheless.' He sighed. 'Fuck it!' he shouted, into the darkness of the empty hall.

'Can I take that as a yes?' the First Minister whispered.

Two

'And you've agreed?'

'What else could I do, Andy? The Police Authority meets tomorrow to confirm it formally, and it'll be announced on Monday. But it's for three months, that's all. I've made that clear.'

There was a silence on Andy Martin's end of the line, until he broke it with a soft chuckle. 'Would that be as clear as you've made it to anyone who would listen that you would never take the job under any circumstances?'

'Yes, okay, I have said that,' Skinner conceded. 'But,' he protested, 'who could have predicted these particular circumstances?'

'Nobody,' his best friend conceded. 'That's why the "any" part of it was a mistake. Now let me make a prediction. However hard it was for you to get into the job, it will be harder for you to get out.'

'Nonsense! I said three months and I meant it. They'll be glad to see me go, Andy. The politicians will hate me here; remember, most of them are followers of my soon to be ex-wife.'

'Your what?' Martin exclaimed. 'Come on, Bob. Alex told me you'd had a row over police unification, but I'd no idea it was that serious. You'll get over it, surely.'

'No, we won't. Too much was said, too much truth told. This isn't like when Sarah and I broke up, or you and Karen. We haven't drifted

away from each other like then, we've torn the thing apart. Besides . . .'
He stopped in mid-sentence. 'No, that's for another time. I have things
to do here. First and foremost, I've got a very messy crime scene to
manage. Second, I've got to face the press.'

'Where are you going to do that?'

'I've told the press office to use the City Chambers. Hanlon, the
Police Authority chair, is going to fix it. I could have done it on the
front steps of the concert hall, but I want to move the media, or as
many as I can, away from there, so the people who were in the
auditorium can leave as easily as we can manage. They're having to go
that way, into Buchanan Street, since there are still three bodies lying
in Killermont Street.'

'I know Hanlon; he'll want to sit alongside you.'

'You're right. He's asked if he could, and not only him. Clive
Graham tried it before him. I've told them both that they're not on.
This is the assassination of a high-profile public figure we're dealing
with and I'm damned if I'm having anything that sniffs of political
posturing alongside it.'

'Hah!' Martin exclaimed. 'That's already happened. I've just
seen that Joey Morocco guy vox-popped on telly, outside in
Buchanan Street. The way he tells the story, the First Minister's
something of a hero, standing up in the line of fire when the emergency
lights came back on. Graham's going to have to give himself a gallantry
medal.'

'Stupidity medal more like.' Skinner paused. 'Did Morocco say
who the victim is?'

'No, but he did say it isn't Aileen, or Paula. They are both unhurt,
yes?'

'Yes, fine, I've spoken to them both, before I had them rushed out
of here. Aileen wanted to stay and wave the red flag, of course.'

'Ouch! Bob, can I do anything? Personally, or through the agency?'

'Yes, you can. I'd like you to take Alex to Sarah's, and stay there with her. I don't believe for a second there's any sort of threat to them, but I'm feeling a bit prickly, and I want all my family under one roof and looked after till I can get to them.'

'I understand. I'll do that. Now, Alex wants to speak.'

Skinner could picture his elder daughter snatching the phone from her partner's hand. 'Dad!' Her voice had the same breathless tone as Sarah's, a little earlier.

'Be cool, kid,' he told her. 'The panic's over; there's no hostage situation or anything like that. Andy will tell you as much as he can. I have things to do and then I have to go to the Royal Infirmary. We have a cop there fighting for his life and I have to see how he's doing. Go now. I'll see you when I can.'

He ended the call and walked back towards the pool of light in front of the stage. The First Minister had been escorted away by his protection officers, and Councillor Hanlon had gone to the Glasgow council headquarters, to have them made ready for the media briefing to come. But Skinner was not standing guard alone.

'I've just spoken to your niece,' he said to Detective Chief Inspector Lowell Payne. 'I didn't tell her you were involved, though, in case she phoned Jean. There's enough anxiety in my family without spreading it to yours.'

There was a personal link between the two men, one that had nothing to do with the job. Ten years after the death of Skinner's first wife, Myra, Alex's mother, Payne had married her sister.

'Thanks, Bob. I appreciate that.'

'Don't mention it. Listen, Lowell, this job I've taken on, temporary or not, I have to be on top of it from the start. That means I need to get up to speed very quickly on the basics of the force, areas where my knowledge may be lacking: its structure, its strengths and its weaknesses, as perceived within the force.

'I'm going to need somebody close to me, to advise me and instruct me where necessary, a sound, experienced guy. You've got twenty-five years plus in the job, all of it in Strathclyde. Will you be my aide, for as long as I need one? Officially, mind; you'll come off CID for the duration and operate as my liaison across the force. You up for it?'

The DCI seemed to hesitate. 'Are you not worried there might be talk, about you and me being sort of related?'

'No, and anyway, we're not. My daughter being your niece does not make you part of my family, or me part of yours.'

'In that case the answer's yes.'

'Good. Now, what's happening outside?'

'Everybody's calm, and they're leaving. They're all potential witnesses, I know, but there's no need to ask them all for contact details, since they're all on a central database. They all booked through the internet, so they all had to leave their details.'

'Good man. Not that we'll need to go back to any of them. None of them can answer any of the questions we need to ask.'

'Those being?'

'Who sent the hit team, and why?'

Payne frowned. 'Why? Does there have to be a why these days, when terrorism is involved, and politicians are the target?'

'Doesn't matter. It's our job to look for it.'

'And mine to help you.'

Skinner turned. He had recognised the voice, from many similar scenes over many years. The man who faced him was clad in a crime-scene tunic, complete with a paper hat that failed to contain the red hair that escaped from it. Looking at him the chief wondered if he would have recognised him in ordinary clothes, or, God forbid, in uniform.

'Arthur,' he exclaimed. 'You're looking as out of water as I feel. What the hell are you doing in Glasgow?'

'You should know, boss,' Detective Inspector Dorward replied. 'You approved the set-up. Ever since forensic services were pulled together into a central unit, we've gone anywhere we're needed and more than that, we've had a national duty rota at weekends. I drew this straw. And bloody busy I've been. I'd not long left a very messy scene in Leith when I got the call to come through here.' He paused. 'But I could ask you the same question. Why are you here?'

'I was following a line of inquiry. It led me here.'

Dorward raised an eyebrow. 'Oh aye,' he drawled. 'I know what that means. So far I've counted four bodies on the ground. Any of them down to you?'

'Just the one.'

Dorward nodded towards the figure under the jacket. 'Not her, though?'

'Definitely not. Now don't push your luck any further, Arthur.'

'Fair enough, Chief; in return, you get your big feet off my crime scene.' He looked at Payne. 'And you.' He paused. 'Here, weren't you at Leith?'

The Strathclyde DCI nodded.

'Then what the fuck's going on here? What's the connection?'

'Never mind that,' Skinner told him. 'This is what matters. For openers, we need you to recover the bullets that killed our victim here, for comparison with the ones that were recovered from the two bodies in Leith.'

'Are you saying they'll be the same?'

Skinner nodded.

'And if they're not?'

'Then we're all going to find out how deep shit can get. Go to work, Arthur.'

'Errr . . .' a deep contralto voice exclaimed from the relative darkness beyond the floodlights, 'can we just hold on a minute here?'

Its owner stepped into the bright light. She was tall, around six feet, and wore, over an open-necked white shirt, a dark suit that did nothing to disguise the width of her shoulders. Her hair was dark, swept back from a high forehead, her eyes were a deep shade of blue, but her nose was her dominant feature. A warrant card was clipped to the right lapel of her jacket.

She eyed Skinner, up and down, no flicker of recognition on her face. 'So who the hell are you, to be giving orders at my crime scene?' she asked, slowly.

The chief constable took his own ID from a pocket and displayed it. She looked at it, then shrugged.

'That doesn't answer my question,' the woman retorted. 'That says Edinburgh. Okay, the earth might have moved for me last night, but not that much. As far as I know, this is still Strathclyde.'

Payne took half a pace forward. 'Cool it, Lottie. This is Chief Constable Bob Skinner, and you know who I am.'

She frowned at him. 'Sure, I know who you are. You're a DCI and you're in strategy. I'm serious crimes, which this as sure as hell is, from what I was told and what I saw outside. That puts me in command of this crime scene.' She nodded sideways, in Skinner's general direction. 'As for our friend here . . .'

'Sir,' Payne sighed, 'I must apologise to you, on behalf of the Strathclyde force. My colleague here, DI Charlotte Mann, she's got a reputation for being blunt, and sometimes she takes it to the point of rudeness. Lottie, get off your high horse. We know what's happened here . . .'

'I don't,' she snapped back. 'I know there's a dead cop outside in Killermont Street, and two other gunshot victims, but I don't know how they got there. I don't know who's under that jacket . . .'

'You'd better take a look, then,' Skinner told her.

'You speak when you're spoken to . . . sir. And don't be trying to tell me my job.' She stepped across to the body.

'Be careful over there,' the blue-suited Dorward warned, but she ignored him as she lifted the jacket from the prone form.

'Bloody hell!' she exclaimed as she observed the shattered head. She peered a little closer, then looked over her shoulder, at Payne. 'Lowell,' she murmured 'is this . . . ?'

He nodded.

'And the two men outside?'

He nodded again. 'The shooters.'

'So you see, Inspector,' Skinner said. 'We do know what's happened here.'

The DI glared at him. 'You might, chum, but the procurator fiscal doesn't, and it's my job to investigate these incidents and report to her. So you can shove your Edinburgh warrant card as far as it'll go. It means nothing to me. As far as I'm concerned, you're just another witness, and for all I know you might even be a suspect. My team should all be here within the next few minutes. Do not go anywhere; they will be wanting to interview you.'

'Aw, Jesus!' Payne laughed, out loud. 'I've had enough of this.' He glanced at Skinner. 'May I, sir?'

'You'd better,' the chief conceded. He moved aside, letting the DCI step up to his CID colleague and whisper, urgently and fiercely in her ear, then catching her eye as she looked towards him, nodding gently, in answer to her surprise.

She walked towards him. 'They didn't waste any time filling the chair,' she said.

'They . . . they being the First Minister and the Police Authority chair . . . felt that they didn't have a choice. I was asked and I accepted: end of story. It'll be formalised on Monday, but as of now you take orders from me and anyone else I tell you to.' He paused. 'Now, Inspector, tell me. How are your traffic management skills?'

Lottie Mann held his gaze, unflinching. 'The traffic will do what I fucking tell it, sir,' she replied, 'if it knows what's good for it. But wouldn't that be a bit of a waste?'

Skinner's eyes softened, then he smiled. 'Yes, it would,' he agreed, 'and one I don't plan to have happen. I know about you, Lottie. ACC Allan told us all about you, at a chief officers' dinner a while back.'

For the first time, her expression grew a little less fierce. 'What did he say?' she asked.

'He said you were barking mad, a complete loose cannon, and that you were under orders never to speak to the press or let yourself be filmed for TV. He told us a story about you, ten years ago, when you had just made DC, demanding to box in an interdivisional smoker that some of your male CID colleagues had organised, and knocking out your male opponent inside a minute. But he also said you were the best detective on the force and that he put up with you in spite of it all. I like Max, and I rate him, so I'll take all of that as a recommendation.'

Mann nodded. 'Thank you, sir. Actually it was inside thirty seconds. Can I take your statement now . . . yours and the guy I was told you arrived with?'

The chief grinned again. 'Mine, sure, in good time. My colleague, no. His name won't appear in your report and he won't be a witness at any inquiry.'

'Spook?'

'Spook. That reminds me.' He turned to Payne. 'Lowell, there is bound to be at least one CCTV camera covering the Killermont Street entrance. I want you to locate it, them if there are others, and confiscate all the footage from this afternoon. When we have it, it goes nowhere without my say-so.'

'Yes, sir.'

As the DCI left, Skinner led Mann away from the floodlight beam and signalled to Dorward that he and his people could begin their work. He stopped at an auditorium doorway, beneath a green exit sign and an emergency lamp.

'Lottie, this is the scenario,' he said. 'On the face of it, a contract hit has taken place here. I can tell you there have been rumours in the intelligence community of a terrorist attempt on a British political figure. So, it's being suggested there's a possibility Chief Constable Field was mistaken for the real target: my wife, Aileen de Marco, the Scottish Labour leader. Aileen usually wears red to public functions. This evening she didn't, but Toni Field did.'

'That suggestion's bollocks,' she blurted out. 'Sir.'

His eyebrows rose. 'Why?'

'A couple of reasons. First, and with respect . . .'

The chief grinned. 'I didn't think you had any of that.'

'I do where it's deserved. I know about you too. And I know about your wife. She's my constituency MSP, and she's a big name in Glasgow, even in Scotland. But not beyond. So, killing her, it's hardly going to strike a major blow for Islam, is it?'

'Go on.'

'Okay. You say this is a contract hit. So, let's assume that the two guys outside weren't amateurs, however dead they might be now.'

'Far from it. They were South African mercenaries, both of them.'

'Right. That being the case, they're going to have seen photographs of their target. Your wife is about five eight and blonde. Toni Field was five feet five with her shoes on and she had brown hair. But even more important, Aileen de Marco is white, and Chief Constable Field was dark-skinned. These people knew exactly who they were here to kill, and they didn't make a mistake. That's my professional opinion. Sir.'

Skinner gazed at the floor, then up, engaging her once again. 'And mine too, Detective Inspector,' he murmured. 'But let's keep it to ourselves for now. The media can run with whatever theories they like. We won't confirm or knock down any of them. Tell me,' he added, 'what did you think of Toni Field?'

'Honestly?'

'I don't believe you could tell it any other way.'

'On the face of it, she was a role model for all female police officers. In reality, she was a careerist, an opportunist and another few words ending in "ist", none of them very complimentary.

'I liked DCC Theakston, but she had him out the door as fast as she could. I more than like ACC Allan, he's the man I've always looked up to in the force, and she had her knife out for him as well. She might have been a good police officer herself, but she didn't know one when she saw one. I have a feeling that you might.'

'I believe I'm looking at one.' He pushed the door open. 'Come on. You're with me.'

'Where? I'm supposed to be in command here.'

'Mmm. True,' he conceded. 'Okay, get your team together, and give them dispositions. You need to search the building for anything the shooters left behind. The weapon they used was a Heckler and

Koch, standard police issue, so the assumption is, they must have worn uniforms to get in.

'Tell your people to find those, and then find out whether they're authentic. If so, we need to establish whose they were, because we're looking for those owners. Beyond that the work here's for Dorward and his people. Once you've got your people moving, I have to do a press conference, and I want you with me.'

'Me?'

'Absolutely. I think Max was wrong to hide you away. You're a gem, Lottie; the Glasgow press deserve you. Just mind the language, okay?'

Three

'Can I get you coffee?' the Lord Provost of Glasgow asked.

Bob Skinner smiled. 'That's very kind of you,' he replied, 'but given that it's nine o'clock on a Saturday evening, if we accepted you'd either have to make it yourself or nip out to Starbucks. No, the use of your office for this short meeting is generosity enough. Now, if you'll . . .'

Dominic Hanlon took the hint. 'Come on, Willie,' he murmured. 'This is operational; it's not for us.'

'Oh. Oh, aye.' The two councillors withdrew.

The Lord Provost was still wearing his heavy gold chain of office. Skinner wondered if he slept in it.

'Right,' he said, as the door closed. 'We'll keep this brief, but I wanted a round-up before we all left.' He looked to his right, at Lottie Mann, and to his left, at Lowell Payne, who had joined them as the press briefing had closed.

The conference had been a frenzied affair. It had been chaired by the Strathclyde force's PR manager, but most of the questions had been directed at Skinner, once his presence had been explained.

'Can you confirm the identity of the victims, sir?' the BBC national news correspondent had asked. She was new in the country, and new to him, sent up from London to make her name, he suspected.

'Sorry, no,' he had replied, 'for the usual next-of-kin reasons, not operational. However,' he had added, halting the renewed clamour, 'I can tell you that the First Minister is unharmed, as is the Scottish Labour leader, Aileen de Marco, who was also present.'

'Joey Morocco says the victim inside the hall was female, and that she was sitting next to the First Minister.'

'Joey Morocco was there. I wasn't. I'm not going to argue with him.'

'Why isn't the First Minister here?'

'Because he was advised not to be.'

'By you, sir?'

'By his own protection staff.'

'Does that mean there's a continuing threat?'

'It means they're being suitably cautious.'

'There are two men lying in Killermont Street, apparently dead. It's been suggested that they were the killers. Can you comment?'

'Yes they were, and they are both as dead as they appear to be.' Skinner had winced inwardly at the brutality of that reply, but nobody had picked up on it. 'As is the police officer they murdered as they left the hall,' he had continued. 'His colleague is in surgery as we speak.'

'Are you looking for anybody else?'

'You're asking the wrong person. I'm here by accident, remember. That's a question for Detective Inspector Mann of Strathclyde. She's the officer in charge of the investigation.'

Lottie Mann had handled herself well. She had given nothing away, but she had made it clear that the multiple killings at the concert hall would be investigated from origins to aftermath, like any other homicide.

The one awkward question had been put by a *Sun* reporter, with whom Mann had history, after arresting him for infiltrating a crime scene.

'Aren't you rather junior to be running an investigation as important as this one?'

She had nailed him with a cold stare. 'That's for others to decide. I was senior officer on duty tonight and took command at the scene, as I would have in any circumstances.'

'By the way, you did fine in there, Lottie,' Skinner told her, in the Lord Provost's small room. 'You did fine at the scene as well; took command, took no shit from anybody, and that's how it's supposed to be.'

'To tell you the truth, sir,' she confessed, as subdued as he had seen her in their brief acquaintance, 'I was in a bit of a panic when I heard that ACC Allan had been taken away. I hope he's all right.'

'He is,' Payne reassured her, 'reasonably so. I called the Royal on my way down here. They gave him an ECG in the ambulance, and there's no sign of a heart attack. They're going to keep him in, though; apparently his blood pressure's through the roof and he's in shock.'

'How about the wounded man?' the chief asked. 'What's his name, by the way?'

'PC Auger. Still in surgery, but the word is that he'll survive. He was shot in the chest, but the bullet missed his heart and major arteries. It did nick a lung, though, and lodge in his spine.'

'And his colleague?'

'Sergeant Sproule. His body's been taken to the mortuary.'

'Who's seeing next of kin?'

'Chief Superintendent Mayfield,' Payne told him. 'She's divisional commander.'

'Okay. And Toni's next of kin? Was she married? I don't know,' Skinner confessed. 'She and I never got round to discussing our private lives.'

'I don't know either, sir. Sorry.'

'No reason why you should, but raise the head of Human Resources, wherever he is, and find out. Whoever her nearest and dearest is needs to be told, and fast.'

'Yes, they do,' Lottie Mann said, 'because the whole bloody world will soon know she was there if it doesn't already. Chief Constable Field was a big Twitter fan. She posted every professional thing she did on it. No way she won't have tweeted that she was chumming the First Minister to a charity gig.' She scowled. 'I'd ban that fucking thing if I could.'

Skinner whistled. 'Thank God you didn't say that to the press.' He smiled. 'Max Allan would never let either of us forget it. Lowell,' he continued, 'do you know where the other ACCs are?'

'Yes,' he replied. 'I thought you'd need to know that. Bridie Gorman's on holiday, in Argyll, I'm told, but ACC Thomas turned up at the concert hall just after you'd left. He was for taking command, but I told him that he'd better speak to Councillor Hanlon down at the City Chambers. He did, and when he'd done that, he went off in what I can best describe as the huff.'

'Oh shit,' the chief constable sighed. 'That I did not need. I know Michael Thomas through the chiefs' association. He was very much in the Toni Field camp on unification of the forces. In fact, at our last meeting, when things got a bit heated, I told him to shut the fuck up unless he had something original to say.' He smiled. 'Don't worry, though, Lowell. I'll make sure he doesn't hold it against you when I'm gone in three months.' He paused. 'Till then, don't worry about him. You might still be only a DCI in rank, but working directly for me as acting chief, you'll be taking orders from nobody else. Now, have you located the CCTV footage?'

'Yes, sir. There was only one camera, and I'm getting the footage. CCTV monitoring in the city is run by a joint body that's responsible for community safety. Councillor Hanlon and ACC Gorman are on the board, and in a situation like this one, we get what we want. In fact, they were expecting a call from us. Their manager said the monitor person crapped himself when he saw what happened.'

'I'm not surprised.'

'What do you want me to do with it?'

'I want you to keep it close to you. I want to see it on Monday, and obviously Lottie has to have access as senior investigating officer, but, Inspector, you and you alone are to view the footage.'

She frowned. 'What am I going to see there?' she asked.

'I don't know for sure, but if I'm right, I'll be in shot . . . Christ,' he chuckled, 'what have I just said? . . . and so will someone else, with me. If that's so, he is absolutely off limits.' He paused. 'Lottie, I hope you didn't have a big date tonight . . .'

'Only with my husband and son,' she said. 'We were going for a Chinese.'

'Well, I'm sorry about that, but I need you to go back up to the concert hall, resume command, and make sure that everything in this operation is done exactly by the book. By now they'll have found shell casings, probably in one of the lighting booths overlooking the stage, and those two discarded police uniforms. Let's just pray they don't have bullet holes in them.' He gave her a card. 'That's my mobile number. Keep me in touch.'

She smiled. Until then Skinner had not been certain that she knew how. 'Yes, boss. But . . . I'm only a lowly DI. There's a whole raft of ambitious guys above me on the CID food chain, including my two line managers. What do I do when one of them turns up and says he's taking over?'

'One, you ask him why it's taken him so long to get there. Two, you tell him he'd better have a bloody good answer to that question for the acting chief constable, first thing on Monday morning. Thing is, Lottie, Max Allan was the ACC responsible for criminal investigation. He won't be around for a while, and in his absence CID will go straight to me. To be frank, even if he was, that's how it would be. It's the way I work. Questions?'

Payne and Mann shook their heads.

'Good. You know where to get me if you have to. Get on with what you have to do. I'm off to stick my head in the lioness's mouth.'

Four

'You really are a fucking fascist at heart, Bob, aren't you?' she hissed.

'If that's how you want to see me,' he retorted, 'then honestly, I don't give a damn. I got you out of there because there was a belief that you, not Toni Field, was the target of those people. And you know what? If they had shot Paula instead, who was sat between the two of you, Toni would have done exactly the same as I did. She'd have got you out of there, and fast.'

'I should have stayed in the building,' she insisted.

'Why? You're not First Minister any more, Clive Graham is. You were a fucking liability in there, Aileen, somebody else to worry about. I couldn't have that. Plus,' he hesitated for a second, 'you happen to be my wife. I didn't bend any rules to protect you, but believe me, if I'd had to, I would have.'

'That's irrelevant,' Aileen de Marco shouted. 'I should have stayed there. It was my duty; I'm the constituency MSP. I should have been there but instead I'm hiding in this bloody fortress like some kid who's afraid of the dark.'

'No, you were hidden, if you want to put it that way, because there was a chance you might still have been at risk.'

'Does that chance still exist?'

'I don't believe so,' he replied, 'although I can't be certain.'

'But I'm free to leave here?'

'To be honest, you always were. Don't tell me that hadn't occurred to you. But you stayed here. Aileen, you're allowed to be scared! A woman has just been shot dead, a few feet away from you. You may not have noticed this, but her blood is spattered on your dress. The assistant chief constable is in hospital suffering from shock. I am strung out my fucking self! So what's your problem?'

'I was detained, man, against my will. Can't you see that? I'm a politician, and as such I can't be seen to be showing weakness in the face of these terrorists.'

He threw up his hands. 'Okay, Joan of Arc, go. There isn't a locked door between you and the street, and I will arrange for a car to take you wherever you want to go, even if it's back to our place in Gullane.'

'Hah!' she spat. 'The only time I'll be back there is to collect my clothes. I've got somewhere to go tonight, don't you worry, and I will not have a police guard outside the door either.'

Skinner stood. 'You bloody will. You may leave here, but you will have protection, wherever you are. That's Clive Graham speaking, not me. He's ordered it, and I've had arrangements made. For the next couple of days at least, you will have personal security officers looking after you. That is not for debate, but don't worry, discretion is included in their training.'

It had been a casual remark, meaning nothing, but she flushed as he said it and he realised that he had touched a nerve.

'I don't want to know, Aileen,' he murmured.

'As if I care,' she snorted. 'Isn't life bloody ironic? You and I go to war because I'm for police unification and you're against it, yet here you are in command of a force that covers half of Scotland.'

'Temporary command,' he pointed out.

'So you say, but I know you better than that. You may not have volunteered for this job, but now you're in it, you won't want to let it go. Up to now you've chosen your own pond, and been its biggest fish. Now one's been chosen for you, by fate, but your nature will still be the same. Once you get your feet under that desk in Pitt Street, Fettes will never be quite big enough for you again. That's how it will be because that's how you are, like it or not!'

Five

'You might have told me you were goin' to be on the telly, Mum,' Jake Mann mumbled, as he disposed of the last of his cereal. 'I'd have told all my pals to watch.'

'I didn't have much notice of it, Jakey,' Lottie replied. 'Anyway, I wouldn't have wanted you to do that, given the subject.'

'You should have combed your hair.'

She raised an eyebrow and glared at the nine-year-old. 'Maybe, but my hairdresser wasn't available at the time. I could have done with a bit of lippie as well, but the make-up room was in use.'

'You were good, though,' Jake said, reaching for his orange juice.

'Good?' she boomed.

'Brilliant,' he offered. 'Pure dead brilliant.'

'You're getting there, kid.'

'Who was that big man alongside you?'

'That was Mr Skinner. He's from Edinburgh, but he's going to be our chief constable for a while.'

'Is that right?' a voice from the doorway asked.

Lottie turned, and frowned. 'Hey,' she exclaimed, 'the Kraken's awake.'

'The Kraken of dawn,' Scott Mann moaned, as he shambled barefoot into the kitchen, in T-shirt and shorts.

'Dawn? It's half past eight, for Christ's sake.'

'Aye, and you didnae get in till midnight.'

'Sorry, but you saw what happened. Didn't you?'

'Not really. The telly didn't show much. They just said the chief constable was deid, that was all, even though you and the guy Skinner wouldnae say so.' He looked at her as he lifted the kettle to check that it was full, then switched it on. 'Izzat right?'

She frowned. 'It's right.'

'How?'

She nodded towards their son. *'Pas devant l'enfant.'*

'Eh?'

'It means "Not in front of the child", Dad,' Jake volunteered. 'Mum's always saying it so I looked it up on the internet.'

'That's your mother all over, Jakey. She got an O grade in French at the high school, and she thinks she's Vanessa Paradis.'

'Hah, and you'd just love it if I was, sunshine. I'm closer to being her than you are tae Johnny Depp, that's for sure.' She paused. 'He's nearer my height and all.' Her husband was stocky in build but he stood no more than five feet eight. 'Yes, that's a deal, you can have Vanessa and I'll have Johnny.'

'Naw!' Jake protested.

Lottie laughed. 'Chance would be a fine thing, wee man. On you go if you're finished; see what's on CBeebies.'

Their son needed no second invitation to watch television. He grabbed a slice of buttered toast and sprinted from the room.

'So?' Scott asked, as the door closed. 'What did happen?'

'Three bullets in the head from a professional. The thing was very well planned. They blew the power as soon as they'd fired. They shot two cops on the way out . . . Sandy Sproule and Billy Auger . . .'

'Aw, Jesus,' her husband exclaimed. 'I ken Sandy. Is he . . .'

'Yes, I'm afraid so. He died instantly. Billy Auger will live, but they're not sure he'll walk again. Spinal damage.'

'Bastards.'

'Ye can say that again. They'd have got away too, had not Skinner and another bloke arrived just seconds after they'd shot them. I've seen the video. The other guy did for one of them straight away. His buddy ran for it, but Skinner picked up Sandy's carbine and put two rounds through him. Never batted a fucking eyelid either, either on the tape or later, inside the hall. The only thing he was sorry about was that if he'd just wounded the guy he might have given us a clue tae who sent him. But he said that from that range all he could do was aim for the central body mass, as per the training manual. That is one fucking hard man. I couldn't have done that, I'll tell you.'

Scott squeezed her hand. 'You know what, love? I'm glad about that.' The kettle boiled. 'Want another?' he asked.

She handed him her mug. 'Quick one. I've got to be out again. I've had crime scene people workin' all night up at the hall and in Killermont Street. I've set up a temporary murder room, I have to get up there to pull everything together. Killermont Street's still closed to traffic and there's another event due in the hall tonight. Some golden oldie rocker; it's a sell-out and they're desperate not to cancel, so time is, as they say, of the essence.'

Her husband stared at her. 'Can they do that? Just open the place the night as if nothin's happened?'

'As long as they put a patch in the carpet,' she said. 'They won't get the blood and the brain tissue out with bloody Vanish, that's for sure. And they'll have to get joiners in to fix the boards in front of the stage. They had to dig a couple of flattened bullets out of there. They'll maybe keep the lights low all the time, that'll help.'

His eyes widened. 'Imagine. Somebody's goin' to be occupying a seat tonight, and last night a woman was . . . Wow.'

'Ah know,' she agreed. 'It's a bit ghoulish. Listen, Scott, if I could, I would close the hall tonight as a mark of respect. Any polis would. But the hall manager says that people will be coming from all over Scotland to hear this guy. Some'll have left already.'

'Not any polis,' he said.

She looked at him, surprised. 'Come again?'

'Ah still have pals in the job,' he replied, 'even though I've been out for five years. From what they tell me, Antonia Field won't be missed by too many people. A lot of people, me included in my time, liked Angus Theakston, the deputy chief, and I know you did too. It's an open secret that she more or less sacked him. A guy Ah know worked in his office. He says they had a screamin' match one day that folk in Pitt Street could have heard, and that Mr Theakston put his papers in next morning, and was never seen in the office again. She treated old Max Allan like shit too, my pal said. The only one she had any time for was Michael Thomas.'

'He's a fucking weasel,' Lottie muttered. She sipped her tea. 'You never told me any of this before.'

'Ah was told on the QT. You're a senior officer; Ah didn't want to get my pal intae bother.'

'Eh?' she exclaimed. 'Do you actually think that I would come down on a guy because of something you told me?'

'Come on, hen,' he protested, 'you're a stickler and you know it. We used tae work thegither, Ah've seen you in action, remember; been on the receiving end too.'

'Aye,' she retorted, 'and had your own back too. Let's not go there, Scott. Just don't keep anything else from me. Okay?'

'Okay.'

'Good, now I've got to go.'

'When'll you be back?'

'Soon as I can.'

'You've forgotten, haven't you?'

'Forgotten what?'

'We promised Jakey we'd take him to Largs.'

'Bugger!' she swore. 'I'm sorry, Scott.'

'Don't say sorry tae me. Save it for the wee man.'

'Aw, don't be like that. You know what it's like. Look, when I say as soon as I can, I mean it. But I will have to put a report on Skinner's desk first thing tomorrow, ready to go to the fiscal. And I will have to work out where the hell we go from here, given that our new acting chief's gone and killed the only possible bloody witness.'

His expression softened. 'Ah know, love, Ah know.'

She picked up her purse from the work surface and extracted three ten-pound notes. 'Here,' she said. 'Take him wherever he wants to go with that.'

He raised an eyebrow. 'You're takin' a chance, aren't you?'

She frowned. 'I'd better not be.' She headed for the door. 'Have fun, the pair of you. See you.'

Six

The bedroom door creaked as she opened it, jerking him from a dream that he was happy to leave. 'Are the kids awake yet?' Bob mumbled, into the pillow.

'Are you joking?' Sarah laughed. 'It's five past nine.'

Their reconciliation, which had come after a burst of truth-talking only a day and a half before, had taken them both by surprise, but the next morning neither of them had felt any guilt, only pleasure, and possibly even relief.

Their separation and divorce had not been acrimonious. No, it had been down to a lack of communication and each one of them had concluded, independently, that if they had sat down in the right place at the right time and had talked their problems through in the right spirit, it might not have happened at all.

'You what?' Bob rolled over and sat up in a single movement. He was about to swing a leg out of bed, but she sat on the edge, blocking him off.

'Easy does it,' she said. 'They don't know you're here.'

'They'll see my car.'

'No they won't. You parked it a little way along the road, remember.'

'Alex and Andy?'

'They left after you crashed. That was quite an entrance; five

43

minutes to midnight. Your first words, "Gimme a drink," then you polished off six beers inside half an hour.' She paused, then murmured, 'I can always tell, Bob, the more you drink, the worse it's been.'

'I know,' he admitted. 'And the bugger is, the older I get, the less the bevvy helps.'

'So I gather. You did some shouting through the night. It's just as well this house is stone, with thick walls. How do you feel now?'

'My love, I do not know.' He reached out and tugged at the cord of her dressing gown. She slipped out of it, and eased herself alongside him.

She held his wrist, with two fingers pressed below the base of his thumb. 'Your heart rate is a little fast.'

'Probably the dream. It was a bastard.'

'Are you ready to tell me what happened?'

He slipped his right arm around her shoulders. 'I told you last night. Toni Field is dead, and somehow I let Clive Graham talk me into taking her place for three months. Three months only, mind, even though Aileen and Andy both say once I'm there they'll never get me out.'

'Hey,' Sarah murmured. 'Maybe the witch knows you better than I thought.'

'You think so too?' He shook his head, and a slight grin turned up the corners of his mouth. 'And here was me thinking you and I were making a new start.'

'Then let me put it another way. Sometimes you don't know where your duty lies until it's brought home to you. You've been frustrated since you became chief in Edinburgh; I can see that. You were never really keen on the job, without really knowing why. When you were talked into taking it, you found out. It was more or less what you'd been doing before, but it made you more remote from your people and more authoritarian.

'But Strathclyde's different. You've always known why you didn't want that job; you grew up there in a different time and you feel that force is too big, and as such too impersonal. Now that you've been forced into the hot seat by circumstances in which, in all conscience, you couldn't decline, you might find the challenge you've been needing is to change that. You get what I'm saying?'

'Yes.' He paused. 'But I'm a crime-fighter.'

'I know,' she agreed, 'but even Strathclyde CID's remote, isn't it? If you can bring that closer to the people in every one of the hundreds of communities within the force's area, then won't they feel safer as a result, and won't that be an achievement?'

'Okay,' he nodded, 'I can see your argument. Maybe you're right . . . and maybe if this new unified force does happen it'll be even more important to have someone in charge who thinks like I do. But probably you're wrong. The chances are I'll be back in Edinburgh by November. The chances are also that the unification will happen and I'll walk away from it.' He hesitated, and his forehead twisted into a frown. 'That's the way I feel right now.'

'So tell me why,' she whispered. 'Although I think I can guess, having seen this before.'

'I killed someone,' he whispered, 'one of the South Africans. His name was Gerry Botha. He probably didn't murder Toni Field, not personally, but he was part of the team that did: not just her, but three other people in the last forty-eight hours, and God knows how many more in other places, before that. I've shot people before in the line of duty . . .' He sighed. 'Christ, darlin', most cops never handle a firearm, but I'm always in the firing line. At the time it's a decision you have to make in a split second. I've never been wrong, or doubted myself afterwards, but there comes a time when you have to think that however evil the life you've just snuffed out, someone brought it into being.

45

'Gerry Botha and his sidekick Francois Smit, they probably have mothers and fathers still alive, and maybe wives and maybe kids who see completely different men at home and who're not going to have them to take them to rugby and cricket or the movies or to the beach any more, like I did yesterday with ours before all this shit happened, and when I start to play with all that in my head I start to think, "Oh God, perhaps that man wasn't all that different from me, just another guy doing the best he can for those he loves." And that's when it gets very difficult.' He leaned back against the headboard, and she could see that his eyes were moist.

She kissed his chest. 'Yeah, I know, love. That's why you, of all people, understand why I prefer to be a pathologist, rather than to work with people with a pulse. But,' she said, 'if I was a psychologist, I'd be telling you to take that thought and apply it to Botha's victims and to imagine how their nearest and dearest are feeling today, then to ask yourself how they'd feel about you if you'd funked your duty? Toni Field, for example; did she have a family?'

'No, she's never been married,' he told her. 'According to the Human Resources director, her next of kin was her mother, name of Sofia Deschamps. He was able to get the mother's details from her file; he accessed it from home. I'm not too happy about that, but it's an issue for later.

'Mother lives in Muswell Hill; a couple of community support officers broke the news to her last night. Apparently there was no mention of a father on her file. The mother was a single parent, Mauritian. Antonia must have Anglicised the name at some point, or maybe the mother did, for she graduated as Field.'

'I guess now they can confirm that she's the victim.'

'Yeah. The press office is going to issue a statement at twelve thirty, after the Police Authority's emergency meeting. That will ratify my . . .

temporary . . . appointment, and I'll be paraded at another media briefing at one.'

'What about your own Police Authority?'

'Good question. The chairperson's a Nationalist, one of the First Minister's cronies. He was going to talk to her last night, but I'll have to give her a call as well, to ask for her blessing, and to get her to nod through Maggie as my stand-in and Mario's move up to ACC Crime.' He took a breath.

'And I'll have to talk to Maggie myself; I can go and see her, since she doesn't live far away. Then I'll need to call in on Mario . . . not to tell him about his promotion, he knows about that . . . but to see how Paula is the day after. And I suppose I'll have to go to Fettes and change into my fucking uniform . . .'

Sarah rolled out of bed and grabbed her dressing gown from the floor. 'Then what the hell are you still doing lying there? Get yourself showered . . . but don't you dare put my Venus leg shaver anywhere near your chin . . . then dress and come downstairs to surprise our children. I'll make you breakfast and then you can get on the road.'

'Yes, boss.' He grinned.

'You'll see,' she added, 'it'll be good for you, this new challenge.'

'If I'm up to it.'

'That's bullshit. You do not do self-doubt, my love.'

Bob frowned. 'No, you're right, not when it comes to work. In everything else though,' he sighed, 'I'm a complete fuck-up. Three marriages; soon to be two divorces. Are you sure you want to get close to me again?'

She put her hands on his shoulders, and drew him to her. 'Even in our darkest moments,' she whispered, 'even across an ocean, I was never not close to you. You see us? We're each other's weakness and strength all rolled into one. This time, strength comes out on top.'

47

He nodded, stood, took hold of her robe, and kissed her. 'Sounds good to me.'

He headed towards the bathroom, then stopped. 'Will you keep the kids here tonight?'

'Yes. Will you come back here?'

'Mmm. What do you think? Do you want me to, I mean? What will the kids be thinking? This has all happened pretty quick; Aileen being gone, you and me . . .'

'What do I think?' she replied. 'To be brutally honest, I think that Mark won't bat an eyelid, that James Andrew will be pleased . . . he didn't like her and, believe me, I never said a word against her to him . . . and that Seonaid will barely notice she's gone.'

He nodded. 'Okay then. I'll see you later.'

He was stepping into the en-suite when she called after him. 'Hey, Bob?'

He looked over his shoulder. 'Yeah?'

'If you did walk away from the job,' she asked, 'do you have the faintest idea what you'd do?'

'Sure. I could collect non-executive directorships, get paid for sitting on my arse and play a lot of golf, but that wouldn't be my scene. No, if I do that I'll become a consulting detective; I'll become bloody Sherlock.'

Seven

*H*e looks tired and tense, Paula Viareggio thought. *But he also looks more alive than I've seen him in a couple of years.*

'I am perfectly fine, Bob,' she assured him. 'Honestly. The police doctor checked me out last night and he said exactly that. He checked both of us out in fact. The baby's good too. For a while afterwards I did wonder if he'd stick his head out to find out what all the fuss was about, but it seems he's keeping to his timetable.'

'You're some woman, Paula,' Skinner chuckled. They were sitting around a table on the deck of the prospective parents' duplex. The sun was high enough to catch the highlights in his steel-grey hair.

'No, I'm just like all the rest. I had my few moments of sheer terror, and I know I'm never going to lose the memory, of the noise more than anything else, the sound of the bullets hitting the poor woman.'

'Hey, enough,' her husband said quietly.

'No, Mario, it's all right; I yelled my head off at the time, because I was afraid . . . I was scared for two, as well. But once something's happened, it's happened. You can't go back, you can't change it, but the danger's over and talking about what happened won't bring it back. So no worries, big fella; I won't be waking up screaming in the night.'

'I'm glad you feel that way,' the chief constable said, 'because there

49

is a formal murder investigation going on in Glasgow and it would be useful if you could give my DI a statement, for the record.'

'I won't have to go through there, will I? I couldn't be arsed with that.'

'No, of course not. You don't need to leave home. Knock it out on your computer, print it, sign it with Mario as witness, then scan it and send it to DI Charlotte Mann.' He dug a card from his pocket and handed it to her. 'Her email address is on that.'

'Will do. Is Aileen having to do the same?' She paused. 'That is the one thing that gets to me, Bob: the idea that she was the real target.'

'Then don't dwell on it,' he told her. 'Because I don't believe she was, and neither does Lottie Mann.' He looked at his colleague. 'How about you, Mario?'

The swarthy detective shook his head. 'Probably not.'

'But what does Aileen think?' Paula asked.

'I've never been good at working that out,' Skinner replied, 'but whatever she believes, she won't mind having people think she was. There's more votes in it.'

She stared at him, shocked. 'Bob, that's not worthy of you. The poor woman was terrified last night.'

'Maybe, but she was spitting tin tacks when I spoke to her last at the thought of Clive Graham taking credit from it.'

'Get away with you, you're doing her an injustice.'

'I wish I was, but I'm not.' His expression changed, became quizzical. 'Did she tell you anything last night about the two of us?'

Paula hesitated. 'No, she didn't say anything specific; but looking back, there was something about her, something different.'

'We're bust,' he said. 'Sorry to be blunt, but it's over. The press will catch on eventually. When they do, we'll call it "irreconcilable differences". That'll be true, as well.'

'The police unification issue? Mario told me you were at loggerheads about it.'

He nodded. 'That's part of it, but not all. She was planning to turn me into a backroom politician. Aileen has ambitions beyond Scotland that I knew nothing about. She had this daft idea that I would help her fulfil them.' He snorted. 'As if.'

He stood, straightened his back, and smoothed his uniform jacket. 'Now I must go. Wouldn't do if I was late for my unveiling.' He turned to Mario once again. 'Okay, ACC McGuire. I have no idea when I'll see you again, but I'm glad the promotion's come through. It probably won't make any operational difference to you, as you'll still be head of CID under the new structure, but you'll be doing the job from the command corridor, where you've belonged for a while now.'

A smile lit up McGuire's face. 'Thanks, boss.'

'You're out of date. Maggie's the boss, for the next three months. She'll need support though; be sure to give her all you can. And have your people do something for me too.'

'Of course.'

'Freddy Welsh. The armourer, the man that young Houseman and I arrested yesterday. The man who supplied the weapons for the concert hall hit and God knows how many others. Clyde and I didn't have time to ask him all the questions we needed to, but they're still relevant. Technically, it's part of Lottie Mann's investigation, but he's in your hands, so your people should handle the interrogation.

'I want to know who placed the order for the weapons. Was it Cohen, the man who put the operation together, or was it someone else? Somebody sent that team after Toni Field . . . yes, Paula, fact is we're certain she was the target . . . and we must find out who it was and why they did it.'

'I'll handle it myself,' the new ACC said. 'But it's a pound to a pinch of pig shit, Bob; his lawyer will have advised him by now to keep his mouth shut.'

'Then keep his lawyer out of it. Welsh is going away for years for illegal possession of firearms, and conspiracy to supply. We don't need to charge him over his involvement in Field's assassination, so you can interview him as a potential witness, not a suspect.'

'Okay, but I'll bet you he still won't talk. His customers aren't the sort you inform on.'

Skinner smiled. 'If that's how it is, you give him a message from me. If he holds out on us, I won't hesitate to hand him over to MI5, and Clyde Houseman. My young friend made quite an impression on Freddy at their first meeting. I don't think Mr Welsh will be too keen on another session. Now, I really am off.'

McGuire saw him to the door. 'Well,' he said as he rejoined his wife in the sunshine. 'Is this our morning for surprises? The big man enticed to Strathclyde, not to mention him and Aileen being down the road.'

'Indeed,' Paula laughed. 'And maybe get yourself ready for another. When she saw that Joey Morocco last night, before the concert, and it was all going off . . . mmm, that was interesting.'

Mario looked at her, intrigued, reading her meaning. 'She looked like she wanted to eat him, did she?'

'Oh, I think she has, in the past. In fact I know so, 'cos she told me. And I'm pretty certain she fancies another helping.'

Eight

'God, but you're hot stuff when you're angry, Aileen de Marco,' Joey Morocco gasped.

She smiled, looking down on him as she straddled him. 'Then look forward to mediocrity, my boy, because I won't stay mad for ever . . . unless you can come up with ways of winding me up.'

'What if I told you I'm a Tory?'

'Hah! That might have worked once, but now I'd just feel sorry for you, 'cos you're an endangered species in Scotland.' She raised an eyebrow, reached behind and underneath her and took his scrotum in her right hand, massaging him, gently. 'You're not, are you?' she asked.

'Absolutely not! Absolutely not!'

'Just as well,' she laughed, releasing him.

'You don't need to stop that, though.'

'Yes, I do. I'm knackered.' She pushed herself to her feet, bounced on the mattress as if it was a trampoline, and jumped sideways off the bed. 'Besides, have you seen what time it is?'

'No; a gentleman removes his Tory Rolex, remember.'

'And this lady keeps on her nice socialist Citizen. For your information it's gone half past twelve.'

'Missed breakfast, then,' he observed, with a cheerful grin. 'Have we still got fairies at the bottom of the garden?'

'My unwanted guardians, you mean?' She crossed to the window and looked outside, taking hold of a curtain and drawing it across her body. 'Yup. They're parked across your driveway too; that's a clear sign to anyone that there's something going on here. I thought the protection people were supposed to be subtle. Here,' she added, 'do you ever have paparazzi hanging around?'

'Yes,' he exclaimed, sitting upright, suddenly alarmed, 'so get your face away from the window.'

She stayed where she was, looking back over her shoulder, and letting go of the curtain. 'Why? Would I be bad for your image? Would your fans not approve of you with an older woman?'

'I'm not worried about my image, Aileen,' he protested. 'I'm concerned about yours. You're married to a bloody chief constable, remember, and you're a top politician. You can't afford scandal.'

She left the window and winked at him. 'Not to "a chief constable", Joey; to "The Chief Constable". Bob's taking over the Strathclyde job; it's an emergency appointment. There was nobody else there anyway.'

Her reassurance was wasted on him. 'Jesus Christ,' he said, 'so these guys outside, they report to him?'

She shrugged. 'I suppose they do. But can you see them being brave enough to go to him and say, "By the way, sir, your wife's shagging Joey Morocco"? Somehow I don't. But even if they did, frankly I would not give the tiniest monkey's. I wouldn't lose my party job over this, for I'm divorcing Chief Constable Skinner just as fast as I can, or he's divorcing me, if he gets in first.' She read his concern. 'Don't worry, Joey. You won't be caught in the middle. The split between Bob and me, it's not about sex, it's about ambitions that could not be further apart. You and me? We're just a bit of fun, right?'

He hesitated, then nodded.

'That's how it was when you were starting out on that soap on BBC Scotland, fun. Now you're in big-budget movies, moved upmarket, and I'm free and soon to be single again, but it's still just fun, convenient uncomplicated nookie, no more than that. You're a sexy guy and I'm a crackin' ride, as my coarser male constituents would say, so let's just enjoy it without either of us worrying about the other. Deal?'

His second nod was more convincing. 'Deal.'

'Good, now what do you do for Sunday lunch these days?'

'Usually I go out for it. Today, maybe not; I'll see what's in the fridge.'

'Do that, and I'll get showered and dressed. No rush, though. I'd like to lie low here for the rest of the day, if I can.'

'Of course. We might even manage breakfast tomorrow?'

'Sounds like a plan. Thanks. You're a sweetheart. It really is good to have somewhere to hide out just now. Actually, I'm a chancer,' she admitted. 'I brought enough clothes with me for two nights.' She shuddered. 'God, was I glad to get out of that dress, with the bloodstains. I felt like Jackie Kennedy.'

He winced at the comparison as she went into his bathroom. She had left her phone there the night before, after brushing her teeth. She switched it on, then checked her voicemail.

There were over a dozen calls. One was from her constituency secretary, one from Alf Old, the Scottish Labour Party's chief executive, another from her deputy leader . . . *Probably cursing that the bastard missed me,* she thought . . . several from other parliamentary colleagues, not all of her party, and three from journalists who were trusted with her number. She had expected nothing from her husband.

As soon as she was showered and dressed she called the secretary, an officious older woman with a tendency to fuss. 'Aileen, where are you?' she demanded, as soon as she answered. 'I've tried your flat, I've tried your house in Gullane. I got no reply from either.'

'Never you mind where I am,' she retorted sharply. 'It would have been nice of you to ask how I was, but I'm okay and I'm safe. Anybody calls inquiring about me, you can tell them that. I may call into the office tomorrow, or I may not. I'll let you know.'

No reply from Gullane? she mused as she ended the call, but had no time to dwell on the information as her phone rang immediately. She checked the screen and saw that it was the party CEO, trying again. 'Alf,' she said as she answered.

'Aileen,' he exclaimed, 'thank God I've got through. How are you?'

'I'm fine, thanks. I'm safe, and I'm with a friend. I'm sorry I didn't call you last night, but things were crazy. The security people got me off the scene, by force, more or less. Even now I have protection officers parked outside, like it or not. The First Minister insisted.'

'Good for him. Now . . .'

'I know what you're going to say. Silence breeds rumours.'

'Exactly. I've had several calls asking where you are, and whether you might have been wounded.'

'Then issue a statement. Have they confirmed yet that it's Toni Field who's dead?'

'Yes. Strathclyde police announced it a wee while ago.'

'In that case we should offer condolences . . . I'll leave it to you to choose the adjectives, but praise her all the way to heaven's gate . . . then add that I'm unharmed, and that I've simply been taking some private time to come to terms with what's happened. I suppose you'd better say something nice about Clive Graham as well, but not too nice, mind you, nothing that he can quote in his next election manifesto.'

'Mmm,' Old remarked. 'I can tell you're okay.'

'I'll be fine as long as I keep myself busy,' she told him. 'I'm sorry if I seem a bit brutal, but even without what happened last night there's a lot going on in my life.'

'Do you want to take some more time out? Everyone would understand.'

'They might,' she agreed, 'but in different ways. There are plenty within the party who'd think I was showing weakness. I don't have to tell you, Alf, as soon as a woman politician does that the jackals fall on her. I've handled stress before; I'm good at it.' She paused. 'I'll be back in business tomorrow; I have to be. The First Minister will come out of this looking like fucking Braveheart, so we have to keep pace. We need to come out with something positive. You know that Clive and I were planning a joint announcement on unifying the Scottish police forces?'

'Yes, you told me.'

'Well, I want to jump the gun. Have our people develop the proposition that what happened in the concert hall illustrates the need for it, that it was a result of intelligence delayed by artificial barriers within our police service that need to be broken down. Then set up a press conference for midday tomorrow. We don't have to say what it's about. They'll be all over me anyway about last night. But I want to be ready to roll with that policy announcement.'

'Will do,' Old said, 'but Aileen, what about your personal security? I know the police don't believe there's any continuing threat to you, because I spoke to the DI in charge this morning, but they can't rule it out completely.'

'I told you,' she snapped, 'I've got bodyguards. But so what? If people want to believe there is someone out to get me, let them. Remember Thatcher at Brighton? The same day that bomb went off she was on her feet, on global telly, making her conference speech and saying "Bring it on". That's the precedent, Alf. I either follow it or I run away and hide. Now get to work, and I'll see you tomorrow.'

As Old went off to follow orders, Aileen thought about returning some of the other calls but decided against it. Instead she trotted downstairs. 'Joey?' she called as she went.

'I'm in the kitchen. Telly's on: you should see this.'

She had had no time to learn the layout of the house when she had arrived late the night before, but she traced his voice to its location. The room looked out on to a large rear garden surrounded by a high wall, topped with spikes. 'No place for the photographers to hide here,' she remarked.

'No. I had the fencing added on when I bought the place. It does the job.'

'So what's on the box that I should see?'

He turned from the work surface where he was putting a salad together and nodded towards a wall-mounted set. It was on, and a BT commercial was running. 'Sky News,' he replied. 'They've been trailing a Glasgow press conference and somebody's name was mentioned. In fact . . .'

As he spoke, the programme banner ran, then the programme went straight to what appeared to be a live location: a table, and two men, one of them in uniform.

'Is that who I think it is?' Joey asked. 'I spoke to him last night; didn't have a clue who he was. No wonder he got frosty when I asked about you.'

She smiled, but without humour or affection. 'That's him. I told you earlier what this is about. Observe and be amazed, for it's one of the biggest U-turns you will ever see in your life. Here, I'll do the lunch.'

As she took over the salad preparation, Joey Morocco watched the bulletin as Dominic Hanlon introduced himself to a roomful of journalists and camera operators. There was a nervous tremor in the councillor's voice, a sure tell that the event was well beyond his comfort zone. He began by paying a fulsome tribute to the dead Antonia Field, and then explained the difficult circumstances in which the Strathclyde force had found itself.

'However,' he concluded, 'I am pleased to announce that with the approval of his Police Authority in Edinburgh, Chief Constable Robert Morgan Skinner has agreed to take temporary command of the force for a period of three months, to allow the orderly appointment of a successor to the late Chief Constable Field. Mr Skinner, would you like to say a few words?' He looked at his companion, happy to hand over.

'In the circumstances,' Skinner replied, 'it's probably best that we go straight to questions.'

A forest of hands went up, and a clamour of voices arose, but he nodded to a familiar face in the front row, John Fox, the BBC Scotland Home Affairs editor.

'Bob,' the reporter began, 'you weren't a candidate for this job last time it was vacant. Are you prepared to say why not?'

The chief constable shrugged. 'I didn't want it.'

'Why do you want it now?'

'I don't, John. Believe me, I would much rather still be arguing with Toni Field in ACPOS over the principles of policing, as she and I did, long and loud. But Toni's been taken from us, at a time when Strathclyde could least afford to lose its leader, given the absence of a deputy.

'When I was asked to take over . . . temporarily; I will keep hammering that word home . . . by Councillor Hanlon's authority, on the basis that its members believe me to be qualified, as a police officer I felt that I couldn't refuse. It wouldn't have been right.'

Fox was about to put a supplementary, but another journalist cut in. 'Couldn't ACC Allan have taken over?'

'Given his seniority, if he was well, yes, but he isn't. He's on sick leave.'

'What about ACC Thomas, or ACC Gorman?'

'Fine officers as they are, neither of them meets the criteria for permanent appointment,' he replied, 'and so the authority took the view that wouldn't have been appropriate.'

'Did you consult your wife before accepting the appointment, Mr Skinner?' The questioning voice was female, its accent cultured and very definitely English. Aileen was in the act of chopping Chinese leaves; she stopped and if she had looked down instead of round at the screen she would have seen that she came within a centimetre of slicing a finger open.

She saw Bob's gaze turn slowly towards the source, who was seated at the side of the room. 'And why should I do that, Miss . . .'

'Ms Marguerite Hatton, *Daily News* political correspondent. She is the Scottish Labour leader, as I understand it. Surely you discuss important matters with her.'

'You're either very smart or very stupid or just plain ignorant, lady,' Aileen murmured. 'You've just lit a fuse.'

A very short one, as was proved a second later. 'What the hell has her position got to do with this?' her estranged husband barked. 'I'm a senior police officer, as senior as you can get in this country. Are you asking, seriously, whether I seek political approval before I take a career decision, or even an operational decision?'

'Oh, really!' the journalist scoffed. 'That's a dinosaur answer. I meant did you consult her as your wife, not as a politician.'

On the screen Skinner stared at her, then laughed. 'You are indeed from the deep south, Ms Hatton, so I'll forgive your lack of local knowledge. I suggest that you ask some of your Scottish colleagues, those who really know Aileen de Marco. They'll tell you that there isn't a waking moment when she isn't a politician. And I can tell you she even talks politics in her sleep!'

'Jesus!' Aileen shouted. 'Joey, switch that fucking thing off!'

'Relax,' he said, 'it's not true.'

The woman from the *Daily News* was undeterred. 'In that case,' she persisted, 'how will she feel about you taking the job?'

'Why should I have any special knowledge of that?' He looked around the room. 'No more questions about my wife, people.'

On camera, John Fox raised a hand. 'Just one more, please, Bob? How is she after her ordeal last night?'

'Last time I saw her she was fine: fine and very angry.'

'Where was that, Mr Skinner?' Marguerite Hatton shouted.

'You've had your five minutes,' he growled. 'Any more acceptable questions?'

The woman beside Fox, Stephanie Marshall of STV, raised a hand. 'You weren't a candidate for the Strathclyde post last time, Chief Constable, but will you put your name forward when it's re-advertised?'

Watching, Aileen saw him lean forward as if to answer, then hesitate.

'If you'd asked me that last night,' he began, 'just after Dominic asked me to take on this role, I would have told you no, definitely not. But something was said to me this morning that's made me change my attitude just a wee bit.

'So the honest answer is, I don't know. Let me see how the next couple of weeks go, and then I'll decide. Now, ladies and gentlemen, I must go. We have a major investigation under way as you all realise, and I must call on the officer who's running it.'

Aileen reached out and grasped the work surface, squeezing it hard.

'What are you doing?' Joey chuckled.

'I'm checking for earth tremors. You might not know it but what he just said is the equivalent of a very large mountain starting to move. I can't believe it. I told him last night he'd never leave Pitt Street once he got in there, but I didn't think for one second that he'd actually listen to me. It's a first.'

He reached out and patted her on the shoulder. 'No, dearie, it's you that wasn't listening to him. His words,' he pointed out, 'were "this morning", not "last night". So whoever made him think again, it wasn't you.'

'You're right,' she whispered. 'Which makes me wonder where the hell he was this morning.'

'While I'm wondering about something else,' Joey said. 'Why did that *News* cow ask where he'd seen you last night?'

Nine

'I'm sorry about that *News* woman, sir,' Malcolm Nopper said. 'I've never seen her before. I can't keep her out of future press conferences, but I'll do my best to control her.'

Skinner looked at the chief press officer he had inherited from Toni Field, and laughed. The media had been escorted out of the conference room in the force headquarters building and the two men were alone. Nopper eyed his new boss nervously, unsure how to read his reaction.

'How the hell are you going to do that?' the chief constable asked. 'Sellotape over her gob? So you didn't know her? I didn't know her either, and it would have been the same if she'd turned up in Edinburgh, on my own patch. She's a seagull; we all get them.'

'A seagull, sir?'

'Sure, you know, they fly in, make a noise, shit on you, then fly away again. As for controlling her, you don't have to. If she turns up at one of my media briefings in future . . . not that I plan to have many . . . I'll simply ignore her. You can do the same at any you chair.'

'I tend not to do that, Chief,' Nopper said. 'When an investigation's in process, I let the senior investigating officer take the lead.'

'Not any more. Lottie Mann will have to go before the media later on. From something that Max Allan told me a while back, I guess she hasn't had any formal media training. Am I right?'

'None that I can recall,' the civilian agreed.

'I know she'll be fine, but I'm not sure she does, so she must have a minder. I'll be there but if I go on the platform it'll undermine her. As you said, she's the SIO. So you'll be there, you'll introduce her and you'll pick the questioners. Ms Hatton will not be one of them. Your regulars won't mind that. In my experience they don't like seagulls either.'

'As you wish, Chief.'

'Mmm. Where will you hold it? Do you have a favourite venue?'

'No. Normally it would be where it's most convenient for the officer in charge.'

'In that case we do it here in Pitt Street, in this room. I spoke to DI Mann on the way through here. She'll be finished at the concert hall by two. She and I agreed that given the nature of this investigation it's best that it be centrally based, rather than in a police office that's open to the general public. Nobody else will be using this room this afternoon, will they?'

'Not as far as I know, but suppose somebody was, you want it, you get it.'

'Okay, set it up for four. That'll give Lottie time to brief me, and it will give me time to get used to my new surroundings.'

As he spoke, a figure appeared in the double doorway.

'Lowell,' Skinner called. 'You found us. DCI Payne is going to be my executive officer during my stay here,' he explained to the press officer. 'When you want to get to me, you do it through him. That'll be the case for everyone below command rank, but be assured, I will be accessible; his job won't be to keep people out, but to help them in.'

He moved towards the exit. 'Your first task, Lowell. Show me to my office. I knew where it was in Jock Govan's time, but I have no clue now.'

As one of her first signs of her new-broom approach, Antonia Field had rejected the office suite used by her predecessors and had commandeered half a floor in the newer part of the headquarters complex. 'Have you decided where you're going to live, sir?' Payne asked as he led the way up a flight of stairs towards the third floor.

Skinner stopped. 'Lowell,' he said, 'I don't expect to be "sirred" all the time by senior officers, least of all by you. You want to call me something official, call me "Chief". When there's nobody else around and you ask me something you'd ask me over the dinner table, call me Bob, like always.'

'Fair enough. Although,' he added, 'it was really a professional question, since I'll have to know where to raise you in an emergency.'

'True. The answer is that as much as possible I plan to live in my own house. I will have a driver and I plan to use him.'

'That's in Gullane?'

'Sure. Where . . .' He halted in mid-sentence. 'Ah, you thought I might stay in Aileen's flat.'

'Well, yes.'

'That won't be happening. It will become apparent soon, if only because we're both public figures, that she and I are no longer together.'

Payne was silent for a few seconds, as they resumed their climb. 'I see,' he murmured. 'I'm sorry to hear that. So that's why you weren't with her at the concert.'

'That was part of the reason. Anyway, it's not public knowledge yet, although I came close to making it so in my press briefing, when that bloody *News* person wound me up. It is something I'll have to deal with, and soon, but not right now. Once we've both calmed down, we may issue a joint statement, but we're both too hot to discuss that just now.

'So,' he continued, 'Gullane is where you'll reach me most of the time. When I have to stay here I'll use a hotel; Hanlon's already said he'll pick up the tab for that . . . without me even asking, would you believe.'

They reached the top of the stairway; Payne turned left, and headed along a corridor that was blocked by a glass doorway, with a keypad. He opened it with four digits and led the way into a complex with more than a dozen rooms around a small central open space, with four chairs surrounding a low table, on which magazines were piled.

'This is it, Chief, your new command suite. Your office is facing us.'

Skinner stared ahead. 'It's got glass walls,' he exclaimed.

'Relax,' his aide said, noting his indignation. 'There are internal blinds between the panels. I'm told that Chief Constable Field kept them open all the time.'

'That will change; they'll be closed permanently. I never did like people watching me think.'

'There's a bathroom and a changing room as well. They have solid walls,' he added.

'Just as well, or I'd be going back to Jock Govan's old suite. Do I have a secretary?'

'Of course, but she isn't here today. I called her and told her what was happening, about you, and your appointment. I didn't want her finding out from the telly. She offered to come in, but I told her not to.'

'What's her name?'

'Marina Deschamps.'

'Mmm,' Skinner murmured, then he blinked. 'Deschamps, you said? Wasn't that Toni's birth name?'

Payne nodded. 'Yes. It's her sister; the chief brought her with her. She insisted on it, apparently, before she accepted the job.'

'Eh? The bloody Human Resources director didn't think to tell me that last night.' He frowned. 'What about the mother? Are we flying her up here?'

'The Met took care of that. They got her on to the first Glasgow flight this morning.'

'I wish to hell they'd left her down there.' He sighed. 'I know I have to pay her a courtesy call, but I'll leave that until tomorrow. Meantime, the sister should be regarded as on compassionate leave. Does she have a contract of employment?'

'I don't know for sure, Chief, but I'd imagine so.'

'She's a civilian, yes?'

'Yes.'

'Okay. Tell the Human Resources director that her contract will be honoured. If she wants to stay here in another capacity, she can. If she wants to leave, then she may do so at once, but she'll be paid as if she'd worked a full notice period, whatever that is. Then tell him to find me a replacement, pronto, someone with full security clearance, mainly to manage my mail and yours.'

They had been walking as they talked, and reached Skinner's new office as he finished issuing his orders. The door was locked, but Payne took a ring with three keys from his trouser pocket and handed it over. 'I had the lock changed,' he said. 'Easier than searching through Ms Field's things and getting Marina's back from her.'

'Good thinking.' He detached a key from the ring, used it to unlock the door, then handed it to the DCI. 'Yours,' he said then stepped inside. As he did so he felt a sudden and unexpected shiver run through him. 'Weird,' he murmured. 'I have never imagined doing this, not once.'

He looked around. The room was larger than the one he had left in Edinburgh, but furnished in much the same way. His desk was on the left, facing a round meeting table, with six chairs that slid underneath it. Beyond, there was another door; he could see through the unscreened glass wall that it led into another office.

He pointed towards it. 'Secretary's room?'

'Yes,' his aide replied.

'Where are you going to go?'

'I hadn't given that any thought.'

'Where's the deputy's office?'

'That's the one beyond the secretary's.'

'Then use that. It's vacant.'

'Okay, Chief, thanks.' Payne walked behind the desk and opened a door behind it. 'Your personal rooms are through here,' he said. 'There's a safe in the changing room, but apparently nobody knows the combination, unless Marina does. I'll ask her. If she doesn't I'll . . .' He smiled. 'Actually I'm not sure what I'll do.'

'Too bad Johnny Ramensky's dead,' Skinner chuckled.

'Yeah: the last of the legendary safecrackers. As for the rest,' the DCI continued, 'all of Ms Field's things have been removed, from the changing room and the bathroom, and everything from the desk as well, that wasn't office-related. Her business diary is still there, so you can see what she had in her schedule. There are also some files. I had a look at them, a very quick look, and then closed them up again. They seem to contain her observations on her senior colleagues.'

'Then take them away and shred them,' Skinner instructed him. 'I don't want to know about her prejudices and her grudges.' He grinned. 'I prefer to develop my own. What's the general view of Michael Thomas?' he asked. 'You can be frank, don't worry.'

'Unfavourable,' Payne replied, without a pause for thought. 'I knew him as a constable, way back, after I'd made sergeant. He was "Three bags full" then, before he started to climb. Much later I was stationed in his division for a while when he was a chief super. He virtually ignored me. He has a reputation for efficiency, but also for being a cold fish. He was a big supporter of Toni Field, at least he kissed her arse regularly enough.'

'I know that from ACPOS. He was her regular seconder in the debate on unification. What about Bridie Gorman?'

'Now she is well liked. She spends a lot of time out of the office, in the outlying areas of the force. I think that suited her, and suited Chief Constable Field as well, for they were complete opposites, as cops and as people.' Payne scratched his chin. 'Obviously I don't know what perceptions were outside Strathclyde, but the view in here was that Field planned to get rid of every chief officer apart from ACC Thomas. She'd already axed the deputy, and it was common knowledge that Mr Allan was next.'

Skinner nodded. 'Yes, I could tell that at ACPOS too. She didn't even try to be civil to him. Any word on him, by the way?'

'Yes, I checked. He's still in hospital, suffering from what they're now describing as shock. They're going to keep him in for a couple of days. I don't know how he'll feel about coming back.'

'Then see if you can find out for me. Go and visit him, this evening if you can. Max is only a few months off the usual retirement age. If he's up to talking about it, tell him that if he'd like to come back, I'll be happy to see him, but if he doesn't, I'll sign him off for enough sick leave to take him up to his due date.'

'Yes, Chief; I was planning to go and see him anyway. He's always been good to me.'

'Fine. Now who's here, in the building now?'

'ACC Thomas is. He said he'd be in his office, and that he'd like to see you as soon as possible. And ACC Gorman's in as well. She came down from Argyll overnight.'

'Does she want to see me too?'

'No, she said to tell you she was about if you needed her, that's all.'

Skinner smiled. 'Okay then, let's talk to her; I can spare a few minutes before I have to see Lottie. Ask her to drop in, then give Mr Thomas my apologies, tell him that I'll fit him in tomorrow morning, and that he's free to salvage what's left of his Sunday.'

As Payne left, he walked over to the desk, tried the swivel chair for height, and found, as he had expected, that it was set far too low. He stayed in it for only a few seconds, then pushed himself out. There was something not right about it, something that made his spine tingle. He knew what it was without any deep analysis. Less than forty-eight hours before, Toni Field had been sitting in it, and at that very moment she was lying in a refrigerated drawer in one of the city's morgues, unless she was being autopsied by Sarah's opposite number in the west.

He knew that he would never feel comfortable in her old seat, and so he wheeled it over to the secretary's office, and left it in there with a note saying, 'Replace, please,' scribbled on a sheet torn from a pad.

He had just stepped back into his own room when he heard a knock on the door. 'Come in,' he called.

'I can't,' a female voice shouted back. 'This door self-locks. It can only be opened with a key or from the inside.'

He stepped across and admitted his visitor. ACC Bridget Gorman was in civvies, light tan trousers and a check shirt. 'Afternoon, Chief,' she said. Her manner was tentative, not that of the Bridie Gorman he knew.

'Hey, Bridie, last week at ACPOS it was Bob,' he told her. 'It still is, okay? Come in and have a seat.' He showed her across to the table and pulled out two of the chairs.

She glanced across to the desk, taking in the missing swivel but saying nothing. 'Wouldn't be right,' he replied to her unspoken question. 'I feel bad enough being here.'

Gorman frowned, and her forehead all but disappeared behind a mop of black but grey-streaked hair. 'I know,' she murmured. 'It's just awful. And it could have been Aileen.'

'No,' he said. 'I don't believe it could, and neither does DI Mann.' He explained why.

She nodded. 'Yes, I can see that. Somebody like them, they'd know exactly who they were shooting, I suppose. But why? Why Toni Field?'

'They didn't need to know that.'

'But they'd know who wanted it done.'

'Not all the way up the chain, not necessarily.'

'Do you think it was related to something here?'

'Come on, Bridie,' Skinner murmured, 'you know the rule: speculation hinders investigation.'

'Aye, I suppose I do. Did you say that Lottie Mann's involved?'

'She was on duty; she took the shout.'

'Granted, but . . . Lottie can be like a runaway train. Max Allan was always careful how she was deployed.'

'I know that,' he conceded. 'But last night was chaos. The hall was full of headless chickens, but she turned up and took charge, even put me in my place. I liked that. It means she's my kind of cop. What's her back story? She said she has a family, but that's all I know about her.'

'That's right,' she confirmed, 'she has. Her husband used to be a cop too. His name's Scott, as I recall. I've got no idea what the wee boy's called.'

'Used to be, you say?'

'Yes. He left the force a few years back. No, that's a euphemism; he was encouraged to resign. He had a drink problem and eventually it couldn't be tolerated any more. The job probably didn't help, for he seems to have got himself together after he left it. The last I heard he was working in security in a big cash and carry warehouse out near Easterhouse.' She smiled. 'There's a story about Lottie and an interdivisional boxing night . . .'

'I've heard it. Max Allan told me.'

'Aye but did he tell you the name of the cop she flattened? It was Scott; that was how they met.'

Skinner laughed, softly. 'There's a love story for you. Somebody should make the movie.'

'Fine, but who would you get to play Lottie?'

'That would be a problem, I concede. Gerard Butler in drag, maybe.' A name suggested itself. 'Joey Morocco?'

'Mr Glasgow? Our movie flavour of the month? He looks good, granted, but I wonder sometimes if there's any real substance to him. I'm pretty sure I'd back Lottie against him over ten rounds.'

'Maybe I'll make that match,' the chief murmured. 'It would fill Ibrox Stadium. Bridie,' he said, his tone changing, 'I know you're as surprised to see me here as I am to be here.'

She contradicted him. 'No, I'm not. What happened, happened. I think they've done the right thing. This force always needs a strong hand; Max is too old, I don't have the experience in the rank, and neither does Michael, whatever he might think.' She frowned, concern in her eyes. 'How is Max, by the way?'

'He's okay, but it remains to be seen whether he'll be back. But whether he is or not . . . I have to get some hierarchy in place here. That means I need to appoint a temporary deputy chief. Even if Max was here, I'd want that to be you. Are you up for it?'

She was silent for a few seconds. 'How can I say no?' she asked when she was ready. 'But what are you going to tell Thomas?'

'I don't plan to explain myself, if that's what you mean, Bridie. The Police Authority gave me the power to designate my deputy, and you are it.'

She smiled, and said, 'This might sound daft, Bob, but . . . what will I have to do as deputy?'

He returned her awkward grin and replied, 'To be honest, I don't know yet, not in any detail, because I don't know yet what the demands of the job will be on me. Mind you, they have just cast doubt on my plans to go to my house in Spain in a couple of weeks' time, something I'll have to break to my children. Holidays might prove to be out of the question.'

'Aw, what a shame,' she exclaimed, like a kindly aunt. 'The poor wee souls.'

'It might not be a complete disaster. I'll ask their mother if she can clear some time to take them instead.' He sighed. 'As for your question, all I can say is that you'll deputise for me whenever it's necessary.'

'I'd better go and practise looking important then,' the ACC chuckled. 'Was there anything else for now?'

'No. My usual practice is to have a morning session with my senior colleagues. I'll probably carry that on here; Lowell Payne will advise everybody. He's going to be my aide while I'm settling in here, maybe for longer.'

'Good,' she declared. 'I like Lowell. He tends to fly below the radar; that may be why he hasn't risen higher.'

'I don't think he's bothered about that. I know him well, from outside the force, and I'm glad to have him alongside me.' He stood. She thought he was indicating the end of the meeting and was in the act of rising, but he waved to her to stay seated.

'I'm just about to call Lottie up here, to give me an update on her investigation. You stay here and sit in; belt and braces. Christ, after what happened to Toni, none of us can be sure we're going to see tomorrow.'

Ten

'I could get to like this,' Aileen said. 'Bob's garden in Gullane is nice too, but it overlooks the beach. He refuses to plant trees to give it a bit of privacy; says he likes the view.' She picked up her glass from the wrought-iron table. 'Well he's bloody welcome to it!'

Don't get to like it too much, Joey Morocco thought. He had been on the astonished side of surprised when Aileen had called him the night before, almost raving about being imprisoned by her husband and seeking sanctuary for a day or two, but they had enjoyed regular liaisons a few years before, and the occasional fling since.

Their history together had been enough to overcome his caution about taking another man's wife under his roof, even when the man was as formidable as Bob Skinner was said to be.

Nonetheless, when she had defined their renewed relationship, *'just fun, convenient uncomplicated nookie, no more than that'*, he had been relieved. He was bound for Los Angeles in a few days, for the film project that was going to make him, he knew, and the last thing he wanted was a heavy-duty woman in Scotland with her claws in him.

'Are you sure that's really what you want?' he asked. 'To end your marriage?'

'Bloody certain,' she replied. 'I don't actually know what drew me to him in the first place.' She grinned. 'No, that's not true, I do. I wanted to find out if he matched up to the waves he was giving out. Very few do, in my limited experience.'

'Did he?'

'At first, yes. Then I made the mistake of marrying him. It all got mediocre after that, but I suppose that's life. I'll learn from it, though; once is enough.'

He smiled.

'And you're relieved to hear that, I know,' she said. 'Don't worry, Joey. My career is all planned out, and it doesn't take me within six thousand miles of where you're going.' She looked around the suntrap garden once more. 'But this is nice. I like it here; it suits me. I'm guessing that when you go to the US, you won't be back here very often, so if you need a tenant, let me know.'

'I will,' he promised. 'The way my commitments are, I won't be back for at least a year, so that might work. You'd be a house-sitter, though, not a tenant.'

'No,' she declared. 'It would have to be formal. I couldn't be seen as your bidey-in, even though you were never here.'

He shrugged. 'Whatever,' he murmured, hoping secretly that it would all be forgotten by the next morning. 'Want another drink?' he asked.

Aileen pressed her glass to her chest. 'No, I'm fine,' she said. 'I'm not a big afternoon drinker . . . or evening, come to that. You've seen me in action before. You know I can't handle it.'

'True,' he conceded. 'If you're sure . . . I think I'll get another beer, if you don't mind.'

'Not a bit.'

He wandered back into the kitchen, and took another Rolling Rock from the fridge. He had just uncapped it when the phone rang. He frowned, irked by the interruption, wondering which of the few people with access to his unlisted number had a need to call it on a bloody Sunday, when they all knew it was the day he liked to keep to himself.

'Yes,' he barked, not choosing to hide his impatience.

'Is that Joey Morocco?' a female voice asked.

'Depends who this is.'

'My name's Marguerite Hatton. I'm on the political staff of the *Daily News*.'

'And I'm a bloody actor, so why are you calling me?' *Hatton, Hatton*; the name was fresh in his mind. Of course, the woman from the press conference, she who had tried to give Aileen's husband a hard time, and had her arse well kicked.

'I'm trying to locate Aileen de Marco,' she replied. 'I'd like to talk to her about her ordeal last night and how relieved she feels that the killer got the wrong woman.'

'So?' he challenged. 'Why are you calling me?'

'You're quoted as saying, last night as you left the concert hall, that you're a friend of hers,' she explained. 'I'm calling around everyone; the Labour Party, Glasgow councillors, anyone who might know her, actually, but she seems to have disappeared. Do you have any idea where she might be?'

'Why should I? And if I did, do you really think that I'd betray her by setting you on her? If you want to find her, ask her husband, why don't you?'

'I rather think not,' Hatton drawled. 'Can you tell me about your relationship with Ms de Marco, Mr Morocco?'

'No,' he snorted. 'Why the hell should I do that?'

'But you did say you're a friend of hers.'

'Yes. So what? Aileen has many friends. She's Glasgow's leading lady. Ask a real journalist and they'll tell you that.'

'Oh, but I'm a real journalist, Mr Morocco,' she told him. 'Be in no doubt about that. How long have you known Ms de Marco?'

'For a few years.'

'How close are you?'

'We are friends, okay? Is there any part of that you don't understand?'

'What's the nature of your friendship?'

'Private. Now please piss off.'

'I don't think so.'

He felt himself boil over. 'Listen, hen,' he shouted, lapsing into Glaswegian in his anger, 'you want to talk to me, you go through my agent or my publicist. By the way, both of those are owed favours by your editor, so don't you be making me have them called in.'

'He owes me a few as well, Joey,' she countered. 'I keep bringing him exclusives, you see. When did you last see Ms de Marco?'

'Fuck off!' he snapped and slammed the phone back into its cradle.

'You've been a while,' Aileen said, as he rejoined her.

'I had a nuisance call,' he replied.

'There's a number you can call that stops you getting those.'

'It doesn't always work. But hopefully that one's gone away to bother somebody else.'

Eleven

'How's the force reacting to Mr Skinner's appointment?' Harry Wright of the *Herald* called out, from the second row of the questioning journalists gathered in the Pitt Street conference room.

'Come on, Harry,' Malcolm Nopper began to protest, but Lottie Mann cut across him.

'How would I know?' she replied, her deep booming voice at a level just below a shout. 'I'm just one member of this force, and for the last,' she made a show of checking her watch, 'twenty hours, minus a few for sleep, I've been leading a murder investigation. I think I can say for everybody that we're all still shocked by what happened to our former chief constable. As for the new chief, he's keeping in close touch with my investigation, but he's confirmed me as the lead officer.'

'Ladies and gentlemen,' Nopper exclaimed, 'people, I know these are unique circumstances, but I remind you that we're here to discuss an ongoing inquiry into a suspicious death.'

A few explosions of laughter, some suppressed, some not, came from the gathering at his blatant use of police-speak. Skinner winced, and reflected on his insistence that the chief press officer should take the chair at the briefing. He had slipped into the room at the first call for order, and was standing at the back, half-hidden behind a Sky News camera operator.

'Okay,' Nopper sighed, shifting in his seat before the Strathclyde Police logo backdrop as he tried to rescue the situation. 'At least that got your attention. My point was that this is a murder we're here to talk about and that it should be treated just like any other, regardless of who the victim is. Now can we stick to the point?' He looked towards the *Herald* reporter. 'Harry,' he invited, 'do you want to ask a proper question?'

The man shrugged. 'I thought that was, but never mind. Detective Inspector, you were able to confirm for us that the police victims are Chief Constable Field and Sergeant Sproule. Now can you tell us anything about the other two men? Do you know who they are . . . were, sorry?'

Lottie straightened in her chair, and took a deep breath, in an effort to slow down her racing heart. 'We believe so,' she replied, speaking steadily. A murmur rippled through the media, and she paused to let it subside. 'They've been identified as Gerard Botha and Francois Smit. They were both South African citizens, and they've been described to us as military contractors.'

'Mercenaries?' a female *Daily Record* hack shouted.

The reporter was so suddenly excited that Lottie suspected she had spent her career waiting to write a crime story that didn't involve domestic violence, homophobia or dawn raids on drug dealers. 'If you want to use that term,' she said, 'I won't be arguing with you.'

'Who gave you that description?' John Fox asked, from his customary front and centre seat.

'Intelligence sources,' the DI told him.

'MI6?'

Lottie looked him in the eye, then gave him the smallest of winks. 'Be content with what I've given you.' She came within a couple of breaths of adding, 'There's a good boy,' but stopped herself just in time, realising that Pacific Quay's top crime reporter was someone she did not need as an enemy.

Fox grinned. 'I had to ask, Lottie. These men were the killers, yes?'

She nodded. 'Yes.'

'To what degree of certainty?'

'Absolute.'

'Do you know as certainly how they came to die?'

'Yes,' the DI said. 'But with the greatest respect, I'm going to tell the procurator fiscal before I tell you. Fair enough?'

The BBC reporter shrugged his shoulders slightly as if in agreement, but some others tried to press the point. She held her position until eventually Harry Wright changed the angle of approach.

'DI Mann, the concert hall had security cover and the event was policed, yet these two men seem to have smuggled a weapon in there regardless. Is your investigation focusing on your own security and on the lapses that allowed this to happen?'

'We know how they did that too, but again I'm not able to share it with you.'

'Same reason, I suppose,' Wright moaned. 'The fiscal gets to know before the public.'

She shook her head, firmly. 'No. It's information that we have to keep in-house for now. There are aspects of it that we need to follow up.'

'Continuing lines of inquiry?'

'Sure, if you want to say that, I'm content.'

'DI Mann, why isn't Mr Skinner sitting alongside you?' Marguerite Hatton cried out from the side of the room.

'Relevant questions only,' Nopper exclaimed. 'Anyone else?'

'I'll decide what's relevant,' the woman protested. 'I'll disrupt this press conference until you answer. Why isn't the new chief constable present?'

'He is!'

Every head in the room, apart from the two seated at the table, turned at Skinner's bellow.

'Satisfied?' he boomed. 'DI Mann is leading this investigation and she enjoys my full confidence.'

'How is your wife today, Mr Skinner?' Hatton shouted back.

Slowly, the chief constable walked towards her. A press office aide stood at the side of the room, holding one of the microphones that were available so that every reporter's questions could be heard. He held out his hand for it and took it, then stopped.

He knew that the TV cameras were running and that still photographs were being shot, but made no attempt to have them stop.

'Lady,' he said, into the mike, 'I don't know who you think you are, or what special privileges you expect from me, but you're not getting any. You're here at our invitation to discuss a specific matter, and now you're threatening disruption, as everyone here has heard. I'm not having that. One more word from you and I'll have you ejected.'

'This is a public meeting,' she protested.

'Don't be daft,' he snapped back at her. 'It's a police press conference. I mean it. One more word and you are on the pavement.' He held her gaze, his eyes icy cold, boring into hers, unblinking, until she subsided and turned away from him.

'Okay,' he murmured. 'As long as we're clear.' He looked at the platform. 'Carry on, Malcolm.'

'Thank you, sir,' the chief press officer said.

The *Daily Record* reporter raised her hand. Nopper nodded to her. 'Can we take it that Chief Constable Field's relatives have been told?'

'Of course,' he replied. 'We released her identity, didn't we? Her mother arrived in Glasgow this morning.'

Shit, Skinner thought, *they're going to love you for that when the media turn up on their doorstep.*

'Did they identify the body?'

Malcolm Nopper put a hand to his mouth, to hide a laugh.

'They knew who she was, Penny,' John Fox pointed out.

Twelve

'So you're the armourer,' ACC Mario McGuire said to the man who faced him across the table in the Livingston police office. There was nobody else in the interview room.

Freddy Welsh was a big man, one with 'Don't cross me' in his eyes, but someone had. There was a deep blue bruise in the middle of his forehead and his right hand was bandaged. For all that, he still looked formidable. 'I don't recognise that name,' he murmured.

'Maybe not, but it seems that other people do. People like Beram Cohen.'

'Never heard of him.'

McGuire leaned back and sighed. 'Look, Mr Welsh, can we stop playing this game? You've never been in police custody before, so I appreciate you're only doing what you've seen on the telly, but really it's not like that. There's no recording going on here.

'You've already been charged with illegal possession of a large quantity of weapons. We have the gun that was used in last night's murder in Glasgow, and we are in the process of proving beyond any doubt that it came from the crate that was found yesterday afternoon in your store. You can take it that we will do that, and as soon as we do, the Crown Office will have a decision to make.'

'And what would that be?' Welsh asked.

'Are you really that naive, man?' McGuire laughed. 'Do I have to spell it out? The kill team that executed Toni Field are all dead.'

The prisoner's eyelids flickered rapidly. He licked his lips.

'You didn't know that?' his interrogator exclaimed.

Welsh shook his head. 'I've been locked up since last night, and I wasn't offered my choice of newspaper with breakfast this morning. How would I know anything? I don't even know who this bloke Tony Field is, or how Glasgow comes into it.'

'Antonia Field,' McGuire corrected. 'The Chief Constable of Strathclyde. She was the victim. Your customer, Mr Smit, put three rounds through her head. You told my colleague Mr Skinner it was a woman he and Botha were after, and you were right.'

The other man frowned, as he took in the information. McGuire had assumed that he knew at least some of it, but it was clear to him that he had been wrong. 'And they're dead?' he said.

The ACC nodded in confirmation. 'Yeah. Cohen, the planner, the team leader, he died of natural causes, a brain haemorrhage, but you knew that much. As for the other two, Mr Skinner and the other man you met,' as he spoke he saw the shadow of a bad memory cross Welsh's face, 'arrived on the scene too late to save Chief Constable Field, but they did come face to face with Smit and Botha as they tried to escape, over the bodies of two other police officers they'd just taken down. They were offered resistance and they shot them both dead.'

The armourer started to tremble. McGuire liked that. 'Yes,' he went on, 'dead. It's one thing being the supplier, Freddy, isn't it? You've been doing that for donkey's years, supplying the weapons to all sorts, but never being anywhere near them when the trigger was pulled. Not like that here, though. You're too close this time, and it's scary. Isn't it?'

He reached into his pocket and pulled out two photographs and laid them in the table. One showed the body of Antonia Field, the other that of Smit.

'Go on, take a good look,' he urged. 'That leaky grey stuff, that's brain matter. Awful, isn't it?'

Welsh pushed them back towards him.

'You don't like reality, do you?' he said. 'It's not good to be that close.' He leaned forward again. 'Well, you are, and far closer than you realise. That woman, her whose photo I've just shown you, when that was done to her, my wife,' his voice became quieter, and something came into it that had not been there before, 'my heavily pregnant wife, was in the very next seat. When I got her home last night she was in a crime scene tunic that Strathclyde Police gave her, because the clothes she'd been wearing before had Toni Field's blood and brains splattered all over them, and she couldn't get out of them fast enough.'

He stopped, then reached a massive hand across the desk, seized Welsh's chin and forced him to meet his gaze.

'So far I know of four people who I hold responsible for that, Freddy. You are the only one left alive, and that puts you right in it, because now only you can tell me who commissioned this outrage. And you will tell me.' He laughed, as he released Welsh from his grasp.

'You know, Bob Skinner suggested that if you didn't cooperate, I should get the MI5 guy here to persuade you. But I don't actually need him. He's just a spook with a gun, whereas I am a husband who's going to wake up in cold sweats, for longer than I can see ahead, at the thought of what might have happened to my Paula and our baby if that sight you supplied with your Heckler and fucking Koch carbine had been just a wee bit out of alignment.

'I've been playing it cool up to now, because Paula's amazingly calm about it and I want to keep her that way, but that's been a front. Inside I've been raging from the moment it happened. Now I can finally let it out. You're a big guy, but you're not tough. There's a hell of a difference. I'm probably going to beat the crap out of you anyway, but what you have to tell me may determine when I stop.'

He sprang from his seat and started round the table.

Thirteen

'So what have your people got?' Skinner's jacket . . . while he disliked any uniform, his hatred for the new tunic style favoured by some of his brother chiefs was absolute . . . was slung over the back of the new swivel chair that had been in place by the time he had returned from the press briefing. He had refused all requests for one-on-one interviews, insisting instead that these be done with Lottie Mann, as lead investigator.

His visitor was as smartly dressed as he had been the day before, but the blazer had given way to a close-fitting leather jerkin. *No room for a firearm there*, the chief thought. Just as well or security would have gone crazy. The garment was a light tan in colour almost matching Clyde Houseman's skin tone, but not quite, for his face sported a touch of pink. 'Have you caught the sun?' he asked.

The younger man smiled. 'Did you think I'd just get browner?' he responded. 'I'm only one quarter Trinidadian, on my father's side. The rest of me gets as sunburned as you. And the answer's yes. I went for a run this morning, a long one; not on a treadmill either but around the streets.'

'Where did you go?'

'Along Sauchiehall Street, then down Hope Street to the Riverside; over the Squinty Bridge, along the other side for a bit then I crossed back further up, past Pacific Quay. Up to Gilmorehill from there, round the university, and then home.'

'Is that your normal Sunday routine?'

'Hell no. Normally I go out for breakfast somewhere. There are a few places nearby.'

'Where is home?'

'Woodlands Drive.'

Skinner's eyebrows rose slightly. 'Woodlands Drive, indeed. I had a girlfriend who had a flat share there, in my university days. Louise.' His eyes drifted towards the unfamiliar ceiling, and then back to his visitor. 'Are you married, Clyde?'

Houseman shook his head. 'Half my life in the Marines and special forces, seeing action for most of it, then on to MI5. No,' he chuckled. 'I couldn't find the time to fit that in. Not that I had any incentive, given the happy home I grew up in.'

The two men's first encounter had been in a squalid housing estate in Edinburgh, when Skinner had just made detective superintendent. Houseman had been a street gang leader, son of a convicted murderer and a thief, until the scare the cop had thrown into him had made him rethink his entire life and join the military.

'Hey,' the chief constable said, 'mine wasn't that great either. It didn't put me off marriage, though, not that I've been very fucking good at it. I've had three goes so far. My first wife died young, car crash, second marriage ended in divorce, and now the third's going the same way.'

'You and the politician lady?'

'Yeah. She had this notion that I should help her fulfil her ambitions, which are substantial. That would have involved me following behind, in the Duke of Edinburgh position. Not my scene, I'm afraid, so we're calling it a day.'

'Won't that be tough on your kids?'

'No. The three young ones are very close to their mother, and as for my adult daughter, she'll wave Aileen a cheerful goodbye. Having made a similar mistake herself she reckons I was daft to split up with Sarah in the first place, and I'm coming to agree with her. They say that Alex and I are absolutely alike, but that's hardly surprising, since I pretty much brought her up on my own.'

He sighed. 'I know why you went for the run, incidentally. To clear your head after what happened last night. We all have our own way of dealing with the shitty end of the job, the things we see, and sometimes the things we have to do; I've been known to go running myself, but usually I get pissed first, to give me something to run off, so it'll hurt that wee bit more. Sometimes I wish I was a Catholic like my friend Andy, so I could go to church and get absolution. But no, not me; I have to do it the hard way.'

Without warning he swung his chair around and sat upright, his forearms on his desk. 'But enough of that. I asked you what your people have got, if anything, on the origin of this hit. We've discounted the notion that Aileen was the target, so, who wanted Toni Field dead?'

Houseman looked back at him, his expression serious. 'I'm not sure I have the authority, sir,' he replied.

Skinner shook his head. 'No, Clyde, I'm not having that. I know there's recent history between your team and Strathclyde and that your deputy director told you to keep your distance from our Counter-terrorism and Intelligence Section. But that was then and this is now.

'Amanda Dennis may have told you she thought it was leaky, but I know damn well that she didn't like or trust Toni Field, and didn't want any involvement with her. I've known Amanda for years, and I worked with her on an internal investigation I did in Thames House a few years ago. I can lift that phone right now and have your order rescinded, but save me the bother, eh?'

The spook gazed at him for a few seconds, then shrugged. 'I'm sure you're right,' he said, 'and I don't fancy breaking into Amanda's Sunday, so okay. The truth is we've got nothing yet. But that's no disgrace, since we've concentrated our efforts since last night on the source of the intelligence that London had, that there was going to be a political hit somewhere in Britain.

'Twenty-four hours ago, that was my colleagues' firm conviction. Today, they're saying they were conned. The threat was bogus; somebody in Pakistan was trying to buy entry into Britain for his family. In short, back to square one.' He smiled. 'Now, since we're sharing, how about you?'

'Fair enough,' Skinner conceded. 'We've been working on the basics. We have one potential witness to interview. You met him yesterday evening: Freddy Welsh. He may have dealt only with Beram Cohen, but it's possible that the order for the weapons was placed by somebody else.'

'Do you want me to talk to him again?'

'I don't think that'll be necessary. Mario McGuire's going to see him.'

'McGuire? Your colleague? The man whose wife was sitting next to Toni Field?'

He nodded. 'The same. Freddy isn't going to enjoy that; not at all.'

'Did you tell him to go hard?'

'No, but I couldn't stop him even if I tried. You and I might have scared Freddy last night, but that was a gentle chat compared to what the big fella's capable of.'

'He won't go too far, will he?'

'He won't have to. I expect to hear from him fairly soon. In the meantime, there is one thing that I will "share" with you, to use your term. Remember, our assumption yesterday was that Smit and Botha were going to get into the hall disguised as police officers?'

'Only too well,' Houseman said, with a bitter frown. 'If the police communications centre hadn't been on Saturday mode, we might have got the message through in time to stop them.'

'That's something I will be addressing now I'm in this chair,' Skinner promised, 'but don't dwell on it. My fear was that those uniforms would have been taken from two cops and that we'd find them afterwards, probably dead.'

'Yes. You're not going to tell me you have, are you?'

'No; the opposite in fact. We've found the uniforms, along with the discarded police-type carbine that Welsh supplied, in the projection room where they took the shot from, but I don't have any officers missing, and the tunics were undamaged . . . no bullet holes, stab wounds or anything else.

'They were also brand new, and were a one hundred per cent match for the kit my people wear. Trousers, short-sleeved undershirt, stab vest with pockets, and caps with the usual Sillitoe Tartan around them. Same for the equipment belt and the gear on it, Hiatt speedcuffs, twenty-one-inch autolock baton, and a CS spray.

'Okay, all British police forces wear similar clothing these days, but all these things were identical,' he stressed the word, 'to ours. The Strathclyde insignia is sewn on the armoured vest, and the man-ufacturer was the same . . . that's telling, for the force changed its stab vest supplier not so long ago. In addition to that, we found two bogus cards on lanyards. Well, they were bogus in that the names were made up, they'd been created from blanks that my people believe were genuine.'

'Could Welsh have supplied the stuff?'

'You saw his store yesterday. There was nothing there other than firearms, boxed.'

'In other words,' the MI5 operative murmured, 'what you're saying is that . . .'

'We're doing a thorough stock check now, but it looks as if the clothing and body equipment came from our own warehouse. I've also asked for checks to be done in every other force that uses Hawk body armour. In other words, Clyde, the hit team had inside help. Somebody in this force supplied them.'

'Then you've got a problem, sir.'

Skinner leaned back in his chair, making a mental note to adjust it to deal with his weight. 'Actually, Clyde,' he murmured, 'I've got two.'

Houseman frowned. 'Oh? What's the other?'

'It's why I asked you to come here,' the chief replied. 'It takes us back to sharing. I need to know what you took from Smit's body yesterday, when I was busy shooting Gerry Botha, and where it led you. I've seen the CCTV, remember. You were very slick, and very quick, but it's there.' He took a deep breath, then let it out in a sigh. 'Fifteen years ago, son,' he said, 'I gave you a serious warning; don't make me have to repeat it, far less follow through on it.'

Fourteen

'You don't need to see the tape, Danny,' Lottie Mann said, in a tone that would have blocked off all future discussion with anyone but Detective Sergeant Provan; he had known her for too long.

He persisted. 'Are you going to show it to the fiscal?'

'She's got it already. The chief had it sent over to her office after he'd shown it to me.'

'So what's on it?' The stocky little detective puffed himself up, his nicotine-stained white moustache bristling, a familiar sign of irritation that she had seen a few hundred times before, mostly when she had been a detective constable on the way up the ladder, before she had passed him by. 'This is a police inquiry and I'm second in seniority on the team. I'm entitled to bloody know.'

'News for you, Dan. You're third in the pecking order. The new chief constable might have told the press that I'm SIO on this one, but make no mistake, he is. This man Skinner is miles different from Toni Field in most ways, but in one they're very much alike. She was on the way to creating a force in her own image, flashy, high-tech.'

'Don't I know it,' Provan grumbled. 'Fuckin' hand-held devices in all the patrol cars. She'd have had us all wearing GPS ankle bracelets before she was done, so she could tell where every one of us was all the time.'

Lottie smiled; she had a soft spot for her sergeant that she never showed to anyone else. While it was a little short of the truth to say that he was her only mentor . . . Max Allan had been that also, if anyone ever was . . . he had always been her strongest supporter, even though he had known from their earliest days as colleagues that he had plateaued, while she was on the rise.

'I wouldn't go quite that far,' she said, 'but aye, that's along the lines I meant. Skinner, if he sticks around, he'll change us too, but it'll be far different from the Field model. And I'll tell you something else, when it comes to CID, it will always go back to him. So, Danny my man, don't you be under any illusions about who's really heading this investigation, 'cos I'm not.'

'Okay,' he replied. 'That's ma card marked. So if Ah want to know what's on that video Ah go an' ask Skinner. That's what ye're saying, is it?'

'Jesus!' the DI exploded. 'You're as persistent as my wee Jakey. I never said I wouldn't tell you. The recording shows four people being shot. Three of them are dead, and Barry Auger could be left in a wheelchair.' She described it in detail, as she had done to her husband a few hours earlier. 'Don't feel left out because you haven't seen it, Danny. I wish I hadn't. Poor Barry and Sandy, they never had a chance.'

'So much for body armour,' the sergeant muttered.

'It's no' going to stop a bullet at close range,' Mann replied. 'Anyway, Sandy was shot in the head, twice. He was a goner before he hit the ground. The guy Smit was getting ready to finish Barry when Skinner and the other bloke arrived.'

'Aye, the other bloke. What about him?'

'Not one of ours. Youngish bloke, maybe mixed race, looked military.'

'You're kidding,' the DS exclaimed. 'When I was coming in, there was a bloke just like that at reception, and I heard him ask for the chief constable's office. Light brown skin, dark hair, creases in his trousers, shiny shoes; a fuckin' soldier for sure. Who is he? What is he?'

'Skinner hasn't said outright, but you can bet he's MI5. I know they've got a regional presence in Glasgow but I've never heard of them being involved with us before.'

'So how come they were this time?'

'The chief had an investigation going in Edinburgh, and this man got pulled in.'

'Linked to this one?' Provan asked.

'Aye. They've got a man in custody, the arms supplier.' She held up a hand. 'Before you get excited, he knows nothing that's going to help us. I just had a call from an ACC in Edinburgh. He told me he just finished interrogating him and he's satisfied he's not holding anything back.'

'So the only possible line of investigation we've got are the uniforms they wore.'

'Right enough; and the fact that they were ours, not fakes,' she confirmed. 'But that's not going to be general knowledge either, Danny. If Smit and Botha did indeed have an inside contact, we know one thing, he'll be on his guard. We have to be careful.'

'Agreed, but can Ah ask, how certain are we they're frae inside?'

'Every single item that we found was what an officer would wear or carry, yet they came from a range of suppliers. If they got them anywhere else they'd have had to know who every one of those is, and some of that stuff isn't public knowledge, not even under Freedom of Information rules. But it's the CS spray that's the clincher; that stuff's military, and each canister has a serial number. We know that the two we found came from our store, because the numbers are in sequence and they were missing from the stock.'

'Right. How do we handle it?'

'Quietly,' Mann declared. 'All police equipment's held in a secure store in Paisley. Operationally, ACC Thomas has oversight of all supplies. He checked on the numbers for me personally . . . he let me know it was a big favour, mind . . . and he's agreed that we can interview the civilian manager, as long as we're discreet. We're off to Paisley, first up tomorrow morning.'

'Just the two of us?'

'Absolutely,' the DI replied. 'Discreet is the word.'

Provan nodded. 'Fair enough. Now, there's one other thing that Ah've been wondering, a question I haven't heard anyone raise since last night.'

'What's that?'

'How did these two fellas get there, and how were they plannin' tae get away? This was a well-planned operation, so I doubt they were going down tae the Central Station to catch the London train.'

Lottie Mann's eyes widened. 'You know, Dan, life's really not fair. You should be the DI, not me. Smit and Botha had nothing on them, nothing at all. No ID of any sort, no wallets, no car keys, nothing.'

'In that case, Lottie,' the DS chuckled, 'maybe Ah should be chief constable, for if the new guy really is runnin' this investigation like you say, then he's missed it as well.'

Fifteen

Clyde Houseman's face grew even more pink, but with embarrassment.

'Come on,' Skinner snapped. 'Out with it.'

'I'm sorry, sir,' the man replied, 'but it's like this. I'm a Security Service officer, and what we were involved in yesterday . . . well, I felt at the time it was one of our operations, and not police, and when I was sent to see you yesterday, by my boss, it was on the basis of bringing you inside, not deferring to you.'

'And you kept thinking that way even though three of our people had been shot?' the chief constable countered.

'Even though. I'd just taken someone down myself, and in those circumstances it was my duty to protect the interests of my service: standard practice. So I did what I did. I meant to report to my deputy director straight away, but I was caught up in the situation and couldn't. I tried to call her this morning, but so far I haven't been able to raise her, and I don't want to go anywhere else. She's my immediate boss.'

'Even Amanda Dennis has to turn her phone off some time,' Skinner said. 'Clyde,' he continued, 'I understand what you're saying, but I'm not buying it. Like it or not, this was a very public crime and the investigation has to be seen to be thorough. I can't have you withholding evidence. So come on, man, and remember this: I've already protected the interests of your service. Only one police officer has seen that tape of you and me taking care of the South Africans, and that's how it's going to stay. She's assuming that I've given it to the procurator fiscal, the prosecutor's office, because I let her believe that, but in fact it's still in my desk. The deputy fiscal in charge of the investigation knows about it, because I've told him; he understands the sensitivity and he's prepared to forget that it ever existed.'

'Where is it now?'

'Locked in my desk, for now, till somebody comes up with the combination of the bloody safe that Toni Field left behind.'

'Thank you for that,' Houseman murmured. 'But do you trust your people? Leaks can happen, and the last thing that either of us wants is for that video to wind up on YouTube.'

'At the moment, I trust them more than I trust you,' Skinner pointed out, 'and I will until you cough up what you took from Smit's body. Look, I don't want to, but I will bypass Amanda and go to your director if I have to, even though he is a buffoon.'

'Sir Hubert would probably back me up.'

'No he wouldn't,' the chief chuckled. 'Do you have any idea of what would happen if I even hinted to the media that MI5 was getting in the way of my investigation? You're forgetting who's been killed here. Toni Field was a big name in the Met, plus the Mayor of London was said to be her biggest fan. All of their weight would come down on Thames House if I dropped the word. Plus,' he added, 'I've got the tape. You're worried about YouTube, son? If I chose I could edit it, destroy the footage of me shooting Botha, and leak the rest myself. If I chose,' he repeated. 'Not that I would, but I won't have to, because you're going to . . .' he smiled, '. . . share with me again. Aren't you?'

Houseman sighed, then reached inside his leather jerkin. For an instant Skinner tensed, but what he produced was nothing more menacing than an envelope.

'I had a hunch our meeting might go this way,' he said, 'so I brought the things along.'

He handed it across to the chief, who took it, ripped it open and shook its contents out on to the desk: a car key, with a Drivall rental tag bearing a vehicle registration number, and a parking ticket.

Skinner picked up the rectangle of card and peered at it with the intense concentration of a man who had reached the age of fifty and yet was still in denial of his need for reading spectacles.

'Have you done anything with this yet?'

His visitor shook his head. 'I decided to wait for instructions.'

'On whether to hand it over to me or not?'

'Yes, more or less.'

'Now you've done it, story's over as far as I'm concerned. If Amanda gives you a hard time, although I don't believe she will, you can tell her I coerced you into it. So,' he held up the ticket, between two fingers, 'you know where this is for?'

'It doesn't say on it.'

'Maybe not, but given the exit they chose, the likeliest is the multi-storey on the other side of Killermont Street, beside the bus station. One way to find out.' Skinner pushed himself to his feet. 'Gimme a minute.'

He picked up his uniform jacket from the back of his chair, and stepped into the private room behind it. When he emerged, three minutes later, he had changed into the same slacks and cotton jacket that Houseman had seen the day before.

'We're going ourselves?' the younger man asked.

'Of course. I seize every chance that comes up to get out of my office; there may not be too many more, now I'm here.'

He led the way out of his room, but instead of heading straight for the exit, he turned left, stopping at the second door. He opened it and called to the occupant. 'Lowell, I have an outside visit; I could use your help.'

Payne had been working on the chief constable's forward engagement diary. He closed it and crossed swiftly to the door. 'Where are we going?' he asked, then reacted with surprise as he saw Houseman for the first time.

Skinner did the introductions on his way to the lift. 'Clyde's come in with some new information,' he added. 'He's found the vehicle Smit and Botha were using yesterday. Well, that's to say, we know where it might be.'

'Should we call Lottie?' the DCI asked.

'Yes, we should, but we won't until we've got something to tell her.'

They rode the lift down to the sub-level that accessed the police headquarters park, then took Payne's car, which he had left in the space allocated to the deputy chief. The journey along Sauchiehall Street and Renfrew Street to the Buchanan Street bus station took only two minutes, five less than it might have on a weekday. Skinner smiled as they passed the McLellan Galleries, his mind going back thirty years to a visit to an art exhibition, in a foursome with Louise Bankier and a couple of their fellow students, when he had spotted, on the other side of the big room, Myra, his fiancée, with a spotty guy he had never seen before. They were heading for the exit, hand in hand, with eyes only for each other. He never had found out who the bloke was, but it had never occurred to him to ask. He had been too wrapped up in his own guilt over Louise; indeed the close encounter had been the beginning of the end of that relationship.

He was still dwelling on the past as they approached their destination. In case his daydream had been noticed, he took out the Drivall car key and made a show of peering at the number written on the fob, until he gave up and handed it to Houseman, and his younger eyes.

'We're looking for a Peugeot,' he announced, after the briefest study, 'registration LX12 PMP. Doesn't say what colour it is.'

Payne ignored the official entry point and drove to the office instead. The way was blocked by a barrier. A staff member, in a Day-Glo jacket, came out to meet them. The DCI showed his warrant card, and the parking ticket that Skinner had handed to him. 'That one of yours?' he asked.

The attendant studied it. 'Aye,' he confirmed. 'It's dated yesterday afternoon. Left overnight, eh, and no' picked up yet. Stolen car? There's nae TV in here so we get them.'

'Not necessarily, but we need to find it. Is the park busy?'

'Jam packed, but go on in.' He pushed a button at the side of the barrier, and it rose.

'Okay. Two ways of doing this,' the chief declared. 'We either drive through very slowly, and hope we get lucky, or we do the sensible thing and split it. Lowell, drop me on level two, Clyde on four and you go to the top and park. We work our way down till we find it. You've both got my work mobile number, and I've got yours; either of you find the car, you call me and I'll alert the other.'

Payne did as he was instructed. As each of them reached his starting point, he realised that the multi-storey was spilt into sub-levels, making it bigger than it had looked from the outside. They searched their separate areas as quickly as they could but nonetheless almost fifteen minutes had passed before Skinner's mobile rang. By that time he was at ground level.

His screen told him that it was Houseman who had made the discovery. 'I'm on level five,' the spook said. 'At the side, overlooking the street.'

'Good spot. Be with you in a minute; I'll tell Lowell.'

'There's no need. The way this place is built he can see me from where he is.'

Skinner took the stairs, two at a time. As he stepped out on to level five he saw Payne, on his left, coming towards him down a ramp.

The Peugeot was a big saloon model, in a dark blue colour. Skinner took the key from his pocket and worked out by trial and error which button unlocked it. Houseman was in the act of reaching for the driver's door handle when Payne called out to him.

'No, not without gloves.' He smiled. 'Sorry,' he said. 'It's a CID reflex.'

'Understood,' the MI5 man conceded. He took a handkerchief from his pocket and used it to open the door.

Skinner stepped up behind him and looked inside, then slotted the key in to light up the dashboard. 'Satnav,' he said.

'So?' Houseman murmured.

'With a bit of luck they'll have used it. With even more, they won't have deleted previous entries. When did they collect the uniforms and equipment? Where? That may give us a clue.'

'Mmm.'

'And if they did pick up the gear from an inside source, he may have left us a print, or a DNA trace.'

'That's if he's on the database,' Payne pointed out. 'If he is inside, how likely is that?'

'Come on, Lowell,' Skinner chided. 'Think positive.' He glanced into the back of the car, saw it was empty, then withdrew the key and closed the driver's door, leaning on it with an elbow. Moving round to the back of the vehicle, which had been left perilously close to the wall of the building, he pushed a third button on the remote. There was a muffled sound and the boot lid sprang open.

'Jesus Christ!' the DCI yelled, jumping backwards in alarm and astonishment.

His companions stood their ground, gazing into the luggage compartment.

'Surprisingly capacious, these things,' the chief constable murmured, 'aren't they, Clyde? You'd get at least two sets of golf clubs in there, no problem. Maybe two trolleys as well.'

'Beyond a doubt.'

Two medium-sized blue suitcases lay on their sides, at the front of the boot, but there had still been more than enough room for the rest of the load to be jammed in behind them: the body of a man, knees drawn up and his arms wrapped around them. The eyes were open, staring, and there was a cluster of three holes in the centre of his chest.

'So, chum,' Skinner wondered. 'Who the hell were you, and why did you wind up here?'

Sixteen

'That's Bazza Brown,' DS Dan Provan announced.

Lottie Mann frowned. 'Are you sure?'

'Trust me. Real name Basil, but nobody ever called him that, unless they wanted a sore face. The first time Ah lifted him he was sixteen, sellin' what he claimed were LSD tabs on squares from a school jotter. They wis just melted sugar, but nobody ever complained; he wis a hard kid even then, and he had a gang.'

'When was that?' Skinner asked. He had never met the wizened little detective before but he found himself taking an instant liking to him, and to his irreverence.

'Goin' on twenty-five years ago, sir. He moved on frae there, though. The next time I picked him up he'd just turned twenty-one and he was sellin' hash. He got three years for that, in the University of Barlinnie, and that, you might say, completed his formal education. He's never done a day's time since, even though he's reckoned . . . sorry, he was reckoned . . . to be one of the big three in drugs in Glasgow.'

'So how come he wound up in a car boot sale?'

'Ah can't tell you that, sir. But Ah know you're going to want us to find out.'

The chief grinned. 'That is indeed the name of the game, Sergeant.'

He and Payne had called in Mann and her squad at once. They

had left the car untouched. Indeed the only change in the scenery since they had made their discovery lay in the absence of Clyde Houseman. Skinner had decided that it would be best if he made himself scarce.

He had expected Lottie Mann to be blunt when she arrived, and had been ready for her challenge.

'Can I ask what the fuck you're doing here, sir? I've got people out showing pictures of Smit and Botha to every car park attendant in Glasgow, and what do I find? You and DCI Payne, with their bloody car key!'

'Inspector!' Lowell Payne had intervened, but his new chief had calmed his protest with a wave of his hand.

'It's okay. DI Mann is well entitled to sound off. I was given some information, Lottie, and I decided to evaluate it myself, and to bring you in if I reckoned it was worth it. Get used to me: it's the way I am.'

'Oh, I know that already, sir,' she retorted. 'Just like I know there's no point me asking who your source was.'

'That's right, but now the result is all yours.'

She had given one of her hard-earned smiles, then gone into action.

The photographer and video cameraman were finishing their work as Provan announced the identity of the victim and he and Skinner had their exchange. They had been hampered slightly by a silver Toyota parked in the bay on the right, but the two to the left were clear.

As they packed their equipment, the elevator door opened, beside the stairway exit, and a woman stepped out, pushing a child in a collapsible pram with John Lewis bags hung on the back. She frowned as she moved towards them. 'What's going . . .' she began.

Payne moved quickly across to intercept her, holding up his warrant card. 'Police, ma'am. Is that your Toyota?'

'Yes, but what . . . It's not damaged, is it? I can move it, can't I?'

'It's fine, but please don't come any closer. If you give me your car key I'll bring it out for you.'

'It's not a bomb, is it?' The young mother was terrified; Payne smiled to reassure her.

'No, no, not at all. If it was I wouldn't be within a mile of it myself. It's just a suspicious vehicle, that's all. We're checking out the contents. You just give me your keys and don't you worry.'

He reversed the Toyota out of its bay and drove it a little way down the exit ramp, then helped her load her bags and her child, who had slept through the exchange.

'Did she see anything?' Mann asked the DCI as he returned.

'No, or you'd have heard the screams. But we need to get a screen round this, now we've got the room.'

'It's on the way, with the forensic people. We'd better not touch anything till they get here. That peppery wee bastard Dorward's on weekend duty and he'll never let me forget it if I compromise "his" crime scene.'

'It's well compromised already, Lottie,' Skinner pointed out. 'Anyone got a pair of gloves?' he asked. 'I want a look at these suitcases. I'll handle Arthur's flak. I've been doing it for long enough.'

Provan handed him a pair of latex gloves. He slipped them on and lifted one of the blue cases from the boot, laid it on the ground and tried the catches, hoping they were unlocked and smiling when they clicked open.

'Clothing,' he announced as he studied the contents, and sifted through them. 'It looks like two changes: trousers, shirt, underwear, just the one jacket, though, and one pair of shoes. Everything's brand new, Marks and Spencer labels still on them. Summer wear. Mmm,' he mused. 'What's the weather like in South Africa in July?'

There was a zipped pocket set in the lid of the case, which also sported a Marks and Spencer label on its lining. He unfastened it, felt inside and found a padded envelope. It was unsealed; the contents slid into his hand.

'Wallet,' he said. 'Looks like at least three hundred quid. One Visa debit card in the name of Bryan Lightbody. A passport, New Zealand, in the same name, but with Gerry Botha's photo inside. Flight tickets and itinerary, Singapore Air, Heathrow to Auckland through Singapore, business class, departure tomorrow evening.'

He lifted the second case from the car and checked its contents. 'An Australian passport,' he announced when he was finished. 'It and the bank card are in the name of Richie Mallett, and the flight ticket's Quantas to Sydney, again Heathrow tomorrow night. So that was the game plan. Drive to London, fly away home and leave us scratching our arses as we try to find them on flights out of Scotland.'

'Well planned,' Lottie Mann observed.

'Yes, but that's not what these guys did. The man Cohen was the planner. He made all the arrangements, bought the air tickets, hired the car.'

'The car,' she repeated, then turned to Provan. 'Get . . .'

'Ah'm on it already,' he retorted, waving the car key with his left hand while holding his mobile to his ear. 'Yes,' he said, 'that's right, Strathclyde CID. I'm standing over one o' your cars just now, and Ah need to know whose name is on the rental contract.' He paused, listening.

'Because there's something wrong wi' it, that's why.' He waited again.

'Maybe there wasn't when it left you, Jimmy, but there is now. There's a fuckin' body in the boot. Or dae all your vehicles come with that accessory? No, Ah won't hold on. The registration's LX12 PMP;

108

you get me the information Ah want and get back to me through the force main switchboard. They'll transfer your call to my mobile. Pronto, please, this is very important.'

As Provan finished, Skinner tapped him on the shoulder. 'Have you ever done a course,' he asked, 'on communication with the public?'

The sergeant pursed his lips, wrinkling his two-tone moustache in the process, and looked up at him. 'No, sir, I can't say that Ah have.'

'Then I will make it my business, Detective Sergeant,' the chief told him, without the suggestion of a smile, 'to see that you never do.'

'Thanks, gaffer,' the little DS replied, 'but even if you did send me on one, at my age I wake up sometimes wi' this terrible hacking cough. Knocks me right off for the day, it does.'

Skinner laughed out loud. 'I could get to like it here,' he exclaimed. Then he turned serious. 'Now prove to me that you're a detective, not some fucking hobbit who's tolerated because he's been around for ever. There's a begged question in this scenario. I'm not wondering about the guy in the boot. You knew who he was, and I know what he was. No, it's something else, unrelated. What is it?'

As Dan Provan looked up at his new boss, two thoughts entered his mind. The first of them was financial. He had over thirty years in the job, and his pension was secure as long as he didn't punch the chief constable in the mouth, and since that struck him as being a seriously stupid overreaction, it wasn't going to happen. So the 'daft laddie' option was open to him, without risk.

But the second was professional, and pride was involved. He had survived as long as he had because he was, in fact, a damn good detective, and as such he was expert in analysing every scenario and in identifying all the possible lines of inquiry that it offered.

A third consideration followed. Skinner hadn't asked him the question to embarrass him, but because he expected him to know the answer.

He frowned and bent his mind to recalling as much as he could of what had been said in the previous half hour. He played the mental tape, piece by piece, then ran through it again.

'It's the flights,' he said, when he was sure. 'The two dead guys had plane tickets out of Heathrow. Yes?'

'Yes.'

'Right. Now if everything had gone to plan, the two hit men, Smit and Botha, or Lightbody and Mallett, or Randall and fuckin' Hopkirk deceased, whoever they were, if it had all gone to plan, they'd have driven straight out of this car park, almost before the alarm had been raised, headed straight down to London, dumping our friend Bazza in some lay-by along the way, and got on a fuckin' plane. Right, boss?'

Skinner nodded. 'You're on a roll, Sergeant, carry on.'

'Thank you, gaffer. In that case, even as we're stood here, they could have been sipping fuckin' cocktails in business class. Except . . . their flights were booked for Monday, for tomorrow. So what were they supposed to be doin' in those spare twenty-four hours?'

The chief constable smiled. 'Absolutely. Top question. You got an answer for that one?'

Provan shrugged, 'No idea, sir.' He nodded towards the boot of the Peugeot. 'But if we find out what they were doing with poor old Bazza Brown there, maybe that'll give us a clue.'

Seventeen

'He's a marginally insubordinate little joker, but I do like him,' Bob chuckled. 'He and that DI, Lottie, they're some team.'

Sarah smiled across the table, on which the last of their dinner plates lay, empty save for the skeletons of two lemon sole. She raised her coffee cup. 'Could it be that Glasgow isn't the cultural wasteland you thought it was?'

'Hey, come on,' he protested. 'I never said that, or even thought it. I'm from Motherwell, remember; I'm not quite a Weegie myself, but close. I have a Glasgow degree; I spent a good chunk of my teens in that fair city. West of Scotland culture is in my blood. Why do you think I like country music and bad stand-up comedians?'

'So part of you is glad to be back there,' she suggested.

'Sure, the nostalgic part.'

'Then why did you ever leave?' she asked in her light American drawl. 'Myra was from Motherwell as well and yet the two of you upped sticks and moved through to Gullane in your early twenties.'

'You know why; I've told you often enough. I liked Edinburgh, and I liked the seaside. I wanted to work in one and live by the other. I've never regretted that decision either, not once.'

'But what made you choose it over Glasgow? I can see you, man, and your pleasure now at being back there. There must have been an underlying reason.'

He leaned back in his chair and gazed at her. 'Very well,' he conceded. 'There was. I didn't like being asked what school I went to.'

'Uh?' she grunted. 'Come again? What's that got to do with anything?'

His laugh was gentle, amused. 'You've lived in Scotland for how long? Twelve years on and off, and you don't know that one? It's code, and what it actually means is, "Are you Protestant or are you Catholic?" Where I grew up that was a key question, just as much as in Belfast, and for all Aileen and her kind might try to deny it, I'm sure it still is in some places and to some people. The answer could determine many things, not least your employment prospects.

'Why the school question? Because through there, education was organised along religious lines; there were Roman Catholic schools and non-denominational, the latter being in name only. They were where the Protestants went. So, your school defined you, and it could mean that some doors were just slammed in your face.'

'Wow,' Sarah murmured. 'I know about Rangers and Celtic football clubs, of course, but I didn't think it went that deep.'

'It did, and for some it still does. Both those clubs condemn sectarianism but they still struggle to eradicate it among their supporters. I decided very early on that I didn't want any kids of mine growing up in that environment, and Myra agreed. That's what was behind our move.'

'But now you're back you like it?'

'Hey, love, it's been one day. My reservations about the size of the Strathclyde force are as strong as ever. What I'm saying is that I like the people I've met so far. Mann and Provan, they're good cops and pure Glaswegian, both of them.'

'What school did they go to?'

'As for Lottie, I have no idea.' He winked. 'But the Celtic supporter's lapel badge that wee Provan was wearing still offers something of a clue. He may miss their next game,' he added, 'if they don't get these killings wrapped up soon.'

'Yeah,' Sarah said. 'The body in the boot must have been a bit of a shaker.'

'It was for Lowell, that's for sure. He jumped out of his skin. Me too, to be honest, but I've gotten good at hiding it.'

'Why was he there, the dead guy?'

'I guess they didn't want to leave him wherever he was killed. The provisional time of death was Friday evening some time; with the hit being planned for Saturday, they may not have wanted to muddy the waters by having him found.'

'Meaning the police might have made a connection to them?'

He nodded. 'It would have been a long shot, but that would have been the thinking.'

'Mmm.' She frowned. 'But I didn't mean why was he in the boot; I mean why were they involved with him at all?'

'We all asked ourselves that one. It seems that the late Mr Brown was a reasonably heavy-duty Glasgow criminal, but I doubt very much that Mr Smit and Mr Botha met him to do a drug deal on the side.'

'Are you still sure those are their real names?'

'Oh yes, we know that. We can trace them all the way back to the South African armed forces. Lightbody and Mallett were aliases. It remains to be seen whether they actually lived under those names, one in New Zealand, one in Australia. We'll need to wait for the passport offices and the police in those countries to open before we can follow them up.' He checked his watch; quarter to nine. 'New Zealand should be wide awake now, Australia in an hour or two. Anyway, whatever their fucking names, what were they doing with a Weegie hood?'

'Yes, any theories?'

'Only one, the obvious. Mr Brown must have been involved in the supply of the police uniforms and equipment, and they must have decided not to leave him behind as a witness.'

'So why did they leave the arms dealer alive?' Sarah wondered.

'Because he's part of that world, I'd guess, and was in as deep as they were. A small-timer they'd have seen as a weakness.'

Sarah refilled her cup from a cafetière. Bob, who had given up coffee at her suggestion, almost at her insistence, topped up his glass with mineral water.

'But the tough questions are, why was he in the chain at all, and who introduced him? There we do not have a Scooby, as wee Provan would probably say.'

'Good.' She smiled. 'Enough for tonight, Chief Constable. No more shop, just Bob and Sarah for a while. I've been thinking about what happened a couple of nights ago, you and me having a nice quiet dinner and ending up in bed together.' She took his hand, studying it as she spoke. 'I have to ask you this, Bob, because it's been gnawing away at me, knowing from personal experience how unpredictable you are when it comes to women. Are you and the witch definitely a thing of the past? Is there any chance of a reconciliation?'

He sipped some water. 'Given our history,' he began, 'I suppose I deserved that "unpredictability" crack. But you can take this to the bank: Aileen and I are through. Sit her across from you and she would give you the same answer. She'd probably add also that we're not going to walk away as friends either. Each of us married a person without knowing them at all. Before too long we found we didn't even like each other all that much.'

'Do you think you know me now?' she asked.

'None of us can live inside someone else's head, but if I don't know what makes you tick by now . . .' He leaned forward and looked deep into her eyes. 'I always did like you; now I know more. I never stopped loving you either.'

'But let's not put it to the test by getting married again. Agreed?'

Bob nodded. 'Agreed. But is that because you don't trust me? If it is, I understand.'

'Amazing as it may sound, I do trust you. No, it's because right now, the way we are . . . I don't think I've ever felt happier, and I don't want to risk that.'

'Fair enough. Now, with the kids upstairs in bed, can we do something old-fashioned, like watching television?'

She laughed. 'How very couple-ish! Yeah, let's.'

She was flicking through the channel choice when Bob's work mobile sounded. 'Bugger,' he murmured. 'I must give this Edinburgh phone back to Maggie and get a new one from Strathclyde. Chances are this is for her.' He looked at the caller identification. 'No, it's not. Lowell,' he said as he accepted the call, 'what's up? News from down under?'

As Sarah watched him, she saw his eyes widen, a frown wrinkle his forehead for a second then disappear. 'You're fucking kidding,' he exclaimed. 'So that's what the bloody woman was leading up to. Don't apologise, man, I know you had to tell me, but worry not; it won't ruin my night. I just wish I could be a fly on a certain wall, that's all.'

He ended the call as Sarah laid down the TV remote.

'Well?' she demanded. 'What bloody woman? Aileen?'

'As it happened, no,' he told her, 'another bloody woman, but not unconnected. What you asked me earlier on, whether there was a cat's chance of the two of us staying together.' He laughed. 'If you doubted me at all, then, by Christ, you're going to be a happy woman tomorrow morning.'

Eighteen

'Are we all set for tomorrow, Alf?'

'Yes, but I've brought it forward to eleven thirty. The phone's never stopped ringing all day, and the place is going to be packed out. If you want to do follow-up interviews and get them on the midday news we'll need to start a bit earlier than noon.'

'Agreed,' Aileen said. 'And the announcement: do they have that ready?'

'Yes,' the party CEO replied. 'I've just sent you a draft by email. If you clear it, I can tell the policy staff to go home for the night.'

'I'll do that right now.'

'Thanks. I must go now, Aileen. For some reason the switchboard's just lit up like a Christmas tree.'

She cradled the phone and turned to Joey Morocco, who was removing silver boxes from a brown paper bag. She smiled. 'You must do this a lot,' she remarked. 'I heard you at the front door; you were on first-name terms with the delivery boy. "Thank you, Wen-Chong." I take it that means we're having Chinese.'

'I see that being married to a detective's rubbed off on you,' he said. 'Sure, first-name terms with him, with Jeev from the Asian up in Gibson Street, with Kemal from the kebab shop and with Jocky.'

'Jocky? Who the hell's he?'

'Pizza. That's the Italians for you; much more interbred with the indigenous population.'

She looked over his shoulder. 'What have we got?'

'Chicken, brack bean sauce,' he replied, mimicking a Chinese accent, 'plawn sweet and sowah, clispy duck and pancakes, and lice; flied of course.'

'Sounds great. I just need five minutes on my laptop and I'll be ready.'

She wakened her computer from the sleep state in which she had left it earlier in the evening, and searched her email inbox. It was full of messages from friends, anxious, she guessed, for news of her safety, but Old's was near the top and she found it with ease.

She opened the attachment, which was headed, 'Draft Statement: Unified Police Force', scanned it quickly, made a few changes to bring it into her delivery style, then sent it back with a covering note that read, 'Final version clear for use.'

She had just clicked the 'send' button when a tone advised her that another message had hit the inbox, once again from Alf Old. Almost simultaneously, her mobile rang, and the screen showed that he was calling. She made a choice; the phone won.

'Aileen.' Even although he had only said her name, the chief executive, famed for his calmness, sounded rattled. 'I've just sent you an email.'

'I know, it just arrived. I haven't opened it yet.'

'Then you'd better do so.'

Not only rattled, she realised; he was angry also.

She opened the message. There was no text, only an attachment, headed 'P1', in PDF form. She clicked on it and an image appeared, as quickly as her ageing laptop would allow.

It was a newspaper front page, with the masthead of the *Daily*

News, and beneath it a headline. 'Road to Morocco: married Labour leader goes to ground.' Most of it was taken up by a photograph, taken from a distance with a long lens, but the face was all too clearly hers, looking out of Joey Morocco's bedroom window, with a curtain held across her, but not far enough to cover her right breast, which the newspaper had chosen to cover with a black rectangle.

'Fuck!' she screamed.

'Exactly!' Old barked. 'What the hell were you thinking about, Aileen?'

'It's not what you think,' she protested.

'Then what the hell else is it? Anyway it doesn't matter what I think, it's what the readers of the *Daily News* think, them and the readers of every other paper that the photographer sells it on to, once they've had their exclusive. They've already given it to BBC, Sky and ITN, for use after ten, to sell even more papers tomorrow morning.'

'Is it on the streets yet? Can we stop them?'

'It will be any minute now, and no we can't. We could go to the Court of Session and ask for an interdict preventing further publication. We might get it, we might not, probably not. Anyway, the damage is done.'

Her anger had risen up to match his. 'But how did they get it?' she asked. 'How did they know I was here?'

'They didn't. I spoke to the editor of the Scottish version; he's a mate and he was good enough to call me, and to send the page across. He said it was taken by a freelance photographer, a paparazzo, who stakes out Joey Morocco's place periodically, just in case.

'She saw a car parked across his driveway, with two guys in it who had Special Branch written all over them . . . her words . . . so she found a vantage point out of their sight and hung around, just in case. She got lucky; saw a face at the window and a bit more, snapped off as many shots as she could, then legged it.

'It was only when she downloaded the photos on to her laptop in her car that she realised how lucky she was. She got straight on to the *News*. That's her best payer, apparently.'

'Bastards!' she hissed, then chuckled, taking herself by surprise. 'It's the wee black sticker I really hate. It's suggesting that my tits are too misshapen for a family newspaper: that they might put folk off their breakfast.'

'Then cheer up,' Old growled. 'There's another one inside, on page three, appropriately enough, with you looking over your shoulder, as if to make it crystal clear that there is somebody else in the room with you. There's a lot more of you on show there, and they haven't covered that up.'

'Who wrote the story?'

'Marguerite Hatton. She's on their political staff. They flew her up from London overnight.'

'That's the bitch that gave Bob trouble earlier on at his press conference. She'll rub his nose in it now.'

'Or he will rub yours.'

'I couldn't care less about him. Why do you think I'm at Joey's?' As she spoke, she became aware of a figure in the doorway, holding a plate in each hand. 'I've got some apologising to do to him.'

'Well, do it on the way to the emergency exit. You have to get out of there, for a fucking army's going to land on his doorstep as soon as the telly news breaks. Get your bodyguards to pull right up to his door, jump in their car and have them get you the hell out of there.'

'To where, though?' Joey had moved in behind her and was studying the image on the laptop. 'It'll be just as bad at my place.'

'To Gullane?' Old suggested. 'Give yourself time to come up with a cover story? Maybe even do a happy families shot tomorrow.'

'Not a fucking chance. I tell you, we're history. Anyway, I'm going to be in Glasgow tomorrow.'

'Eh?' he exclaimed. 'You're not going ahead with the press conference, are you?'

She gasped. 'Of course, man. We'll never have a bigger crowd. I will not back down from this. It's not going to kill me, any more than that guy did last night, so it can only make me stronger.'

'Then go to my place. Nobody will think to look there. I'll call Justine and tell her you're coming.'

Nineteen

'She's done what?' Sarah looked at him, astonished. 'Let herself be photographed in a lover's bedroom the morning after she's come within an inch of her life?'

'That's what they're going to say,' Bob acknowledged.

'She will argue, of course, that Morocco's an old family friend and that his girlfriend was there too.'

'I don't think so,' he replied. 'She won't lie her way out of it; too big a downside if she's caught, as many a politician's found out to their cost. She'll front it up; I know her.'

'And blacken your name in the process?'

He shook his head. 'She'll have a tough time doing that. She doesn't realise it but I have more friends in the media than she has. Speaking of whom, I expect that some of them will be calling me in the next hour or so, on my mobile and at Gullane. I think it would be best if I go home, so that I'm there to answer them.'

'Aww!' she moaned. 'I was looking forward to you staying.'

'Me too, but if I do, there's an outside chance that someone might doorstep me here in the morning. I don't want you and the kids caught up in this, in any way.'

She stood with him as he rose to leave, picking up his jacket from the back of the sofa. 'How do you feel about this?' she asked.

'Her being all over the tabloids.'

'I've had some of that myself in my career,' he answered, 'and I didn't like it. Am I embarrassed by it? Not a bit. People may talk about me behind my back, but none will to my face, so fuck 'em. Am I angry? No, because I don't have a right to be. It could have been me looking out of your bedroom window and all over the papers in the morning.'

'Are you sorry for her?' she murmured.

'Only if he's a lousy fuck, and not worth it. She will win out of this. I don't know how, but she will.'

She walked him to the door and hugged him there, looking up into his eyes. 'So what do we do?'

'Tomorrow we go to work, each of us, and Trish takes care of the kids as usual. I'm going to be as busy as the Devil's apprentice all this week, so we'll see each other when we can. With a bit of luck we'll be able to keep the weekend free.'

She kissed him. 'That's a plan,' she said. 'Now be on with your way and answer those phone calls.'

The first came, on his work mobile . . . he had switched his personal phone off as he left Sarah's . . . as he was turning on to the Edinburgh bypass. He had been expecting it.

'Bob.' The voice that filled the car through its speaker system was no longer aggressive, as it had been the last time he had heard it, but there was nothing fearful or tentative about it. 'I have something to tell you.'

'No, you don't,' he replied, speaking louder than usual, to allow for road noise.

'You've heard, then.'

'Of course I have. The editor of the *News* called my people. I don't know him but he said that he'd given you advance warning and was offering me the same courtesy. Of course, he also asked me for a comment.'

'And did you give him one?'

Skinner laughed. 'Shouldn't I be asking you that question, in a different context? Not that I need to; from what I've been told the answer's pretty fucking obvious. Oops, sorry, unfortunate choice of word. Bet you're glad now I persuaded you to spend that time in the gym.'

'Bob!' she snapped. 'Did you give the man a quote?'

'Don't be daft,' he retorted. 'Of course I didn't. Nor will I to anyone else, and I'm bloody sure quite a few people will be asking over the next couple of hours. What about you?'

'Nothing so far; they don't know where I am now. But I'm seeing the press tomorrow morning.'

'How about Joey? What's he going to be saying?'

'That I'm an old friend and that he offered me a place where I could recover from my ordeal in private.'

'Is he going to refer to me?'

'What would he say about you?'

'Not about me: to me. Some people might expect him to say "Sorry". That's the big media word these days, isn't it? People under the spotlight all have to utter the "S" word, whether they are or not.'

'Do you expect that?'

'Hell no. I'm sorry for him, if anything. He didn't bargain for all this crap.'

'Well,' she said, beginning to sound exasperated, as if she thought he was playing with her, as he was to a degree, 'what are you going to say?'

'Tonight, nothing. Not a fucking word, about you or against you, or anything else. What time's your press briefing tomorrow?'

'Eleven thirty.'

'In that case,' he declared, 'at ten o'clock, we're going to issue a joint statement through Mitchell Laidlaw, my lawyer at Curle Anthony Jarvis. It will say something along these lines: on Thursday . . . or whenever, you pick the day . . . you and I agreed to separate permanently because of profound and irreconcilable differences that have developed between us. You draft it, let me see it and we'll take it from there. You okay with that?'

'Mmm.' The car was silent, for long enough to make him wonder if the connection had been lost.

'Aileen?' he exclaimed into the darkness.

'I'm still here,' she replied. 'Thinking, that's all. I'm not sure I want it going out through your daughter's law firm.'

'Listen,' he retorted. 'You don't have a regular bloody lawyer that I know of. I can hardly use the Strathclyde Police press office for this, and I'll be damned if I'll have the end of my marriage announced by the Labour Party. Alex will have no sight of the statement, I promise.'

She drew in a deep breath, loudly enough for him to hear it clearly. 'Okay,' she agreed. 'What else do you want to put in it?'

'The minimum.'

'Should I say that we intend to divorce?'

'I include that among the minimum. Don't you? If you want you can say that we'll do it when we've completed the legal period of separation. Unless you want to marry Joey straight away, that is.'

'Don't be funny.'

'Sorry. How's the guy taking it anyway?'

'He's been lovely,' she said.

'I'm assuming that you and he had been over the course in the past. Yes?'

'For God's sake!' Aileen protested. 'Do you think he was a quick pick-up?'

'Not at all; hence the assumption. What else is he likely to say?'

'Nothing beyond what I told you. And he's going to leave for America tomorrow, a few days earlier than planned.'

'He probably thinks that's very wise on his part. I mean, hanging around in a city after being caught banging the chief constable's wife, all sorts of misfortunes might come your way. But tell him not to worry, if he is worrying, that is.'

'I will. And I'll tell him as well that he's probably done you a favour.'

'What do you mean by that?' he asked.

'Isn't it obvious? When you show up somewhere with another lady on your arm, everybody's going to say, "Aw, is that no' nice, after what the poor man went through." I could even hazard a guess as to who she might be.'

'Don't bother yourself, Aileen. You just get on with your brilliant career. I wish you every success.'

'And you get on with yours, my dear. And you remember what I said. Now you're wedged in the Stratchlyde chief's chair, you'll find it impossible to leave. And when the new single force is created, and your case against it has been knocked back, as you know will happen, you'll want that job too, because you won't be able to help yourself. The one and only thing that you and I have in common, my dear, is this: we are both driven by ambition.'

'You could not be more wrong. I have only one motivation.'

'Oh aye,' she said, mockery in her voice. 'And what's that?'

'Love.' He continued, cutting off her gasp of derision. 'Send me your draft. I'll be home in fifteen minutes.' He ended the call.

He thought about his final exchange with Aileen for the rest of the journey to Gullane. Never before had he encapsulated his driving forces in one word, but he realised that it was entirely appropriate. He loved his children, all of them with equal intensity, and he loved Sarah. And he loved his job as well, because it was his vocation, and it enabled him to be the best he could be for all of them.

He had never loved Aileen. He realised that. He had been attracted to a personality as powerful as his own, but had discovered that they could not co-exist in the same union. Eventually each had sought to dominate the other and the marriage had broken apart. This was not to say that Aileen was incapable of love herself. She had her tender side, but she would always be a leader, never a follower, and her soulmate, if he existed, would have to know that and be compliant.

The draft joint announcement was waiting for him as an email attachment when he reached home and turned on the computer in his small office. He read through it, found it factual and unemotional, and forwarded it, unamended, in a message to Mitchell Laidlaw asking him to issue it to the media at 10 a.m. next morning through his firm's PR company. He copied the mail to Aileen, then sent Laidlaw a text message from his personal mobile advising him that it was on its way.

He had expected no reply until the morning, but within a minute, his phone rang.

'Bob,' Mitch Laidlaw exclaimed. 'What a shocker. This is completely out of the blue. This will shake a few people.'

'Clearly you haven't seen the telly news tonight. From what I'm told it has already.'

'No, I missed that. We were watching a film. Why, has it leaked?'

'Not in the way you mean, but . . . go online and look at the *Daily News* website, you may find that explains a lot.'

'Intriguing, but I will. There's no chance of any . . .'

'No, chum; not a prayer. We both know what we want to say and we're not backing off from it. When your PR people put it out, they can add that I'm making no further comment. What Aileen chooses to do is up to her.'

'What about the legal side of it?' the solicitor asked.

'We haven't discussed that. Look after my kids' interests if it becomes necessary; that's all the instruction I'll give you at this stage.'

'I will do. The fact is, you're pretty much divorce-proofed after the last time.'

'Ouch!' Skinner winced. 'You make me sound like a recidivist.'

'Two's above average in our community, Bob.'

He laughed. 'I know, but I'm coming round to the view that the first one doesn't count.'

'Oh yes? What does that mean?'

'Nothing; just idle banter. Now, go on with you.' As he spoke his landline rang out, on his desk. He peered at the caller display. 'Incoming from my daughter,' he said. 'I suspect she has seen the TV news.'

He killed the mobile call and picked up the other. 'Yes, Alex.'

'Pops,' his elder daughter exclaimed in his ear, 'what the hell is this about Aileen and tomorrow's press? I've just had a call from Andy. He's been watching . . .'

'I know. Kid, go easy on her; it wasn't her fault.'

'Wasn't her . . .'

'Alexis,' he said, using her Sunday name for added emphasis. 'Stop and think back, not very far back, to a time when someone was out to make trouble for me, and you left your bedroom curtains open. You with me?'

'Yes, Pops,' she murmured. 'I suppose I live in a glass house.'

'We all do,' he replied. 'Fortunately, you've minimised the chances of a repeat by moving to a penthouse.'

'I know. I suppose I'm only angry because of the effect her behaviour might have on you.'

'Well, don't be. While she was with Morocco, whose bed do you think I was sleeping in? Where did I go on Saturday, when I got free of the concert hall and Glasgow? Where did you and Andy see me?'

'At . . .' she paused. 'You and Sarah? You're back together?'

'Let's just say we've got a hell of a lot in common, with three kids and a lot of personal mileage.'

'Plus the fact that she loves you,' his daughter pointed out, 'and that's the main reason why she came back from America and took the job at the university.'

'Plus the fact that I love her,' he conceded. 'But the key word, darling, is "discreet". Aileen will find out eventually, and the last thing I want is for her to get vindictive. So neither I, nor any member of my family or circle of friends, is going to say a single hard word about her. She had every right to be with Morocco, with or without the horror at the concert hall, but as it happens the guy was there for her when she chose to go to him. So be cool, promise me.'

'I promise. What are you going to do?'

'We, that's Aileen and me, have done it already through Mitch, but you're not to be involved. Don't talk to anyone, not even people within the firm. Understood?'

'Yes.'

He heard a sound, indicating that there was a call waiting. 'On you go now,' he said. 'I'm in for a busy hour or so.'

'Pops,' she sighed. 'Don't be so Goddamned conscientious; do what anyone else would to and unplug the phone from the socket.'

'Is that your legal advice?' he chuckled.

'No, it's pure Alex, and I'm not advising, I'm ordering. Just bloody do it.'

'Yes, boss,' he replied, then, not for the first time in his life, did as she had told him.

Twenty

'I think I preferred it when you were just another DI, and Max Allan kept you in the background.' Scott Mann stared at the kitchen wall clock; it showed five minutes to midnight. 'What the hell time's this tae be comin' in?'

His wife stared at him. 'Don't you bloody start,' she warned. 'The number of times I've asked you that question. That and "Where the hell have you been?" although it was always all too obvious.'

'Ye'll never let me forget, will ye?'

'Bloody right I won't; not when you start digging me up about my work. I've had the day from hell and I don't need you narking at me. I didn't ask to catch the shout to the concert hall last night, but I did and that's the end of it. Okay?' She barked out the last word.

He winced and glanced towards the ceiling. 'Shh,' he whispered. 'Ye'll wake the wee man. He's no' long asleep. He tried to stay awake for you. Ah made him put his light out at half nine, but he did his best tae hang on.'

She smiled, with a gentleness that none of her colleagues would have recognised. 'Wee darlin',' she murmured. An instant later she glared at her husband. 'As well for you though that it's the holidays, and tomorrow's not a school day.'

'Well it's no',' he shot back, 'and that's an end of it.'

'Aye fine,' Lottie sighed, deciding that further hostilities were pointless. 'Where did you go, the pair of you?' she asked.

'We got the bus out tae Strathclyde Park. There's a big funfair there; he had a great time. Ah got him a ticket . . . a wristband thing, it was . . . for all the rides.'

'What about you? Did you go on any?'

'Shite, no! Me?'

'Come on, Scottie,' she chuckled. 'You're just a big kid at heart. What was it? Too dear for both of you?'

'No, Ah just didnae fancy it.'

'Did I not give you enough money?'

He shook his head. 'No, no,' he insisted. 'I had enough if Ah'd wanted.' He paused. 'Have you eaten?' he asked.

'Yes,' she lied. 'I had a sandwich earlier. I just want a cup of something then I'm off.'

In truth, she would have considered committing murder for a brandy and dry ginger, but she refused to keep alcohol in the house, unless they were entertaining, when she bought wine for their guests. She had seen her husband drunk too often to do anything to undermine his constant, daily, effort to stay sober.

'Ah'll make you a cup o' tea,' Scott said. 'Go and take the weight off your plates.'

She did as he told her, slipping off her shoes and her jacket, then slumping into her armchair. She was almost asleep when he came into the living room a few minutes later, carrying what she saw was a new mug, with the theme park logo, and a plate, loaded with cheese sandwiches and a round, individual, pork pie.

'Eaten?' he laughed. 'My arse! Where are you going tae get a sandwich anywhere near Pitt Street on a Sunday night? Wee Danny Provan's no' going to run out and get you something, that's for bloody sure.'

She squeezed his arm as he laid her supper on a side table. 'You're a good lad, Scott,' she murmured.

'Ah do my best,' he replied. 'Honest, Ah really do.'

'I know.'

'So,' he continued, 'how's it goin'? Have you solved the case yet? No' that there's much to solve.'

She laughed. 'Oh, but there bloody is. For a start, we've established who the two dead guys were.'

'Ah thought you knew.'

'We knew who they had been, through our "intelligence sources",' she held up both hands and made a 'quotation mark' gesture with her fingers, 'so called. But now we know about them. That's why I'm so late in. One of them went under the name of Bryan Lightbody. He lived in Hamilton, New Zealand, with a wife and a wee boy Jakey's age, and he owned four taxis there.

'The other one was known as Richie Mallett, single, well-off, low-handicap golfer. He lived in Sydney, in an apartment near somewhere called Circular Quay, and he had a bar there. Both of them seem to have been very respectable guys, apart from when they were moonlighting and killing people.'

Scott whistled. 'They'll no' kill any more, though.'

'No, but they did leave us a wee present.' She broke off to demolish half of the pork pie. 'Do you remember when you were in the job,' she continued, when she was ready, 'hearing of a guy called Bazza Brown?'

He frowned. 'Remind me,' he murmured.

'Gangster. Fairly small time in your day, but come up in the world since then.'

'Mmm,' he said. 'Aye, but vaguely.'

'Well, they'd heard of him,' Lottie declared. 'We traced their car this afternoon, and we found Bazza shut in the boot.'

'Eh?' her husband exclaimed. 'So he must have been in it all night. Was he still alive?'

'No.'

'Did he suffocate?'

'I don't think so. I doubt if he'd time before they shot him in the chest.'

His eyes widened. 'Fuck me!' he gasped.

She chuckled. 'Those may very well have been his last words.' She ate the other half of the pie and washed it down with a mouthful of tea.

'No' much use to you dead, though, is he?' Scott remarked, recovering his composure. 'He'll no' be much of a witness.'

'He's not going to tell us a hell of a lot,' she conceded. 'But nevertheless, even dead, he's a lead of sorts. We think we know why he was involved with them. I don't believe for a minute that he was behind the whole thing, too small a player for that, but if we can find who he was in touch with before he died, that may lead us to whoever ordered Toni Field killed.'

'My God,' he whispered. He looked at her, frowning. 'You're sure she was the target, and no' the de Marco woman?'

Lottie nodded. 'Oh yes,' she replied. 'There's no doubt about that now, sunshine. The crime scene team found her photo, tucked away in Botha's false passport.'

Twenty-One

'Sod this!' Skinner muttered. When he had plugged his landline into the wall ten minutes before six o'clock, it had told him that nineteen messages had been left for him. In theory his number was private and unlisted; he knew that some of the Scottish news outlets had acquired it by means he had chosen not to investigate, but he had no idea how many. The call counter gave him a clue. Making a mental note to have it changed, he held his finger on the 'erase' button until the box was empty. If any friends or family had called him, he guessed they would have rung his personal mobile as back-up.

He switched that on; there were no message waiting, but he had only just stepped out of the shower when it rang. He answered without checking the caller. No journalists had the number . . . no active journalists, but there was a retired one who did.

'Bob,' a deep familiar voice rumbled, the accent basically Scottish but overlaid with something else.

'Xavi,' Skinner exclaimed. 'How are you doing, big fella? And those lovely girls of yours?'

Xavier Aislado, and his ancient half-brother, Joe, were the owners of the *Saltire* newspaper. Their father had escaped from Civil War Spain to Scotland, and eventually they had chosen to return, although in different circumstances and at different times.

Xavi, after a promising football career cut short by injury, had been the *Saltire*'s top journalist, and had been responsible for its acquisition by the media chain that Joe, thirty years his senior, had built in Catalunya.

Their family structure was complicated. Xavi's mother had left him behind as a child, and had gone on to have twin daughters, by a police colleague of Skinner. One of the two had taken over from Xavi as the *Saltire*'s managing editor, although she had been completely unaware of their relationship until then.

'We're all fine,' he said. 'Sheila and Paloma are blooming and Joe's hanging in there. He wasn't too well during the winter, but he's got his love to keep him warm too. But more to the point, what is happening in your life? June called me at some God-awful hour about a story that everybody's chasing, about your wife. She and I want you to know that we owe you plenty, so if it's all balls, you have open access to the *Saltire* to help knock it down. If it's true . . . we'll ignore it if that's what you want.'

'I appreciate that, Xavi,' Bob assured his friend. 'As it happens it is true, but we're proposing to deal with it like two grown-ups. Tell June to be ready for a joint statement this morning; that should put a lid on it.'

'How about this man Morocco? Look, I've been there; I know how you're liable to be feeling about him.'

'Liable to be,' he agreed, 'but I'm not. Morocco's a relative innocent in this carry-on, so don't go looking to give him an editorial hard time. Let him stay a Scottish celebrity hero. Between you and me, the guy's done me a favour.'

'If that's what you want, I'll pass it on to June.' He chuckled, a deep sound that made Skinner think of one of his vices, a secret that he shared with Seonaid, his younger daughter: a spoonful of Nutella, scooped straight from the jar. 'I don't tell her anything, you understand. On the *Saltire*, she's the boss.'

'I'm sure.' Bob frowned. 'Has she brought you up to date with what happened on Saturday, in the Glasgow concert hall?'

'Yes, she has. From what she told me, it rather complicates the Aileen situation. She had a narrow escape and went running to Morocco, not you.'

'She didn't. Have a narrow escape, that is. She wasn't the target.'

'You can say that for certain? I thought there was still some doubt about who they were after. A couple of our Spanish titles are running the proposition that the First Minister himself was the target, and they missed.'

'Then you should kick someone's arse. Clive Graham might not mind the publicity, but the truth is that the one thing we did know for sure was that the target was female, and we said so at the time. Now we know definitely that it was Toni Field. My team in Glasgow haven't announced it yet, but they will this morning. Press conference at ten o'clock, the same time as my lawyer will issue our statement, Aileen's and mine, about our decision, last week, to pull the plug on our marriage.'

'Now there's a coincidence. Sorry,' the Spanish Scot murmured, 'that was my cynicism showing through.'

'Hey, Xavi,' Skinner laughed, 'I've learned many things from you. One of them is how to minimise a story, as well as how to maximise it. Tell June . . . sorry, suggest to her, that she forget about us and concentrate on Glasgow this morning. There were developments yesterday, significant developments, and they're going to blow political marriages off the front page.'

'Any hints?'

'Just one. I don't want anyone approached before the press

conference, but your crime reporter might be well employed doing all the research he can on a man named Basil "Bazza" Brown.'

'Thanks for that. Will you be at the media briefing?'

'No, I have someone else to see before then. I'll need to go, in fact; my driver's due to pick me up in under fifteen minutes.'

'Fine.' Aislado paused, then added, 'You and Strathclyde, Bob. I know how you've always felt about it, so how the hell did that happen?'

'A chapter of accidents, mate. Aileen says that now I'm there it'll be my Hotel California. You know, I can check in any time I like but I can never leave. I'm not so sure about that, though. I have many things to sort out in my head over the next few weeks.'

'Well, if you'd like somewhere to sort them out undisturbed, you're welcome to visit us. I know you have your own place in L'Escala, but we have a guest house here now, and it's yours for as long as you need it, if you don't want anyone to know where you are.'

'Cheers, appreciated. I may take you up on that.'

'Okay. Bob, one last thing. If we do go looking for this man Brown after ten o'clock, where are we likely to find him?'

'In the fucking mortuary, mate.'

Twenty-Two

'I'm too old for this shit, Lottie,' Dan Provan moaned.

'Agreed,' DI Mann retorted. 'But you're here and you're all I've fucking got as a second in charge, so get on with it, eh? Oh and by the way, you're not too old to collect the overtime.'

'There is that,' the sallow sergeant conceded. He smiled. 'Keeps us both out the house as well. How's your Scottie gettin' on?'

'He's fine. Moans a bit but he's doing great in the battle against the bevvy; that makes me happy. He took the wee guy to the big shows in Strathclyde Park yesterday. A year ago, even, I'd never have trusted him to do that.'

'Theme park,' Provan corrected her. 'The shows are what you and me went to when we were kids.'

'Maybe you did. My dad never took me anywhere. All his spare money went on that bloody football team. "Follow, Follow",' she sang, off-key. 'I remember my mum making me hide from him many a Saturday night . . . well, maybe not that many, for they didn't lose all that often, but when they did and he got in with a couple of bottles of Melroso in him, nobody was safe.'

'No' even you?' He looked her up and down, trying to tease her. In all the time they had worked together she had never before mentioned her childhood.

'Not when I was eight or nine. If my mum gave me and my big brother money for the multiplex on a Saturday night, we knew there was going to be trouble.'

Provan frowned. 'Did he . . .'

'Batter my mum? Oh yes. Don't get me wrong, he was a quiet man all the rest of the time.' She shook her head. 'Listen to me, defending him.'

'What happened to him?'

'Stomach cancer happened to him, when I was twelve. Then I grew up, joined the police, got married, and found myself in the same situation as my mother had. She warned me, ye know, but I never listened.'

'Scott was like him? Is that what you're saying?'

She nodded.

'Just as well you could handle him,' the sergeant said, 'like you proved at that daft boxing night.'

'Not all the time. There were re-matches, Danny, without the gloves and the head guard. I didn't always win. That was around the time when he was fuckin' up his police career through the drink. When that finally happened I gave him an ultimatum. I gave him two of them, to be honest. The first was that if he ever raised a hand to me again, I would leave him. The second was that if he ever raised a hand to Jakey, I'd kill him. He believed both of them; he's been off it, more or less, ever since. He still goes AWOL every now and then, but he comes back sober, and that's the main thing.'

'Then good for him. He's gettin' on fine at work too, is he? In that cash and carry place o' his?'

'Yes. He's a supervisor now. The head of security's due to retire in a couple of years, and Scottie's in with a chance of getting the job.'

'Mibbes he could find somethin' for me if he does,' Provan muttered. 'Like Ah said . . .'

She sighed. 'I know, I know, I know. You're too old for this shit: but you're here, and we're both standing in it, so just you keep on shovellin', Danny. I've got another press briefing at ten o'clock. By then I'd like an answer from that car rental company.'

The sergeant nodded; a small shower of dandruff settled on the shoulders of his crumpled, shiny jacket. 'Aye,' he said. 'They should have been back tae us by now. Time tae rattle their cage.' He checked the number on the key-ring fob, then snatched his phone from its cradle and punched it in.

'Drivall Car Hire,' a young female voice chirped. It made him feel older than ever.

'DS Provan, Strathclyde CID,' he announced. 'Ah spoke to somebody in your office last night. The lad said his name was Ajmal; Ah wanted some information about one of your cars that we found in Glasgow. He was going to get back to me, but I'm still waitin'. I need tae speak to him, now.'

'I'm sorry, caller,' the irrepressible youth replied, sounding anything but regretful. 'Ajmal's off duty today.'

'Then go and get him,' Provan barked, 'or dig up your manager! This is a major inquiry Ah'm on.'

The girl sniffed. 'There's no need for that tone of voice, sir. If you hold on I'll see if Mr Terry's available; he's our manager.'

'You do that, hen.' He sat and waited, but not for too long.

'Sergeant err . . .' a querulous male voice began. 'I'm sorry, Chantelle didn't catch your name.'

'Provan,' the Glaswegian growled. 'Detective Sergeant Provan.'

'Thank you, sorry about that; I'm John Terry, the general manager. This will be about our vehicle LX12 PMP, is that right?'

'Indeed.'

'We have been acting on this, I assure you,' Terry declared. 'My colleague Ajmal left me a note when he went off duty. The vehicle hirer has died and you're trying to find out who he was through us, is that the case?'

'I suppose it might be possible, sir,' Provan said, 'that a guy hired a vehicle, shot himself three times in the chest, shut himself in the boot and disposed o' the gun, but we don't really believe that.'

The manager gulped. 'Pardon? I didn't quite catch all of that.'

'Okay, mate. Let me spell it out for ye', in words of one syllabub.'

'My God,' Terry exclaimed, before he was finished. 'Mr Provan, I think we've had a little language difficulty here. Ajmal's English is not the best, and your accent is, let's say, quite regional.'

No, let's fuckin' no' say! With difficulty, the detective managed to keep his thought to himself, as the manager continued. 'Ajmal left me a note with the registration number of the vehicle and the information that a man had been found dead in the vehicle and that the Glasgow police wanted the name of the hirer. What you've just told me is news to me and shocking news at that.'

'Well, now that we understand each other,' Provan said, weighing each word to avoid further 'language difficulties', 'maybe yis can get me the information Ah need.'

'Oh, I have that already, Sergeant. The office where the vehicle was hired . . . it's in Finsbury Park . . . was closed last night. I spoke to the person in charge five minutes ago. The vehicle was rented a week ago yesterday, for return by five p.m. yesterday evening. The hirer's name was Byron Millbank, address number eight St Baldred's Road, London. I happen to know where that is; it's very close to what was Highbury Stadium, the old Arsenal football ground, before they moved to the Emirates.'

'Did he have a UK driving licence?'

'I don't know, but I assume . . .'

'We don't deal in assumptions, Mr Terry. Will they have a record in your other office?'

'Oh yes. And a photocopy. Not everyone does that but we always do; take a photocopy of the plastic licence and the paper counter-part.'

'In that case,' Provan told him, 'I need you tae get back on to your other office and get those photocopies faxed up to me. Haud on.' He found a number that he had scrawled on a pad on his desk for another inquiry, a week before, and read it out to Terry.

'I'm afraid we don't have fax machines in our regional offices any more,' he said. 'Old technology these days.'

'Well, find one, please. Go to the Arsenal if ye have tae; they're bound tae have one.'

'Oh, we won't have to do that. We can scan the copies and send them.'

'Eh?'

'Scan them, Mr Provan. Turn them into JPEGs.'

'Eh?'

'Photographic images. Then we can send them to you as email attachments.' Terry giggled. 'Or don't you have email in Scotland?'

Nancy! Provan, an old-school homophobe, kept another thought to himself. 'Oh aye, sir, we have. It runs on gas, right enough, but we get by.' He read his force e-address, then spelled it out, letter by letter. 'Soon as ye can, please; Ah need it within the next half hour.'

'You'll have it in ten minutes.' Terry paused. 'Can I send somebody along from our Glasgow Airport depot to collect our car?'

'Eventually,' the DS told him. 'Ah'm afraid your car's a crime scene, sir. Ah'm no' sure how long we'll need to hold it for. When we're done with it, we'll bring it back to you. We'll even clean aff the bloodstains fur ye.'

He hung up and turned to Mann. 'A name for ye, Lottie. The car was hired by somebody called Byron Millbank.'

'What do we know about him?' she asked.

'Eff all at the moment, but we should have a wee picture soon, off his driving licence. Meantime, his name's enough tae go searchin' for his birth certificate.'

'Maybe,' the DI cautioned. 'That's assuming it's his real name. Let me see the image as soon as you get it, and blow it up as large as you can. I want to let the big boss see it.'

Twenty-Three

'When it arrives, have them forward it to my email,' Skinner told Lowell Payne, raising his voice slightly as his car overtook three lorries that were travelling in convoy along the busy motorway that links Scotland's capital with its largest city. 'I'd like to see it as soon as I get to the office, although I'm not sure when that will be. I'm not looking forward to my next visit, although it's one I have to make.'

'I'll do that, Chief. I was planning to attend the press briefing. Should I do that?'

'Mmm.' He considered the question for a few seconds, as he held his phone to his ear. His Strathclyde driver was new to him; Bluetooth was not an option. 'Maybe not. The media will be aware by now of your role as my exec, and I've been dodging the buggers since last night. But tell DI Mann she should make it clear that we now know for sure that Field was the target. She doesn't need to say how, but she should rule out any other possibility one hundred per cent. Do we video these events ourselves?'

'I don't know,' Payne admitted. 'I've never been involved in one as formal as this.'

'Then find out. If they don't, make sure it happens. I've always done it in Edinburgh. I like my own record of events.'

'Understood. I'll tell Malcolm Nopper.'

'Thanks. Something else I'd like you to do. The force area is massive, as we all know; I don't plan or expect to set foot in every police station on a three-month appointment, but nonetheless I imagine I'm going to be travelling quite a bit. I want to be in complete touch at all times, so I'd like you to fix me up with a tablet computer.'

'An iPad?'

'That or equivalent, as long as it gets me internet access everywhere I go and has a big enough screen for me to read. With one of those I'll be able to read emails at once, wherever I am.'

'You'll have one before the day's out.'

'Thanks.' As he spoke, his driver signalled then eased to the left, leaving the motorway. Skinner knew where they were, well enough; Lanarkshire had been his territory until he was into his twenties, even if it had changed since his departure.

'Why the hell do they call this Motherwell Food Park?' he mused aloud.

'No idea, sir,' his driver replied, believing that an answer had been required. 'Why would they not?'

'Because it's in bloody Bellshill, Constable; it's miles away from Motherwell.'

'Is that right, sir?'

'Trust me on it; I was born in Motherwell, and my grandparents, my father's folks, they lived in Bellshill. Where are you from, Constable Cole? What's your first name, by the way?'

'David, sir; Davie. I'm from Partick; that's in Glasgow, sir.'

Skinner laughed. 'I know that well enough. I did some sinning there or thereabouts in my youth. Used to hang out in a pub called the Rubaiyat, in Byres Road.'

'That's not quite Partick, sir, but I know where you are. It's still there.'

144

'But not as it was; it was gutted, or "refurbished" to use the polite term for architectural vandalism, back in the eighties. It had a lounge bar . . . where you could take your girlfriend; never to the public bar, mind, men only there . . . called "The Bowl of Night". Very few of the punters had a clue where the name came from, but it was famous nonetheless. There was never any trouble there, either.'

Careful, Bob, he told himself. *Steer well clear of memory lane, or you could get to like this bloody place all over again.*

'Were you Chief Constable Field's driver, Davie?' he asked.

In the rear-view mirror, he saw the young man's eyes tense. 'Yes, sir. I wasn't on duty on Saturday, though. She told me she was being collected by the First Minister's car. I think she was quite chuffed about that.'

'So you've been to her home before?'

'Oh yes, sir, often. We're not far from it now.'

They were moving down a steep incline that led to a complex motorway interchange. To his left, he saw a series of fantastic twisted shapes, the highest of them a wheel. 'What the hell's that?' he asked.

'Theme park, sir,' his driver informed him. 'They call it M and D's.'

'My younger son would love it,' he chuckled. 'He's the family action man. The older one would turn his nose right up; he's our computer whizz kid.'

'That whole area's called Strathclyde Park, sir,' Constable Davie went on.

'Oh, I know that,' Skinner murmured. 'It used to be wilderness. In fact, the Motherwell burgh rubbish tip was there, right next to a football ground that used to be covered in broken glass and all sorts of crap. It was all taken away when the park was created and they diverted the River Clyde to make the loch. I was a kid when they did it, but I remember it happening.'

Nostalgia, nostalgia, nostalgia. Stop it, Skinner! And yet, he reminded himself, none of those he thought of as his second family, Mark, James Andrew and Seonaid, had ever set foot in the town that had raised him.

He shook the thoughts from his head as Davie drove through the interchange and off by an exit marked 'Bothwell'. Almost immediately he took a left, then made a few more turns, the last taking them into a leafy avenue called Maule Road. 'This is it, sir,' he said, drawing to a halt outside a big red sandstone villa, built, Skinner estimated, in the early twentieth century.

'Pretty substantial,' he remarked. 'When did Chief Constable Field move in here?' he asked his driver. 'Given that she was only in post for five months.'

'Three months ago, sir. For the first few weeks she and her sister lived in an executive flat on the Glasgow Riverside.'

'Right.' He stepped out of the car, then leaned over, beside the driver's window; it slid open. 'I can't say for sure how long I'll be,' he murmured. 'If I'm any longer than half an hour, I want you to toot the horn. I'll pretend it's a signal that I've had an urgent message.' He smiled. 'I'll never ask you to lie for me, Davie, but it's always good to have an escape plan.'

'I understand, sir.' Constable Cole frowned, as if wanting to say more, but hesitant.

The chief read the signal. 'Out with it,' he said.

'Thank you, sir. It's presumptuous of me, but I wonder if you'd express my sympathies to Marina and her mother.'

'Of course I will. You've met them both?'

'Yes, sir. I saw Marina pretty much every day, with her working so close to the chief, and I met Miss Deschamps when she stayed with them a couple of months ago. I think she came up to see the new house,' he added.

'What are they like?' Skinner asked. 'Mark my card, Davie.'

'They're both very nice ladies. Marina's younger than the chief by a few years and not all that like her physically, or in personality, come to that. Miss Deschamps . . . she's very particular about that, by the way, sir. Marina's a Ms but her mother is definitely Miss . . . Miss Deschamps is quiet, doesn't say much, but she was always very polite to me. She tried to tip me when we got here.' He grinned at the memory. 'The chief did her nut, but she just smiled and shook my hand instead.'

'Thanks.' The chief constable stood straight, walked through the villa's open gateway and up to the vestibule. He rang the bell and waited.

He was about to press the button again when the front door opened. A tall, slim woman stood there; her hair was honey-coloured, and her skin tone almost matched it. The overall effect, Skinner mused, had the potential to cause traffic accidents.

She looked up at him, but not by much. 'Yes?' she said.

'Bob Skinner,' he told her. 'I believe you're expecting me. My aide called yesterday, yes?'

Her hand flew to her mouth. 'Of course,' she exclaimed. 'I'm so sorry. It's just . . .' She broke off, looking at his suit.

'I'm sorry,' he murmured. 'I should have thought this through. It's my habit to leave my uniform in the office and travel in civvies. Please don't feel slighted.'

'I don't, honestly,' the woman assured him. 'I always thought my sister overdid the uniform bit.' She extended her hand. 'I'm Marina Deschamps,' she said, as they shook. 'Come in, my mother is through in the garden room.'

She led the way and he followed, through a hallway, then along a corridor. He guessed at her age as they walked. A few years younger than her sister, Davie had said. Toni had been thirty-eight, so Skinner placed Marina early thirties, somewhere in age between her sister and his own daughter.

The corridor led them into a small sitting room that might have been a study at some time in the life of the old house, before what most people would have called a conservatory was added. As far as the chief could see it was unoccupied.

'Mother,' Marina called out, 'our visitor is here.'

Sofia Deschamps had been seated in a high-backed wicker armchair, one of a pair, looking out into a garden that was entirely paved and filled with potted plants of various sizes, from flowers to small trees. She rose and stepped into view. She was almost as tall as her younger daughter; indeed they were very much alike, twins with a thirty-year age difference.

'Mr Skinner,' she said, as she approached him. 'Thank you for calling on us.' Her accent had strong French overtones, and she held her hand out in front of her, as if she expected him to kiss it, in the Gallic manner. Instead, he took it in his.

'I wish I didn't have to,' he replied. 'I wish that Saturday had never happened, that Toni was still in Pitt Street and I was still in Fettes, in my office in Edinburgh. My condolences to you both.'

'Thank you.'

It occurred to him, for the first time, that both women were wearing black; inwardly he cursed himself for his pale blue tie. Sofia's face was drawn, and her eyes were a little red, but there was an impressive dignity about her, about both of them, for that matter. 'It's still fairly early,' she murmured, 'but please, allow me to fetch us some coffee.'

'No, no, ma'am,' he protested, 'that isn't necessary.'

'I insist.' She stood her ground; refusal would have been impolite.

'In that case, thank you very much, but if I may I'll have water, sparkling if you have it, rather than coffee. My . . .' He paused; he had been about to describe Sarah as 'My wife'. '. . . medical adviser says I drink far too much of the stuff, and she's made me promise to give it up.'

'A pity,' Miss Deschamps murmured, with a hint of a smile. 'We should allow ourselves the occasional vice.'

'My medical adviser is my vice.' He said it without a pause for thought. 'That's to say,' he added, searching for an escape route, 'she's my former wife, and I've learned that it's too much trouble to disobey her.'

'In that case I will not press you further. Excuse me, I will not be long.'

His eyes followed her as she headed for the door. She might have left sixty behind her, but she had lost no style or elegance; even at that early hour she was dressed in an ankle-length skirt and high heels.

Marina was less formal, in black trousers and a satin blouse. 'Please,' she said, 'sit down.'

Skinner listened for French in her accent; there was some but less than in her mother.

'Maman is being discreet,' she continued. 'She knows I want to ask you about my employment situation, and she doesn't want it to appear as if we're ganging up on you.'

'That's very decent of her,' the chief said, as he sat, facing her, on a couch that matched the armchairs, 'but there's no rush to consider that. I know that you acted as Toni's personal assistant. My assumption has been that you wouldn't want to continue in that role with her successor, but that's a decision you can take in your own time.

'I've already given instructions that you can have all the time you feel you need. My temporary appointment is for three months; if you want to take all that time to decide what you want to do, or at least until a permanent successor to your sister is selected, that'll be fine by me.'

Marina shook her head. 'There's no need, sir,' she replied. 'I have a job, and I'd like to carry on doing it.'

Skinner stared at her, unable to keep his surprise from showing. 'You want to work for me?' he exclaimed.

She nodded.

'Look,' he said. 'I have to be frank about this. You know your sister and I were not exactly the best of friends.'

Marina smiled, then nodded. 'Oh yes. She was very clear about that. But that was more political than anything else. You had different views on certain things, but that didn't affect what she thought of you as a police officer. We both know she was a big supporter of a unified Scottish force.'

'Sure, she made that clear enough in ACPOS, and I made my opposition equally plain. We had some robust discussions, to say the least.'

'Oh she told me. But what you probably do not know is, her big fear was that she would talk you round to her view. She rated you very highly as a police officer; in fact she said you were the best she'd ever met. She wanted the top job, no mistake about that, but she didn't think she'd have a chance if you went for it.'

'Indeed?' Skinner murmured.

'Indeed.'

'So where does that take us, Ms Deschamps?'

'I have no personal issues with you, sir,' she replied. 'Fate has put you in what was my sister's office. I'm a top-class secretary with personnel management qualifications, and I like to work with the best. Therefore . . .' She held his eyes with hers.

'Let me think about it,' he said. 'I like to have a serving officer as my assistant, and I've already appointed someone to that position, pro tem. To be frank, I'll need to get to know the job before I can judge whether there will be enough work left for you. But first things first; you and your mother have a funeral to organise, albeit with all the help that the force can give you. Once that's over, we can talk. Fair enough?'

'Fair enough,' she agreed.

Out of nowhere, Skinner remembered a problem. 'There is one thing, though. Do you have the combination of the safe in the chief's office?'

Marina sighed. 'I did,' she replied. 'It was seven three eight two seven six. But Antonia always changed it at the end of the week. It was usually the last thing she did on a Friday; sometimes she'd tell me the new number there and then, but if she didn't have a chance it would wait until Monday. Last Friday she didn't tell me. You can try the old number, just in case she forgot to make the change, but if it doesn't work, I fear I can't help you.'

She looked up as her mother returned carrying a tray, loaded with two tiny espresso cups, and a bottle of Perrier with a glass.

'No ice,' Sofia Deschamps declared as she placed them on a small table at the side of the couch. 'I refuse to dilute the mineral with melted tap water, as so many do.'

'I couldn't agree more,' Skinner told her. 'When my late wife and I were very young, we went on a camping holiday to the South of France. Everybody told us not to drink the water there, so we didn't. But we had ice in everything, so everything tasted of chlorine.'

'If that was the only side effect,' she countered, 'you were lucky.'

He winced. 'It wasn't; I was being delicate, that's all.'

'Your late wife,' she repeated. 'And earlier you mentioned your former wife.'

'Three,' he said, anticipating the question. 'Three and still counting.'

'Maman!' Marina exclaimed, her tone sharp.

'Ah yes.' Her mother held up a hand. 'I am sorry. That was indiscreet; we have seen this morning's papers.'

'No apology necessary,' he assured her. 'All it means is that our separation is public knowledge. It wasn't the way I'd have chosen for it to be revealed, but these things happen. Have you ever been married, Miss Deschamps? Or am I making a false assumption? Have you reverted to your birth surname?'

'No, you are correct. I have always chosen to avoid marriage. Antonia's father, Anil, was a member of the Mauritian government of the day . . . you see, we have politicians in common. Marriage with him was never possible, since he had a wealthy wife, to whom he owed his position.

'Marina's father was an Australian, with business interests in Port St Louis. He spent part of the year there, the winter, usually, and the rest in Australia, or travelling in connection with his business. He was something of an entrepreneur.' She pronounced the word with care, balancing each syllable.

'We had a very nice apartment there, and a very pleasant life. Not that I was a kept woman,' she was quick to add. 'I had a very good job, in the Mauritian civil service, and I maintained my own household. He did not contribute, because I would not allow it, even though we were together for seventeen years. I had a good income. We are a wealthy country, you know; close to Africa and yet a little distant from it too.'

'I know,' Skinner replied. 'Mauritius is one of the many places on my "To do" list.'

'You will like it.'

'Why did you leave?' he asked her.

'To be with my daughters. Marina's father was very good to both my girls; he more or less adopted Antonia, and when she came to university age, he got her a place in Birmingham, where she did a degree in criminology.'

'She first joined the police in Birmingham as well,' Marina added. 'She had a specialised degree and that got her fast-tracked. Well, you'll have seen her career record, I'm sure. She never looked back.'

'How about you?' he put to her. 'Were you ever tempted to join the force?'

'That never really arose, not in the same way. My father died when I was sixteen. I was very upset, and any thought of university went out of my mind ... not that I had Antonia's IQ anyway. I stayed in Mauritius and went to college; I did a secretarial course and a personnel management qualification. I came to Britain eight years ago, when Antonia was senior enough to point me at a job with the Met support staff.'

She smiled. 'That's not as bad as it sounds; I had a very stringent interview, and I must have been vetted, for I was attached to SO15, the Counter-Terrorism Command, for a little while. But when Antonia became a chief constable ... back to Birmingham again ... things changed. She insisted that I go with her, to run what she always called her Private Office. The rest you must know.'

Skinner nodded. 'I've been told. Ladies,' he continued, 'you'll be aware that since Saturday evening, a full-scale murder investigation has been under way. I'm keeping in close touch with it, and I know that DI Mann, the senior investigating officer, will want to visit you fairly soon to interview you for the record. Meantime, is there anything you would like to ask me?'

'Of course,' Sofia exclaimed, 'but why would he need to interview us?'

'Detective Inspector Mann is a lady, Maman,' her daughter murmured.

'Then she, if you must. Why would she? What do we know? In any event, can this not be an interview? You're her boss now, after all, as my dear Antonia was.'

'Yes but she is in day-to-day charge.' He paused. 'If it makes you happy, I can go over some of the ground she'll want to and report what you say to her. If she's comfortable with that, fine. If not, she can come and visit you again. Okay?'

'Yes,' Marina Deschamps replied, at once. 'But Maman is right. Why do you need witness statements from us?'

'Because we're now certain, beyond any doubt, that Chief Constable Field was the target. These men weren't after my wife, or the First Minister. They were pros, hit men; they knew exactly who they were there to kill, and they did.'

'*Oui*,' Miss Deschamps whispered. 'We saw my daughter's body yesterday. They covered half her face with a sheet, but I made them take it off. We know what was done to her. So yes, I understand you now. What do you need to know?'

'Her private life,' Skinner said. 'I can tell you that we'll be going back through her entire career, looking at what she's done, people she's put away, enemies she may have made along the way who have the power and the contacts to put together an operation like this.'

'Such an impersonal word: "operation". You make it sound like a military thing.'

'It was,' he told her. 'Smit and Botha were former soldiers, and Beram Cohen, the planner, had an intelligence background. They didn't work cheap, and they weren't the sort of men you can contract in a pub. The very fact that the principal, as we'll call the person who ordered your daughter's death, was able to contact Cohen, tells me that he is wealthy and well-connected.

'I know about some of the successes that Toni had as a police officer and I'm aware that she may have upset some very nasty people in her time. Trust me, we will look at these, using outside agencies wherever we need to.'

'Outside agencies?'

'He means the British Security Service, Maman,' Marina volunteered.

'Not only them. The FBI, the American DEA; we'll go anywhere we need to. But alongside that I need to know about any personal relationships your sister may have had. Unlikely as it may seem, did she ever have a romance that ended badly?' He hesitated. 'Did she have any personal weaknesses?'

'Of course not!' Sofia exclaimed.

'I'm sure she didn't,' Skinner said, deflecting her sudden anger, although privately he counted naked ambition and ruthlessness towards colleagues as ranking fairly high on the weakness scale. 'But the questions must be asked if we are to do our best for you in finding the person who had that done to her, what you saw yesterday. Marina, you understand that, don't you?'

'Yes, I do. I knew my sister well enough. Personal weaknesses? Was she a gambler, closet drinker? No, she was tight with her money and she didn't touch a drop. She didn't mortgage beyond her means either; she was shrewd with the property she bought. For example, she picked up this pile at the bottom of the market, after making a big profit from her house in Edgbaston.'

She stopped and looked at her mother. 'Personal relationships?' she repeated. 'Maman, cover your ears if you like, but this is the truth. I don't think Toni ever had a romance in her life, certainly not in the years that I've lived with her in Britain.

'Relationships, yes; she's had six of them. Make no mistake, she was robustly heterosexual. But none of them were about love; all of them were about her career. I'm not saying that she bedded her way to the top, but every lover that she had was a man of power or influence, one way or another.'

'Might any of them have been the sort of man to take it badly when she pulled the plug on him?' the chief asked.

'No, I would not put any of them in that category. Everyone she brought home . . . and she told me she never played away . . . was as cynical as she was.'

'Were they cops?'

'A couple were. There was a DAC . . . deputy assistant commissioner . . . in the Met, about five years ago, and an assistant chief from Birmingham before him. I'm sure that neither of those two were in a position to advance her career directly, but they knew people who were.

'More recently, from what she told me, the men she's been involved with have been . . . how do I put it? . . . opinion formers, movers and shakers outside the police force. There was a broadcast journalist, a civil service mandarin in the Justice Ministry, and another man she said was a very successful criminal lawyer.'

'You're telling me what they were but not who,' Skinner pointed out. 'Can you put names to any of them?'

Marina smiled. 'No, because Antonia never did, and since we didn't live together until she became the chief in Birmingham, I never saw any of them. "No names, no blames", was what she always said, whenever I asked her. It used to annoy me, until I realised that given her background and mine . . .' She broke off and looked at her mother. 'I'm sorry, Maman,' she said, 'but this is the truth. She never had a proper father as such, far less than I did. We were secret daughters in a way, both of us, but her most of all.

'Given that history, that upbringing, it was perfectly natural that Antonia should have woven a cloak of secrecy around her own personal life. And me? I am exactly the same. Most observers, looking at me, would say that my life is a mystery.'

Sofia nodded. Her eyes were sad. 'I wish I could deny that,' she sighed, 'but it is true. That is my legacy to both of my daughters.'

Twenty-Four

'Bingo,' Skinner exclaimed, as he gazed at the photograph on his monitor. He turned to his exec. 'It may say Byron Millbank on his driving licence, and that may not be a top-quality image, but I rarely forget a face . . . and never, when I've seen it dead. That is Beram Cohen, one-time Israeli paratrooper, then a Mossad operative until he was caught using a dodgy German passport while killing a Hamas official, most recently for hire as a facilitator of covert operations.

'As you know, Lowell, he's the guy who recruited Smit and Botha, procured their weapons through Freddy Welsh in Edinburgh, then went and died, inconveniently for them, of a brain haemorrhage a few days before the hit.'

'Could we have stopped it if he hadn't?' Payne asked.

'There would have been even less chance. The evidence we had would still have led us to Welsh, but no sooner; we probably wouldn't have got to the hall as quickly as we did.

'Even if we had been lucky and got the two South Africans, my guess is that Cohen would have been in the car and would have taken off. He'd have been on the motorway inside two minutes. He would have got clear, dumped the guy Brown's body, so it would never have been linked to our investigation, and we'd have had no clue at all, nowhere to go.'

He scratched his chin. 'Cohen dying might have been convenient for us, but as it turned out it wasn't a life-saver. Speaking of Bazza Brown's body,' he continued, 'lying a-mouldering in the boot of a Peugeot, and all that, I'd like an update on that side of the investigation.' He checked his watch. 'Mann's press briefing should be over by now; ask her to come up, please.'

The DCI nodded and was about to leave when Skinner called after him. 'By the way, Lowell, are we any nearer being able to open that bloody safe, or do we seriously have to explore the Barlinnie option? Toni's sister gave me a number, but as she warned me, it had been changed. She did it weekly, apparently; there's security,' he grumbled, 'then there's fucking paranoia.'

Payne laughed. 'It's in hand, gaffer, but the Bar-L route may be quicker than waiting for the supplier to send a technician.' He paused. 'By the way, how did your visit go? How are the mother and sister?'

'As bereft as you would imagine,' the chief replied, 'but they're both very calm. I was impressed by Marina,' he added. 'She's not a bit like her half-sister. Toni, it seems, was the love child of a Mauritian politico; she must have inherited the gene. Marina, on the other hand, struck me as one of nature's civil servants, as her mother was.'

'And her father? Is he still around?'

'No, not for some years; he never was, not full-time. Sofia seems to have valued a degree of independence.' Skinner pointed to the anteroom at the far end of his office, the place that Marina Field had filled. 'Have you lined up any secretary candidates yet?'

'Yes. Human Resources say they'll give me a short list by midday.'

'Then hold back on that for a while. We can call up a vetted typist when we need one. Marina says she wants to carry on in her job, working for me. I've stalled her on it, until I decide whether I want that.'

'How long will you take to make up your mind?'

Skinner grinned. 'Ideally, three months, by which time I'll be out of here.'

Twenty-Five

'It is for these reasons,' Aileen de Marco concluded, reading from autocue screens in the conference room of the ugly Glasgow office block that housed her party's headquarters, 'that I am committing Scottish Labour to the unification of the country's eight police forces into a single entity. The old system, with its lack of integration and properly shared intelligence and with its outdated artificial boundaries, bears heavy responsibility for the death of Antonia Field.

'Not only do I endorse the proposal for unity, I urge the First Minister to enact it without further delay to enable the appointment of a police commissioner as soon as possible to oversee the merger and the smooth introduction of the new structure.'

'Any questions, ladies and gentlemen?' Alf Old invited, from his seat at the table on the right of the platform, then pointing as he chose from the hands that shot up, and from the babble of competing voices. 'John Fox.'

'Is this not a panic reaction, Ms de Marco,' the BBC reporter asked, 'after your narrow escape on Saturday?'

'Absolutely not.'

'What would you say to those people, and there may be many of them, who think that it is?'

'I'd tell them that they're wrong. Scottish Labour took a corporate decision some time ago to support unification; we're quite clear that it's the way forward. On the other hand, the party in power seems less committed. Yes, I know the First Minister says that it's the way forward, but there are people on his back benches who aren't quite as keen.

'We've been reading a lot this morning about the First Minister's personal courage . . . and I have to say that I admire him for the way he displayed it on Saturday, when even the senior Strathclyde police officer on the scene collapsed under the strain.

'What I'm saying today is that it's time for him to bring that courage into the parliament chamber and join with us in getting important legislation on to the Scottish statute book.'

She paused, for only a second, but Marguerite Hatton seized on her silence.

'Do you have anyone in mind for the position of police commissioner, Ms de Marco?' she asked.

Aileen glared down at her from behind her lectern. 'There will be a selection process,' she replied, 'but I won't have anything to do with it.'

'Would you endorse your husband's candidacy?'

'I repeat,' she snapped, 'I will not have anything to do with the selection process. I'm not First Minister, and even if I was, the appointment will be made by a body independent of government. The legislation will merge the existing police authorities into one and that will select the commissioner.'

'Then my question still stands,' the journalist countered. 'Will you endorse your husband's candidacy?'

'I'm sorry, Ms Hatton,' she maintained, 'I'm not going there. I'm the leader of the Scottish Labour Party, and I'm sure that I'll have political colleagues on the new authority, but it won't be my place to influence them in favour of any candidate.'

'Or against one,' she challenged, 'if you believed he was entirely wrong for the job?'

Aileen paused. 'If I believed that strongly enough about someone,' she replied, 'I'd say so in parliament.'

'So do you believe your husband would be the right man for the post, even though he's an authoritarian bully?'

'Now hold on a minute!' Alf Old barked, from the platform. 'This press conference isn't about individuals. It's about important Labour Party policy. However, I have to tell you that I've met the gentleman in question and I don't recognise your description. Now that's enough out of you, madam. Another questioner, please?'

Hatton ignored him. 'But isn't that why you and he have just announced your separation, Aileen?' she shouted. 'Isn't that why you ran into the arms of another man after your terrifying ordeal on Saturday, because Bob wasn't there for you?'

Aileen de Marco had known more than a few intense situations in her life, and she was proud of her ability to stay calm and controlled, whatever the pressure. And so, it was agreed later, her outburst was entirely atypical, which made it all the more shocking.

'Bob's never been there for me,' she yelled. 'Why the hell do you think I'm divorcing him, you stupid bloody woman?'

Twenty-Six

'John, go easy on her, will you?'

'Bob, I'm BBC. We don't run big lurid headlines on our reports and we don't editorialise on politicians. We just run what we've got on the record, and in this case that's Aileen screaming at the Hatton bitch then storming out of the room. We can't ignore that, because it's there. STV have got it, and that means it'll be on ITN national at lunchtime. Sky have got it and they won't hold back. Plus I saw a couple of freelance cameras there, so it could even go international.'

'Bugger,' Skinner sighed. 'And you're the nice guys, aren't you?'

'Exactly,' John Fox said. 'You know what Hatton will do with it, and the rest of the tabloids. Thing is, Bob, it's not just Aileen that's been caught up in it.'

'Don't I know it. I was never there for her, she said.'

'Do you want to react to that?'

'To the media in general, no, because anything I say will be used in evidence against either Aileen or me. To you, because I trust you or we wouldn't be speaking right now, I'll say I'm sorry she feels that way, and I'll add that lack of communication is one of the factors behind our separation.' He paused, then added, 'Hell, you can use this as well, on the record. I find it contemptible that she was goaded into her outburst after what she went through on Saturday night.'

'I will use it too. How about Hatton calling you an authoritarian bully?'

Skinner laughed. 'Jesus, John, I'm the acting chief constable of the UK's second biggest police force. If that doesn't make me an authority figure, I don't know what would. As for me being a bully, I appreciate Alf Old putting her straight, and I hope that others will as well.'

'I wouldn't worry about that,' Fox told him. 'It's a wee bit close to defamation, so most sensible editors . . . including Hatton's . . . won't repeat it. I was only covering my back by asking you about it. Besides, no tabloid editor in his right mind's going to want to fall out with you.' He laughed. 'Not that that implies you're a bully, mind.' He was silent for a second or two. 'Can I ask you something else? he murmured.

'Sure.'

'I told you what she said about Max Allan. Do you want to counter it?'

'I'd like to, but I can't, because it's true. Max was first into the hall when the emergency lighting came on. He could see very little, and at first he thought it was Paula Viareggio who'd been shot, not Toni. Max has known Paula since she was a kid; he and his wife live closer to Edinburgh than Glasgow and so they do nearly all their shopping there. They've been customers of the Viareggio delicatessen chain for twenty years, since the days when Paula worked behind the counter.

'He thought that was her on the floor, and he just buckled. The poor guy's career's probably at an end, and an ignominious one at that, thanks to Aileen. The next time I speak to her she and I are going to have very serious words about it. You can be sure of that.'

'I agree,' the journalist murmured. 'True or not, it was well out of order. But Bob, off the record this time, why did she put herself up there to be shot at? Sorry, that was an unfortunate choice of words in the circumstances.'

'Maybe but I know what you mean. My informed guess would be that her reasons were purely political.'

'Did you know about Labour supporting unification?'

'Of course I did. This is very much between us, chum, but it was the last straw as far as our marriage was concerned.'

'I guessed as much. There's a piece on the *Saltire* website that nobody's noticed yet. It was blown out of the printed edition by the Field shooting, but it's got your stamp all over it. Everybody knows that paper's your house journal, with June Crampsey being a retired cop's daughter.'

'Mmm,' Skinner murmured, 'do they indeed? I'll need to watch that, but I won't lie to you about my input to that article; you're right. I was a bit steamed up at the time. But if you're going to have a girn about me playing favourites, don't, because I'm doing it just now. Nobody else is getting past the switchboard here and I'm taking no other media calls anywhere else.'

'I appreciate that,' Fox chuckled. 'In the spirit of our special relationship, is there anything else you'd like not to tell me? About the Field investigation, for example.'

'Not a fucking word, mate; you're not that special. However, you might like to call another chum of yours, the First Minister. I reckon Aileen will have put his nose mightily out of joint.'

'Thanks for that, and the rest. Cheers.'

The chief was unfamiliar with the telephone console on his desk, but he had noticed a red light flashing during the last couple of minutes of his conversation with Fox. As he hung up he discovered what it was for as the bell sounded, almost instantly. He picked up the receiver, expecting to hear the switchboard operator, or Lowell Payne, but it was neither.

'Yes,' he began.

'Bob,' a male voice snapped back at him, 'can't you keep that bloody wife of yours under control?'

'Hello, Clive,' he replied. 'Funny you should call. Your name just came up in conversation.'

'I'm not surprised. Your ears must have been burning too. Do you know what Aileen's done?'

'Yes.'

'When did you know?'

'I first became aware of it about ten minutes ago, Clive,' Skinner asked, 'what the fuck are you on about? Haven't you read any newspapers today?'

'No I haven't. I'm not in the office. I've spent the last thirty-six hours incommunicado, comforting my distraught wife. She's under sedation, Bob. I'm still trying, but failing, to make her believe that I wasn't the target . . . although the truth is, I'm not a hundred per cent sure of that myself.

'But more than that, it's not just the thought of me with my brains on the floor that's got to her, it's the notion that if she had come with me, and not Toni, she'd have copped it. So you'll see, Bob, reading the press hasn't been at the top of my agenda. My political office has only just emailed me the unification press release Labour have put out.'

'And that's all they've sent you?'

'That's all.'

'Then you should shake up all your press people, in the party and in government. Somebody should have told you that two hours ago my dear wife and I announced that we've split. They should also have told you to check out today's *Daily News*. You're going to have fun with that come next First Minister's Questions at Holyrood, I promise you.'

He heard the First Minster draw a deep breath, then let it out slowly. 'Then I apologise, Bob,' he said, quietly. 'The government people are supposed to brief me constantly on what's happening in the media, partly to ensure that I don't make any embarrassing phone calls like this one. I told them, firmly, to leave me alone, but when the troops are afraid to override your orders when necessary, that makes you a bad general.'

'Or an authoritarian bully,' Skinner murmured.

'What?'

'Nothing. You can tell Mrs Graham to calm down. We have absolute proof that Toni was the target. They were set up and waiting for her.'

'Are you certain?'

Skinner snorted. 'I appreciate that you're a politician, but even you must know what "absolute" means.'

'But how did they know she'd be there?' the First Minister asked, sounding more than a little puzzled.

'When did you invite her to accompany you?'

'Two weeks ago.'

'Yeah, well, one day later Toni posted the engagement on bloody Twitter, and on the Strathclyde force website. She set herself up.'

'But who'd want to kill her? I know she was abrasive, but . . .'

'I've got a team of talented people trying to find that out,' the chief replied, 'and I imagine that right now they're waiting in my assistant's office.'

'Then I won't delay you further. Again, I'm sorry I went off at half cock.'

'No worries. For what it's worth, I reckon I know why Aileen broke ranks on unification. You might not realise it, if you've been cloistered since Saturday, but you've become something of a media hero, thanks to Joey Morocco's eyewitness account. He's seen a few things up close in the last couple of days, has our Joey. With the election coming up, Aileen couldn't let that go uncountered. It's the way she thinks.'

'I suppose it is, and I might even understand it. It won't do her any good though. I've seen our private polls: Labour will be crushed, and her career will be over.'

Bob laughed. 'Don't you believe it, Clive. She has a plan for every contingency. She's like Gloria Gaynor: she will survive. Get on with you now. Go and give your wife the good news.'

Twenty-Seven

'Will I survive this, Alf?' Aileen asked, leaning forward across the table, with a goblet of red wine warming in her cupped hands.

'I'll treat that as rhetorical,' the chief officer replied. 'You've just locked up the female vote within the party; as for the men, they were eating out of your hand anyway.'

'But tomorrow's coverage will be all about me dropping the bomb on that twat Hatton, and not about the policy initiative I announced.'

'Aileen, you and I both know that is bollocks; the announcement doesn't matter. We don't make policy any more, the SNP do.'

'But they need us to get unification through fast,' she countered.

'No, they don't. You and Clive Graham agreed to rush it through before the election so that it doesn't become an issue that the Tories could score with, but the Lib Dems are for it as well, and even in a minority situation their votes would see the bill through. That's if he tables it at all. The poll's in a few weeks, and you've just removed police structure as an issue anyway by announcing that we're for it.'

'You're saying that if I've pissed him off with my challenge he might walk away from our agreement.'

'Indeed I am.' He glanced around the basement restaurant to which they had retreated, checking that they were still alone and that no journalists had followed them there. 'But so what? It's irrelevant alongside the campaign that's ahead of us. With everything that's happened, are you sure you're ready for it?'

She looked him in the eye. 'How long have you known me, Alf?'

He scratched his chin. 'Twenty years?' he ventured.

'Exactly, since our young socialist days. And in all that time have you ever known me not to be up for a battle?'

'No,' he admitted. 'But you've never been in circumstances like these before. You've had a horrendous forty-eight hours.'

'Horrendous in what way? My marriage has broken up. That happens to more than ten thousand of my fellow Scots every year, and probably as many again who end cohabiting relationships. And although the statement Bob made me agree to was bland and consensual, the idiot woman Hatton just succeeded in portraying me as the partner who's been wronged. Don't you imagine that was in my mind when I staged my walk-out?'

'Are you saying that wasn't spontaneous?'

She hesitated. 'No, I'm not, but even before I reached the door I could see the positives in it. Can't you?'

'I suppose so,' he admitted.

'Exactly. So, my other personal disaster: what of that? My body was all over today's *Daily News*, and by now it'll have gone viral on the internet. But I've read the story, there and in all the other papers. Not one has said that Joey was actually in the room, because no way can they prove it, so their lawyers wouldn't let them. Neither of us will ever admit that he was, so what am I, Alf? A victim of the paparazzi, that's what, and that's how the party has to spin it. Understood?'

'Understood,' he agreed, 'but you didn't have to spell it out. Our communications people have been doing that since the story broke, both here and in London. You probably don't know this, but the shadow Culture Secretary in Westminster is going to demand that the government legislates to make invasion of privacy a go-to-jail offence. They won't do that, of course, because it can't afford to piss off the *News*, but they'll make sympathetic noises.'

'I'll bet they will. The last thing they want is Clive Graham with an absolute majority.' She smiled. 'Do you still think I'm not up for a fight?'

Old grinned back at her. 'No, and I never did. So, why did you ask me if you'd survive?'

'I only meant within the party, man. What's the feeling in our shadow cabinet and on the back benches? Are they scared by what's happened? Is my sleekit deputy Mr Felix Brahms likely to seize the day and challenge me for the leadership?'

'As far as I can tell, there won't be a revolt. You certainly needn't worry about Felix. I spoke to him last night. Yes, he was making opportunistic noises, but I put a stop to that.'

She frowned. 'How?'

'You don't want to know.'

'Yes, I bloody do. Out with it.'

He looked around again; a waiter was approaching with an order pad, but he waved him away. 'A friend of mine in Special Branch up in Aberdeen, the Brahms fiefdom, dropped me a word about him. They were worried about him being a security risk as shadow Justice Secretary.

'He's been having it off with a woman, a well-known local slapper called Mandy Madigan, whose brother Stuart is currently remanded in custody charged with the murder of a business rival, that business being prostitution and money-lending.'

'What a creepy bastard!' Aileen exclaimed. 'I like his wife, too. What are we going to do about it?'

'Nothing,' he replied, firmly. 'You've put a hint of sex into the campaign; that's just about okay, given the way that you and Bob have dealt with it. We do not need any more sleaze, though. When Brahms called me about your situation, I had a sharp word with him, told him what I knew. He swears he didn't know about her family background, and he's going to put an end to it. The Grampian cops will keep the affair to themselves, but he'd better be a choirboy from now on.'

'My God,' she chuckled. 'You're making me feel like the singing nun by comparison. Well, maybe not quite, shagging a movie star and all, but still.' She paused. 'Poor Joey; he called me this morning, on his way to the airport. He's quite upset, worried that he might have done for my career. I must call him once he gets to Los Angeles, and tell him he's probably put my approval rating up a few points.'

'Any chance of him supporting you in the campaign?'

'Hell no, he's a Tory. I know, before you say it, I seem to be making a habit of sleeping with the enemy. At least I'm not going to marry this one!'

'Is Bob going to make trouble down the line?'

'For me, no. I've got a funny feeling that I've done him a favour by cutting him loose. Not politically, either. He's got nothing to gain from it.' She frowned, suddenly. 'That said, I must ring him and apologise for what I said at the press conference. He'll have heard by now, for sure, from one of his inner media circle, Foxie, or June Crampsey. I don't want to fall out with him any more than I have done.'

'Why should that bother you?' the chief executive asked. 'You don't think you can win him over on unification, do you? He made his views pretty clear in the *Saltire* at the weekend.'

'Did he? That passed me by, not that I care. It'll go through regardless. And once it's there, who knows what he'll do. I'm quite convinced that if Toni Field was still alive he'd go for it. He's a cop first, second and third; it's all he knows, and most of what he cares about, apart from his kids.

'He's also a pragmatist. If that's right, that he said his piece in the press, all he was doing was getting at me. He knows he won't win. Deep down he also knows that if Field had been there to go for the police commissioner job, he'd have done whatever was needed to stop her, and that would have meant putting himself forward.'

'Christ, you're making it sound as if he was behind the shooting.'

Aileen smiled, but her eyes stayed serious. 'He's shown himself capable of pulling the trigger, on Saturday and more than once before that in his career. But no, I wouldn't go that far.'

'Now she's dead, what will he do?'

'My guess is that he will go for it, and I've told him as much. He spent years telling himself he didn't want to be chief in Edinburgh. Since he was talked into it, he's been saying the same about Strathclyde, but I sensed a change in him when his refusal to put his name forward last time left the field clear for Toni Field, and he saw what a political operator she was. He said something to me once about power only being dangerous if it was in the wrong hands. He could have been talking about her.'

'And his are the right hands, are they?'

'He'd never say so. He'd leave it to the politicians he dislikes so much, and the media he uses so skilfully, to do that. But he believes it all right. He hides it well, but Robert Morgan Skinner has a massive ego, tied to an absolute belief in his own rectitude. And when it comes to power, he's the equivalent of an alcoholic; one taste and he's hooked. Mind you, he'd tell you the same thing about me, and he'd be right too.'

She sipped her wine. 'I want to stay on good terms with him,' she continued, 'because I will need to be. Whatever the polls say, and however badly our colleagues in London have fucked things up for all of us, I intend to be First Minister after the election and, as such, we will have to co-exist.'

Old nodded. 'I can see that.'

'But,' she added, 'there's something else. I want to stay as close to his investigation as I can, because I want to know who killed Toni Field just as much as everyone else does. Who'd want her dead?' she asked. 'She hadn't been in Scotland long enough to have upset the criminal fraternity that badly. Yes, she may have hacked off someone dangerous in her earlier career. But can you recall another case of a senior British cop being assassinated by organised crime? I can't. However, like I said earlier, the late Toni was an intensely political animal. Who knows who she's crossed in that area. Make no mistake, politics can get you killed, and if there is any whiff of that, I want to know about it.'

Twenty-Eight

'I'm fine, Bob, honestly. I lost it for a second or two in there, but that's enough when the red lights are on the cameras. I'm simply calling to apologise for what I said about you. It was unforgivable; if you want, I'll put out a statement through my press office retracting it and saying that I was provoked.'

'Let it be, Aileen. I'm not worried about it. What you said is bloody true, anyway, so I won't ask you to lie for me.'

'Thanks,' she said. 'I appreciate that. You couldn't do something about that Hatton woman, could you?'

'No need. She's done it to herself. I've just taken yet another call from her editor, made no doubt on the advice of his lawyer. This time he was grovelling over what she called me. He's ordered her back to London this afternoon, even offered to sack her if I insisted on it. I said I didn't want that, but that he should tell her, so she can see that I have a magnanimous side after all.'

'But if she ever comes back to Glasgow, she'd better not have any drugs in her handbag?'

He laughed. 'You said that, I didn't. Now, I must go; I've got people outside waiting to brief me on the Toni Field investigation, and I cannot get off the fucking phone.'

'Then I won't keep you. How's it going, by the way? I gather from

176

Alf . . . I'm with him just now; we're hiding out in the Postman's Knock, the bistro down the road . . . that they've determined that she was the target.'

'That's right. My turn to apologise; you should have heard that from us, not him. I'll know more when I've seen the team, but we have several lines of inquiry. Not least, we want to know what the hell a dead Glasgow gangster was doing in the boot of the shooters' getaway car.'

'My God!' she exclaimed.

'Indeed, and you should be pleased to hear it. Lottie Mann was going to break that news at her press briefing. It should deflect some of the coverage of yours. By the way, you'd better call Clive Graham. He practically blew the wax out of my ears a few minutes ago, in the ludicrously mistaken belief that I've got any influence over you.'

'Oh, sorry again,' Aileen said. 'I was planning to do that anyway. Bob, will you keep me up to date on the inquiry?'

'Eh?' he exclaimed. 'Why should I do that?'

'Well,' she murmured, 'I do have a personal interest in knowing why I've had to throw away a very expensive evening dress.'

'There is that,' he admitted. 'Yes, I suppose we could. I'll be briefing the First Minister, so I could persuade myself that I should do the same for the leader of the Opposition, given that the election's coming up.'

'Thanks, you're a love.'

'No, I'm not. I'm chief constable and you're a constituency MSP on my patch. When are you seeing Joey again?' he asked.

'Maybe next time we're in the same city, maybe not, maybe never.' His question took her by surprise; she returned the challenge. 'When are you seeing Sarah?'

His reply took one second longer than it should have. 'Next time I pick up the kids.'

'Sure,' she sniggered, 'sure. Bob, I didn't get where I am by being stupid.' She let her words sink in, realising that her shot in the dark had found a target. 'But don't worry about it, I don't care. Whatever works for you, that's fine by me. As for her, just you be certain that getting even with me isn't her main aim.'

'It isn't,' he said, 'but let's not discuss it further. Now please, let me speak to my team. I promise I'll keep you informed, as far as I can.'

'Thanks, I appreciate that.' He thought the conversation was at an end, but, 'Bob, one more thing. I don't want to have to go back to Gullane again, ever. I'd like you to pack up everything I have there, clothes, jewellery, books, music, personal papers, everything that's mine, and have it couriered through to my flat. Would you do that for me?' She laughed, without humour. 'What am I talking about? Would you do it for us? I imagine you don't want me there again either.'

'Of course I'll do that. I'll deliver them myself.'

'Thanks for the offer, but no, let's keep it impersonal.'

'If that's what you want, fine; I'll do it as soon as I can.'

He hung up, then dialled Lowell Payne's extension number, ignoring the 'call waiting' light that continued to flash on his console. 'I'm clear,' he told his exec as he answered. 'Ask Mann and Provan to join me. Have the sandwiches I ordered arrived yet?'

'Yes, they're on a trolley outside your door; and tea in a Thermos.'

'Good. Listen, I want you to get on to the switchboard and tell them that from now on nobody gets through to me without being filtered through you; not the First Minister, not the Prime Minister, not even the monarch. Most of them won't get through; whenever you can, please refer them to Bridie Gorman or, where it's his area, to

Thomson. Also I've changed my mind about having an office mobile through here; I don't want one. You've got my personal phone number. If anything's urgent and I'm not in the office, you can use that.'

'Yes, Chief.'

Skinner headed for the side door to retrieve the sandwich trolley; Lottie Mann and Dan Provan were entering through his anteroom as he returned. 'Welcome,' he greeted them. 'Sit at the table.'

He pulled the trolley alongside them, then poured three mugs of tea. 'Help yourself to sandwiches,' he said. 'Sincere apologies for keeping you waiting so long, when you have other more important things to do. Bloody phone! Bloody journalists! Bloody politicians! The least I can do is feed you.'

Provan grunted something that might have been thanks followed by a grudging 'Sir'. The chief looked at him, pondering the notion that if he judged a book by its cover, the scruffy little DS would be heading for the remainder store.

'How long have you been in the force, Sergeant?' he asked.

'Thirty-two long years, sir.'

'It's a bind, is it?'

'Absolutely, sir. Ah have to drag ma sorry arse out o' bed every morning.'

'So why are you doing it, for what . . . fourteen or fifteen grand a year, less tax and national insurance? That's all you're getting for it in real terms. With your service, you must be in the old pension scheme, the better one, and you'll have maxed out. It'll never get any bigger than it is now as a percentage of final salary. You could retire tomorrow on two-thirds of your current pay level. Tell me,' he continued, 'where do you live?'

'Cambuslang, sir.'

'How do you get to work?'

Provan reached out and took a handful of sandwiches. 'Train usually, but sometimes Ah bring the car.'

'But no free parking in your station, eh?'

'No, sir.'

'No. So retire and that travel cost is no more. Are you married?'

'Technically, but no' so's you'd notice. She's long gone.'

'Kids?'

'Jamie and Lulu. He's twenty-six, she's twenty-four. He's a fireman, she's a teacher.'

'That means they're off your hands financially. So why do you do it, why do you drag your shabby arse out of bed every morning for those extra few quid?' He laughed. 'Jesus, Sergeant, if you stayed at home and gave up smoking you'd probably be better off financially. You're more or less a charity worker, man. You're streetwise, so you'll have worked this out for yourself. So tell me, straight up, why do you do it?'

'Because I'm fuckin' stupid . . . sir. Will that do as an answer?'

'It will if you want to go back into uniform, as a station sergeant. Somewhere nice. How about Shotts?'

'Okay,' Provan snapped. 'I do it because it's what I am. Ma wife left me eight years ago because of it, before Ah'd filled up the pension pot, when Lulu was still a student and needin' helped through uni. Sure, Ah could chuck it. Like you say, I'd have more than enough to live on. Except I'd give myself six months and ma head would be in the oven, even though it's electric, no' gas. The picture you're paintin's ma worst nightmare, Chief.'

He paused and for the briefest instant Skinner thought he saw a smile. 'Besides,' he added, 'the big yin here would be lost without me. Ah'm actually pretty fuckin' good at what Ah do. But why should Ah go and advertise the fact?'

'The suit's a disguise, is it?'

'No,' Lottie Mann intervened. 'Dan wears clothes, any clothes, worse than any human being I have ever met. Even when he was in uniform they used to call him Fungus the Bogeyman.' She dug him in the ribs with a large elbow. 'Isn't that right?'

The DS gave in to a full-on grin. 'It got me intae CID though.' Then it faded as he looked the chief constable in the eye. 'What you see is what you get, Mr Skinner. No' everybody's like you or even Lottie here, cut out to play the Lone Ranger . . . although too many think they are. Ah don't. Every masked man on a white horse needs a faithful Indian companion, and that's me, fuckin' Tonto.'

The chief picked up a sandwich, looked at it, decided that the egg looked a little past its best, and put it back on the plate.

'Nice analogy, Dan,' he murmured, 'but it doesn't quite work for me. I speak a wee bit of Spanish, just restaurant Spanish, you under-stand, but enough to know that "Tonto" means "Stupid", and that, Detective Sergeant, you are not. I'm not a uniform guy myself, as the entire police community must know by now, so the wrapping doesn't bother me too much as long as it doesn't frighten kids and old ladies, but what's inside does.

'I took a shine to you yesterday, but to be sure you weren't just the office comedian, I pulled your personnel file and the first thing I did when I got here today was to read it. As far as I can see the only reason you're still a DS is because that's what you want to be. You've never applied for promotion to inspector, correct?'

'Correct, and you're right, sir. Ah'm happy where I am. It's no' that I'm scared of responsibility, I just believe Ah've found my level,' he paused, 'Kemo Sabe.'

Skinner chuckled. 'In which case, Dan, I'll value you for as long as I'm here. So, how much of the trail have you two sniffed out?'

'Thanks to you, Chief,' Mann replied, as soon as she had finished the last sandwich, the one that he had rejected, 'we now know that the man who rented the Peugeot was the planner of the operation, Beram Cohen, the guy you've got in the mortuary through in Edinburgh.

'We've established through HMRC that under the name Byron Millbank he's lived and worked in London for the last six years, for a mail order company called Rondar. It operates one of those tele-shopping channels on satellite telly. Three years ago he married a woman called Golda Radnor, the boss's daughter, we're guessing, going by the fact that her name's the company's reversed, and eighteen months later they had a wee boy, named Leon Jesse. According to the General Register Office, Byron was born in Eastbourne thirty-two years ago, father unknown, mother named Caroline Anne Millbank, died on the last day of the last century.'

'Pity,' Provan muttered. 'She missed the fireworks.'

'I doubt if she was ever alive to see them,' Skinner countered.

'Do you think those records are faked, sir?' Mann asked.

He nodded. 'And clumsily, by somebody with a knowledge of poetic history. I studied it as an option in my degree. Look at the names: Byron Millbank, out of Caroline Anne. Lord Byron the poet, and two of his most famous women, Lady Caroline Lamb and her cousin Annabella, the one he wound up marrying.'

'Where does Millbank come from?'

'That was Annabella's family name, only it was spelled differently, as I recall.' He laughed. 'I don't know where all that came from. I must be turning into Andy Martin; he's got a photographic memory for everything. However,' he continued, 'there's a second context, and one that's more likely to be connected. It used to be a secret, but now one of the most famous buildings in London is Thames House, on

Millbank: it's the MI5 headquarters. Whoever set up Cohen's identity practically signed their name.'

'Aye, sir, but,' Provan interposed, 'how do you know that Cohen's no' the alias?'

'I know because I'd never heard of him until Five told me who he was, and told me about his career in the Israeli military and then its secret service. I guess,' he continued, 'that Mr Millbank had a driving licence.'

Mann nodded.

'And a passport?'

'Yes, sir.'

'Neither of them more than six years old?'

The DI opened the folder she had brought with her, searched through her notes, then looked up. 'That's right. Both issued a couple of months before he shows up on the payroll of Rondar, and on the same day.'

'To make absolutely sure,' Skinner instructed, 'I want you to go to the DSS and see if his records go any further back with them. My dollar says they don't. Before then Cohen was in Mossad, until he was caught up in an illegal operation and got thrown out.'

'But what does it mean, sir?' Dan Provan asked.

'Probably nothing at all, as far as our investigation's concerned. My reading is that British intelligence did the Israelis a favour by looking after one of theirs. They gave him a legitimate front and if he continued to take on black ops under his old identity, that was all right with them. They told me about one where he had used Smit and Botha; that was American-sponsored, in Somalia. I suppose he was what the spooks call an asset, but now it looks as if he wasn't fussy who he worked for.'

The sergeant blew out his cheeks. 'This is a' new stuff for us, gaffer. How do we go about investigatin' MI5, for Christ's sake?'

'You don't,' the chief told him. 'Yes, Byron Millbank, he'll need to be followed up, but I'll take care of that. I want you two and your team to focus on Bazza Brown. Am I right in believing that the media haven't made any connection between his murder and the Field assassination?'

'So far they haven't. As far as they know, Ronnie Edgar from Townhead's the SIO on that case, and they've only just found out it's Bazza that's dead. They've been told we're still tryin' to identify the victim.'

'Good. From what I've heard of Brown's history, now that we have released his name, the first thing the press will do will speculate that it's gang wars. That'll be fine by me. Let them chase that hare as long as they can. Meantime, you need to look at his family and his associates. Do you know them?'

'I know the main one; that would be Cecil, his brother,' Lottie Mann replied. 'Younger by two years, but they were as inseparable as twins.'

'Cecil?' Skinner repeated. 'Basil and Cecil? Not exactly Weegie names.'

Provan's eyes twinkled. 'Remember that old Johnny Cash song, about a boy called Sue? Their old man, Hammy, he had the same idea. He gave them soppy names, and the pair of them grew up as the hardest kids in Govan. The muscle was equally divided, but Bazza got a' the brains. Ah've lifted Cec in my time. He's no' likely tae help us.'

'Lift him again; tell him it's on suspicion of conspiracy to murder Toni Field. If the brothers were that close, we have to go on the assumption that whatever the connection was to Smit and Botha, Cecil was part of it. See how he reacts under questioning. Whether he was involved or not, he'll be thinking revenge. If you tell him there's nobody left for him to kill, he might just cooperate.'

'He might, sir. Just don't build your hopes up, that's all Ah'm sayin'.'

'Understood. Now, what else do you have to tell me?'

'The satnav in the rental car, sir,' the DI said. 'We've looked at it and it was used. Since they've had it, they've been to several locations. One was in Edinburgh, and another in Livingston.'

'The first would be when they first met up with Freddy Welsh, their armourer, when Cohen upped and died on them. The second was when they collected the weapons from Welsh's store. We know that already. Anything we don't know?'

She nodded. 'We've found out where they were living. Their journeys were to and from a hotel out on the south side; it's called the Forest Grove. It's a quiet place, family run, with about a dozen bedrooms. They were booked in for a week, Sunday to Saturday, full board, signed in as Millbank, Lightbody and Mallett. Millbank said they were there for a jewellery convention, and that the other two worked for the South African branch of his firm. The owner knew him; he'd stayed there before, a couple of times.'

'Do we have dates?'

'Yes, boss. And yes, we've checked for unsolved crimes to match them. There were none, neither in Glasgow, nor anywhere else in Scotland. But there was a watch fair in the SECC each time, so it looks like he was there on legitimate business.'

'Fair enough; good on you, for being thorough. Who paid the bill?' he asked.

'The man the hotel people knew as Lightbody. He settled up on Saturday lunchtime, then they left. The owner, his name's MacDonald, remarked to him that he hadn't seen Mr Millbank for a couple of days, and that his bed hadn't needed making. Lightbody said that he'd been called away to a meeting in Newcastle and that he'd flown back to

185

London from there. Mr MacDonald thought that was odd, for his daughter had serviced the room the first morning he was gone and his stuff was still in it. Thing about the bill, though, sir, it was settled in cash, old-fashioned folding money.'

'New Bank of England fifties?'

Mann's looked at him, surprised. 'How did you know that?'

'Our investigation in Edinburgh last week, after we found Cohen's body, led us to a kosher restaurant in Glasgow. The three guys ate there, and that's how they paid. Does MacDonald still have the notes?'

'I'm afraid not, sir. They went straight into his bank's night safe. I've got somebody contacting his branch though; they're probably still there.'

'Good. The notes from the restaurant are in Edinburgh. If we can match them up with these and they are straight from the printer, we might be able to trace them to the issuing bank and branch.'

'Wouldn't that have been Millbank's?' the DI pointed out.

Provan shook his head, causing another micro snowstorm. 'Ah don't see that. If he's had two identities, he's going tae have kept them completely separate.'

'For sure,' Skinner agreed. 'It may be that he had a separate Beram Cohen account, or a safe deposit box, but there's also a chance the cash came from the person who bought the operation. If we can trace its movement in the banking system, you never know.'

'If we can recover them,' Mann said. 'I'll chase it up.'

'Do that, pronto. Anything else from the satnav?'

'Yes, one other journey, but I'm not getting excited about it. On Friday, they went from the hotel to the Easthaven Retail Park, not far from the M8 motorway.'

'Indeed?' the chief said. 'Why are you writing that off?'

'Because it seems they went there to shop and to eat, that's all. We found receipts in the car for two shirts, and a pack of underwear from a clothes shop, and for two pizzas, ice cream and coffee from Frankie and Benny. The next journey programmed was the second last, the one to Livingston; the last being from their hotel to the car park next to the concert hall, where we found the car.'

'Yes, you're probably right; sounds like a refuelling stop, no more.' He frowned. 'Forensics. What have they given us?'

'They say that Bazza was shot in the car. They dug a bullet out of the upholstery, and found blood spatters. Other than that, they've given us nothing we didn't have before.'

'Post-mortem report? What about that? Has Brown been formally identified? I don't want as much as a scratch in him until that's done. If we ever do put anyone in the dock for this, he can't be allowed to walk out on a technicality.'

'That's done,' she said. 'His wife did it first thing this mornin'. Pathology's not holding us up but still I'm not pleased about it. Either Dan or I will have to be there as a witness. That's going to use up the rest of the day for whoever it is, with there being two of them.'

'Two?'

'Yes, there's Bazza, and there's the one on Chief Constable Field.'

'Of course.'

'Yes, I'd hoped that could be done yesterday, but it turns out it wasn't.'

'Bugger that,' the chief grumbled. 'What was the problem?'

'The chief pathologist was away on what he said was "family business", then this morning the so-and-so went and called in sick. I don't fancy his deputy, not since his evidence cost me a nailed-on conviction in the High Court last year. I said I wasn't having him do them, so they've called somebody through from the Edinburgh University pathology department.'

'Professor Hutchinson?'

She shook her head. 'No, sir. I asked for him but he wasn't available either. Instead they've sent us his number two. A woman, they said. I hope she's up to the job.'

Skinner's eyebrows rose. 'Oh, she is, Inspector, she is. I can vouch for her. As for you being there,' he continued, 'your priority has to be keeping the investigation up to speed.'

'Fair enough, sir. I never mind not going to post-mortems. Do you want me to send a couple of detective cons along instead?'

'No, Lottie, you leave that to me to sort out. The autopsies may be only formalities, but given that my predecessor's going to be on the table, our representative has to be appropriate in rank. Luckily, I know the very man for the job.'

Twenty-Nine

Every so often, in the office where he spent most of his time, Detective Chief Superintendent Neil McIlhenney would find himself daydreaming. When he awakened it was always with a start as he looked out of his window. He was still well away from being used to life in the Metropolitan Police Service, and he wondered if he ever would.

When a move south, on promotion, had been offered to him he had taken no time at all to accept. There had been more involved than his own future. Louise, his wife, had taken time out of her acting career to have a family, but he had known there would come a time when she would want to go back to work, and London was where she was known and where the opportunities arose.

As she had put it, she was beyond the 'age of romance', in that lead roles in major movies were no longer being offered, but it had always been her intention to go back to the stage when she passed forty, as she had a few years earlier. They had been in London for only a few weeks, yet she was in rehearsal for a major role in a West End play and the arts sections of the broadsheets were trumpeting her return.

The sound of his mobile put an end to his contemplation; he looked at the screen and smiled when he saw who was calling.

'Good morning, Chief Constable,' he said. 'I'm guessing this isn't a social call.'

189

'Why shouldn't it be?' his former boss challenged. 'We have lunch breaks in Strathclyde too. I take it you've heard what's happened.'

'How could I not, even if I hadn't had my best mate call me on Saturday night, as soon as he got Paula back to Edinburgh? He was crying, Bob; Mario. Can you believe that? He started to tell me what had happened and then he broke down, sobbing like a baby. Was Paula really that close to the victim?'

'Their heads couldn't have been any more than three feet apart when Toni Field's was blown open,' Skinner told him.

He shivered. 'God, it doesn't bear thinking about. How is she?'

'Most people, put in her situation, would be under sedation right now. Clive Graham's wife still is, and she wasn't even there. Maybe at another time Paula would be too, but at the moment she's completely focused on the baby, so, once she was sure he was okay in there, she was fine. I was with them yesterday morning and saw no sign of a delayed reaction. She's still on course to deliver in a couple of weeks.'

'Yes,' McIlhenney said. 'That's something else I won't be around for, but I'll get up to meet wee Eamon as soon as I can. You know Mario's calling him after his father, don't you?' He paused. 'It's not plain sailing for me, you know, being down here. To move or not to move, it was my choice; Lou didn't put any pressure on me. If I'd said no, we'd have got by, but I want what's best for all of us, Lauren, Spence and wee Louis, and this is it. That said, I miss you lot and not being around for Mario when he really needed me, that was tough.'

'I can imagine. But I admire you nonetheless, for making the move. I have to admit, you're so Edinburgh that I didn't think you'd have the balls.'

'Thanks, pal.' The DCS chuckled. 'By the way, does Joey Morocco still have his? He had a small part in one of Lou's movies a few years back. She says he had a reputation for nose candy and shagging anything female and alive, the latter probably being optional.'

'Fu—' Skinner snorted. 'You are one of the few guys in the world who could say that and get away with it. Yes he has, maybe more by luck than judgement. Aileen and I are history, but what you saw in the papers probably happened because of that, rather than the other way round. I've got no beef with Morocco, but there's a freelance photographer here in Glasgow who should leave town sharpish.'

'That sounds as if you're planning to be there for longer than the three months Mario told me about. I called him back yesterday,' he explained, 'just to make sure he was all right.'

'Ach, Neil, I'm not planning anything. This whole thing . . . it's so bizarre, so bloody terrible, and with the Aileen situation too, I haven't had time to gather my thoughts. I just don't know any more. What I do know is that I'm at the head of the highest profile investigation of my career, and I'm going to consider nothing else until it's done. Speaking of which . . . you were right. This isn't a social call.'

'Some things never change. Go on, Chief, let me hear it.'

'Okay, but you're not due anywhere soon, are you? It's best that I fill you in from the start, and it'll take a while.'

'No, I'm clear for an hour. I was just about to go for lunch, but I can do without that.'

'Thanks. Knowing how you like your chuck, I appreciate that.'

He ran through the events of the previous few days, from the discovery of a body in a shallow grave in Edinburgh, through the chain of events that led to the assassination of Chief Constable Antonia Field, then gave McIlhenney the story of the investigation as it stood.

The chief superintendent stayed silent throughout, but when Skinner was finished, he asked, 'Am I right in thinking that you've run all these checks on your planner, this man Cohen, alias Byron Millbank, without any reference to my outfit?'

'You're spot on, chum. I chose not to involve the Met until I absolutely had to, and that time is now. Make no mistake, this is a Strathclyde operation, but I am going to need to interview people in London, and I will need assistance. I propose to phone your commissioner and ask for it, but what I do not want is for the job to be handed to anyone who might have been personally acquainted with Toni Field. I know she had an affair with a DAC, but I don't have a name.'

'Couldn't you ask the Security Service for help? I know you're well in with them.'

'I could but I don't want to. Their paws are all over Beram Cohen's false identity.'

'Forgive me for asking the obvious, but couldn't Beram Cohen be the false name? They told you about him, after all.'

'No, because there's no trace of Millbank any further back than half a dozen years.'

'Right, box ticked. So, boss . . . listen to me; old habits and all that . . . cut to the chase. Why are you calling me? As if I can't guess.'

'I'll spell it out anyway,' Skinner told him. 'When I call my esteemed colleague, I want to ask him to lend me someone I know and who knows the way I work. But I don't want you press-ganged. Do you want to take this on, and can you?'

'Of course I want to,' McIlhenney replied. 'Can I, though? I'm heading up a covert policing team down here. I have officers operating under cover, deep and dangerous in some cases. I don't run them all directly, but I have to be available for them, and their handlers, at all times.'

'Not a problem. All I'm talking about here is partnering one of my guys in knocking on a few doors. Millbank was a family man, so there's a wife to be told. He had a legitimate job, so that will have to be looked at. I need to know whether there was any overlap between his life and that of Beram Cohen, and if there was, to see where it takes us.'

'Who will you give me? You can't know anyone through there yet, apart from the assistant chiefs.'

'Wrong, I do. I'm going to send my exec down. He's a DCI and his name is Lowell Payne.'

'That's familiar. Isn't he . . .'

'Alex's uncle, but our family link is irrelevant. He's been involved in this operation almost from the start. He's the obvious choice.'

'In which case,' McIlhenney exclaimed, 'I'll look forward to meeting him.'

Thirty

Anger writhed within Assistant Chief Constable Michael Thomas like a snake trapped in a jar. He had seen enough of Bob Skinner, and the way he dominated ACPOS meetings, to know that he did not like the man.

He was ruthless, he was inflexible, he was politically connected and in Thomas's mind he had an agenda: Skinner was out to mould the Scottish police service in his own image, planting his clones and protégés in key roles until they came to dominate it.

He had done it with the stolid Willie Haggerty in Dumfries and Galloway, with quick-witted Andy Martin in the Serious Crimes and Drug Enforcement Agency, and most recently in Tayside, with Brian Mackie, 'The Automaton', as some of his colleagues had nicknamed him.

When Antonia Field had been appointed chief constable of Strathclyde and he had taken her measure, he had been immensely pleased. Finally there was someone on the scene with the rank, the gravitas and the balls to tackle his enemy head on. The truth, that he was afraid to do so himself, had never crossed his mind.

She had identified him from the beginning as her one true supporter among the command ranks in Pitt Street, and he had demonstrated that at every opportunity. She had been in post for less than a month when she took him to dinner, and laid out her vision of the future.

'Unification is coming, Michael,' she began. 'My sources among the movers and shakers tell me that the Scottish government is going to create a single police force, as soon as it deems the moment to be right. I will make no bones about it; I want to be its first chief.

'As head of Strathclyde I should be the obvious choice, but we both know there's a big obstacle in my way. I need allies if I'm going to overcome him, and in particular I need you. You're the only forward-thinking policeman in the place. Theakston, Allan, Gorman, they're all old-school thinkers; they're not going to be around long. Back me and you'll be my deputy inside a year, and again when the new service comes into play. Are you up for that?'

'Of course, Toni, of course.'

After dinner she had taken him to bed, to seal their alliance, she said, although there were times later, after he felt the rough edge of her tongue, as everyone did, when he wondered whether it had been to give her an even greater hold over him, insurance against his ambition growing as great as hers. It had been a one-off and when it was over she had more or less patted him on the bum and sent him home to his wife. There had been no hint of intimacy from then on; he wondered whether there was a new guy in the background, but that was one secret she did not share with him.

For all that, she had been as good as her word and he had been almost there: DCC Theakston gone to enforced early retirement, and Max Allan with his sixty-fifth birthday and compulsory departure only four months in the future. Within a few weeks he would have been deputy. And beyond that?

She had been right about the new force. It had come up in ACPOS, and while Skinner had won the first battle, by a hair's breadth, the next round would be theirs, and the First Minister would be able to claim chief officer support as he moved the legislation. The enemy would be marginalised and unable to go forward as a candidate for commissioner, having fought so hard and publicly against the creation of the job.

Toni had promised him that she had no ambition to grow old, or even middle-aged, in Scotland. She was bound for London, back to the Met when its commissioner fell out with the Mayor, as all of them seemed to do. 'I have levers, Michael, and I will use them, when the time comes. When I go, the floor will be yours.'

Three shots, inside two seconds, that was all it had taken to put the skids under his entire career. He had been doing a spot of evening fishing with his son near Hazelbank when the call had come through. 'An incident reported at the concert hall, sir,' the divisional commander had told him. 'A shooting, with one reported casualty.'

He had known that Toni would be at the hall that night . . . for the previous fortnight she had been full of her 'date' with the First Minister . . . and so he had almost stayed on the river, but a moment's reflection had convinced him that the smart thing would be to tear himself away and rush to the scene. He had arrived to discover that Toni was the reported casualty, and that Max Allan was another, having suffered some sort of collapse, suspected heart attack, they were saying. Her body was still there, with crime scene technicians working all around it in their paper suits and bootees. He had tried to take charge of the shambles, and that was when DCI Lowell bloody Payne had told him about Skinner being there.

He hadn't believed the man, until Dom Hanlon had told him Skinner had taken command, and that he would have to live with it, even though the guy had no semblance of authority. Outrageous, bloody outrageous. Then next day, to cap it all, they'd gone and appointed him acting chief.

That was when the grief had set in, for his own foiled prospects as much as for his fallen leader. He knew where he stood with Skinner, a fact confirmed when he had chosen Bridie Gorman, whom Toni had sidelined almost completely, as acting deputy. He had been considering resignation, quite seriously, when he had been called to the chief constable's office, urgently. Twenty-four bloody hours and suddenly it was urgent.

There he had been, Toni Field's arch-enemy behind Toni Field's desk. God, it had been hard to take.

He hadn't expected subtlety and there had been none. 'Michael,' Skinner had begun, 'you don't like me, and I don't like you much either. But that's irrelevant; if everyone in an organisation this size were bosom buddies it would get sloppy very quickly. Far better that some of us are watching out for each other, and that there are some rivalries in play.

'I had two CID guys in Edinburgh who could have been twins, they were so close; indeed, twins they were called, by their mates. Eventually they rose until they were at the head of operations. It didn't work out; things started to slip through the net, because each one overlooked the other's weaknesses and mistakes. At least that's not going to happen with you and me, in the time I'm here.'

'In that case,' Thomas had ventured, 'wouldn't that make me an excellent deputy?'

The response, a frown. 'Nice try, but no. In my ideal world, people like you and me would be elected to our post by the people we seek to command, not appointed by those who command us, or by boards of councillors. I've been here a day and I've worked out already that if we did that, you wouldn't get too many votes.

197

'I don't doubt your ability as an officer, not for a second, but what I've seen in ACPOS and heard since I've been here make some believe that you're not a leader. Forgive me for being frank; it's the way I'm built.

'However,' Skinner had continued, 'even though I chose ACC Gorman as my deputy when necessary, you are still my assistant and that I respect. So let's work together, not against each other, for as long as I'm here. I'd like to meet with you and Bridie tomorrow morning, so that you can both brief me on your areas of responsibility. Mean-time . . . there's something quite important that I'd be grateful if you could handle. It's not going to be pleasant, but it needs a senior officer.'

And that was how Michael Thomas had come to be standing, seething with anger, in an autopsy theatre, gowned and masked, looking, not for the first time, at the naked body of Antonia Field. The pathologist had followed him into the room. She was a woman also, a complete contrast to Toni, and not only in the fact that she was alive. She was tall, fair-skinned, and the strands of hair that escaped her sterile headgear were blonde.

'You're the duty cop with the short straw in his hand, I take it,' she said. 'I'm Dr Grace.' She turned and nodded towards a young man. From what Thomas could see of his face, his skin tone looked similar to that of Toni. 'And this is Roshan, who'll be assisting me.'

He realised, to his surprise, that she was North American, possibly Canadian, possibly US; he had never been able to distinguish the respective accents.

'ACC Thomas,' he replied. 'Given the circumstances, I felt it was appropriate that I come myself.'

'And I don't imagine Bob tried to talk you out of it,' she murmured, through her mask.

He looked at her, puzzled. 'I'm sorry?'

'Chief Skinner. He's my ex, my former husband. The older he gets, the more squeamish he gets.'

'I see.' The bastard had set him up!

'That said, he's been to more than his fair share. How about you?'

'I've spent most of my career in uniform,' he told her, avoiding a straight answer.

'Ah, so you'll have seen mostly suicides and road fatalities. They have a pretty high squeamishness quotient.'

'Mmm.'

She looked at the man. His eyes told her what the rest of his face was saying. 'You've never been to an autopsy in your life, have you?'

'No,' the ACC confessed.

'So here you are, looking at somebody you knew and worked with, who's now dead and you're going to have to watch me cut her open and take her insides out, all in the line of duty?'

Thomas felt his stomach heave, but he mastered it. 'That sums it up pretty well,' he conceded. 'I suppose your ex would say "Welcome to the real world", or something like that.'

'That sounds like a Bob quote, I admit. Since he didn't, I assume you didn't tell him you've never done this duty before.'

'Of course I didn't.'

'Ah,' she exclaimed, 'the macho thing. The traditional pissing contest, in yet another form. As a result I've got somebody in my workplace who's liable to faint on me or, worse, choke himself to death by barfing inside a face mask. You should have told him, and he'd have sent someone else, because he knows that's the last thing I need. And by the way, he isn't an ogre, either.'

'Well, I'm here now, Doctor,' he replied stiffly, 'so we might as well take the chance. I'll make sure I don't land on anything important when I fall over.'

'Not necessary.' She peeled off her mask. 'You're a legal necessity but in practice don't have to watch every incision or every organ being removed. This is not going to be a complicated job. Cause of death is massive brain trauma caused by gunshot wounds; we know that before I touch her. But the law needs a full report and that's what it will get.

'You can go sit in the corner and read a book, or listen to your iPod. If I find something I believe you need to look at up close, I will tell you and you can look at it. But that's not going to happen. And from what I've seen of our next customer, that's going to be the case with him as well. He was shot from so close up that some of his chest hairs are melted. So go on, get out of my space.'

He looked at her, gratefully. 'Thank you,' he said. He started to move away, then paused. 'Doctor Grace,' he ventured, 'this is a silly thing to ask, I know, but Toni and I, well, we were friends as well as colleagues. Be gentle with her, yes?'

'As if she were an angel,' Sarah replied, feeling pity for the man, then adding, in case he thought she was being sarcastic, 'Who knows, by now she may be one.'

Thirty-One

'Ye cannae do this,' the prisoner protested, 'ma lawyer's no' here. I'm saying nothin' till he gets here. And this charge! What the fuck yis on about? Conspiracy tae fuckin' murder? That's pure shite. Ah never murdered onybody.'

'Technically that's true, Cec,' Dan Provan admitted. 'The jury was stupid enough tae convict you of culpable homicide, and the judge was even dafter when he gave you five years. But the boy ye killed was just as fuckin' deid, so let's no' split hairs about it.'

'We can do it,' Lottie Mann assured him. 'We can do pretty much what we like.'

'Oh aye?' Cecil Brown stuck out his jaw, with menace, then took a closer look at the expression on her face and realised that aggression was not his best option.

'Oh aye.' She pointed at the recorder on the desk. 'That thing is not switched on. When your brief gets here it will be and we'll get formal, but until then, tell me what business you and your brother had with the South Africans.'

He stared back at her. When they had arrested him, the DI's impression had been that he was genuinely surprised. As she studied his big, dumb eyes, that feeling moved towards certainty. 'What fuckin' South Africans?' he asked.

Provan leaned forward. 'Son,' he murmured, 'off the record, who's your biggest rival in Glasgow?'

'Ah don't know what you're talkin' about.'

He laughed. 'Of course you do. Don't fanny about, Cec. I'm askin' you who you've got in mind, what mind ye have, that is, for toppin' your brother. Paddy Reilly? Specky Green? Which of those have you crossed lately? Which of those are we liable tae find in the Clyde any day now?'

When the sergeant floated the second name he saw Brown's eyes narrow; very slightly but it was enough. 'It's Specky, right? Let me guess; you and Bazza ripped him off on some sort of a deal, or moved gear intae one of his pubs. So you're thinkin' it was him that bumped off the boy. Well, if ye are, ye're wrong.'

'Aye, sure.' The tone was a mix of scepticism and contempt. 'Ah might be thick, but no' so thick Ah'd believe youse bastards.'

'He's not kidding, Cecil,' Lottie Mann assured him. 'This is how it was. We found your brother's body yesterday afternoon crammed into the boot of a car in the multi-storey park next to the Buchanan Street bus station. It had been there for a day, and it was starting to hum.

'It was a hire vehicle from London, and it was meant to be the getaway car for the two men, those South Africans I mentioned, who shot and killed our chief constable in the Royal Concert Hall on Saturday evening. Unfortunately for them, they didn't get away, and they're no longer,' her eyes narrowed and she smiled, 'in a position to assist us with our inquiries.' She paused, letting the slow-moving cogs of his mind process what she had said.

'Now we don't actually believe,' she went on, 'that you and your brother were the masterminds behind a plot to kill Ms Field, but the fact that we found him where we did, and also that our forensic team will prove that he was killed by the same gun that was used to shoot two police officers outside the hall, that puts you right in the middle of it.'

Cecil Brown's mouth was hanging open.

'Yes,' she continued. 'I can see you get my point. So we need you to tell us what your role was, and how Bazza came to meet up with those guys. You help us, before your brief gets here to shut you up, and your life will be a hell of a lot better. For openers, you will have a life.

'We are going to put somebody in the dock for this, make no mistake, and at the moment you're all we've got. I'm not talking about five soft years for manslaughter here, Cecil. If you're convicted of having a part in Chief Constable Field's murder you'll be drawing your old age pension before you get out.'

'Personally, laddie,' Dan Provan yawned, 'Ah'd love tae see that happen. You sit there and say nothing and we'll build a case against ye, no bother.'

'Ah don't know anything!' the prisoner shouted. 'Honest tae Christ, Ah don't. Bazza said nothin' tae me about any South Africans.'

'What did he tell you?'

'Nothin'.'

'Come on,' the DS laughed, 'when did your big brother keep secrets from you? The pair of you wis like Siamese twins. You lived next door tae each other, drove the same gangster motors . . . what are they, big black Chrysler saloons . . . ye both married girls ye'd been at the school with, ye shared a box at Ibrox. Come on, Cec. You cannae expect us to believe that Bazza was involved in the shooting of the chief bloody constable and he kept you in the dark about it.'

'Man,' the surviving Brown brother protested, 'ye're off yir heid. Bazza would never have got involved in anything as crazy as killin' the chief constable, or any fuckin' constable. The amount of shite that would have brought down on our heids! It's the last thing he'd have wanted. He had nothin' to do with it.'

'But he had, Cecil,' Lottie Mann boomed. 'Like it or not, he was with Smit and Botha, the two men who shot Ms Field. He was involved with them, and he could have identified them, so they killed him when they had done whatever business they had with him.'

'If you say so,' the prisoner muttered, his lip jutting out like that of a rebellious child. 'But he never telt me about it, okay?'

She sighed. 'Yes, right. Let's say I accept that, for the moment. Did Bazza keep a diary?'

'Eh?'

'Did he keep any sort of written record of his life; his meetings, deals, and so on?'

'In a book, like?'

'Book, computer, tablet.'

'Ah don't know. Maybe on his phone.'

'We don't have that,' Mann said. 'Would he have had it on him?'

'Oh aye, a' the time.'

'Did he have a contract or did he use a throwaway?'

'He had a top-up. He took it everywhere, even tae the bog.'

'Then Smit and Botha must have dumped it after they killed him.' She leaned closer to him. 'Cec, we want whoever was behind them. So do you, for your brother's sake. Help us.'

He met her gaze. 'How can Ah, if Ah don't know anything?'

'Where's Bazza's car?'

Brown turned, at Provan's question. 'Parked outside his hoose,' he replied.

The DS looked at the DI, eyebrows raised, as if inviting a response.

It came. 'Did Smit and Botha pick him up from home?' she asked.

'Naw. Ah'd have seen them,' Cec volunteered, with certainty.

'We've got CCTV. It covers both houses. Ah checked it this mornin', as soon as Senga told me he was deid. Ah was looking for Specky, or his boys. There was nothin', other than us, the paper boy and the postie.'

'So that makes us wonder. How did he get to wherever he met them?'

'Ah suppose Ah must have took him.'

'Where? When?'

'Friday evenin'. Ye know that big park with a' the shops, beside the motorway? Bazza asked me if Ah'd take him there for seven o'clock. He said he was meetin' a burd. He always had bits on the side,' he added, in explanation. 'Our cars are a wee bit obvious, so if he is . . . when he wis . . . playin' away he liked tae use taxis. Ah took him there and Ah dropped him off, in the car park, must hae been about seven, mibbes a wee bit after.'

'And that was the last time you saw him?'

'Aye.'

'But you didn't see the woman?'

'Naw.' His eyes were fixed on the table. 'There couldnae have been one, could there? Ah must have delivered him tae the guys that killed him.'

'Then it's too bad for him he didn't tell you what was going on. You could have hung around and watched his back.'

'Fuckin' right,' Cec muttered.

'Is there anything else?' Mann asked him. 'Anything that could help us?'

'I wish there wis. If Ah could, Ah would, honest.'

'You know what,' she said, 'I think I believe you. Cec, you're free to go, but I warn you, we've got search warrants for Bazza's house, and for yours, and for the office of that so-called minicab company that you run. We're enforcing them right now, going through the records, and looking for anything that'll tie your brother to those guys. If we find something, and you're involved after all, you'll be back in here before you've even had time to take a piss.

'In the meantime, my advice is to watch your back. If the man we're after gets it into his head that Bazza might have confided in you, he might decide that it's too big a risk to leave you running around loose.'

Brown's eyes seemed to light up with a strange intensity, that of a man with two bells showing on a one-armed bandit and the third reel still spinning. 'Ah hope he does, Miss. Ah'd like tae talk tae him.'

Thirty-Two

'So there you have it. Sir Bryan Storey, the Met commissioner himself, has approved your trip. Funny,' Skinner mused, 'I met that man for the first time at a policing conference a few weeks ago. D'you know what he said, "Ah, you're Edinburgh, are you?" as if he was a Premier League manager and I was mid-table Division Three. Just now when I spoke to him, he was almost deferential. It seems that this office does have clout nationally, more than I'd realised.'

'I don't have to report to him when I get there, do I?' Lowell Payne asked.

'No, not even a courtesy call. I doubt if he's spoken to a DCI since he got the final piece of silver braid on his cap. You just catch the first London flight you can tomorrow, go to New Scotland Yard and ask for Chief Superintendent McIlhenney. He'll be waiting for you.'

'What's he like, this man?'

The chief smiled. 'Try to imagine a quieter, more thoughtful version of Mario McGuire; but when he has to, Neil can be almost as formidable. The division he works in, covert policing, has some tough people in it. He'd never be any good in the field himself because he's too conspicuous, but he will always have the respect of the people who are.'

'How do we play it with Millbank's family?'

'You should take the lead in the questions. You're the investigator, in practice; Neil's just your escort. He knows that and he's okay with it. I'd suggest you begin by being circumspect. Remember, we've only just identified Cohen under the name Byron Millbank. Now we have done, Storey's going to send two female family support officers to break the news to his widow, but you'll be going in soon after.'

'How much will they have told her?'

'Only the basic truth, that he died suddenly, of a brain haemorrhage, and that he had no identification on him at the time, hence the delay in getting to her. It's your job to fill in the rest, and find out as best you can whether she has a clue that her old man had another identity. The book's open on that. My bet is that she doesn't, but you reach your own conclusions, gently.'

'Once we get past gentle, what then?'

'You don't,' Skinner told him, with emphasis. 'You ask to see her husband's computer, to check his calendar, recent contacts, all that stuff. Kid-glove stuff, Lowell. It's only if she doesn't play ball that you have to make the request formal, and take it all away.

'It should be the same with his workplace, this teleshopping outfit. It's pretty obvious that it's a family business, given the similarity with the wife's maiden name, so unless you find a box of Uzis in his desk, you maintain the front that it's a formal sudden-death inquiry, required by Scottish law, and that all we're doing is confirming his appointments, movements, etc.'

'Understood.' Payne stood up. 'When do you want me back?' he asked.

'When you're done; that's all I can say. I have no idea how this thing will go, but I do know this. An outside agency has an interest in it, and I want to head it off. So, any leads that are thrown up have to be followed up, fast. If you need to stay tomorrow night, or even beyond that, so be it.'

'Okay, I'll take enough clothes and stuff for a couple of days.' He smiled. 'There's just one thing, though, Bob. It's our wedding anniversary on Thursday, and I've got a table booked at Rogano. If it comes to it and I have to cancel, I'd appreciate it if you call Jean and tell her, and say that it was your fault.'

Skinner whistled. 'There ought to be no absolutes in the field of human courage,' he said, 'but it would take an absolute fucking hero to do that. If necessary, her niece and I will take her to Rogano ourselves, and I'll pick up the tab.'

'That's a deal. Hopefully it won't come to that. Here,' he added, 'what will you do for an assistant while I'm away? You're still on a learning curve here.'

'Yes, and I'm going to rely on my ACCs to instruct me. Mr Thomas and I had a getting to know you session earlier on. I asked him to attend the post-mortem on Toni Field and to sit in on Bazza Brown's while he was there.'

'Oh shit,' Payne murmured.

The chief frowned. 'What?'

'Maybe I should have told you, but I never thought to, because it was no more than office gossip. Not long after Field arrived, when she lived on the Riverside, a couple of PCs in a Panda car saw Michael Thomas leaving her apartment block at three in the morning. The story was all round the force inside a day. ACC Allan heard about it and put the word out that anybody who even thought of posting it on Twitter or Facebook would wind up nailed to a cross.'

'Indeed?' Skinner murmured, with a thin smile. 'Typical Max; he's too nice a guy for his own good. Yes, it sounds like I really have put Thomas on the spot. Was this a continuing relationship?'

'I'm pretty sure it wasn't.'

'How sure?'

'Not a hundred per cent, I admit. Why?'

'Oh nothing. Between you and me, Marina Deschamps gave me a rundown on her sister's sex life. It hadn't occurred to me till now, but the numbers didn't quite add up.' He nodded, as if he had reached a conclusion, then spelled it out. 'That's made my mind up,' he said. 'I'm going to tell Marina she can come back to work. If any more Toni skeletons pop out during this investigation, it'll be useful to have her around.'

'Do you want me to . . .'

'No, I'll call her myself, after I've told the fiscal that I want the body released tomorrow morning.'

'The fiscal here doesn't like to be told, Chief,' Payne warned.

'Then I'll make it seem as if it was his idea all along.'

'He's a she.'

'Aren't they all these days? When my dad was in practice just after the war, there wasn't a single female solicitor in the burgh. Now the majority of law graduates are women, like our Alex. It's magic; it hasn't half shaken up the establishment. What's her name?'

'Reba Paisley. Mrs.'

'Get her on the phone for me, please. Then you'd better get off home, once you've booked your flight.'

'Will do. By the way,' he volunteered, 'that bloody safe; you were right. It was installed at Chief Constable Field's request and we do not have the technical capability in-house to open it. I've asked our plant and machinery people to source the supplier and get someone to deal with it.'

As Payne headed back to his own office to make the call to the procurator fiscal, the regional chief prosecutor, Skinner moved from the table to his desk. As he eased himself into his seat . . . not a patch on my Edinburgh chair, he grumbled, mentally . . . his mobile buzzed and vibrated in his pocket, signalling an incoming text. He dug it out and read it.

'In Glasgow. Can I blag a lift? We came in Roshan's car. Be about 6. Sarahx.'

He keyed in a reply, awkwardly because of the thickness of his index finger; he had never mastered using his thumbs on the mini-keyboard.

'I know, & what ur doing. Sure. Take a taxi to Pitt St when ur done. L Bob.'

He had no sooner sent the message than the phone rang. 'Chief Constable,' he said as he picked up.

'Procurator fiscal,' an assertive female voice replied. 'What can I do for you, Mr Skinner?'

'Nothing, Mrs Paisley. I don't ask for favours. Let's get that clear from the start.'

'So this is a social call?'

'Yes, partly.'

'Even "partly" makes a change. In the time she was here I never once heard from your late predecessor.'

'You won't be wanting to hang on to her then,' Skinner chuckled.

'To tell you the truth,' the fiscal replied, 'I hadn't given that any thought.'

'What's your normal procedure with homicide victims?'

'I don't have one. I make my judgement on a case by case basis, but it's my judgement, I stress. It's not a call that I delegate to a deputy. In this case . . . is the PM done?'

'As we speak.'

'Who are the immediate family?'

'Mother and sister.'

'Are there any prospects of further arrests?'

'Further?' Skinner repeated. 'We never actually got round to arresting Smit and Botha.'

He heard a sound that might have been a chuckle. 'You know what I mean. Because if there are, defence counsel might want access to the body.'

'I know that, but it isn't an automatic right. I can't say for sure we will ever trace the people in this chain of conspiracy, let alone guessing when. We're interviewing the brother of the man found dead in the getaway car, but I don't believe he will be able to help us.'

'Why not?'

'Because he's still alive. If Cec knew anything, he'd probably be in the cooler next to his brother.'

'How about if I authorise release for burial only?'

'Toni Field was born in Mauritius. What if her mother wants to take her home there?'

'It would be a lot easier in an urn than a coffin. Is that what you're saying?'

'I'm not saying anything, only asking questions.'

'But good ones,' Paisley said. 'Tell you what. If the post-mortem report satisfies me that there are no unresolved questions about the death, the family can have her, and do whatever they like with her.'

'That's fair enough,' Skinner agreed. 'I'll tell them. The only unresolved questions about the death aren't related to the autopsy. There are only two: who wanted her dead and why.'

'Do your people have any ideas about either of those issues?'

'I don't encourage my people to deal in ideas, only evidence. As I speak they're looking for any that's to be found. When they have more to report, they will, to both of us. Good to talk to you; you must come here for lunch some time.'

'That will also be a first,' the fiscal remarked. 'I'll look forward to it.'

As he hung up, Skinner scribbled, 'Lunch Pitt St with fiscal: arrange,' then called the switchboard and asked to be connected with Marina Deschamps. It was her mother who came on the line. 'I regret that Marina is unavailable,' she said. 'Will I do?'

'Of course, Miss Deschamps. I want to talk to you about Antonia's funeral.'

'Good, for we were going to call you about that. We contacted an undertaker, but he said that he had no access to her body.'

'Not yet,' he agreed. 'There are issues in any homicide, but once the fiscal has some paperwork in place, everything should be all right. What I want to talk to you about is the form of the funeral. Antonia was a chief constable, and she died in office. If you want a private family funeral, so be it, but it's only right that her force should pay its tribute. I'm happy to organise everything for you, if that's what you would like. Did she have a religion?'

'She was raised in the Roman Catholic Church,' she fell silent for a few seconds, 'although she was not a regular visitor, I must admit.'

'Nonetheless. Cardinal Gainer, in Edinburgh, is a friend of mine. I'm sure he would officiate, or approach his opposite number in Glasgow.'

'That is very generous of you, Mr Skinner. I would like to talk to Marina about it when she returns.'

He heard a sound, in the background, as if someone was calling out. 'Is that her now?' he asked.

'No, it's just street noise. We will call you, Mr Skinner. Thank you very much.'

Thirty-Three

'Anything on Bazza's computer, Banjo?' Lottie Mann called out to a detective constable who was seated at a table on the other side of the inquiry office, working on the confiscated PC. He rose and crossed towards her.

'No email account that I can find, and that's disappointing. He was very big on porn sites, though,' he advised her. 'Nothing illegal, nothing that Operation Amethyst would have hit on; all grown-ups, all doing fairly monotonous and repetitive stuff. Strange; from what I saw of Mrs Brown when we raided the house, he shouldn't have needed any diversions like that. There are some pictures of her on the computer that bear that out, and a couple of videos.'

'*Chacun à son goût.*'

The DC nicknamed Banjo . . . his surname was Paterson, but none of his colleagues made the connection to the man who wrote the words of 'Waltzing Matilda' . . . stared at her. 'Eh?' he exclaimed.

'It's the only French I know,' she said. 'It means there's no telling what you'll find under a guy's bed when you take a look. Or something like that.'

'I'll take your word for it, boss. I only speak Spanish and a wee bit of Mandarin Chinese.'

'Smart bastard,' she snarled. 'What else?'

'Video games; the thing was wired up to a big high-def screen. And casinos, he was quite a gambler, was our Bazza. He played roulette and blackjack mostly, but poker as well, from time to time. He also had an account with an online bookie, and bet heavily on the horses and on boxing.'

'Was he any good at it?'

'He seems to have been. He paid through a credit card; I've looked at the records and most months there was more going in than coming out. He had a system for roulette and he only ever backed favourites.'

'That's not a complete surprise; Bazza's old man had a bookie's licence and a couple of betting shops. As I recall, Bazza ran them for a while after he died, then sold them on to a chain. So yes, he'd a gambling background. He backed the wrong horse, though, when he took up with the South Africans. How about Cec?' she asked. 'Did he have a PC?'

'Cec couldnae spell PC,' Dan Provan muttered.

'Possibly not,' the detective constable agreed. 'He's got a PlayStation and that was it. He likes war games; anything where people get blown to bits. He also likes porn, but DVDs in his case. We could nick him for a few of those if you want.'

'Can't be arsed,' Mann said. 'What about their office?'

'Definitely non-ecological. They don't give a shit about how many trees they kill. All their records are on paper. However, they did fail to hide a list of addresses. They didn't connect to anything so we're having a look. Our search warrant was broad enough to let us go straight in.' Paterson smiled. 'Now for the good bit. Uniform have visited just one so far, a four-bedroom villa in a modern estate near Clydebank; it's a cannabis farm, and you can bet the others are too.'

She laughed. 'Poor old Cec; it's not his week. He's probably home by now; have him rearrested and brought in, then hand him and that address list over to Operation League. He's their business now.' She turned to Provan. 'Bilbo,' she began.

He glared at her. 'The chief wis bad enough,' he growled. 'No' you as well.'

'What do we have on Bazza as a force? Is there an intelligence report on him?'

'Now there's a hell of a question to be askin' a garden fuckin' ornament like me.'

'Okay, Dan,' she laughed, 'I'm sorry.'

'No more funnies?'

'No more funnies.'

'Good, because that really was a hell of a question. Ah've got a mate, a good mate, in what we're no' supposed to call Special Branch any more, in Counter-Terrorism Intelligence Section. He's jist told me that the chief . . . the old chief, no' the new one . . . asked for updated files on all organised crime figures as soon as she came in. When SCT went to work on Bazza, they asked the National Criminal Intelligence Service for input, and a big red sign came up, warnin' them off.'

'What does that mean?'

'It means he wis a fuckin' grass, Lottie; he was protected. And if it wasnae for us, and it wasn't, it must have been for MI5. They've got a serious crime section.'

'Jesus!'

'You'll get brownie points wi' the new chief when ye tell him that, eh?'

'Maybe. But have you thought through the implications?'

'Sure,' Provan admitted, 'but Ah'm no' paid enough to spell them out. Ye'd better go and see the gaffer.'

'I will do. While I'm up there, you concentrate on the only other line of inquiry we have with Bazza. Have we got the CCTV tapes from the Easthaven Retail Park yet?'

'Aye, and I've cleared up something; nothin' major, just a point for the record. We know that Smit and Botha were at Easthaven and that Bazza went there too, to meet them. We know from the gaffer that the South Africans were in Livingston on Friday, collecting their weapons. Ah've checked with the team in Edinburgh, spoke to a DC called Haddock, bright-soundin' kid . . .'

'Nothing fishy about him?' Mann murmured.

'Whit . . . ach, be serious, Lottie. He said that there was no mention of a third man bein' with them. So, Bazza must have been in the boot o' the motor by then.'

'Fair enough, fills in the timeline. Take a look at that video and see if it shows them meeting, then we'll join all the dots. What does the recording cover?'

'Two cameras, all day Friday, midnight to midnight. But there's a clock on it so Ah'll speed run it back to just before seven and go from there.'

'Fine, you do that. I'll go and see the boss.'

Thirty-Four

'You do realise, Lottie,' a frowning Skinner said, 'that I should be water-boarding the wee man until he tells me who his contact in CTIS is. That section is supposed to be completely confidential. Information like that shouldn't be passed on outside the reporting chain.'

'That's why I didn't bring him up here with me,' the DI replied. 'But you'd be wasting your time, boss. He'd drown before he told you. Dan's old school.'

'Don't I know it. That's why the tap's not running. I won't press the point, for now, but I won't forget it either. Make sure he knows that, so that his mate, whoever he is, will get to hear about it.'

'Understood, boss. I'll drop a word in his ear.'

'Don't be too friendly about it. I know he was your mentor, but you're his line manager, not the other way around. Now, since he has given us this information . . . you know what it suggests?'

'I think so,' she said, 'if it was the Security Service that flagged Bazza Brown as off limits . . . and who else would it be?'

'Drugs enforcement,' the chief suggested, 'but that's unlikely. I can and will check it, though. If that was the cause of the red notice, it would have come from Scotland. The head of the SCDEA and I are close. He'll tell me if it was his mob that were running Brown. Indeed,

I've got a feeling that if it was them, he'd have been in touch with me by now to let me know.

'So, let's say that Bazza was on the books of MI5's serious crime section. If our speculation that they fixed Beram Cohen up with a new identity is well founded, then he would have as well, and that's our link.'

'What do you want me to do about it, boss?'

'Absolutely nothing,' Skinner replied, almost before she had finished her question. 'As far as you're concerned, you never had the information you just brought me and neither did Dan. He shouldn't have been given it in the first place, and if he made any written note of his conversation, it must be destroyed.'

'Yes, sir.' She rose from the chair that faced the chief constable's desk. It was low set, so that whoever sat behind the desk was always looking down on his visitors, an intimidating tactic that Skinner disliked, and vowed that he would change. 'Since I was never here,' she said, 'I'd better make myself scarce.'

He laughed. 'You do that, Lottie. Concentrate on the video you told me about. If you can show Bazza Brown meeting Smit and Botha, you can wrap up the inquiry into his murder, and pass that on to Reba Paisley's office. Why he met them, if we're right about that, she doesn't need to know. How they came to know him, that's completely off limits.'

'Fine, I'll report back on the first part as soon as we've nailed it down.'

He watched her as she left then reached across his desk for the phone, only to be interrupted by his mobile signalling another incoming text. 'Done here. Scrubbing up, then on my way. Sarahx.'

No reply needed; he smiled as he put it back in his pocket, then picked up the other instrument, selected 'direct dial' and made the call he had been intending.

'Mario? How are you settling into my old office? Do you like the view? You can see every bugger who comes in and goes out. Useful at times.'

'Sure,' the newly appointed ACC conceded, 'but they can see me.'

'Not if you angle the blinds right.'

'I'll try that. Have you got any other advice for me?'

'Yeah, keep your eye on David Mackenzie; he's after your job.'

'I worked that one out for myself, Bob, quite some time ago. Anything else? Anything serious?'

'No, but a question. How's Paula?'

'Blooming. No sign of delayed shock, post-traumatic stress or any of that crap, I'm relieved to say. Maybe because she's got too much on her mind. She saw her consultant again this morning, at his request. When he checked her over yesterday, he thought he might have got her dates wrong. Now he's sure, he's given her to the end of the week to get the job done herself, or he's going to induce labour.'

'They did that with Myra, when she had Alex. As I recall, it started with castor oil. Tell her that; the threat alone might be a trigger.'

'I will. Now let me ask you one. How's Aileen? First off, I'm sorry about you two, and about all the other shit. She's had a very tough forty-eight hours, man.'

Skinner felt his forehead tighten. 'Are you saying I made it worse?' he asked.

'No, absolutely not,' McGuire insisted. 'I wasn't implying that. I understand how things are between you. It was a straight question.'

'In that case, she's fine. She and I spoke not that long ago and everything's okay. We've put our situation on the record, so the press will have to be very careful with what they say about her. I know she had that bother at her press conference this morning, but given the trouble the Hatton woman's been making, it'll work for her rather than agin her.'

'Good. Now would you like to come to the point?'

'What makes you think there is one?' Skinner asked.

'How long have we known each other? About fifteen years? I'm not saying you never call me just to pass the time of day, but I don't recall you ever doing it from the office, not once.'

'Christ, is that true? You know, McIlhenney said much the same earlier. What does that say about me?' He sighed. 'The sad thing is, you're right. I've got a situation here, I need it resolved, but I can't be bothered going through channels. It would take too long. Instead, I'm looking for a simpler solution. Do you remember a wee guy called Johan Ramsey?'

'Wee Jo? Of course. A master of his craft, if ever there was one.'

'It didn't stop him getting lifted a few times though. Do you know where he is now?'

'As a matter of fact I do. He's here in Edinburgh, on parole after his last sentence. We were advised when he was released.'

'Good,' Skinner declared. 'That's what I wanted to hear.'

'How come?' McGuire laughed. 'What do you want with him?'

'I want to employ him.'

'You what?'

'I mean it. I've got a job for him. There's a safe in my office here. Toni Field had it installed, and only she knew the combination. I don't have the time to wait for some bloody company in the south of England to free up one of their specialists, so I want to hire one of my own. I'd like you to pick him up, and invite him to join me here tomorrow morning, to see what he can do. Tell him there's a hundred in it for him, regardless, cash, and that his probation officer will never know. Can you do that for me, ACC McGuire? Make it work and I'll buy you lunch after your first ACPOS meeting.'

'Hell, Bob, you don't need to bribe me to get me to do that. That's a first, and it's going in my memoirs.'

'That's fine,' Skinner grunted, 'but you'd better make it clear to wee Jo that if it winds up in his, then next time he gets sent down, I will make certain, personally, that parole is off the table.'

Thirty-Five

'In my office, please, Dan,' Lottie Mann said as she returned to the investigation suite.

'Absolutely,' Provan muttered, but too quietly for her to hear, and he rose from his seat and followed her into a small room at the end of the open area.

'See that friend of yours in CTIS?' she began, without preamble. 'Whoever he is, you'd better warn him that where he works careless talk costs lives, and in this case it's his that's on the line. On Toni Field's watch there would probably have been a leak inquiry over what he told you. There won't be this time, but probably only because Skinner likes you too much to use a nutcracker to get the name out of you.

'We are not to follow up what you were told. Instead we're to wrap up Bazza's murder, pass the file to the fiscal and mark it case closed, then get on with the main investigation, which is still, unlike Field, very much alive. That's the way it is, Dan. You are from Barcelona. You know nussing.'

'Ye've got the accent wrong,' the DS said. 'Ah'm old enough to have seen *Fawlty Towers* when it wis new. Unfortunately, Lottie, Ah don't know nothin'. In fact, Ah know too fuckin' much.'

'Oh, I know that,' she laughed. 'Too much for your own good.'

'No, love,' he sighed, 'for yours.'

She stared at him. 'What are you on about, Detective Sergeant? Can we just keep up the pretence that I'm your senior officer?'

'No, we can't.'

Her eyes narrowed. A spasm of something strange ran through her, and she realised that it was fear. 'Dan,' she murmured, 'what is this?'

'This, Lottie, is me doin' something Ah shouldn't. By rights Ah shouldn't be talking to you alone. There should be a senior officer in this room right now, probably the chief constable himself. There isn't, because Ah care about you, lassie, and I want you to know about this from me, first. This might have to be another of those conversations that never happened, like mine with Alec in CTIS, but this is a hell of a lot more serious.'

He reached across her desk and switched on her computer; it was an old-fashioned tower type, probably on its last legs, and took an inordinate length of time to boot up.

'Dan,' she said once more, as they waited, but he hushed her, with a finger to his lips.

'They store the CCTV recordings on DVDs,' he told her, as he loaded a disk on to the computer's player tray, and slid it into position, then settled into the DI's chair so that he could control playback.

'I started at the end, like Ah said,' he began. She looked at the screen and saw a still image of an empty car park, and with numerals in the bottom right corner. 'These things can hold eight hours at a time,' he explained. 'They have a bank of recorders tae cover the whole park. When one disk gets full, another starts, so it's constant. Ah thought I'd have to go a' the way back tae seven, but . . .'

He clicked a rewind icon, three times; the image began to move, as did the time read-out, fast, backwards. Provan's finger hovered above the mouse until the clock showed seven twenty-eight, when he clicked again, freezing the recording once more.

'Ah nearly missed this first time. Watch.' He clicked on the 'Play' arrow and the images started to move.

Mann peered at the screen. The park was almost as empty as it had been before; only a few cars remained. Then she saw a silver saloon roll into view, moving jerkily, for the camera was set to shoot only a few frames per second. It came to a stop and as it did so, a figure walked towards it, his speed enhanced. He was carrying a large parcel. She could just make out a face in the front passenger seat, and a hand, beckoning.

'Bazza,' Provan murmured. 'Now see what happens.'

The man she took to be Brown opened the rear door, slid into the back seat, and closed it behind him. Everything was still for a few seconds. Then she saw what seemed to be three flashes, inside the Peugeot, as if someone was sending a Morse message with a torch. Immediately afterwards, the car zoomed off, at high speed.

'That was the execution of Bazza Brown,' the DS said.

'No doubt about it,' his DI agreed. 'So?'

'So, what was wrong with that picture?'

'Enlighten me,' she growled. 'Stop playin' games, Dan.'

'This is no game, kid. The parcel.' He emphasised the word. 'Where did Brown get the fuckin' parcel? Cec never mentioned that. As far as he was concerned he was takin' his brother to meet a bit on the side. And what was in it? Did he take her chocolates? If he did, it's the biggest box of Black Magic Ah've ever seen.'

'True,' she murmured. That cold feeling revisited the pit of her stomach. Her old crony was taking her somewhere, and she had a bad feeling about their destination.

'Then there was the time,' the DS continued. 'Bazza wanted to be there for seven, yet the South Africans never turned up for another half hour. So Ah ran the recording back to the time Cec told us, like

225

this.' He rewound once more, stopping at six fifty-eight, with a large black car in shot, near to where the Peugeot had pulled up.

Provan let the recording go forward, and Mann saw Bazza Brown step out of his brother's Chrysler, and into the last half hour of his life. He went nowhere, but stood his ground, pacing up and down, waiting, as Cec drove away.

And then a door opened; it was set in the side of a large warehouse building at the top of the frame. A figure stepped out. He was carrying a large parcel, and he walked towards Brown. There was no handshake between the two, barely a glance exchanged, it seemed, as the bundle was handed over. The second man seemed about to turn on his heel, when Provan froze the screen.

'I need you to confirm, ma'am,' he said, 'that the man with Brown is who I think he is.'

Standing behind him, Lottie leaned over and grasped his shoulder, and the corner of the desk, for support.

'Oh no,' she moaned. 'Oh my God, no. You know it is, Danny. You know it's my Scott.'

The sergeant let out a sigh that seemed bigger than he was. 'Ah've never wished in ma life before,' he murmured, 'that Ah wasnae a cop. But I do now, so that somebody else could be doin' this.'

He stood, and gave her back her own chair. Then he went to the door, opened it and beckoned to Banjo Paterson, who crossed the office and joined them.

'Detective Inspector,' Provan announced, his accent vanishing in the formality of his voice, 'in view of what we've just seen, and what you've confirmed, in spite of my subordinate rank I have got no choice but to ask you to remain here with DC Paterson while I take this matter to senior officers.'

Thirty-Six

'So this is where it all happens,' Sarah Grace said, with a smile in her tone as she looked round the room that had become his. 'This is the nerve centre of Scottish policing.'

'A week ago,' Bob told her, 'I would have denied that suggestion, with all the vehemence at my disposal. Today, I'm forced to agree with you.'

'I prefer the command suite in Edinburgh,' she confessed. 'It has a more, I dunno, a more lived-in feel about it. This is all very antiseptic, very impersonal.'

'Honey child,' he laughed, 'don't you think that might be because I haven't had time to stamp my personality on it?'

'Maybe. I'm sure you will . . . as long as that doesn't involve importing that coffee machine you inherited from your old mentor Alf Stein.'

'It won't, I promise you. You told me I should give myself a caffeine holiday and that's what I'm doing. I haven't had a coffee this week. Are you pleased with me?'

She grinned. 'Yes and no. If you really are sticking to it, that might mean I have to give up too. When you're around, at least. Speaking of which,' she added, 'do you want to stop off tonight? The Gullane house will be empty, since the kids are with me.'

'I think I would like that very much, although I do have something to do there, before the place can be truly empty.'

'Can I help?'

'Mmm,' he mused. 'No, I don't think so. I don't reckon either of us would feel right if you did.'

'Ah,' Sarah whispered. 'I think I can guess what you mean. Clearing out all the evidence, yes?'

'Yes, at the other party's request.'

'Then you're right. That is something you should do on your own . . . unless it involves a bonfire, in which case I'll be happy to help.'

'Hey, hey!'

'I'm joking,' she said. 'The strangest thing happened to me this morning. I saw the newspapers and all of a sudden I found that I don't bear that woman any ill-will, not any more, however she might feel about me.'

'To be honest with you, Sarah,' Bob confessed, 'I don't believe she feels any way about you, and I doubt that she ever did. She thought I was somebody I'm not. Now she's found out the truth, she's happy to make me, and everything to do with me, part of her past.'

'Does that include not trying to take you for plenty in the divorce?'

'That hasn't been mentioned,' he grinned, 'and I'm not going to raise the subject.'

He loaded a handful of documents and files into his attaché case, an aluminium Zero Halliburton that Sarah had given him as a birthday present a few years before, clicked it shut and picked it up. 'Come on,' he said. 'Constable Davie, my driver, will be waiting for us in the car park.'

He turned, and was in the act of heading for the door that led directly into the corridor when he saw a small, crumpled, moustachioed figure in his anteroom, his hand raised as if he was about to knock on the door.

'What the hell?' he murmured. 'Hold on a minute, love,' he told his ex-wife. 'There's something up here. Detective sergeants don't turn up uninvited in the chief's office without a bloody good reason.'

He signalled to Dan Provan to enter, but the little man stood his ground. 'What the fu—' Skinner muttered. 'Sit down for a minute, Sarah,' he said. 'Maybe the wee bugger's scared of strange women.'

He walked towards the glass doorway, then stepped through it into the outer office. 'Yes, Dan?' he murmured. 'Where's your DI and what can I do for you?'

'She's detained, sir, downstairs in the office.'

Skinner had a low annoyance threshold. 'What the fuck's detaining her? Has it paralysed her phone hand?'

'No, sir, you don't understand. Ah've detained her. Out of bloody nowhere she's become involved in the investigation. The rule book requires that Ah do that and report the matter to senior officers, plural. In this case, Ah don't think that means a couple of DIs.'

The chief's face darkened; looking up at him, Provan, experienced though he was, felt a chill run through him.

'Where is she?' Skinner murmured.

'She's in her private office, boss. DC Paterson's with her; Ah've ordered him not to allow her to make any phone calls or send any texts.'

'You've done that to Lottie?' Skinner said, and as he did he realised how upset the sergeant was. 'Right, let's hear about it, but not here.'

He opened the door behind him and called out to Sarah, 'Urgent, I'm afraid. Hang on please, love; I'll be as quick as I can.' Then he led the way into the corridor and along to ACC Gorman's office, relieved to see through the unshaded glass wall that she was behind her desk. He rapped on the door, and walked straight in.

'Bridie, sorry to interrupt, but something's arisen that DS Provan feels he has to bring to the top of the reporting chain. He's been around long enough to know the rule book off by heart, so we'd better hear him out.'

'Of course.' Skinner's deputy rose. 'Hi, Dan,' she said. 'You look as though the cat's just ett your budgie.'

The little sergeant sighed. 'Ma'am, if it would make this go away Ah'd feed it the bloody thing maself.'

'So what do you have to tell us?' she asked.

'To show you,' he corrected her. 'Is your computer on?'

'Give me a minute,' she said, then pressed a button behind a console that sat on a side table.

The command suite computers were of more recent vintage than those in the floors below, and so it was ready in less than the time she had requested.

Provan inserted the DVD he had brought with him into a slot at the side of the screen. 'This is CCTV footage,' he explained to the two chief officers, 'from the Easthaven Retail Park. It was taken on Friday evening. Our investigation established that the two men who killed Chief Constable Field went there at that time, and later Bazza Brown's brother, Cec, told us that he took Bazza there as well. Now, please watch.'

He played the recording in the same way that he had shown it to his DI twenty minutes earlier, stopping as the Peugeot roared away from the park.

'That's your homicide wrapped up,' Skinner remarked. 'But where did the parcel come from?'

'Watch again,' Provan replied, rewinding the recording by half an hour, showing Brown's drop-off by his brother, the unexpected encounter, and the handing over of the package. Once again, he froze the action to show the newcomer's face.

'I see,' the chief constable murmured. 'Are you going to tell me who that is, now?'

It was Bridie Gorman who answered. 'I can tell you that,' she hissed. He looked at her and saw that her eyes, normally warm and kind, were cold and seemed as hard as blue marble. 'That is Scottie Mann, one-time police officer until the bevvy got the better of him, and still the husband of Detective Inspector Charlotte Mann. What's the stupid fucking bastard gone and done? Dan, what was in the parcel? Do you know?'

'I would bet my maxed-out pension, ma'am,' the veteran detective declared, 'that it was two police uniforms and two equipment belts.'

Thirty-Seven

'I'm sorry that took so long,' Bob told Sarah as he stepped back into his office, 'but it had to be done straight away, and by nobody other than my deputy and me.'

'What's happened?' she asked. 'Can you tell me?'

'In theory no, I can't, but bugger that. If I don't I'll be brooding over it for the rest of the night. Bridie Gorman and I have just found ourselves in the horrible position of having to interview, under caution, the senior investigating officer in the Toni Field murder. Her husband turned up not just as a witness, but as a suspect in the conspiracy. That's what wee Provan came to tell me, and it must have been bloody tough on him, because the two of them are bloody near father and daughter.'

'Oh my. How did it go?'

'We put the question directly to her and she swore that she had no knowledge of her husband's involvement, and that if she had she would have declared it.'

'Do you believe her?'

He nodded. 'Yes, we do. The poor woman's in a hell of a state. She alternates between being tearful and wanting to rip her old man's heart out . . . and she's big enough to do that too.'

'What happens now?'

'Scott, the husband . . . the ex-cop husband,' he growled, his face twisting suddenly in anger, 'will be arrested. In fact it's under way now. Provan's taking a DC and some uniforms to their house to pick him up. Their son will see that happen, I'm afraid, but there's no way round that. DC Paterson and the uniforms will take him away and Dan . . . he's the boy's godfather . . . will stay with him till Lottie gets back.' He chuckled, savagely. 'She wanted to make the arrest herself! I almost wish that was possible. It'd serve the guy right. No chance, though; she's out.'

'You mean she's suspended?' Sarah looked as angry as he did.

'No, of course not.' He smiled to lighten the moment. 'Calm down. No need to get the sisterhood wound up. She's on an unanticipated holiday, that's all. She can't continue on the inquiry, because she's been hopelessly compromised.'

'Who'll take over from her?'

'Dan will,' Skinner replied, 'reporting to me, just as she's been doing. I could parachute in another DI, indeed maybe I should, given his closeness to the family, but Scott was a cop himself and it would be difficult to find someone who had never crossed his path.

'Anyway, Provan's forgotten more about detective work than most of the potential candidates will ever learn, and he's still got enough left in his tank to see him through. He won't interview Scott, though. Bridie and I will do that, tomorrow morning. Not too early, though, I want him to stew in isolation for a while. Now,' he declared, 'let's you and I get out of here. Change of plan; we'll take the train, then a taxi to yours. I can't have PC Davie drive me through to Edinburgh at this time of night.'

They took the lift down to the headquarters car park, where PC Cole was waiting. The chief constable introduced the extra passenger, 'Doctor Grace, the pathologist, from Edinburgh University,' then apologised for the delay, a gesture that seemed to take his driver by surprise. His reaction rose to astonishment when Skinner told him that the destination was Queen Street Station.

'Are you sure, sir?' he exclaimed.

'Certain. You can pick me up from there tomorrow as well. I'll let you know what train I'm on.'

The train was on the platform five minutes from departure as they settled into its only first-class compartment. Sarah grinned. 'I'm on expenses, or I would be if you hadn't bought my ticket. What's your excuse?'

'I'm not quite sure,' he confessed, 'since everything happened very quickly at the weekend, but I think I am too. But the truth is that I prefer first, on the rare occasions that I take the train, simply because there's less chance of me meeting an old customer, so to speak.'

'And that would worry you?' she asked, eyebrow raised. 'Are you feeling your age?'

'No to both of those, and not that it's likely to happen, but I'd rather avoid those situations. I'm not just talking about people I've locked up; there's councillors, journalists, defence lawyers. I don't like to be cornered by any of them, because I don't care to be in any situation where I have to watch every word I say.'

'I can see that,' she conceded.

No other passengers had joined them by the time the train left the station.

'This preference of yours for privacy,' Sarah ventured, as it entered the tunnel that ran north out of Queen Street, 'would it have anything to do with you not wanting to be seen with me?'

'What?' He laughed. 'Don't be daft.' He reached out and took her hand. 'There is no woman in the world I would rather be seen with.'

'Apart from Alex.'

'Alexis is my daughter, and so is Seonaid, our daughter, yours and mine. We made her and I am very proud of that, even though I was fucking awful at showing it for a while. You are different, you are you, and I love you.'

'This hasn't happened too soon, has it?' she wondered. 'A week ago, if you'd asked me, I'd never have imagined you and me, here like this, now.'

'Me neither,' Bob admitted, 'but I am mightily pleased that we are. It should never have been any other way. I was stupid, and not for the first time in my life. Feeling my age, you asked. Well, maybe I am, in a way. It's led me to a point where I'm honest with myself about my weaknesses, and the things I've done wrong in the past, and strong enough to be able to promise you that I will never let you down again.'

'You realise that if you do,' she whispered, as the train passed out into the open with leafy embankments on either side, 'I will do your autopsy myself, before they take me away?'

He gave her a big wide-open smile, a rarity from him. 'Yes, but I don't need that incentive.'

When the door slid open, they were both taken by surprise. 'Tickets please.'

The guard's intervention ended the moment. They were passing through the first station on the route before Sarah broke the silence. 'When did you eat last?' she asked.

'Good question; probably sometime between one and half past; sandwiches with Mann and Provan, my office. They were crap. The bread was turning up at the edges by the time we got round to them.'

'That sort of a day, uh?'

He nodded. 'That sort. How about yours?'

She scrunched up her face for a second or two. 'Usual blood and guts, but pretty run-of-the-mill, as my job goes.'

'No surprises? No complications?'

'None, in either case. The two cadavers I'll be looking at tomorrow . . . remind me of their names again? Not that it matters.'

'Smit and Botha, also known as Mallett and Lightbody.'

'Well, one thing I can tell you about them right now is that they were very good at their job, and humane too. Neither of their victims had any time to think about it. Mr Brown died on Friday evening. He may have seen the man who was killing him, but he died instantly. He still had a surprised expression on his face.'

'I know,' Bob reminded her. 'I saw him in his second-to-last resting place. And,' he added, 'I've just seen a recording of him being shot.'

'Why didn't they kill the detective inspector's husband?'

'Because he never saw them, otherwise, you're right, poor Lottie would be a widow.'

'Then too bad for Mr Brown that he did, otherwise his life expectancy would have been pretty good. He was a fit guy.'

'And how about Toni?'

'Same with her, as you might expect, given her job. She was killed even more humanely than Brown, if I can use the term. She would not have had the faintest idea of what had happened to her. Well,' she corrected herself, 'maybe a few milliseconds, but no more than that. She'd have been brain-dead even before the force of the impact threw her out of her seat. If that's some small comfort to her family, you might like to tell them.'

'I have done already. I saw her mother and sister this morning.'

'How were they?'

'Very dignified, both of them. I've let the fiscal talk herself into releasing the body as soon as she gets your report.'

'Then I'll complete it and send it to her before I move on to Smit and Botha.' She paused. 'But how about her husband? How about the child?' she asked. 'Or is it too young to understand?'

He stared at her, a slight, bewildered smile on his face. 'Husband?' he repeated. 'Child? What child?'

'Hers of course, Antonia Field's. I assumed she was married or in a familial relationship.'

'No, never,' Bob said. 'She was never married, and she lived with her sister. What makes you think she had a child?'

'Hell,' she exclaimed, 'I might not be a professor of forensic pathology yet, but I do know a caesarean scar when I see one.'

He sat up straight in his high-backed seat. 'Well, honey, that is news to me, and neither her mother nor her sister . . . who wants to come back to work for me . . . gave me the slightest hint of its existence.'

'Then tread carefully if you decide to tackle them about it. Yes, she has a scar, and there were other physical signs of child-bearing. However, there is no way I could guarantee that her baby was delivered alive.'

'I accept that, but the odds are heavily in favour of that. If a kid goes full-term or almost there . . .'

'That's true, but Bob, where are you going with this? Suppose she did have a baby and kept quiet about it in case it harmed her career; that's not a crime.'

'In certain circumstances it might be. An application for the post of chief constable requires full disclosure.'

'But honey, she's dead. Does it really matter?'

'Probably not at all.' He grinned. 'But it's a mystery and you know how I feel about them. How old was this scar? Can you tell?'

'I can take a guess. I'd say not less than one year old, and not more than three.'

'Okay. One year ago she was chief constable of the West Midlands;

if she had it then it would have been a bit noticeable. But hold on.'

He raised himself from his seat and took his attaché case down from the luggage rack. He spun the combination wheels and opened it.

'I've got Toni's HR file in here. Let's take a look and see what that tells us.' He removed the thick green folder, then closed the case again, putting it on his knee to use as an impromptu table.

'Let's go back three years. Then she was a Met commander, on secondment to the Serious and Organised Crime Agency; she built her legend there knocking over foreign drugs cartels. If she'd taken time out to have a kid, that would have been noticed and recorded. It isn't, so we can rule it out. So where does that take us?'

As he read, a smile split his face. 'It takes us to her becoming the chief constable of West Midlands, just over two years ago.'

'She couldn't have been there long,' Sarah remarked.

'She wasn't. She barely had time to crease her uniform before the Strathclyde job came up. But, it says here that before she was appointed to Birmingham she took a six-month sabbatical, which ended a week before she was interviewed. That fits like a glove,' he exclaimed.

'It does,' Sarah agreed. 'But what do you do about it?'

'I could simply ask her family, but you're right; there could be sensitivities there. It's even possible they don't know about it. Marina gave me a pretty full rundown of her sister's sex life and didn't mention her being pregnant. She may have assumed that I knew from her record, but on the other hand, is there any reason why she should? If the child was safely delivered, it could have been put up for adoption. Toni was the sort of woman who wouldn't have fancied any impediment to her career ambitions.

'So no,' he decided, 'I won't take it to Sofia or Marina. Instead I'll do some digging of my own. I have a timeframe, her full name,

Antonia Maureen Field, and her date of birth; they'll be enough for the General Register Office to get me a hit. But I'm not counting on it.'

'No?'

'No. I have a feeling that there's another possibility, one that might even be more likely.'

'You love this, don't you?' Sarah chuckled. 'The thrill of the chase, and all.'

'It's what I do, honey,' he replied. 'It's the part of the job that I've always loved. These days, I don't have too many chances to be hands on, so I take every one that's going.'

'Including interviewing the guy tomorrow morning? Surely you don't really have to do that. An ACC alone's pretty heavy duty, isn't she?'

'Oh, I have to do it, make no mistake. Not only was he a police officer until a few years ago, his wife still is. I've come to rate her in the last couple of days, and to like her a lot too. This bastard's gone and compromised her career and even put her in a situation where she had to be formally detained for a short while.

'Tomorrow morning, he's going to have me across the table, and if he thinks that his obligatory lawyer will prevent me from coming down on him like an avalanche, he's kidding himself.'

'It's a new thing in Scotland, isn't it, the prisoner's right to a lawyer?'

Bob nodded. 'Indeed, but to be frank, I don't know how we got away with the old system for so long. It doesn't bother me anyway; I'm at my best when I don't say a word.'

Sarah grinned, as a gleam came into her eye. 'You can say that again, buddy,' she murmured.

Thirty-Eight

'Where is ma daddy, Uncle Dan?' Jake Mann asked, not for the first time. His godfather realised that there was no ducking the question.

'I told ye before, Jakey, it's all hush-hush, but maybe this'll explain it. Ye know your daddy used to be a policeman.'

The child nodded, with vigour. 'M-hm.'

'Well, it's like this. They've asked him to go back and help them again. Yer mum and I, we've been asked no' tae talk about it, not even tae you.'

'Wow! Secret squirrels?'

'That's right, secret squirrels; undercover.' He ruffled Jake's hair. 'Now away ye go to your bed, like yer mum asked ye to a while back.'

'Okay.' He hugged his honorary uncle and ran into the hall, heading for the stairs, as if he was fuelled by excitement.

'You're a lovely wee man, Danny Provan,' Lottie said, from the kitchen doorway. 'I'd never have thought of that.' She was carrying two plates, each loaded with fish and chips still in the wrapper. She handed him one and settled into her armchair. 'It won't hold up for long, though,' she sighed. 'Eventually, this is going to hit the press.'

'Eventually,' he conceded, 'but these are special circumstances. The husband of the SIO bein' lifted? Okay, it's bound to leak within a

240

day or two, but Ah'd expect the fiscal tae go to the High Court and get an interdict against publishing Scott's name, at least until the trial begins, maybe even till he's convicted.'

'There's no doubt he will be, is there?'

'Ah'd love tae say he's got a chance, but Ah can't. We found the wrapping from the parcel in the car. You know as well as I do that the forensic people will find fibres on it and match them to a police uniform.'

'It's as well for him he is done,' she barked. 'I could bloody kill him, for what he's done to Jakey; it'll be hellish for him at school. Ye know what kids are like. I tell you this, even if by some miracle he does get out of this, he and I are done. He's never coming back here. Never!'

'Come on, Lottie, Scott wouldnae harm his laddie for a' the tea in China.'

'And what about me? Do you think he hasn't harmed me?'

'No, Ah don't,' the sergeant admitted. 'I concede that. Ah want you to know, hen,' he added, 'that this has been the worst day of my police career. What I had to do this afternoon . . .' His voice trailed away, as if he had run out of words.

'But you had to do it, Dan,' she countered. 'As you say, you had to do it. If you hadn't, I'd have thought the worse of you, and so would you and all, for the rest of your life. You've always been a hero to me, since I was the rawest DC in the team, but never more so than this afternoon.'

Thirty-Nine

'You'll be DCS McIlhenney, then,' Lowell Payne said as he approached the hulking, dark-suited stranger who stood at the entrance to the platform at Victoria Station where the Gatwick Express arrived.

'How do you work that out?' the other countered.

'The boss's description was enough. That and the fact that you've got his warrant card hung around your neck.'

'Ah. I deduce that you are a detective. DCI Payne?'

They shook hands. 'That's me. It's a pleasure to meet the other half of the Glimmer Twins.'

'You know my Latino compatriot?' he asked, surprised. 'Bob never mentioned that.'

'Yes, I do. I was involved in the investigation in Edinburgh that led up to the shit that happened at the weekend. That's how I met Mario. He and I got to the Glasgow concert hall not long after the shooting. Now I find myself right in the middle of the follow-up.'

'You were there?' McIlhenney's eyes flashed. 'How's Paula? McGuire says she's all right, but I couldn't be quite sure that he wasn't spinning the truth to keep me off the first plane.'

'Trust me, he wasn't,' Payne assured him. 'She's a tough lady. Everything happened so fast that I don't think she had time to be scared. She was fine when we got there, shaken, but well in control of herself. From what the boss said when he called me last night she still is. Mind you, you can think about booking a flight this weekend, from what I hear. The baby's expected by the end of the week.'

'Is that right? That's terrific.' He laughed. 'Mario has no idea how much his life is going to change. He reckoned nothing could ever slow him down, but this will. Who knows? I might even get to overtake him.'

He read the question written on Payne's face. 'He's always been first to every promotion,' he explained. 'Then when I get one, he lands another. It's the same again this time. I come all the way to London to make chief super, he stays in bloody Edinburgh, and gets the ACC post.' He beamed. 'There's a longer ladder here, though; he'll be struggling from now on. He's got one more rung left in him, max, while I could have two in the Met.'

'Good for you guys,' Payne said. 'I'm not on a ladder any more. I won't see fifty again, I've reached my level, and I'm happy with it.'

'Don't write yourself off,' McIlhenney murmured, 'not if you're working for Bob Skinner.' He frowned, rubbing his hands together. 'Now,' he continued, 'enough career planning. You and I have got a grieving widow to interview.'

'Does she know she's a widow yet?'

The chief superintendent checked his watch, as they walked towards the station exit. 'She should by now. We ran some checks on her and found that she's not in employment, so we guess that she's a full-time mum. The family support people were going to call on her at nine thirty, and I've had no message to say that she wasn't in. It's going on ten now, so hopefully by the time we get there, she'll have had time to absorb what's happened.'

'Or not, as the case may be,' the visitor countered. 'It's the worst possible news they'll have given her. She might not be capable of talking to anyone.'

'In that case, we get a doctor, we sedate her and while she's in the land of nod we search the place, quietly but carefully.'

'Can we do that?' Payne wondered. 'Legally, I mean?'

McIlhenney opened his jacket, displaying an envelope in an inside pocket. 'I've got warrants,' he said. 'Everything the Met does these days has to be watertight. We are all book operators now. I hate to think how Bob Skinner would get on down here. He'd do his own thing, because that's all he knows, and wind up on page one . . . just like his bloody wife! That was a shocker; it blew me right out of my seat when I saw those pictures. Some of my brother officers think it's funny, fools that they are, to see the big man embarrassed like that. How's it going down in Pitt Street?'

'Very quietly. The new chief's reputation travels before him. One of our ACCs might be found chortling in a stall in the gents, but he's got his own secret to protect, so he's poker-faced in public.'

'Sensible man.' McIlhenney slowed his pace as they approached a waiting police car. 'I can't get over Aileen getting herself compromised like that. She always struck me as super-cautious, given her political position. What doesn't surprise me, though, is that the marriage was up shit creek even without the Morocco complication.'

'No?'

'No. Those are two of the most powerful people, personality-wise, that I've ever met. I never thought it would last. Just as I never thought he and Sarah would actually split, even though she can be volatile and though Bob doesn't have quite the same control over his dick that he has over everything else. McGuire tells me that Sarah's back in Edinburgh. Is that right?'

'So I believe. I have met her, you know. For example, a few years back, at my niece's twenty-first . . . well, she's my wife's niece, really. Sarah and Bob weren't long married at the time. She was well pregnant at the time.' McIlhenney was staring at him, puzzled. 'Alex,' he explained. 'Alexis, Bob's daughter. I'm married to her mother's sister, although Myra had died well before I came on the scene.'

The chief superintendent beamed, then laughed. 'Jeez,' he exclaimed, 'the man's like a fucking octopus; his tentacles are everywhere. He's had a family insider in Strathclyde CID all this time and he's never let on.'

'Oh, come on,' Payne protested, 'you're making it sound like I was his snitch. I rarely saw him, other than a few times when he came with Alex to visit our wee lass, or family events, like weddings and such, and before now our paths only ever crossed the once professionally, way back when I was a uniform sergeant and he'd just made detective super.'

'Maybe so, but I'll bet when you did see him, you spent a hell of a lot more time talking about policing than about Auntie Effie's bunions.'

'Mmm,' the DCI murmured. 'We don't have an Auntie Effie, but yes, I suppose you're right. It was mostly shop talk. Mind you, I'm not a golfer, and I don't follow football, so there wasn't much else on the agenda.'

'Wouldn't have made any difference,' McIlhenney assured him. 'Come on, let's get on our way.' They slid into the back of the waiting police car. 'You know where we're going?' he asked the constable at the wheel.

'Yes, sir,' the driver replied. 'There was a message for you while you were away,' he added. 'The family support gels say it's okay for you to go in. The lady's been advised, and she's okay to speak to you.'

'I hope she's still okay after we've finished,' the chief superintendent grunted.

The car pulled out of the station concourse and into the traffic. 'Tourist route, sir?' the constable asked.

'Not this trip. We can show DCI Payne the sights later.'

The visiting detective had no more than a tourist's knowledge of London, and so he sat bewildered as they cut past New Scotland Yard and along a series of thoroughfares that might have been in any developed city in the world, had it not been for the omnipresence of the Union flag and the Olympic rings, and for the Queen's image beaming from shop windows displayed on a range of souvenir products from clothing to crockery. The sun told him that they were heading roughly north, and occasionally a sign would advise him that Madame Tussaud's lay a mile from where they were at that moment, or that they were passing an underground station called Angel, or that the Mayor of London wished him an enjoyable stay in his city.

They had been on the road for twenty minutes when McIlhenney pointed out of the window to his left, indicating a modern steel edifice, its clean lines sharp against the sky. 'The Emirates Stadium,' he announced. 'Home of Arsenal Football Club.'

'Are you a fan?'

'No,' he chuckled. 'Spence, my older laddie, won't allow it. He plays rugby, pretty well, they say, and I usually follow him on winter Saturdays. Not that we've had too many of them down here, not yet. Next season, though; he's been accepted by London Scottish. Dads on the touchlines can be bad news at junior rugby, but they like me, being a cop.'

And a brick shithouse into the bargain, Payne thought. 'The stadium. Is that where we're heading?'

'Not quite. We're going to the Gunners' old home, Highbury. In fact,' he paused as they made a turn, 'there it is.'

Ahead the DCI saw a tall building with 'Arsenal Stadium' emblazoned in red along its high wall, with a wheeled gun underneath.

'Who plays there now?' he asked. As he spoke he glanced forward and caught in the rear-view the constable driver giving him a look that might have been scornful, or simply one of pity.

'Nobody, sir,' he volunteered. 'It's been turned into flats and stuff. They weren't allowed to knock down the front of the main stand . . . more's the pity. Should have bulldozed the lot, if you ask me.'

'I take it you're not a follower.'

'God forbid! No, I'm Totten'am, till I die.'

'You don't want to get into that, Lowell,' McIlhenney advised. 'Serious London tribalism.'

'When you've been on uniform duty at an Old Firm match,' the visitor countered, 'nothing else can seem all that serious.'

'Before I came down here, I might have agreed with that.'

The driver indicated a right turn, then waited for oncoming traffic to pass. Reading the street sign, St Baldred's Road, McIlhenney tapped him on the shoulder. 'Don't turn in there. Pull over here and we'll walk the rest; this vehicle would tell the whole neighbourhood that something's up.'

'Sir.' The PC changed his signal, then parked twenty yards further on. The two detectives climbed out, and crossed the street.

St Baldred's Road told a story of comfortable middle-class prosperity. The Millbank family home was four doors along, on the left, a brick terraced villa, smart and well-maintained like all of its neighbours.

A blue Fiesta was parked outside, out of place between a Mercedes E-class, and a Lexus four-wheel drive with a child seat in the back. Payne glanced inside the little Ford and saw two female uniform caps on the front seats. *Discretion seems to be the watchword in the Met these days*, he thought.

The door opened before they reached it; one of the pair, a forty-something, salt-and-pepper-haired sergeant, stood waiting for them. 'How is she?' McIlhenney asked, quietly, as they stepped inside.

'Shocked, but self-controlled,' the woman replied. 'She's got a kid, little Leon. In my experience that usually helps to keep them together.'

'The child's here? Not in a nursery?'

'He's here, outside in his playground. Molly, PC Bates, my colleague, is looking after him. I'm Rita,' she added 'Sergeant Caan.'

'Has she called anyone? Friends, family?'

'No, not yet. She said something about having to phone her mother, to let her know. I said we could do that for her. She felt she had to do that herself, but she hasn't got round to it yet.'

'Do you know,' Payne began, 'if we're right in our assumption that the husband worked for her family business?'

Rita Caan nodded. 'Yes, spot on. The mother runs it; Golda's father's dead.'

'Thanks, that's helpful; one less question for us. Have you picked up anything else?'

She frowned at him. 'Other than the fact that she's four and a half months pregnant, no.'

'Doctor on the way?' McIlhenney asked.

She sighed. 'Of course he is. It's standard in a situation like this. She didn't want to bother him, but we persuaded her that he'd want to be bothered. He's coming after his morning surgery.'

'Good. Sorry, Sergeant. I wasn't doubting you; I just had to know for sure. Let's see her, then, before the doc gets here.'

'Okay. She's in the living room. This way.' She led them to a solid wood door, as old as the house, tapped on it gently, then opened it. 'Golda,' she called out. 'My colleagues have arrived. Chief Super-intendent McIlhenney and Mr Payne, from Scotland. Mr McIlhenney is too, as you'll realise very quickly, but he's one of ours.'

The widow was in the act of rising as they stepped into the room, which extended for the full length of the house, with double doors opening into the garden. As Payne looked along he saw a ball bounce into view, and heard a toddler's shout, as Caan's colleague retrieved it.

'Don't get up, Mrs Millbank, please,' McIlhenney insisted. 'I'm the local,' he added, 'he's the visitor. First and foremost, we are both very sorry for your loss.'

'Thank you,' Golda Millbank, née Radnor, said. Her voice was quiet, but strong, with no hint of a quaver. 'Please, can you tell me what happened to Byron? All that Rita could say is that it was a brain thing.'

'That's correct,' Payne confirmed. 'An autopsy was performed; it showed that your husband suffered a massive, spontaneous subarachnoid cerebral haemorrhage. Death would have been almost instantaneous, the pathologist said.'

'When did this happen?'

'Last week.'

'Last week?' she repeated. 'Then why has it taken so long for you to tell me?'

'When your husband's body was found,' the DCI explained, 'he had no identification on him. It took the police in Edinburgh some time to find out who he was.'

'What does Edinburgh have to do with it?'

'That's where he was found.'

'But he was supposed to be in Manchester, then in Glasgow, at a jewellery fair, and then in Inverness, visiting one of our suppliers. I don't understand why he would be in Edinburgh.'

'When was he due home, Mrs Millbank?' McIlhenney asked.

'Not until today; I expected him back this evening.'

'When was the last time you spoke to him?'

'On the day he left for Scotland. Byron doesn't like mobile phones; he won't have one. When he's away on business, I don't expect to hear from him, unless he sends me an email. He tends to do everything through his computer. He has a laptop, a MacBook Air. It goes everywhere with him; he says that all his life is on it.'

'When did you meet him?' The DCS kept his tone casual.

'When he came to work for my parents' business; I called in there one day, a few months after he started. Neither my father nor mother were there but he was. He introduced himself and,' she smiled, 'that was that.' She shook her head. 'He was such a fit, strong man. I can't believe this has happened.' She stared at McIlhenney, and then at Payne. 'Are you telling me the truth?' she asked. Her voice was laden with suspicion. 'Has somebody killed my husband?'

It was Payne who replied. 'No, absolutely not. I assure you, his death was completely natural. I can get you a copy of the post-mortem report, if it'll help you. I can even arrange for you to speak to the pathologist, Dr Grace. She's one of the best in the business, I promise you. If there had been any sign of violence, or anything other than natural causes, she'd have found it.'

'Then why are you here?' she demanded. 'You two, you're detectives, you're not wearing uniforms like Rita and Molly. And you, Mr Payne, you've come all the way from Scotland. Would you do that if there was not something more to this?'

'When he died, Mrs Millbank, he was unattended, not seen by a doctor,' the DCI explained. 'That makes it a police matter; nothing sinister, a formality really, but we have to complete a report.'

'Very good, but such things must happen every day. For a senior officer to come down to London . . . please, Mr Payne, don't take me for a fool.'

He glanced at the DCS, who nodded. 'Very well, there is more to it,' he admitted. 'Can I ask you, Mrs Millbank, how much do you know of your husband's background, of his life before you two met?'

'I know that he was born in Eastbourne, that he never knew his father and that his mother is dead. He spent some time in Israel, was a lieutenant in the army, but left because of his opposition to the Iraq war, worked in mail order and finally for an investment bank, before he joined Rondar . . . that's our family business.'

'How about friends, family? Did you ever meet any of them?'

'He has no family, and as for friends, when he left the army, he left them behind too. We have friends, as a couple, but that's it.'

'Has he ever mentioned a man called Brian Lightbody, from New Zealand, or Richie Mallett, an Australian? Or have you ever heard of either of them indirectly?'

She shook her head. 'No. Those names mean nothing to me. Why do you ask?'

'Because we know that your husband ate with them in a kosher restaurant in Glasgow, on the day he died, and that they were all registered in the same hotel, and that the other two told staff they were there for the jewellery fair.'

'So?' she retorted. 'That's your explanation surely. I don't know everybody in the business, and if they were jewellery buyers also, they do tend to be in the same place at the same time.'

'Sure, but . . . Mrs Millbank, Lightbody and Mallett weren't jewellery buyers, and those weren't their real names. I'm not free to tell you at this stage who they were, but we do know, and we do know their real business.'

'Are you saying they killed Byron?'

'No,' Payne insisted, 'I am not, but they were with him when he died. There is physical evidence that one or both of them tried to revive him after he collapsed. When they failed, they removed all the identification from his body, including his clothing, and concealed

251

him. Then, after a day or so, they called the police and told them where he could be found.'

Golda Millbank opened her mouth but found that she could not speak. She looked towards Rita Caan, as if for help. 'Is this . . .' she whispered.

'I don't know any of it,' the sergeant told her. 'It's not what I do. Molly and me, we're only family support, honest.'

'It's true, Mrs Millbank,' McIlhenney said. 'We're here to find out everything you knew about your husband and about what he did.'

'I know all about him,' she insisted. 'He was a good husband and a faithful family man. Or are you trying to tell me that he had a piece on the side?'

'Not for a second, but suppose he did, that wouldn't be our business. Let me chuck another name at you. Beram Cohen; Israeli national. Mean anything?'

Both he and Payne gazed at her, concentrating on her expression, looking for any twitch, any hint of recognition, but neither saw any, only utter bewilderment.

'No,' she declared. 'I've never heard of him.' She rose from her chair. 'I have to phone my mother. She needs to know what's happening here.'

'Where will she be at this moment?' the DCS asked.

'She'll be at work.'

'In that case, I'm sorry, but we'd rather you didn't contact her.' He paused. 'Look, Mrs Millbank, I'm as satisfied as I can be that you know no more about your husband than you're telling us. But let me ask you, how successful is the family business? I could find out through Companies House, but if you know, it would save time.'

She took a deep breath, frowning. 'I can tell you that. I'm a director, so I know. Frankly, it's been on its last legs since my father died three years ago. We're being out-marketed by other companies and we don't have the expertise in the company to reverse the trend. Mummy's trying to sell it, but there are no takers.'

'Byron wasn't a director?'

'No, Mummy wouldn't allow that. She didn't want a situation where she could be outvoted. There's just the two of us on the board; I'm unpaid of course.'

'How about Byron? Was he on a good salary?'

'Thirty-five thousand. He had to take a pay cut at the beginning of last year, down from fifty.'

'In that case, living in his house must be a stretch,' McIlhenney suggested. 'This isn't the cheapest part of London, from what I'm told. How long have you lived here?'

'We bought it when Leon was on the way, and moved in just after he was born. But it's okay, we get by easily, because we don't have a mortgage.'

'Lucky you. Did your father leave you money?'

'No. It was Byron. He made a pile in bonuses working with the bank, and never spent it. He wasn't the type to buy a flashy sports car or anything like that. No, one way or another we've always been comfortably off.' Her eyes narrowed. 'Are you saying . . .'

'I'm not saying anything,' the DCS replied. 'I'm asking. We're trying to build up a complete picture of Byron. To do that we need to search, where he lived, where he worked, everywhere we can. Was he a member of a sports club, for example?'

'He played squash, but otherwise he wasn't the clubbable sort. He ran, on the streets, he cycled and he did things like chins and press-ups . . . he could do hundreds of those things . . . but always on his own.'

'So all his private life was here in this house?'

'Yes.'

'Did he have a computer here?' Payne asked.

'We have one, yes, but it's mine and he never used it. I've told you, he had his laptop, his MacBook, and he took that with him when he left.'

'Can we look in your machine nonetheless? Just in case he was able to access it without you knowing about it.'

She let out a sigh, of sheer exasperation. 'Yes, if you must, but honestly, Byron wouldn't do that, any more than I would look in his. That's assuming I could get into it. He used to laugh about it and say that breaking his password was as likely as winning the Lottery.'

'If that's so,' McIlhenney said, 'I wouldn't like to try to access it, just in case it spoiled my luck for the jackpot.'

'No worries of that happening,' Payne pointed out.

'You mean you didn't find it,' the widow asked, 'among his effects?'

'I told you, we didn't find anything, Mrs Millbank. Not even his clothes.'

She shuddered and for a second her eyes moistened, her first sign of weakness. 'How awful,' she whispered. 'Robbing a dead man. How could they have done that? Of course I'll help you in any way I can. What do you need to see?'

'That computer for a start,' the DCS replied. 'If you could take us through it, looking for any files you don't recognise, and at its history, its usage pattern. Then if we could look though his belongings, and examine any area where he might have worked at home.'

'There wasn't one. He never did. But you can look. If it'll help, you can look; anything that'll help you find those so-called friends of his.'

'Oh, we know where they are,' Payne said.

'Then what are you looking for?'

'I'm afraid it's one of those situations where we won't know until we find it. And if we do,' he added, 'we might not be able to tell you, for your own protection.'

Her forehead wrinkled. 'That sounds a little scary. You can't tell me anything?'

'No more than we have already.'

'Nothing? What about that name you mentioned, the Israeli man, Beram Cohen. Where does he fit? Who is he?'

The DCI looked at his escort colleague, raising his eyebrows, asking a silent question. McIlhenney hesitated, then nodded.

'I'm sorry, Mrs Millbank,' Payne replied, 'but he was your husband.'

Forty

'Thanks, Bridie,' Skinner said, as the ACC rose from her chair at his meeting table, their morning briefing session having come to an end. 'I'll give you a shout when I'm ready to start interviewing Scott Mann. He can stew for a bit longer.'

'His lawyer's not going to like that,' she pointed out.

'Then tough shit on him. The Supreme Court says he has a right to be there, but we still set the timetable, up to a point, and we haven't reached that yet. He can wait with his client.'

Gorman liked what she heard; her smile confirmed it.

'Do something for me,' he continued. 'Ask Dan Provan to come up here, straight away. With Lottie being stood down, he's carrying the ball, and I need to speak to him.'

The third person in the room was on his feet also, but the chief waved him back down. 'Stay for a bit, Michael, please. I'd like a word.'

ACC Thomas frowned, but did as he was asked.

'I want to apologise to you,' Skinner began as soon as the door had closed behind Gorman.

'For what, Chief?' *For which of the many ways I've been offended?* he thought.

'For asking you to attend Toni Field's post-mortem. It's been suggested to me since then that your relationship might have been more than professional. If I'd been aware of that at the time, no way would I have asked you to go.'

'Even if the suggestion was untrue?'

'Even then, because I wouldn't have been quizzing you about it. If you and she had a fling away from the office, so what? When I was on my way up the ladder, and widowed, I had a long-standing relationship with a female colleague. Nobody ever questioned it and if anyone had they'd have been told very quickly to fuck off.'

'Then I accept your apology, and I appreciate it, sir . . . although it wasn't really necessary, since it was my duty as a senior officer to attend the autopsy.'

Skinner grinned. 'Which means, by implication, that if it was yours, then it was mine even more, and I shirked it.'

'I didn't say that.'

'No, but if you had I couldn't have argued, 'cos you'd have been right. The truth is, I've seen more hacked-about bodies than you or I have had years in the force, combined, and I tend not to volunteer to see any more. I should have stood up for that one, though.'

Thomas shook his head. 'No, you shouldn't,' he said.

'How do you work that out?' the chief asked.

'Because the examination was performed by your ex-wife, who still speaks of you with a smile and a twinkle in her eye; in my book that disqualifies you as a witness. Suppose that she'd made a mistake, and her findings had been challenged by the defence in a future trial and you'd wound up in the witness box. You'd have been hopelessly compromised.'

Skinner stared at him. 'Do you know, Michael,' he murmured, 'you are absolutely right. It's years since I attended one of Sarah's autopsies, but I have done, when we were married. I shouldn't have, unarguably. I should have known that, so why didn't it dawn on me?'

'I'd guess because the possibility of her slipping up didn't enter your head,' Thomas suggested. 'She does seem very efficient.'

'She's all that. She gave up pathology for a while, when we went our separate ways, but I'm glad she's back. I confess that the very thought of what she does turns my stomach from time to time, but I can say the same about my own career.'

'Is it public knowledge?'

The chief blinked. 'What?'

'Toni and me. Does everybody know?'

'From what I gather, most of the force does.'

'Jesus!' The ACC stared at the ceiling. 'It's never got back to me, then. I've never heard a whisper, not once. And once is the number of times it happened so how the . . .'

'You were unlucky. You were seen by the wrong people, the kind whose discretion gene was removed at birth. Max Allan did what damage limitation he could, but for what it's worth, when Lowell Payne gets back from a wee job I've given him, I'm going to ask him to root out the people who started the story. Then I'm going to draw them a very clear picture of their futures in the force. What's the shittiest part of our vast patch, Michael? Where does no PC want to be posted?'

'I'll give it some thought,' Thomas growled.

Skinner nodded and pushed his chair back. 'You do that,' he declared. 'Let's you and I start again, with a clean sheet,' he added, extending his hand.

As the two men shook, Skinner's phone rang. 'Need to take this,' he said. 'It might be Payne.'

It was.

'We've just left Mrs Millbank, Chief,' his exec told him. 'We got nothing from it. Neither of us believe that she had a clue about her husband's previous, or any idea about his sideline. It helped their lifestyle, though; the family business is pretty well fucked, but they live debt-free and drive a nice Lexus.'

'But no clue to where he kept his Cohen money?'

'Yes and no. The wife, widow now, told us that he had a computer, an Apple MacBook Air laptop that he was never parted from. His life was in it, was how she put it. Am I right in thinking that hasn't shown up anywhere?'

'You are,' Skinner agreed. 'Nothing of his has turned up. He was buried naked, wrapped in a sheet. Leave that with me, Lowell. I'll check it out and get people moving if I have to. Where are you off to now?'

'To check out his workplace, in the Elephant and Castle, wherever that is. It'll be a shock for his mother-in-law, or maybe not, depending on how she felt about him. From what I gather, Byron, or Beram, wasn't much bloody good as a buyer. That's what the father did, and the business has been suffering since his death.'

'Let me know how you get on. Then we can decide whether there's anything else to be done in London.'

'Will do, boss.'

The chief constable flicked a button on his console to end the call, another for an outside line, then dialled a number that was ingrained in his memory, yet which he had never called before.

A female voice answered. 'Yes?'

'Bet you got a shock when that rang,' he said. 'Theory being that it's for your private calls, and not routed through the comms centre.'

'Are you kidding?' Maggie Steele replied. 'This is the fourth call I've had on it. One was from Chief Constable Haggerty in Dumfries, another was from Archbishop Gainer, and the third was from old John Hunter, the freelance journalist, who's got onset dementia and asked me for a prawn biryani with naan bread. He got me mixed up with the

Asian takeaway. Are there any of your friends who don't have this number, Bob?'

'One or two. How are you getting on?'

'Okay, but I still feel a wee bit overawed. It feels strange, sitting in this chair, and you on the other side of the country. Only for three months though, yes?'

'That's the duration of my appointment,' he agreed, 'or my loan if you'd rather put it that way.'

'Can I have a straight answer to that question? You will be back, won't you?'

'That's my intention.'

'Bob! Don't prevaricate. Have you been seduced by the bright lights and the glitter balls of Glasgow already?'

'No, but . . .'

'I knew it!' she declared.

'No, really. I still have three months in my head, for reasons that are more than just professional.'

'The kids, I imagine.'

'And Sarah,' he added, 'but keep that very much to yourself. I know that you and she didn't always see eye to eye, but much of that was my fault. It's best for us as a family that she's here, and that we get along.'

'But? I can still hear it, hanging there.'

'But, there are good people through here, Mags, and they need leadership. There is no successor here, from within, and frankly, nobody else in Scotland either, except possibly for Andy, and he wouldn't want it.

'The force has already been disrupted and demoralised by Toni Field, God rest her, by her blind ambition and her half-arsed ideas. I'll hear about the likely runners when the job is advertised. If I don't fancy any of them, I won't rule out applying for the post myself.

'As I say that, I'm thinking that it sounds incredibly conceited, but I am a good cop and I do believe that I'm capable of doing the job, in spite of the misgivings I've always held about the size of this effing force.'

'That's not conceited,' she retorted, 'it's the plain truth. And beyond that,' she asked, 'will you go for the police commissioner post, if unification happens?'

'I haven't thought that far, but if I can overcome my doubts about policing half of Scotland, I suspect I'll be able to do the same about the rest.'

Maggie laughed. 'Now there's a sea change, after what you were saying in the press last weekend. If it's what you want, Bob, or what you feel you have to do, good luck, although I'll worry about who we might get here as your permanent successor.'

'I'm listening to her,' he said.

'Nice of you to say so, but I don't have the seniority. The councillors on the Police Authority won't have it.'

'The councillors will have it, because I'll bloody tell them. Their political parties all owe me favours and I will call them in, make no mistake.'

'But maybe I don't want it,' she suggested.

'Bollocks,' he laughed. 'You do, because your late husband would have insisted on it.'

He heard her sigh. 'You've got me there. Stevie would. Hell, though, my in-tray's stacked high here, and yours must be even bigger.'

'True, but I didn't just call you to shoot the breeze. I need your help in our top-priority investigation, Toni Field's assassination. You weren't really involved when it began, but are you up to speed now?'

'Yes,' she confirmed, 'fully.'

'In that case, you'll know it all began when we found the body of a man in Edinburgh, having been directed by the people who left him there, his ex-soldier buddies. They're now dead, having been killed on the scene after the Field hit. We've found their car, and what was in it, including the body of a well-known Glasgow hoodlum. Although we haven't linked his death to them, but there was nothing there that referred back to Cohen. Everything that he had is missing. That includes a MacBook Air laptop . . . you know, the super-light kind . . . and that's what we would most like to find.

'It may no longer exist. Freddy Welsh told me he burned his clothes but he didn't mention the computer. Maybe that went into the fire as well, but maybe not. Either way, Freddy needs to be asked; use Special Branch. Have George Regan go to see him. He's been well softened up, so he'll talk with no persuasion.

'If he can't help us, I would like you to institute a search, city-wide, but looking initially at the area near Welsh's yard, where Cohen died, and around Mortonhall, where he was found. Will you do that for me?'

'Of course. What's on the computer?'

'I don't know; his wife in London said his whole life was on it, but maybe that means nothing more than his iTunes collection and photographs of her and their kid. On the other hand, there may be the key that unlocks all the fucking boxes.

'We know already all there is to know about Byron Millbank; that's the alias he was given by somebody's friends at MI5. If what the widow told Lowell Payne and Neil McIlhenney is literally true, the MacBook, if it still exists and we can find it, may tell us everything we need to know about Beram Cohen, including the name of the person who paid him to kill the chief constable of Strathclyde, and why.'

'We'll get on it right away,' Steele promised.

'Thanks,' Skinner said. 'It's a long shot, I know, but if you don't buy a ticket, you won't win the raffle.'

Forty-One

'Where have you been, Sarge?' Banjo Paterson asked, as Provan came into the room. 'The DI was on the phone looking for you.'

'Did ye tell her I'll call her back?'

'No. I thought you might not want to. It's awkward with her being suspended.'

'She's not fuckin' suspended!' Provan yelled, flaring up in sudden fury. 'She's on family leave. If I hear that word used once more Ah'll have your nuts in a vice, son.'

The DC backed off, holding up his hands as if to keep the little man at bay. 'Sorry, sorry, sorry.'

'Aye, well . . . just mind your tongue from now on.'

'Understood. So,' he continued, 'where have you been? You went out that door like a greyhound. I've never seen you move so fast.'

'Doesnae do tae keep the chief constable waiting,' the DS said, a smirk of bashful pride turning up one corner of his mouth.

Paterson whistled. 'A summons from on high, eh? What did he want?'

'He wants us to do a wee job for him. Ah need you to get intae your computer and find me a phone number for the equivalent of the General Register Office in the Republic of Mauritius . . . wherever the fuck that is.'

'It's in the Indian Ocean. Give me a minute.'

Provan looked on as he bent over his keyboard, typed a few words, clicked once, twice, a third time, then scribbled on a notepad. 'There you are,' he announced, as he ripped off the top sheet and handed it over. 'That's the number of the head office of the Civil Status Division, in the Emmanuel Anquetil Building, Port Louis, Mauritius.' He glanced at the wall clock. 'I make that fifteen seconds short of the minute.'

'Since you're that fuckin' clever, can you access birth records through that thing?'

'I doubt it, but I'll have a look.' He turned back to the screen and to his search engine, but soon shook his head. 'No, sorry; not that I can see. You'll have to call them.'

'Will Ah be able to speak the language?'

'Possibly not; it's English.'

'Cheeky bastard,' the DS growled, but with a grin. He dialled the number Paterson had given him. The voice that answered was female, with a musical quality.

He introduced himself, speaking slowly, as if to a child. 'I am trying to find the record of a birth that may have taken place in your country two years ago.'

'Hold on please, sir. I will direct you to the correct department.'

He waited for two minutes and more, becoming more and more annoyed by the sound of a woman crooning in a tongue he did not understand, but which he recognised as having Bollywood overtones. Finally, she stopped in mid-chorus and was replaced by a man.

'Yes, sir,' he began. 'I understand you are a police officer and are seeking information. Is this an official inquiry?' His voice was clipped and his accent offered a hint that he might have understood the lyrics of the compulsory music.

'Of course it is,' Provan replied, his limited patience close to being exhausted, 'as official as ye can get. It's a murder investigation.'

'In that case, sir, how can I be of help?'

'Ah'm lookin' for a birth record. Ah don't know for certain that it'll be there, but ma boss has asked me to check it out. All we have is the name of the mother, Antonia Field.'

'What is the date?'

'We don't know that either, just that it was two years ago, in the period between January and June. The lady took six months off work tae have the child, so our guess is that it was probably born round about May or early June.'

'Field, you said?'

'Aye, but when she lived in Mauritius she was known as Day Champs.'

'Pardon?'

'Day Champs.'

'Are you trying to say Deschamps, officer?' He spelled it out, letter by letter.

'Aye, that's it.'

'Very good. I will search for you. If you tell me your number, I will call you back. That way I will know that you really are a policeman.'

'Fair enough.' Provan gave the official the switchboard number, and his own extension, then hung up.

With time to kill, he wandered into Lottie Mann's empty office, sat at her desk, picked up the phone and dialled her number.

She answered on the first ring. 'Dan?'

'Aye. How're ye doin', kid?'

'Terrible. Wee Jakey isn't buying the story about his dad any more. I've had to tell him the truth, and it's breaking his wee heart.'

'Maybe he'll be home soon,' the sergeant suggested, knowing as he spoke how unlikely that was.

'Get real, Dan,' she sighed. 'There's more. On Sunday I gave Scott thirty quid to take the wee man out for the day. They went to that theme park out near Hamilton. It occurred to me, that's a hell of a lot more than thirty quid's worth, so I had a rummage in his half of the wardrobe. I found an envelope in a jacket pocket, with four hundred and twenty quid in it. The envelope had a crest on the back: Brown Brothers Private Hire.'

Provan felt his stomach flip. 'Lottie,' he murmured. 'What are ye telling me this for? Ah'll have tae report it now.'

'No you won't. I've done that already, I called ACC Gorman and told her.' She paused. 'Here, did you think I was going to cover it up? For fuck's sake, Danny!' she protested. 'Don't you know me better than that?'

'Aye, right,' he sighed. 'Ah shouldae known better. Sorry, lass.'

'Have they interviewed him yet?' she asked. 'The big bosses?'

'They'll just be startin' about now. Ah'm no long back frae seein' the chief. He was just gettin' ready to go down there, him and Bridie.'

'Then God help my idiot husband. There's no prizes for guessing who'll play "bad cop" out of that pair, and I would not like that bugger sitting across the table from me. Why were you seein' him anyway?' she asked. 'Are you telling me there's been a development?'

'No, just something he asked me to handle for him.' As he spoke he heard a phone ring outside, then saw Paterson pick up his own line. The DC spoke a few words, then beckoned to him. 'I think that's ma contact now,' he said. 'Ah'll need tae go. Ah'll call ye if I hear anything from the interview.'

Forty-Two

The chief constable paused outside the door of the interview room. 'Who's his solicitor?' he asked his deputy.

'Her name's Viola Murphy,' Bridie Gorman told him. 'She's a hotshot in Glasgow, a solicitor advocate . . . that means . . .'

'I know what it means. She takes the case the whole way through, from first interview to appearing in the High Court. I know about her too. She was one of my daughter's tutors when she did her law degree. Alex couldn't stand her.'

'Will she know you?'

'Not personally. She might from the media, though.'

'Of course, she's bound to. How do you want to play this?'

'Very simply. We're going to walk in there and inside five minutes Mr Mann is going to be singing like a linty. He'll tell us everything we want to know. And you know what? It might even be true.'

Gorman was sceptical. 'Mmm. I know Scott. He used to be a cop, remember, a DC. He's interviewed people in his time, so he'll know what's going on in here. He'll know that he has a perfect right not to say a single word, and you can bet that's how Viola bloody Murphy will have advised him to play it.'

'We'll see. You keep her in her box and let me have a go at him. Remember, the right to silence goes both ways.' He opened the door and stepped into the interview room.

Scott Mann was seated at a rectangular table. His solicitor was by his side, but she shot to her feet. 'I don't appreciate being kept waiting like this,' she protested.

Skinner ignored her. He and Gorman took their places and she reached across and switched on the twin-headed recorder, then glanced up and over her shoulder to check that the video camera was showing a red light.

'I mean it,' Viola Murphy insisted. 'I am a busy woman, and you've kept me sitting here for an hour and a half. I promise you, as soon as this interview is over I'll be complaining to your chief constable.'

Now there's a real kick in the ego, Skinner thought. *She doesn't know who I am after all.*

'For the purposes of the tape,' the deputy began, 'I am ACC Bridget Gorman, accompanied by acting Chief Constable Bob Skinner, here to interview Mr Scott Mann, whose legal representative is also present.'

Murphy glared at Skinner, but could not hide her surprise at his presence. He could read her mind. *If the top man is doing this interview himself, my client is in much deeper shit than I thought.*

'Well? Get on with it,' she snapped.

'Ms Murphy,' Gorman said, 'you're here to advise Mr Mann of his legal rights and to ensure that these aren't infringed. But you don't speak for him, and you don't direct us.'

As they spoke, Skinner fixed his gaze on Scott Mann, drawing his eyes to him and locking them to his as if by a beam. He held him captive, not blinking, not saying a word, keeping his head rock steady. The silent exchange went on for almost a minute, until the prisoner could stand the invisible pressure no longer and broke free, staring down at the desk.

'Look at me,' the chief murmured, just loud enough for the recorders to pick up. 'I want to see what we're dealing with here. I want to see what sort of person you are. So far I've seen nothing; a nonentity in the literal sense of the word. They say you were a cop once. They say you're a loving husband and father. I don't see any of those people; they're all hiding from me. Look at me, Scott.'

'Mr Skinner!' Viola Murphy yelled, her voice shrill. 'I won't bloody have this! I protest!'

His head moved, very slightly, and his eyes engaged hers. She stared back, and shivered, in spite of herself.

'No you don't,' he told her, in a matter-of-fact voice. 'You sit there, you stay silent and you do not interfere with my interview. If you raise your voice to me again and use any more abusive language, I will suspend these proceedings and charge you with breach of the peace, and possibly also with obstruction. Then we will wait for another lawyer to arrive to represent both Mr Mann and you.'

'You're joking,' she gasped.

'I have a long and distinguished record of never joking, Ms Murphy. I advise you not to test me.' He turned back to Mann who was looking at him once more, astonished. 'Okay,' he said. 'I have your attention again.'

He fell silent once more, then reached inside his jacket, and produced what appeared to be three rectangles of white card. He turned the top one over, to reveal a photograph, of Detective Inspector Charlotte Mann, then laid it in front of her husband.

'For the tape,' he said, 'I am showing the prisoner a photo of his wife, a senior CID officer.'

He turned the second image over and placed it beside the first.

'For the tape,' he said, 'I am showing the prisoner a photo of his son, Jake Mann.'

He turned the third over and put it beside the other, watching Mann recoil in horror as he did so.

'For the tape,' he said, 'I am showing the prisoner a close-up photo of the body of Chief Constable Antonia Field, taken after she was shot three times in the head in the Royal Concert Hall, Glasgow, on Saturday evening.'

He paused, as the shock on the prisoner's face turned into something else: fear.

'What I'm asking you now, Mr Mann,' he continued, 'is this. How could you betray your wife and compromise her career, how could you condemn your wee boy to the whispers and finger-pointing of his school pals, by being part of the conspiracy that led to Toni Field lying there on the floor with her brains beside her?' His gaze hardened again; in an instant his eyes became as cold as dry ice. He reached inside his jacket again and produced a fourth image. It was grainy but clear enough.

'For the tape,' he said, 'I am showing the prisoner a photograph of himself in the act of handing a parcel to a second man, identified as Mr Basil Brown, also known as Bazza.'

He glanced at the solicitor. 'To anticipate what should be Ms Murphy's next question, we know that Mr Mann was not receiving the package because that image was taken from a CCTV recording that shows the exchange. However, Ms Murphy, your client did receive something from Mr Brown and that is also shown on the video.'

His hand went to his jacket once more, but this time to the right side pocket. He produced a clear evidence bag and slammed it on to the table. 'For the tape,' he announced, 'I am showing Mr Mann an envelope which his wife discovered today in their home and sent to us. It bears the crest of Mr Brown's taxi firm and contains four hundred and twenty pounds.

'It hasn't yet been tested for fingerprints and DNA but when it is we're confident it will link the two men. We can't ask Mr Brown about this as he was found dead in Glasgow on Sunday. However, Mr Mann, we don't need him, or even that evidence. We've recovered the paper from the package you handed over and we've got your DNA and prints, and his, from that. We can also prove that the package contained two police uniforms, worn as disguises by the men who assassinated Chief Constable Field.'

He stopped, and locked eyes with Mann yet again. His subject, the former detective, and veteran of many interviews, was white as a sheet and trembling.

'All that means,' Skinner continued, 'that we can prove you were an integral part of the plot to murder my predecessor, and it is our duty to charge you with that crime.

'You'll be lonely in the dock, Scott; it'll just be you and Freddy Welsh, the man who supplied the guns. Everybody else in the chain is dead, bar one, the man who gave the order for the hit, recruited the planner and funded the operation.' He paused. 'I think we've reached the point,' he went on, 'where you bury your face in your hands and burst into tears.'

And Mann did exactly that.

Skinner waited, allowing the storm to break, to run its course and then to abate. When the prisoner had regained a semblance of self-control, he asked him, 'What's your story, Scott? For I'm sure you have one.'

'My client,' Viola Murphy interposed, 'isn't obliged to say anything.'

The chief sighed, then smiled. 'I know that as well as you do,' he replied. 'And you know as well as I do that given the evidence we have against him, if your client takes that option and sticks to it, then the best he can hope for is a cell with a sea view.

'Silence will be no defence, Ms Murphy. The best you will be able to offer will be a plea in mitigation, and by that time it will be too late, because once he's convicted, the sentence will be mandatory. I'm offering the pair of you the chance to make that plea to me now, and through me to the fiscal, before he's charged with anything.'

'He said he was only borrowin' them,' Scott Mann blurted out. 'He said he would give me them back.'

'Okay,' the chief responded. 'Now for the big question. Did he tell you why he was borrowing them?'

'He said it was for a fancy dress dance, for charity. He told me that he and Cec wanted tae go as polis, and that they wanted it to be authentic.'

Skinner leaned forward. 'And you seriously believed that?' he exclaimed.

'I chose to. The fact is, sir, Ah didn't want to know what they were really for, because I didn't have any choice.'

'What do you mean by that? You had a very simple choice. You could have told your wife that Bazza Brown had asked you to acquire two police uniforms for him, and let her handle his request. Jesus, man, even if your half-arsed story is true, by not telling Lottie and co-operating with Brown, you condemned a woman to death.'

'I ken that now,' Mann wailed. 'But like I said, I didnae have any choice. Bazza's had a hold on me from way back, since I was a cop. It's no' just the drink that's a problem for me. Ah'm an addictive personality. Anything I do, I do it to the limit and beyond.'

'Drugs?'

'Not that: gambling. Horses, mostly, but there was the cards too. Bazza's old man was ma bookie, and then he died and the brothers took over. Bazza gave me a tab, extended credit, he called it, but what he was really doin' was lettin' me pile up debt. One night he introduced me to a poker school. Ah did all right early on, but I think that was rigged, to suck me in. Then I lost it all back, but Ah was beyond stoppin' by then. Bazza kept on stakin' me, letting my tab get bigger and bigger. It got completely out of control, until before I knew it I was about seventy-five grand down, on top of twelve and a half that I'd owed him before.'

He paused, and his eyes found Skinner, reversing their earlier roles. 'That was when I was truly fucked. He pressed me for the money, even though he knew I didnae have it. He got heavy. He threatened me, he threatened Lottie and he even threatened wee Jakey, even though he was only a baby then.

'I threatened him back, or Ah tried to, told him he was messing wi' a cop and that I could have him done. He laughed at me; then he put a blade to my throat and told me that it would be the easiest thing in the world for me to be found up a close in an abandoned tenement with a needle hangin' out my arm and an overdose of heroin in ma bloodstream. And Bazza did not kid about those things. So I agreed tae pay him off in kind.'

'How?' the chief murmured.

'I became his grass, within the force. I told him everything we knew about him. Every time he was under surveillance he knew about it. If one of his boys was ever done for anything, Ah'd fix the evidence, or I'd give Bazza a list of the witnesses against him and he'd sort them.'

'You mean he killed them?'

'No, he never needed to go that far. That would have been stupid, and he wasn't.'

'So you were his safety net within the force?'

'Aye. And I got uniforms for him, once before.'

'You did? When?'

'About six months before I was kicked out. He gave me the same story: a fancy dress party. That time he did give me them back, after they'd been used in a robbery at an MoD arms depot. All the guys that were in on it were caught eventually, apart from Bazza.' He frowned. 'That was a funny one, a Special Branch job rather than our CID.'

And I know why, Skinner thought. *Bazza was off limits on the NCIS database because he'd grassed on his accomplices in the robbery . . . or possibly set the whole thing up for MI5.*

'How did you get the uniforms, then and this time?' he asked.

'I've got a friend who works in the warehouse. I asked for a favour.'

'I don't imagine it was done out of the goodness of your friend's heart.'

Mann shot him a tiny smile. 'It was, as it happened.'

'Eh?' The chief constable was taken aback. 'So why did you have that cash from Bazza Brown?'

'Ah told him that Ah had to pay the supplier.'

'What's your friend's name?'

'Aw, sir. Do ye really need it?'

Skinner stared at him, then he laughed. 'Are you kidding me? Of course we do. The guy's as guilty as you are, almost. Name, now.'

'Chris McGlashan,' the prisoner sighed. 'Sergeant Chris McGlashan. And it's no a guy; it's Chris, as in Christine. Please, sir,' he begged. 'Can ye no' leave her out of it? Can you not say I broke intae the warehouse and stole them?'

'Why the bloody hell should I do that?'

'She'll deny it.'

'I'm sure she will, but we'll lift her DNA as well, from the package and the equipment.'

'Aw Jesus, no! Lottie . . .'

The obvious dawned. 'Aw Jesus, indeed!' Skinner exclaimed. 'You stupid, selfish, irresponsible son-of-a . . .' he snapped. 'This Chris, she's your bit on the side, isn't she? You're an addictive personality right enough, Scott. The booze, the horses, the women . . . Is she the only one you've been two-timing Lottie with, or have there been others?'

Mann seemed to slump into himself. 'One or two,' he sobbed.

'Mr Skinner,' Viola Murphy ventured, 'is this relevant to your investigation?'

'Probably not, but it does demonstrate what a weak, untrustworthy apology for a husband and father your client is . . . let alone what a disgrace he was as a serving police officer.'

He turned back to his subject. 'How did Bazza react when you were chucked out of the force, Scott? I don't imagine you could have worked off all that ninety-odd grand, just in doing him favours.'

'He was okay about it, more or less. He told me he'd still come to me for info, and that he'd expect me to get it through Lottie, but he never really did, no' until this business. To tell you the truth, I half expected tae wind up in the Clyde, but nothin' happened.'

'No, you idiot,' Skinner's laugh was scornful, 'because the debt was never real! The poker school, where you supposedly lost all that dough. Did it never occur to you that it wasn't just the first few hands that were rigged in your favour, but that the whole bloody thing was rigged against you, to set you up? Who were the other guys in the school? Did you know them?'

'A couple of them; they were Bazza's drivers in the taxi business.'

'Then they must have been on bloody good tips, to be able to sit in on such a high-roller card game. You got taken, chum, to the cleaners and back again, just like everyone else who was involved with your friend Mr Brown. Did you really never work any of this out?'

'No. Now you say it, I can see how he done it, but honest, sir, he had me scared shitless most of the time and on a string. He was even the reason I got chucked off the force.'

'What? Are you saying he fed you the booze?'

'It had nothin' tae do wi' the booze. The station commander caught me liftin' evidence against Cec, one time he got arrested for carvin' up a dope dealer that had crossed the pair of them. I photocopied the witness list. He walked in on me while Ah was doing it, and saw right away what it was about. He gave me a straight choice: either Ah resigned on health grounds and blamed alcoholism, or I'd go down for pervertin' the course of justice.'

'Why did he do that?'

'For Lottie's sake, he said.'

'And who was this station commander, this saviour of yours?'

'Michael Thomas,' Mann replied. 'ACC Thomas, he is now. He was a superintendent back then.'

'Indeed?' Skinner murmured. 'And what happened to Cec? I don't recall any serious assault convictions on his record.'

'The charges were dropped anyway. The two key witnesses withdrew their evidence. They must have got to them some other way.'

'Not through you?'

'No. I never knew who they were. Ah never got that far. They must have had another source in the force.'

Forty-Three

'Do you ever feel like you're in a movie, or a TV series?' Lowell Payne asked.

Neil McIlhenney laughed. 'All the bloody time. My wife's an actress, remember. As a matter of fact, she's just been offered the lead in a new TV series, about a single mother who's a detective, but it would have meant spending months at a time out in Spain, so she turned it down. Why d'you ask? Are you a frustrated thesp?'

'Hell, no. No, it's being down here, in this place, where all the names come straight off the telly. Highbury earlier on; now it's the Elephant and bloody Castle, for God's sake. Makes me feel like Phil Mitchell.'

'Nah, you've got too much hair, mate.'

'Where does the name come from anyway?'

'I'm told by my cockney colleagues that it goes back to one of the worshipful companies that had an elephant with a castle on its back on its coat of arms. Somehow that became the name of a coaching inn on this site, about two hundred and fifty years ago.'

'So it's got fuck all to do with real elephants, or castles.'

'Absolutely fuck all.'

The two detectives were standing on the busy thoroughfare they had been discussing, having been dropped off by their driver in the bus lane that ran past the Metropolitan Tabernacle Baptist Church, a great grey pillared building.

'Where's the office?' the visitor asked.

'On the other side of the road, on top of that shopping complex; that's what I'm told.'

Payne looked at the dual carriageway, and at the density of the fast-moving traffic. 'Crossing that's going to be fun,' he complained.

'No. It's going to be dead easy,' his companion replied, heading towards a circular junction. At the end of the road was a subway, running under the highway and surfacing through the Elephant and Castle tube station. 'The office should be just around the corner here,' he said, as they stepped out into the sunlight once more.

They walked up a ramp that led into a shopping centre, and found the block without difficulty, and the board in the foyer that listed the tenants, floor by floor.

'There we are,' McIlhenney declared. 'Rondar Mail Order Limited, level three, north. Just two floors up.'

They took the elevator, at Payne's insistence. 'I'd an early start, and I am knackered. Buggered if I'm walking when there's an option.'

As they stepped out, they saw, to their left, the Rondar logo, emblazoned across double doors of obscured glass. There was no bell, no entrance videophone, so the two officers walked straight through them, into an open space furnished with half a dozen desks and a few tables. At the far end, there were two partitioned areas, affording privacy. They counted five members of staff, all female, all white, all dark-haired, all in their twenties.

'Fuck me,' Payne whispered, 'it's like a room full of Amy Winehouses. I'm sure you don't have to be Jewish to work here, for that would be illegal, wouldn't it, but I'm even surer it helps.'

The woman seated at the desk nearest to the entrance looked up at them. They judged that she was probably the oldest of the five. 'Yes?' she said.

'Mrs Radnor, please,' the DCS replied, showing her his warrant card. 'Police. I'm Chief Superintendent McIlhenney, from the Met, and this is Chief Inspector Payne, from Strathclyde.'

'Aunt Jocelyn's busy, I'm afraid. She's making a new product video, and can't be disturbed.'

McIlhenney smiled. 'I think you'll find that she can. But we'd all prefer it if you did it, rather than us.'

For a moment or two, the niece looked as if she might put up an argument, but there was something in the big cop's kind eyes that told her she would lose. And so, instead, she sighed and stood. 'If you'll follow me.' They did. 'Can you tell me what this is about?' she asked as they reached the private room on the right.

'Family matter,' Payne told her.

'But I'm . . .' she began, swallowing the rest of her protest when he shook his head. 'Wait here, please.' She rapped on the door and stepped inside.

They waited. For a minute, then a second, and then a third. McIlhenney's fist was clenched ready to knock, when it reopened and Jocelyn Radnor, glamorous, late fifties and unmistakably Golda's mother, stepped out. She did not look best pleased, even under the heavy theatrical make-up that she wore.

'Gentlemen,' she exclaimed, 'I haven't a clue what this is about, but it had better be worth it. I've been trying to get that bloody promo right for an hour now, and I had finally cracked it when Bathsheba came in and ruined it.'

'We're sorry about that,' McIlhenney said, lying, 'but it is important, and better dealt with in your office.'

'If you say so,' she sighed. 'Come on.' She led them into the other room; they found themselves looking down the Elephant and Castle, back towards the tabernacle. The furniture had seen better days, but it was quality. She offered them each a well-worn leather chair and sat in her own. 'What's it all about, then? "A family matter," my niece said.'

'We want to talk to you about your son-in-law,' Payne replied.

She tilted her head and looked at him. 'You're one too?' She chuckled. 'Scotland Yard is finally living up to its name. What about my son-in-law?' she asked, serious in the next instant. 'Why are you asking about Byron?'

'We'll get to that. Can you tell us, how did he come to work for you?'

'We needed a buyer, simple as that. Jesse, my late husband, always handled that side of the business, from the time when he founded it. That was the way it worked; he bought, I sold. Eventually, there came a time when he decided to plan for what he called "our retirement". What he really meant was his own death, for he was twenty years older than me and had heart trouble, more serious than I knew. So he recruited Byron.'

'How?'

She frowned at the DCI. 'I don't know; he recruited him, that's all. I can't remember.'

'Think back, please. Did he place an ad in the newspapers, or specialist magazines? Did he use headhunters?'

Her eyebrows rose, cracking the make-up on her forehead along the lines of the wrinkles that lay underneath. 'That was it. I asked where he found him and he said he had used specialists.'

'Do you know anything about his career before he joined you?'

'Jesse said he had worked for other mail order firms, in his time, and for a bank, but he never specified any of them.'

'Doesn't he have a personnel file, Mrs Radnor?' McIlhenney asked.

'Please, officer,' she sighed, with a show of exasperation. 'This is a family business. We don't need such things. I know he was born somewhere on the south coast, although I can't remember where, I know that he never had a father and that his mother is dead, I know that he's nowhere near as good a buyer as my husband was, I know that he's a very good husband to my daughter, and I know that he spent some time in Israel, a lot of time.'

'How do you know that last bit?'

'The accent would have told me, if he hadn't. He didn't get all of that in Sussex. I asked him about it, not long after he joined us; he said that after his mother died he went to work in a kibbutz.'

'Do they have mail order in kibbutzes?' Payne murmured.

'Of course not, but after that he stayed in Tel Aviv for another few years, or so he said.'

'You didn't believe him?'

'Let's say he was never very specific.' She paused. 'Look, to be absolutely frank, my guess has always been that when Jesse took him on he was doing a favour for a friend from the old days.'

'The old days where?' the DCI asked.

'My late husband was a soldier in his earlier life, a major in the Israeli army. He fought in the Six Day War, back in sixty-seven. He didn't come to Britain until nineteen seventy-two.'

'But he kept his links with Israel? Is that what you're saying?'

'Yes, through work with Jewish charities. He had a couple of friends at the embassy as well.'

'So, Mrs Radnor,' McIlhenney murmured, 'if we told you that the man you've known all these years as Byron Millbank was known before that as Beram Cohen, am I right in thinking you wouldn't be all that surprised?'

'Not a little bit.' She gazed at the DCS. 'So what's he done, that you're here asking about him?'

'He's died, I'm afraid.'

Jocelyn's hands flew to her mouth, but she regained her composure after a few seconds. 'Oh my. That I did not expect. Golda, my daughter, does she know?'

'Yes, we've just left her. You'll probably want to go to her when we're finished here.'

'Of course. When did this happen? Where? And how?'

'Last week, in Edinburgh, of natural causes.' He carried on, explaining how it had happened and what his companions had done with his body.

She listened to his story without a single interruption. 'What was he doing with these men?' she asked, when he was finished.

'Planning a murder,' he replied. 'You've probably heard of the shooting of a senior police officer in Glasgow on Saturday evening. Your son-in-law organised the whole thing. The two guys who buried him were his comrades, soldiers like he was in Israel, working these days for money, not for flags.'

'Yes,' she acknowledged, 'I read of it. His buddies, they're dead too, yes?'

'Killed at the scene.'

'So Byron was a soldier. That's what you're saying?' McIlhenney nodded. 'Israeli army, I guess.'

'That and more. Latterly he was Mossad, the Israeli secret service.'

'So was my husband,' she told them, 'in the old days, and for a while after he came to Britain. It all fits. So why did they send him over here?'

'From what I'm told, he'd become an embarrassment, so he was relocated. He kept in touch with his old community though. The concert hall killing wasn't the only job he did, not by a long way. I guess it all helped pay for your daughter's lifestyle.'

'I have wondered about that,' she admitted. 'And Golda, does she know any of this?'

'Only that her husband had another identity.'

'Am I allowed to tell her the rest?'

'If you want to, but do you? Isn't being widowed enough for her to be going on with?'

'True,' she agreed. 'So why did you tell me?'

'Because you don't strike me as the sort of person who'd fall for a phoney cover story when we say we need to take Byron's computer and all the other records he kept in this office.'

'I'll take that as a compliment,' Jocelyn said.

'So, can we have it?'

'I imagine that's a rhetorical question, and that you have a warrant.'

'Call it a courteous request, but yes, we do.'

'Warrant or not,' she retorted, 'I'd be happy to cooperate, and let you take everything you need. Unfortunately, someone's beaten you to it.'

'Eh?' Payne exclaimed. 'What do you mean? Nobody else knows about this branch of the investigation.'

'That's irrelevant. This is London, Chief Inspector, and there's a depression. Two nights ago we had a burglary. The thieves took a few pieces of not very valuable jewellery, and they took Byron's computer. Of course, I reported it to your people, as we have to for the insurance claim, but frankly, they didn't seem too interested. That's how it is these days.'

Forty-Four

'What do you think, Bridie?' Skinner asked. They were in her office; she held a mug of coffee in a meaty hand, he held a can of diet Irn Bru.

'I think,' she began, 'that I accept his story about the fancy dress. Okay, he knew he was being spun a line, and that he chose not to ask questions, but I don't believe that Scott Mann would knowingly be a part of any conspiracy to murder, or that if we charged him with that, we'd get a conviction.

'However, we can tie him to those uniforms beyond reasonable doubt, so he's not walking away. I would propose that we charge him with theft, and his girlfriend, assuming we do get her DNA from the packaging. We'll get guilty pleas for sure, I could read it in Viola Murphy's dark Satanic eyes.'

The chief gave a small nod. 'I agree with that. What about McGlashan? Do we let her resign quietly or do the full disciplinary thing?'

'Formal,' Gorman replied, without hesitation. 'If I could I'd put her in the public stocks in George Square.'

Skinner laughed. 'I once suggested to my soon to be ex-wife that her party should propose that as a way of dealing with Glasgow's Ned hooligan problem. She took me seriously, started arguing that the rival gangs would turn out in force to throw rocks at them. So I started arguing back to wind her up. She got angrier and angrier, wound up calling me a fucking fascist. Looking back, it was maybe the beginning of the end. We won't go that far with this lady, but yes, I agree, she has to be made an example of.' The humour left his expression. 'The consequences might be worse than an hour being pelted with rotten fruit. Imagine how Lottie's going to react when she finds out.'

His deputy sighed. 'Need she?'

'She's bound to. Her husband's going to court and so's his girlfriend. We'll make sure there's no mention of a relationship during the hearing, but she'll figure it out, for sure. It might be best for the pair of them if the sheriff puts them out of her reach for a few months.'

'Do you think he will?'

'I'm bloody sure of it. They've got to go down.'

'And what about the elephant?' she asked.

'Which one would that be?' he murmured.

'The great big one in this bloody room: Michael Thomas.'

'I've been trying to pretend it isn't there,' the chief admitted.

'But it is,' Gorman insisted. 'Scott Mann claims that Thomas caught him photocopying a witness list for the Brown brothers, and hushed it up. For Lottie's sake, indeed. Do you buy that?'

'No. Not for a second. If what Mann says is true, then he had an obligation to call in another officer to corroborate what had happened and then to charge him.'

'So why didn't he?'

'I'll let you speculate on that, Bridie,' Skinner said. 'I'm too new here.'

'If you insist. The witnesses against Cec Brown were nobbled anyway, and as Scott said, that suggests Bazza had another source. According to his story, Michael Thomas saw the list, and we know that he kept quiet about Mann nicking it. That has to raise the possibility that he was that source. If he'd done what he should have, the investigation would have gone all the way to Brown, the witnesses would have been protected and both brothers would have been finished.'

'I can't argue against that. So what do you suggest we do about it? Get the brush out again and sweep it under the carpet? After all, Brown's dead and it will only be Scott's word against his.'

'We couldn't do that, not even if we wanted to, and I don't believe that either of us do. Viola Murphy heard the accusation, and she has the copy of the recording that we were bound by law to give her. She's riding the bloody elephant in the bloody room!'

'Colourful but true. What's your recommendation?'

'We take a further statement from Mann, not as an accused person, but as a witness, and we give it to the fiscal. What do you say? New or not, you are where the buck stops.'

'Yes and no,' the chief said. 'Action has to be taken, but not by us. I suggest that you call in Andy Martin, and the Serious Crimes Agency. I don't want to do it myself, or to be involved, because Andy's in a relationship with my daughter. That might not have mattered in the past, but we have to be spotless here. His people have to take the statement, and have to decide what happens after that. Almost certainly that will not involve the local fiscal. For all we know she could be a member of the Michael Thomas fan club. See to it.'

'Will do, Bob. After the statement's taken, what will we do with Scott?'

'We charge him, and his girlfriend as soon as we have a DNA match. Murphy will probably apply for bail. Likely she'll get it, since we have no strong grounds for opposing it, so we might as well let them go, until their first court appearance.'

'What about Lottie?' Gorman asked. 'Are you going to tell her about this . . . new development?'

'Hell no! Dan Provan can do that. I'm nowhere near brave enough.'

Forty-Five

Detective Sergeant Dan Provan sat at his absent boss's desk staring at the notes he had made. He was unsure of the significance of what he had discovered. Instinctively he doubted that it had any relevance to the investigation on which he was engaged. But one thing he did know: it was well outside his comfort zone as a police officer.

He had spent most of his thirty-something year career catching petty thieves and putting them out of business, sorting out those who thought that violence was an acceptable means of self-expression, or in one short but horrible chapter, pursuing and prosecuting those he would always refer to only as 'beasts', sicko bastards who preyed upon children, their own on one or two occasions, leaving them with physical and emotional scars they would carry through life.

Always, those issues had been clear, and he had known exactly what he was doing and why. But this stuff, Glasgow hoodlums coming up with big red 'hands off' notices on the national intelligence database, and the latest, Mauritian mysteries, it was all unfocused, and way outside the rules of the game that he was used to playing. Yet it excited him, gave him the kind of thrill he had experienced as a young man, before it had been washed away by a river of sadness and cynicism.

When the door opened he did not look up. Instead he growled,

'Banjo, will you fuck off! Did Ah no' say Ah want to be alone in here?'

'Indeed?' a strong baritone voice replied. 'Anyone less like Greta Garbo I cannot imagine.'

Provan gulped and shot to his feet. 'Sorry, sir,' he said to the chief constable. 'Ah thought it was DC Paterson. Around here we're no' used to the brass comin' tae see us. Always it's the other way around, and usually for the wrong reasons. As a matter of fact,' he continued, 'I was just about tae ask for an appointment wi' you.'

Skinner laughed. 'You make me sound like the fucking dentist. Sit down, man, and relax. Before we get to your business, I've got another task for you. Not a very pleasant one, but I reckon you'd rather do it that anyone else.'

'Sounds ominous, gaffer.' He took a guess. 'Scott Mann?'

'Got it in one. ACC Gorman and I have not long finished interviewing him. He's going to be charged.'

'Conspiracy to murder?' the DS murmured.

'No, he'll only be charged with theft. We're satisfied that he had no specific knowledge of why Bazza Brown wanted the uniforms. He's heading for Barlinnie though, or Low Moss.'

'Still,' Provan countered, 'all things considered, that's a result for him. It'll no' be nice for Lottie and the wee fella, but a hell of a lot better than if he got life.'

'True, but it's not as simple as that. There will be a co-accused, Sergeant Christine McGlashan, who works in the store warehouse.'

Provan stiffened in his chair. 'Christine McGlashan?' he repeated. 'She used to be a DC, until she got promoted back intae uniform. She worked alongside Scott in CID and it was an open secret that he was porkin' her. But that was before he met Lottie. Are you gin' tae tell me he still is?'

The chief constable nodded. 'I'm afraid so. You'll see that's why

289

you're the best man to explain the situation to Lottie. That said, if you think it's Mission Impossible, you don't have to accept it. This tape will self-destruct in five seconds and I'll handle it myself.'

'No, sir, Ah'll do it. You're right; it's best she hears that sort of news from someone who knows the both o' them.'

'Thanks, Dan. None of this is going to go unnoticed or unrewarded, you realise that?'

'Appreciated, boss, but that "Thanks", that was enough. There's no way you could reward me, other than promotion to DI, and I wouldn't accept that. I am where Ah want to be. If you can make sure that for as long as Ah'm here Ah'll be alongside the Big Yin, tae look after her, that'll be fine.'

'For as long as I'm here myself, I'll make sure that happens. That's a promise, Dan.'

'In which case, Ah hope you stick around.' He frowned. 'What's happenin' tae McGlashan?'

'She'll have been arrested by now, and on her way here. You and Paterson can interview her, but make sure you listen to the recording of Mann's interview first. Once you've done that, you can charge them both, then release them on police bail, pending a Sheriff Court appearance.' He took a breath, then went on. 'Now, what were you coming to tell me?'

'The thing you asked me tae do, sir,' Provan responded. 'Ah've got a result, sort of. There's a hospital in Port Louis . . . that's the capital of Mauritius,' he offered, with a degree of pride. 'It's called the Doctor Jeetoo. Its maternity department has a record of a patient called Antonia Day Champs. She had a baby there, a wee girl, on May the twenty-third, two years ago. It was born by caesarean section, and she was discharged a week after. The address they had for her was in a place called Peach Street. I checked the local property register; it said it's owned by a woman called Sofia Day Champs.'

'Toni's mother,' Skinner volunteered. 'She got knocked up and went home to Mum.'

The sergeant sniggered. 'Makes a change from goin' tae yer auntie's for a few months, like lassies used tae do in the days before legal abortions. Ah wonder why she didnae have one herself, given that she was such a career woman. Her clock must have been tickin' Ah suppose.'

'Who knows?'

'I spoke to the ward sister. She said she remembered her. She said that a woman came to visit her when she was in, but no husband. There was one man came to visit her, though; much older, about seventy. The sister heard Sofia call him "Grandpa". She said his face was familiar, like somebody she'd seen in the papers, but that whoever he was he was pretty high-powered, because the consultant was on his best behaviour when he was there, and Antonia had a room tae herself.'

'Then I guess that could have been her father. Marina told me he was a bigwig in government, and Sofia was his mistress. So what about the birth registration, Dan?' the chief asked. 'That's what I'm really interested in.'

'Then you're no' goin' tae like this. Mauritius is more modern than ye'd think. All the latest records are stored on computer. The doctor who attends the birth gives the parents a form tae say that it's happened, but that's the only written record, apart from the official birth certificate that the parents are given when they register it. And you have tae do that; it's the law. The government guy Ah spoke to checked the whole period that she was out there after the twenty-third of May, and there is no record of a birth bein' registered. He's in no doubt about that.'

'Bugger!'

The DS held up a hand: it occurred to Skinner that one day he would make an excellent lollipop man. 'However,' he declared, 'he did say that he'd found an anomaly. On the thirtieth of May, a week later, there were forty-six births notified, but when he looked at the computer, he noticed that number seven two six four is followed by seven two six six. There's a number missing; he had his computer folk look at it. They said it had been hacked. How about that then, boss? D'ye think Grandpa was powerful enough to have the record removed?'

'I doubt it, Dan,' Skinner replied. 'But I know someone who is.'

Forty-Six

'So much for the tour of the capital,' Lowell Payne grumbled.

'We drove past the Tower of London, didn't we?' Neil McIlhenney pointed out. 'And if you went up on the roof here and found the right spot, you'd be able to see the top of Big Ben. Not only that, you've seen the home of the mighty Arsenal Football Club. All for free too, in the most expensive city I know.' He grinned. 'Tell you what. You check in with the King in the North and I'll take you for a pint and a sandwich. It's getting on past lunchtime and I'm a bit peckish myself.'

'I've been trying but he's not in his office, and his mobile's switched off.'

'Maybe he's still doing that interview you told me about.'

'If he is and the bloke hasn't been charged yet, he'll be entitled to get up and walk out.'

'He's probably still hiding under the table. Big Bob doesn't like bent cops, even ex ones. Try him again, go on.'

The DCI took out his phone and pressed the contact entry for Skinner's direct line. He let it ring six times, and was about to hang up when it was answered.

'Lowell?'

'Yes, Chief.'

'How's it going down there? Got anything useful?'

'Some, but don't get excited. We've worked out how an Israeli ex-paratrooper and disgraced spook hit man came to get a job as a jewellery buyer with a London mail order company. His late father-in-law was Mossad, once upon a time.'

'Surprise me,' Skinner drawled, with heavy sarcasm. 'How did you find that out?'

'We decided to be forthcoming with his mother-in-law. She was equally frank in return; she told us.'

He chuckled. 'Giving the guy a job, that's one thing; marrying your daughter off to him might be taking it a bit too far.'

'You'd think so, but the impression we're getting is of a popular, charming bloke. The wife's devastated. It was just starting to hit home when we left.'

'How about the mother-in-law? How did she take it?'

'Calmly. She was upset, of course, but it didn't come as a bombshell to find out that poor Byron had a second line of business. Before we left, she told us she hoped he was better at that than he was at the jewellery buying.'

'Did you get anything else from your visit, apart from a compendium of Jewish mother-in-law jokes? Did you take his computer?'

'No, and that's the real news I have for you. Somebody beat us to it; Rondar Mail Order had a break-in last Friday night. A few small items were taken, but the main haul was Byron Millbank's computer. I'm sorry about that, boss, but this trip's been pretty much a waste of time.'

'Like hell it has,' the chief retorted. 'There are three possibilities here, Lowell. One, the break-in was exactly that, a routine office burglary. Two, it was an inside job, staged to hide something incriminating from the sharp eyes of the VAT inspectors. Three, someone who knew about Byron's background, and the fact that he was no

294

longer in the land of the living, decided to make sure that nothing embarrassing had been left behind him. I know which of those my money's on. You've had a result, of sorts, Lowell. What was only a suspicion until now, it's confirmed in my book. The cleaners have been in, and not just in London.'

'But what have they been covering up?'

'Work it out for yourself. It's too hot for any phone line, especially a mobile that can be easily monitored. The thing that's getting to me is that they've been too damn good at it. If I'm right, I know what the big secret is, but I can't even come close to proving it, and the bugger is that I don't believe I ever will. Our investigation into Toni Field's murder is dead in the water, as dead as she is.'

'Are you sure?' Payne asked.

'I don't believe in miracles, brother.'

'What do you want me to do, then?'

'You might as well come home. Get yourself on to an evening flight. I'll see you tomorrow.'

As the DCI ended the call, he realised that McIlhenney was gazing at him. 'How did he take it?' he asked.

'He reckons that's it. We're stuffed. He's going to close the inquiry. He sounded pretty pissed off. I know he hates to lose.'

The chief superintendent shook his heard. 'No,' he said. 'You don't know. He refuses to lose. You wait and see. He's not finished yet.'

'He says he doesn't believe in miracles.'

'Then he's lying. When he's around they happen all the time.'

Forty-Seven

'Bastards!' Skinner exclaimed. The room was empty but there was real vehemence in his voice. 'It's like someone's farted in a busy pub. You're pretty sure who it was but you've got no chance of proving it and the more time passes, the more the evidence dissipates.'

Frustrated, he reached for his in-tray and began to examine the pile of correspondence, submissions and reports that his support team had deemed worthy of his attention. He had planned that it would go to Lowell for further filtering but his absence had landed it all on his desk.

'Commonwealth Games, policing priorities,' he read, from the top sheet on the pile. 'One, counter-terrorism,' he murmured. 'Two, counter-terrorism, three counter-terrorism, four, stop the Neds from mugging the punters.' He laid the paper to one side for consideration later, probably at Sarah's, and picked up the next item, a letter.

It was addressed to Chief Constable Antonia Field, from the Australian Federal Police Association, inviting her to address its annual conference, to be held in Sydney, the following December.

He scribbled a note, 'Call the sender, tell them about Toni's death. If he asks me to do it, decline with regret on the ground that I have no idea where I'll be in December,' clipped it to the letter and dropped it into his out-tray.

He worked on for ten minutes, finding it more and more diffi-cult to maintain his concentration. He felt his eyes grow heavy and realised for the first time that he had missed lunch. A week before he would have poured himself a mug of high-octane coffee, but Sarah had made him promise to give up, and he had promised himself that he would never cheat on her again, in any way. Instead, he took a king-size Mars Bar from his desk drawer and consumed it in four bites.

As he waited for the energy boost to hit his system, he picked up his direct telephone, found a number and dialled it.

He hoped that it would be Marina who answered rather than Sofia; and so it was.

'Bob Skinner,' he announced.

'Good afternoon. This is a pleasant surprise . . . do you have something to tell us about Antonia's death?'

'No, sorry. In fact I have something to ask you. When were you going to get round to telling me about Toni's child?'

He counted the silence; one second, two seconds, three . . .

'Ah, so you know about that.'

'Of course. You must have realised that the post-mortem was bound to reveal it.'

'Yes, I suppose I did. Maman and I hoped you wouldn't regard it as relevant. It isn't really, is it?'

'Probably not,' he agreed, 'but when we set out to create a picture of someone's life, it has to be complete. We can't leave things out, arbitrarily, for personal, or even for diplomatic, reasons.'

'No, I accept that now. We should have volunteered it.'

'What happened to the child?'

'She's here, with us. When you visited us the other day, she was upstairs, playing in the nursery that Antonia made for her there. She was born in Mauritius, two years ago. Her name is Lucille; she's such a pretty little thing. Normally she lives in London, with Maman, in a house that Antonia's father bought for them. He is widowed now, and when he heard of the child he was overwhelmed. He had never recognised my sister as his daughter, not formally, not until then.'

'Does he know she's dead?'

'Oh yes. Maman called him, straight away. She said he was very upset. So he should have been. I don't care for the man, even though I've never met him.'

'Who's Lucille's father?' Skinner asked.

'I don't know,' Marina confessed. 'Antonia never told me, and she never told Maman. But she registered the birth herself, in Mauritius. You should be able to find out there.'

'That's right,' he agreed, 'we should.' *We should*, he thought, *but some bugger doesn't want us to.*

'When you do, will you let me know, please. Maman and I have been looking for Lucille's birth certificate among Antonia's papers, but we can't find it.'

'Sure, will do. But until then we're guessing. Those men friends you told me about, her lovers: she never gave you any clue to their names?'

'No, not really. She gave one or two of them nicknames. The DAC in the Met, for example, she called him "Bullshit", for whatever unimaginable reason. The mandarin she called "Chairman Mao", and the QC was always "Howling Mad". Other than that, she never let anything slip.'

'You mentioned five men in her life,' the chief said, 'but when we met you said she'd had six relationships in the time you lived with her. Was the sixth Michael Thomas?'

She laughed. 'Him?' she exclaimed. 'You know about that?'

'The whole bloody force seems to know about that. He was seen leaving the flat she was renting, far too late for it to have been a work visit.'

'Then that was careless of her, and not typical. It was very definitely a one-night stand. It was also the only time that she ever had a man when she and I were under the same roof. Actually, I found it quite embarrassing,' she confessed. 'The walls were thin.' He heard what might have been a giggle. 'It's very off-putting to hear your sister faking it. Next morning I complained. She laughed and said not to worry, that it had been what she described as "tactical sex" and wouldn't happen again.

'No,' she continued, 'her most recent relationship was still going on, and had been for at least three months. I'm more than a little surprised that I haven't heard from the poor man; he must be distraught, for they were close. For the first time I sensed that there was no motive behind the relationship, nothing "tactical" about it.'

'I don't suppose she told you his name, either.'

'Ah, but this time she did,' Marina exclaimed. 'That's why I believe it was serious. She told me he is called Don Sturgeon, and that he works as an IT consultant. She never brought him home and she never introduced us, but I saw him once when he came to pick her up. He is very attractive: clean-cut, well-dressed, almost military looking.'

Skinner felt his right eyebrow twitch. 'Indeed?' he murmured. 'Anything else that you can recall about him?'

'Yes,' she replied at once. 'His skin tone; it's almost the same as mine. It made me wonder if he was Mauritian too, and that's what she saw in him.'

'In this life,' the chief observed, 'anything is possible. Marina,' he exclaimed as a picture formed in his mind, 'are you doing anything, right now?'

'No. Maman is with Lucille, so I'm free.'

'Then I'd like you to come into the office, quick as you can.'

Forty-Eight

Lowell Payne had seen the interior of Westminster Abbey several times, but only on television, when it had been bedecked for royal weddings or draped in black for funerals, and packed with celebrants or mourners. As he stepped inside the great church for the first time, he found himself humming 'Candle in the Wind' without quite recalling why.

It was the sheer age of the place that took hold of him, the realisation when he read the guide that its origins were as old as England itself, and that the building in which he stood went back eight centuries.

He knew as little of architecture as he did of history, but he appreciated at once that the abbey was not simply a place of worship, but also of celebration, a great theatre created for the crowning of kings and, occasionally, of queens.

In common with most first-time visitors, he paused at the tomb of the Unknown Soldier, wondering for a moment whether the occupant's nearest and dearest had been told secretly of the honour that had been done him. 'Somebody must have known,' he whispered as he looked down, drawing an uncomprehending smile and a nod from a Japanese lady tourist by his side.

He moved on and found a memorial stone, commemorating sixteen poets of the First World War, recognising not a single name.

Charles Dickens he knew, though, and the Brontë sisters, and Rabbie Burns, and Clement Attlee. Stanley Baldwin was lost on him, but somewhere the name Geoffrey Chaucer rang a bell.

His mobile did not ring, but it vibrated in his pocket. He took it out, feeling as if he was committing a form of sacrilege, until he realised that half of the tourists in the place were using smart-phones as cameras.

He read the screen and took the call. 'Chief,' he said, keeping his voice as low as he could, and moving away from the throng of which he had become a part.

'Where the hell are you?' Skinner asked. 'You at the station already?'

'No, I've got time to kill, so I'm doing the tourist thing. Does the name Stanley Baldwin mean anything to you?'

'Of course. He was a Tory prime minister between the wars, and even less use than most of them. He took a hard line on Mrs Simpson and made the King abdicate, but he didn't mind Hitler nearly as much. Bloody hell, Lowell, what did you do at school? You'll be asking me who Attlee was next.'

'No, I know about him. What can I do for you?'

'Cancel your return flight. I'd like you to stay down there overnight. Can you do that?'

'Sure. Has there been a development?'

'Maybe. I'm not sure. But if something plays out . . .' His voice drifted off with his thoughts for a few seconds. 'I'll know in a couple of hours, but meantime you just hang on down there. I'll be back in touch.'

The conversation ended with as little ceremony as it had begun, leaving Payne staring at his phone. 'If you say so, Bob,' he murmured. 'I wonder if I can put a West End show on expenses.'

Forty-Nine

Skinner smiled as he gazed at the ceiling. *Stanley Baldwin,* he thought. He guessed where Payne had been when he had reached him. The abbey was one of his favourite stopping-off places when he was in London.

London. For all that the prospect of an independently governed Scotland was looming, the great monolith in the south remained the centre of power. He had decided that he would vote 'Yes!' with his heart in the referendum, but he had no illusions over the difficulty his country faced in extricating itself from the British state, if that was what the majority chose.

Scotland might become a nation, fully self-governing, a member of both the European Union and the UN, but it would still share a head of state and an island with its English neighbours and their common problems of security would remain. He knew better than most what that would mean. MI5 would continue to operate north of what would have become a national border.

Even if a future first minister had access to its work and to those of its secrets that affected his interests, he would have a very small voice in decisions that affected its remit and its funding, and no control at all over its activities. Strings would continue to be pulled in secret, by secret people, like his friend Amanda Dennis and her immediate boss,

Sir Hubert Lowery, the director of the service.

It would be up to the new Scotland to come to terms with the need to have its own counter-espionage service, to protect itself against potential threats from wherever they came, even if that was Westminster. He had discussed this with Clive Graham, at a meeting so private that he had kept it from Aileen. Whatever their differences on the unification of the police forces, the two men were agreed that if the time came, their country would need its own secret service. There was also an understanding over the man who would head it.

His smile was long gone when the phone sounded; he flicked the switch that put it on speaker. 'Yes?'

'Sir,' a woman replied, 'it's PC May in reception. I'm very sorry to bother you, and I wouldn't normally, but there's a man here, an odd-looking wee chap, and he's asking to see you. He won't give me his name but he says to tell you that he's been sent by Mr McGuire in Edinburgh. What should I do?'

'He's okay,' Skinner told her. 'He's a tradesman I need to solve a practical problem. Take him to the lift, then come up with him to this floor, straight away. I'll meet you there and take charge of him.'

He hung up and walked from his office. He was waiting by the elevator door when it opened less than two minutes later. A small wiry man with a pinched face and a jailhouse complexion stepped out.

The chief looked towards his escort. 'Thanks, Constable. I'll call you to come and collect him when we're done. By the way,' he added. 'I'm expecting another visitor quite soon. Let me know directly he arrives.'

She was nodding as the lift door closed, leaving Skinner alone with his visitor. 'Well, Johan,' he exclaimed. 'It's good to see you, under different circumstances from the usual.'

Johan Ramsey was dressed in baggy jeans and brown jerkin, over a

Rangers football top that his host judged, from its design, to be at least three seasons old. He was one of those people whose only expression was furtive. 'Is this legit?' he asked.

Skinner laughed. 'Johan, I'm the chief fucking constable; of course it's legit. A wee bit unorthodox, that's all. Come on.'

He led the way to his office, and into his private room, where he pulled aside the door that concealed the safe. 'That's the problem,' he said. 'My predecessor took the combination to her grave, and I can't open it. Six digits, I'm told.'

Ramsey took a pair of spectacles with one leg from a pocket in his jerkin, and perched them on the narrow bridge of his nose. He appraised the task for a few seconds, then nodded, and declared, 'A piece of piss,' with a degree of pride. 'If you'll just step into the other room, sir, Ah'll have it open in a couple of minutes.'

The chief's jaw dropped, then he laughed. 'Jo, if you think I'm leaving you alone in here, you're daft.'

The little man pouted. 'Professional secrets, Mr Skinner,' he protested.

'My arse! Jo, you're a professional fucking thief! I don't know what's in the bloody thing. Tell you what, I'll stand behind you, so I can't see your hands.' He took five twenty-pound notes from his wallet and waved them before the safe-cracker's eyes. 'And there's these,' he added.

'What about ma train fare?'

Skinner snorted, but produced another twenty. 'There you are: and a couple of pints when you get home. Now get on with it.'

'Aye, okay.'

He turned and hunched over the safe. The chief saw him reach inside his jacket again then insert a device that could have been a hearing aid in his ear. Everything else was hidden to him; all he could see were small movements of Ramsey's shoulders.

'A couple of minutes' he had said, and it took no longer, until there was a click, and the safe swung open.

'Piece of piss, Ah told ye. Three four eight five's the combination. Four digits, no' six.'

Skinner smiled as he handed over the notes. 'Do you know what "recidivist" means, Johan?' he asked.

'No, sir,' Ramsey replied as he pocketed them.

'No, I didn't think so. Do me one favour, even though it'll be a big one for you. Try not to get nicked again on my patch, whether it's here or in Edinburgh. This can't get you any favours, and I really don't want to have to lock you up again. Come on, let's get you back home. Remember, you were never here.'

His desk phone rang again as they stepped back into his office. He picked it up.

'PC May again, sir. Your next visitor's arrived.'

'Good timing,' he said. 'Bring him up, and you can take this one back.'

Fifty

'When will they be in court?' Viola Murphy asked, as soon as Dan Provan had finished reading the formal charges, and the two accused had been taken away to complete the bail formalities.

'Ah can't say,' he replied, 'but we'll let you know. Will you be defending them both?'

'Probably, unless either one of them changes their mind and decides to plead not guilty; in that event, there could be a conflict. Does Skinner mean it? Will he press for custodial sentences?'

'From what Ah hear you got on the wrong side of him. Did you think he's the kind that bluffs?'

'No,' the lawyer conceded.

'It's no' just him. ACC Gorman's of the same mind.'

'And you?'

'Listen, Viola, we all are. It's tough for me, personally, you must know that, but we cannae let this go by wi' a slap on the wrist, especially for McGlashan. If she goes down, he has tae and all. That would be the case suppose he wasn't an ex-cop and married to somebody who still is. The fact that he is just underlines it. The fiscal will demand jail. The best you can hope for is a soft-hearted sheriff that gives them less than six months.'

'I'll ask for a suspended sentence.'

'Ye better no'. He might hang them.' He winced. 'Bad joke, Ah know, but you know the bench. Sometimes, the more that lawyers chance their arm, the harder they go. Would ye like some advice?'

'I'll listen to it,' she said. 'Whether I'll act on it . . .'

'Okay. If I was in the dock, I'd want the youngest, freshest kid in your firm tae do the plea in mitigation. Ah'd even be hopin' that they made an arse of it, and the judge took pity on them. Because that's the only way those two will get anything like sympathy from any sheriff in this city.'

'Mmm,' she murmured. 'You may well be right. I suppose you should be; you've been around long enough to have seen it all. I'll have a word with my partners, and see what they think. Thanks, Sergeant.'

The door had barely closed behind her when it opened again. Provan looked up, to see Scott Mann framed there.

'Dan,' he began. 'Sarge.'

The older man bristled. 'Don't you fuckin' call me Sarge.' He jerked a thumb in the direction of DC Paterson who stood beside him, gathering notes and papers and putting them in order. 'That's reserved for colleagues, like Banjo here; for police officers, and that you're no'. And don't "Dan" me either. Mr Provan, it can be, but frankly Ah'd prefer nothing at all. Ah'd rather no' see you again.'

'Will ye put a word in for me?' Mann begged.

'What? Wi' the high heid yins? You must be joking.'

'No, I meant wi' Lottie.'

The DS started round the table towards him, only to be restrained by Paterson's strong hand, grabbing him by the elbow. He stopped, gathering himself.

'There is even less chance of that,' he said when he was ready. 'From now on, I will do all I can to protect Lottie from you. Now you fuck off out of here, boy, get off wi' your tart. And be glad you're leavin' in one piece. In the old days ye wouldn't have.'

Fifty-One

'Who was that little guy?' Clyde Houseman asked, as he settled into the chair that Skinner offered him. 'He wasn't the sort you expect to see on the command floor of the second largest police force in Britain.'

'Just a technician,' the chief replied. 'I had a wee problem, but he sorted it out for me.'

'Computer?'

He shrugged. 'You know IT consultants, they live in a different world from the rest of us. Some of them turn up and they're dressed like you, others, they're like him. I know which ones I trust more. I'm not a big fan of dressing to impress.'

The younger man winced and his eyes seemed to flicker for a moment. 'I do . . .'

Skinner laughed. 'Don't take it personally. I wasn't getting at you. You're ex-military, an ex-officer; you've had years of training in taking a pride in your appearance. Plus, you're not a computer consultant; you're a spook. Whatever, you look a hell of a lot better than you did as a gang-banger in Edinburgh half a lifetime ago.'

'Thank God for that.'

'Me, now? I've never changed. I joined the police force because I felt a vocational calling, and I followed it even though I knew that my

310

old man had always hoped I would take over the family law firm eventually. I think he died hoping that. I never let myself be swayed, though. I applied to join the Edinburgh force, they saw my shiny new degree and they accepted me. And you know what? The first time I put on the uniform, I realised that I hated it. The thing was ugly and uncomfortable and when I looked in the mirror I didn't recognise the bloke inside it.

'It didn't kill my pride in the job, but it did make me want to get into CID as fast as I could. Look at me now; I'm a chief constable, but my uniform is hanging in my wardrobe next door. I'm only wearing a suit because I feel a wee bit obliged to do that, at least until I get settled in here.

'The real me might dress a wee bit sharper than the guy you passed at the lift, but it would still be pretty casual. So what you see here, to an extent it's a phoney. Old George Michael got it right; sometimes clothes do not make the man.

'But yours, though, they do. They mark you out, they define you. The military defined you. It made you; you became it. Before that you were no more than eighty kilos of clay waiting to be given proper form.

'I could see that when I came across you in that shithole of a scheme in Edinburgh. That's why I gave you my card that day: I thought you might see the light and get in touch. You didn't, but you still went in the right direction. If you had . . . you'd still be the man you are, but you'd just look a bit different, that's all.'

Houseman laughed. 'Scruffy at weekends, you mean? How do you know I'm not?'

'I know, because I've met plenty of soldiers in my time and quite a few were officers who rose through the ranks, like you. I'll bet you don't have a pair of jeans in your wardrobe. Am I right?'

'You are, as a matter of fact. Is that a bad thing?'

'In a soldier, no. In a lawyer, no. In an actuary, for sure no. When I hang out in Spain I see these fat blokes on the beach in gaudy shirts and ridiculous shorts, with gold Rolexes on their wrists and all of them looking miserable because their wives have dragged them there and they're starting to panic because they don't know who anyone else is and, worse, nobody knows what they are. My golf club's full of people who've never worn denim in their fucking lives, and that's okay, because if they did they'd be pretending to be something they're not.'

'Exactly. So what are you saying?'

'I'm trying to tell you,' Skinner said, 'that conformity is fine for normal people. But you, Clyde, you're not a normal person, you're a spook. You're a good-looking bloke, of mixed race, so you have an inbuilt tendency to be memorable. The way you dress, the way you present yourself, makes you unforgettable, and in your line of work, my friend, that is the very last thing you want to be. If they didn't teach you that when you joined up at Millbank, then they failed you.'

Houseman's eyebrows formed a single line. 'Point taken, sir. Any suggestions?'

'Nothing radical; the obvious mostly. Vary your dress, and when you go casual, don't wear stuff with big logos or pop stars on the front. Shop in Marks and Spencer rather than Austin Reed. Let your hair grow a bit shaggy. Don't shave every day. Wear sunglasses when it's appropriate, the kind that people will remember rather than the person behind them. Choose what you drive carefully.'

He smiled. 'That day you and I met, back in the last century, I was driving my BMW. That was an accident; normally I'd have been in my battered old Land Rover. If I had, you and your gang wouldn't have given it a second glance, and I wouldn't have had to warn you off.'

312

'Then whatever caused that accident, I'm grateful for it. You gave me the impetus to get out of there. Otherwise I might not have. I might have stayed a stereotype and wound up in jail.'

'Nah, I think you'd have made it. You were a smart kid. You'd have worked it out for yourself, eventually.'

'Maybe.' He pulled himself a little more upright. 'However, I'm sure you didn't call me here to give me fashion advice.'

'No,' Skinner agreed, 'that's true. I felt I should give you an update on the investigation, since you were in at the death, so to speak.'

'Thanks, sir. I appreciate that. How's it going?'

'It's not,' the chief sighed. 'It's stalled. All our lines of inquiry have dried up. There is no link between Beram Cohen and the person or organisation who sponsored the hit. We know how it was done, and even if it points in a certain direction, the witnesses are all dead. That's probably my fault,' he added. 'You had no choice but to take down Smit, but if I was a better shot I'd have been able to stop Botha without killing him.'

'There will be no further inquiries about our part in that?' Houseman asked.

'None. Everything is closed.'

Skinner rose to his feet, and his visitor followed suit. He moved towards the door, then stopped. 'I'm aware,' he said, 'that in Toni Field's time MI5 policy was to keep our counter-terrorism unit at a distance. It's okay, I'm not asking you to comment. Toni may not even have been aware of it, but I know it was the case. I just want you to know that while I'm here, I won't tolerate that. You can keep secrets from anyone else, but if they affect my operational area, not from me. Understood?'

Houseman nodded. 'Understood, sir.'

They walked together to the lift. The chief constable watched the doors close then went back the way he had come, but walked past his own room, stopping instead at the one he had commandeered for Lowell Payne. He knocked on the door then opened it halfway and looked in.

'Come on along,' he said.

Marina Deschamps put down her magazine, stood and followed him. 'This is all very surprising,' she murmured, with a smile. 'Even a little mysterious. By the way, did you solve the mystery of the safe?'

He nodded. 'This very afternoon. I've still to check its contents, but if there's anything personal in there I'll let you have it. As for the rest, you're right, but now I can show you what this visit's all about.'

He sat behind his desk and touched the space bar on his computer keyboard to waken it from sleep.

'This room has a couple of little bonuses,' he began. 'Having worked next door, you're probably aware that there's a security system. There's a wee camera in the corner of the ceiling and when the system is set, anyone who comes in here is automatically filmed, without ever knowing it.'

'Yes,' she agreed. 'Some evenings I would be last out of here, and so I had to be shown how to set it.'

'Yes, I imagine so. But did Toni tell you that it's more than an alarm?'

'No, she never did. It is? In what way?'

'It can also be used to record meetings. Clearly, if that happens, all the participants should be made aware of it, but if they weren't they'd never know.' He used his mouse to open a program then select a file. He beckoned to her. 'Come here and take a look at this.'

As she walked round behind him he clicked an icon, to start a video. There was no sound, but the image that she could see was clear and in colour. The chief constable with his back to the camera and

314

facing him a sharply dressed, immaculately groomed man, whose skin tone was almost identical to her own.

'Ever seen him before?' Skinner asked, hearing an intake of breath from over his shoulder.

'Yes,' she whispered. 'That's Don Sturgeon. What's he doing here?'

Fifty-Two

'What d'you think of the beer?' Neil McIlhenney asked.

'It's okay,' Lowell Payne conceded. 'What's it called?'

'Chiswick Bitter. I don't drink much, not any more, but when I do it's the one I go for.'

'That's because it doesn't take the top of your head off,' one of their companions remarked, 'unlike that ESB stuff. Bloody ferocious that is. I've seen tourists staggering out of here after a couple of pints of that stuff. Not like you Jocks, though. You'd drink aviation fuel and never feel it.'

'I used to,' the DCS chuckled. 'Me and my mate. In those days we used to say that English beer was half the strength of a Scotsman's piss, but since I came down here I've developed an occasional taste for it. Travelling to work on the tube has its compensations.'

The other Londoner glanced at him. 'Where do you live?'

McIlhenney raised an eyebrow. 'Was that a professional inquiry? I've heard about you guys; you're never off duty.'

'No, not at all.'

'Richmond, actually.'

The man had his glass to his lips, he spluttered. 'You what? On a copper's pay? Maybe it should have been a professional question.'

'My wife's owned the place for years. When we lived in Edinburgh

316

it was rented out. We used her flat in St John's Wood if we ever came down.'

'You're shitting us.'

'Oh no he's not,' Payne laughed. 'Ask him who his wife is.'

As he spoke, the phone in the pocket of his shirt vibrated against his chest. He knew who the caller would be without looking at it. He excused himself as he took it out, and stepped out into the street.

'Where are you now?' Skinner asked.

'I'm in a pub called the Red Lion, in Whitehall, with Neil McIlhenney and two guys he says are part of the Prime Minister's protection team. This might be a good night to have a go at him.'

'Given what happened on Saturday,' the chief pointed out, 'that's not very funny. Have you got a hotel?'

'Yes, the Met fixed me up with one near Victoria Station.'

'Good. I want you to meet me tomorrow morning. Victoria will do fine. I'll be coming up from Gatwick, same flight as you caught today.'

'I'll see you there. Where are we going?'

'I have a meeting, and given where it is and what's on the agenda, I'm not going in there unaccompanied.'

'Sounds heavy. Where?'

'Security Service, Millbank. I'm just off the phone with my friend Amanda Dennis, the deputy director. She's expecting us.'

Payne gasped. 'Jesus Christ, boss. Why are we going there? What's happened?'

'Nothing that I can slam on the table, point at and say "He did it", but enough for me to fly some kites and see how they react. I can see a chain of events and facts that lead to a certain hypothesis, but I can't see anything that resembles a motive. Still, what we've got is enough for some cage-rattling. I'm good at that.'

'I think I know that.'

'Then you can sit back and learn.'

'At my age I don't want to.'

'You're a year older than me, Lowell,' Skinner chuckled, 'that's all. One thing I want you to do in preparation for the meeting. When you call Jean, as I'm sure you will, tell her where you're going. I'll be doing the same with Sarah. I know, I said that Amanda's a friend, and she is, but in that place, friendship only goes so far.'

Fifty-Three

'Are you going to work in Glasgow for good, Dad?' Skinner's elder son asked, ranging over three octaves in that single sentence.

Mark McGrath, the boy Skinner and Sarah had adopted as an orphan, was at the outset of adolescence, and the breaking of his voice was not passing over easily or quickly. James Andrew, his younger brother, laughed at his lack of control, until he was silenced by a frown from his mother.

'I dunno, mate,' Bob confessed. 'Last week I'd never have imagined being there. On Sunday, when I agreed to take over, the answer would still have been no. But with every day that passes, I'm just a little less certain. But remember, even if I did apply for the job, so would other people. There's no saying I'd be chosen.'

Both of his sons looked at him as if he had told them Motherwell would win the Champions League.

'No kidding,' he insisted. 'There are many very good cops out there, and most of them are younger than me. I won't see fifty again, lads.'

'You'll get it, Dad.' James Andrew spoke with certainty, his father's certainty, Sarah realised, as she heard him. 'Will we have to move to Glasgow?'

'Never!' The reply was instant, and vehement.

'Come on, guys,' Sarah interrupted. 'It's past nine, time you headed upstairs. And don't disturb your sister if she's asleep.'

'She won't be,' Mark squeaked. 'She'll be practising her reading.'

'That's a bit of an exaggeration surely,' Bob chuckled. 'She might be looking at the pictures.'

'No, Dad. She's learning words as well; I've been teaching her. There's a computer program and I've been using it.'

Skinner watched them as they left, and was still gazing at the door long after it was closed. Sarah settled down beside him on the sofa, tugging his arm to claim his attention. 'Hey,' she murmured, 'come back from wherever you are. Whassup, anyway?'

'Ach, I was just thinking what a crap dad I've been. I should be teaching my daughter to read, not subcontracting the job to Mark. Last week I was all motivated, pumped up to do that and more. We had a great morning on the beach on Saturday, the kids and I, then I had a phone call, the shit hit the fan and I had to go rushing off, didn't I, and get it splattered all over me. Now I'm thinking seriously about taking on the biggest job in Scotland, when I've already got a job that's far more important than that.'

She turned his face to her, and kissed him. 'Bob,' she said, 'I love you, and it's good to see you taking your kids so seriously. But you always have done. You've been great with the boys all along, and you've never neglected Seonaid. It's taken you a while to realise that she isn't a baby any more, that's all. Me living in America didn't help, since that meant you missed a big chunk of her infancy, but I'm back now, and we can help her grow together.' She put a hand on his chest. 'That does not mean I expect you to become a house husband, because you couldn't. There's too much happening, too much at stake just now, and if you don't get involved in it, you'll regret it for the rest of your life.

'You can't walk away anyway, it's not in your nature. This thing tomorrow, this high-stakes meeting at MI5 that you're so worked up about, even if you're not saying so, you don't have to go there, do you? But you want to, you feel you have to. Isn't that right?'

'I set it up,' he admitted. 'Yes, it is a bit of a fishing trip, and there are other ways I could have played it. For example, I could just write a report, a straight factual account of the things that we know, and suggest certain possibilities. Then I could give that report to the Lord Advocate, who's my ultimate boss as a criminal investigator in Scotland, with a copy to the First Minister.'

'Why don't you?'

'Because they'd burn it. If I told them what I know to be fact and what I see as a possibility, they'd be scared stiff. If they acted on it, it could provoke a major conflict between them and the Westminster government. All in all, it's best that I keep it from them, and that I go and have a full and frank discussion with Amanda.'

'Bob,' Sarah ventured, 'are you suggesting that MI5 had something to do with Toni Field's murder?'

'No, I'm not, because the evidence doesn't take me there. Even if I thought they were capable of doing that, I can't see why they would. But I do know that they created the conditions for it to happen, and that they've been doing what they can to cover up. There's a piece of that I still don't understand, but I never will because they've been too good at it.'

'Okay,' she said. 'Here's what I think you should do. See this thing through to its conclusion, and let it go, however unsatisfactory the conclusion may be. Then apply for the Strathclyde job. You'll get it; even the boys know that. And once you're there, be everything you can be. Build your support staff so that you can delegate and not have to change every light bulb. Work the hours a normal man does, and be the father that a normal man is expected to be.'

He grinned. 'And the husband?'

'Nah,' she laughed in return. 'You were always lousy at that; we're fine as we are.'

'Yeah,' he agreed. 'I'll go with that.'

'Would you like a drink? I put some Corona in the fridge for you. I take it it's still your favourite beer.'

'Absolutely, but I'll give it a miss tonight. Early start tomorrow. Hey,' he added, 'you realise that from now on I'll be able to tell whether you've got another bloke just by checking the fridge?'

'Yes, but how will you know I don't have another fridge somewhere, one with a combination lock just in case you do find it?'

Her joke triggered a memory. 'Bugger,' he exclaimed. 'I finally got into my own safe this afternoon, in the office. I haven't had a chance to check the papers that were in it. They're in my briefcase; mind if I go through them now?'

'No,' she replied, jumping to her feet, 'you do that, and I'll check that Madam Seonaid isn't halfway through *War and Peace* by torchlight under the duvet.'

As she left the room, he reached for his attaché case and opened it. He had brought the remnants of his in-tray with him, to be worked on during his flight to London, but the contents of Toni Field's safe were in a separate folder. He took it out and set the rest aside.

His dead predecessor's papers were contained in a series of large envelopes. He picked up the first; the word 'Receipts' was scrawled on the outside. He shook out the contents and saw a pile of payment slips, two from restaurants, three from petrol stations, five for train tickets, two for books on criminology bought from Amazon, another from a hotel in Guildford, *double room, breakfast for two,* he noted, recalling a policing conference in the Surrey town two months earlier that he had declined to attend. *Maybe she took Marina,* he thought.

Or possibly not. Might Toni have been capable of taking the so-called Don Sturgeon along for the ride, and slipping him on to her expenses?

He stuffed the slips back into the envelope and picked up the next. His eyebrows rose when he saw his own name written on the front. He was about to open it when he found a second envelope attached, stuck to it by the gum on its unsealed flap. He prised them apart and read another name, 'P. Friedman'. He looked inside, but it was empty, and so he laid it aside and slid out the contents of his own.

He found himself looking at two photographs of himself. From the background he saw that they had been taken surreptitiously at ACPOS, probably by Toni, with a mobile phone while his attention had been elsewhere. They were clipped on to a series of handwritten notes.

As he read them he saw that they were summaries of every meeting they had ever attended together, and one that had been just the two of them, when he had paid a courtesy call on her in Pitt Street in the week she had taken up office. That note was the most interesting.

Robert M. Skinner (Wonder what M stands for?)

The top dog in Scotland he thinks, come to let me know no doubt that he could have had my job for the asking . . . if he only knew. Tough on him; this is the season of the bitch. Sensitive about his politician wife. Eyes went all cold when I asked about her. Wonder if he knows what I do, about her screwing the actor guy every time he's in Glasgow. Or if he'd like me to show him the evidence. If he knew about the other one! But that definitely stays my secret, till the time is right.

Skinner's eyes widened as he read.

The man has testosterone coming out of his pores, which makes it all the more ironic that his wife plays away, as did the one before, from what I hear. As a cop, old school. He will not be an ally over unification. Question is, will he be an opponent for the job? Think he will, whatever he says; he's a pragmatist, used to power, and not being questioned. Also, will he stand for Scotland's top police officer being a woman, and a black one at that? Sexist? Racist? His sort usually are, if old Bullshit is anything to go by. Must work out a way to take him out of the game. Main weakness is his wife; use what I know and work on getting more on her. Other weakness his daughter, but she's protected by the dangerous Mr Martin so too much trouble. Summary: an enemy, but can be handled.

'No wonder this fucking woman got herself killed,' he murmured to himself. 'I might have been tempted to do it myself.'

He replaced the notes and the photographs, then turned to the next envelope. It was inscribed 'Bullshit'. It contained nothing but photographs, of Toni Field and a man. In one they were both in police uniform, but in the others they were highly informal. It was all too apparent that at least one of the participants had been completely unaware that they were being taken, most of all in one in which he was clad only in his socks.

Skinner stared. He gaped. And then he laughed. 'Bullshit,' he said. 'B. S. for short. B. S. for Brian Storey, Sir Brian bloody Storey, deputy assistant commissioner then, going by his uniform, but now Commissioner of the Metropolitan Police. And weren't he and Lady Storey guests in the royal box at Ascot a few weeks ago?'

His smile vanished. Was Brian Storey a man to be blackmailed and take it quietly? Maybe, maybe not.

He moved on to the next envelope. It was labelled 'Brum', another collection of candid camera shots of the star of the show with a West Midlands ACC, in line with Marina's account. Skinner knew the guy by sight but could not remember his name, a sign that the days when he might have been of use to Toni lay in the past.

The same was true of the men featured in the next two. The broadcast journalist had been a name a couple of years before but had passed into obscurity when he had signed up with Sky News. As for Chairman Mao, the only thing for which he was remarkable was the size of his penis, since Toni had been able, easily, to swallow it whole.

The fifth envelope in the sequence was 'Howling Mad'. There was something vaguely recognisable about the man, but if he was a QC as Marina had said, he would normally be seen publicly in wig and gown, as good a disguise as the chief constable had ever encountered. In addition, he was the only one of the five who was not seen completely naked, or in full face, only profile. However, there were a series of images possibly taken from a video, in which the pair were seen under a duvet, in what looked to be, even in the stills, vigorous congress.

'Howling Mad,' Skinner repeated. 'Who the hell are you, and why is that name vaguely familiar?'

His question went unanswered as he refilled the envelope and turned to the last. It was anonymous; there was no description of its contents on the outside. He upended it and more photographs fell out. They showed Toni Field as he had never seen her, out of uniform, without make-up, without her hair carefully arranged. In each image she was holding or watching over a child, at various ages, from infancy to early toddler.

He felt a pang of sadness. Little Lucille, who'd never see her mother again. One photograph was larger than the rest. It showed Toni, sitting up in a hospital bed, holding her child and flanked by Sofia and a man, Mauritian. He had given his daughter his high forehead and straight, slightly delicate nose. *And how much of his character?* Skinner wondered.

He was replacing the photographs and making a mental note to hand them over to Marina, after burning four of the others . . . the 'Bullshit' file was one to keep . . . when he realised that something had not fallen out when they did. He reached inside with two fingers and drew out a document.

He whistled as he saw it, knowing at once what it was even if its style was unfamiliar to him. A birth certificate, serial number ending seven two six five, recording the safe arrival of Mauritian citizen Lucille Sofia Deschamps, mother's name, Antonia Maureen Deschamps, nationality Mauritian, father's name Murdoch Lawton, nationality British.

In the days when Trivial Pursuit was the only game in town, Bob Skinner had been the man to avoid, or the man to have on your team. There was never a fact, a name or a link so inconsequential that he would not retain it.

'Murdoch,' he exclaimed. '*The A Team*, original TV series not the iffy movie, crazy team member, "Howling Mad" Murdock, spelled the American way but near enough and that's how Toni would have pronounced it anyway, played by Dwight Schultz. Hence the nickname, but who the hell is he?'

Sarah's iPad was lying on the coffee table. He picked it up, clicked on the Wikipedia app, and keyed in the name of the father of little Lucille Deschamps.

When Sarah came back into the room he was staring at the tablet's small screen, his face frozen, his expression so wild that it scared her.

'Bob,' she called out, 'are you all right?'

He shook himself back to life. 'Never better, love,' he replied, and his eyes were exultant. 'Can you print from this thing?' he asked.

'Of course. Why?'

'Because the whole game is changed, my love, the whole devious game.'

Fifty-Four

'Are ye sure you're all right, kid?' Since his visit earlier in the evening he had called her three times and on each occasion he had put the same question. Lottie understood; she knew that he was hurting almost as much as she was, but was incapable of saying so.

'I promise you, Dan, I'm okay. That's to say I'm not a danger to myself, or to wee Jakey. Nobody's going to break in here tomorrow and find me hanging from the banisters. Ask me how I feel instead and I'll tell you that I'm hurt, embarrassed, disappointed and blazing mad, but I'll get over all that . . . apart, maybe, from the blazing mad bit. I've made a decision since you called me earlier. Jakey's going to his granny's tomorrow and I'm coming back to work.'

'But Lottie,' Provan began.

She cut him off. 'Don't say it, 'cos I know that I can have nothing to do with the Field investigation, but there's other crime in Glasgow; there always is.'

'The chief constable said ye should stay at home until everything's sorted.'

'As far as I'm concerned it is sorted. Scott's been charged, right?'

'Right.'

'He's no longer in custody, right?'

'Right.'

'And I'm not suspected of being involved in what he did, right?'

'Right.'

'Thank you,' she said. 'In that case, there is no reason for me to be stuck in the house twiddling my thumbs. The longer I do that the more it will look like I'm mixed up in my husband's stupidity. So, Detective Sergeant, I will see you tomorrow. If the chief doesn't like it, the only way he'll get me out of there is by formally suspending me, and as you've just agreed, he doesn't have any grounds to do that. I won't come into the investigation room in Pitt Street. I'll go to our own office in Anderston instead.'

'Then ye'll see me there. The chief's told me to shut down the Pitt Street room. He says the investigation's went as far as it can, and there's no point in our bein' there any longer.'

'Why?' she asked, surprised. 'Have we run out of leads?'

'Worse than that. Everywhere we've gone, some bugger's been there before us. See ye the morra.'

As Lottie hung the wall phone back on its cradle in the hallway, her eye was caught by a movement. She looked at the front door and saw a figure; it was unrecognisable, its shape distorted by the obscure glass, but she knew who it was. She felt a strange fluttering in her stomach, and realised that she was a little afraid. She thought of calling Dan back. She thought of going back into the living room and listening to loud music through her headphones.

But she did neither of those things. Instead her anger overcame her nervousness, and she marched to the door and threw it open.

Her husband stood on the step, with a key in his hand, wavering towards the Yale lock that was no longer within reach. She snatched it from him.

'Gimme,' he protested.

'No danger. You'll not be needing it any longer.' She grabbed him by one of the lapels of his sports jacket and pulled him indoors.

'Aw thanks, love,' he sighed, misunderstanding her.

'Thanks for nothing,' she replied. 'You won't be staying. You're as drunk as a monkey and I'm not putting on a show for the neighbours, that's all.'

'Ach Lottie, gie's a break. I'm goin' tae the fucking jail, is that not enough for you?'

'That's the last thing I want, you pathetic twat,' she hissed. 'What do you think that's going to do for your son at the school? Every kid in the place will be pointing fingers at him and calling him names. The only thing that'll save him from being bullied is that all of them know me. As for your slapper, though, that McGlashan, they can stick her in Cornton Vale for as long as they like.'

'Leave Christine out of this,' Scott snarled, lurching towards her.

'I'd leave her out of the human race,' she retorted, her voice filled with scorn. 'And you take one more step towards me,' she added, 'and it won't be a police car that'll come for you, it'll be an ambulance. It was you that brought her into it. I hope you're happy that you've ruined her life as well as your own. If I didn't feel the contempt for her that any woman would feel, and that any good police officer would feel five times over, I could actually find it in my heart to be sorry for the poor cow. Do you have the faintest idea how cruel you've been in even asking her to do what she did, far less in talking her into it?

'I know you and she were at it before we met, and I suspect that you always have been, behind my big stupid plodding back. That can only mean that the daft bitch actually feels something for you. And that you've let her down just as badly as you've betrayed and shamed Jakey and me.'

She took him by the arm, as if she was arresting him and began to push him towards the door. 'Now go,' she ordered, 'and don't you ever come back here.'

'Lottie,' he pleaded, 'gie's a break.'

'Certainly. Which arm would you prefer?'

'Ah've got nowhere else tae go!'

'No? Why don't you just go to her place?'

'Aye, that'll be right. Her husband's lookin' for me as it is.'

'Her what? Well, I'll tell you what, you go down to the riverside and find yourself a nice bench to sleep on, so that if he comes here, I can tell him where to find you.' She opened the front door and thrust him outside. 'As soon as I get inside,' she warned him, 'I'm going to phone the station. If you're seen within a mile of this house for the rest of the night, you'll be lifted. But I won't tell them to arrest you. Oh no, I'll have them drive you to Christine McGlashan's house, drop you there and ring the doorbell. You think I wouldn't do that, you snivelling bastard?' she challenged.

He shook his head.

'Aye, damn right I would. You know, Scott, what I feel right now, looking at you? I feel ashamed that I let you father my son. Well, I tell you this. There is no way that I will let you pass your weakness on to him. It might hurt him for a bit, but you're never going to see him again.'

With that, Charlotte Mann slammed the door on her husband, walked quietly into her living room, slumped into an armchair, and wept as she had never wept before.

Fifty-Five

'It's bloody warm in this city,' Lowell Payne remarked, as they stood on the pavement outside Thames House.

'It can be in the summer,' Skinner conceded. 'I have this theory that all big cities generate their own heat. Mind you, it can be cold here too. I remember, oh, must be twenty years ago now, standing here on Millbank one evening in February, with a wind whistling up the Thames that felt as if it had come all the way from Siberia. That's still the coldest I've ever been in my life.'

'Are we going to get a chilly reception in here, d' you think?'

'No, I don't, but things may cool down quite a bit once we get going.'

'Who are we meeting?'

'I'm not absolutely certain. As things stand, our appointment is with Amanda Dennis, the deputy director of the service. Whether she has anyone with her, that may depend on whether she guesses why we're here.'

'What's my role?'

'You're a witness,' Skinner told him. 'Did you do what I suggested?'

'Tell Jean, you mean?' Payne frowned. 'No, I didn't, I'm sorry. You've known her for longer than I have, so I shouldn't have to tell you that if I just happened to mention casually that you and I were off to a top-level meeting with MI5 but I couldn't tell her what it was about, she'd have gone into full worry mode, and not slept a wink. Did you tell Sarah?'

'Of course. Sarah gave up worrying about me years ago.'

'Did you tell her what the meeting's about?'

'No, and she didn't ask. She's used to me moving in mysterious ways. She calls me God, sometimes.'

The DCI grinned and shook his head. 'What is it with you two?'

'What do you think?'

'Honestly?'

'Always. I'd expect nothing else.'

'I think that Aileen getting caught out with Joey Morocco came in very handy for both of you.'

'What does Jean think?' Bob asked.

'There's nothing for her to think about,' Lowell told him, 'as far as you and Sarah are concerned, not yet, but she'll be fine. They didn't know it at the time, but I heard her and Alex compare notes one day. Neither of them were too keen on Aileen.'

'I know that now.'

'I've got nothing against her, mind, but on the two occasions that I've met Sarah, I thought that she was a sensational woman and that the two of you together just filled the whole room.'

'Maybe we did at that, Lowell. We lost our way for a while, that was all. I hope we've found it again.'

'What's made the difference?'

'I've stopped living in the past. Recently, somebody very close to me told me that for the last twenty and a bit years, since Myra was killed in that bloody car, I've been in denial, that I've never accepted it, never moved on. I've come to accept that's true. It drove Sarah and me apart, and with Aileen . . . I made myself see Myra in her, when in fact they couldn't be more different. Myra was wild, self-indulgent and she lived her life on the spur of the moment. She was also promiscuous, as Jean may have told you, more than I ever was, even when I was single.

'Aileen, on the other hand, is one of the most calculating people I have ever known. I don't mean that unkindly, not any more, but everything she does is to a plan, and everyone around her must conform to it, even me.

'She supports police unification for two reasons. One, she does believe in it, but two, she thought that it would make me leave the force and help her achieve her real ambitions, which don't lie in Scotland, but down here, in Westminster.

'I'm sure she'll get there, but not with my help. As for me, as was said to me, my soul's been broken, but Sarah's helping me fix it, and I feel more at peace with myself than I have in years.' He checked his watch. 'And I'll be even more so when we've done our business here. Are you all set?'

'Yes, I'm ready.'

'Good. Come on then, I like to be bang on time when I visit this place.'

They entered the headquarters of the Security Service through a modest door to the right of the building's great archway, and stepped up to a reception desk that might have belonged to any civil service department. Skinner announced them to one of the uniformed staff. When he told the man that he had an appointment with Mrs Dennis, there was a subtle change in his attitude. He checked a screen that the police officers could not see, then nodded.

'Yes, gentlemen,' he announced. 'I'll let the DD know you're here and she'll send someone down to collect you.' He made a quick phone call, then filled in two slips, which he inserted in plastic cases and handed them over, one to each. 'These must be surrendered on leaving. Now, if you'll follow me, I'll check you in through our electronic security. It's just like an airport, really.'

'I know,' Skinner said. 'But I have a pacemaker so you'll have to pat me down.'

'That won't be necessary, Rashid,' a woman called out.

The chief constable looked over towards a line of lift doors and saw Amanda Dennis approach. 'Oh, but it will,' he insisted. 'I'm not having your lot plant a gun on me when we get upstairs then say I carried it in.'

She laughed. 'Damn it! There goes Plan A.'

The deputy director of MI5 was not what Lowell Payne had been expecting. In his mind he had pictured Dame Judi Dench, or someone like her. Instead he saw someone who was around fifty, with dark, well-cut hair and sparkling eyes that had none of the chilly aloofness that were a feature of her film and television equivalents.

'Hi, Mandy,' Skinner greeted her when the security search was over and he and Payne had retrieved their bags from x-ray. 'Good to see you; this is DCI Payne, Lowell, my sidekick, but you'll know that by now.' He kissed her on the cheek. 'You're looking better than ever. Still finding time for the toy boy?'

She winked. 'Shows, does it?'

'Does he still think you work in a flower shop?'

'No, it closed down. Now he thinks I'm a proof-reader in a law firm.' She grinned. 'Actually he knows exactly what I do. He's a bright enough chap to read the parliamentary reports where my name crops up occasionally. You know how it is, Bob. It's the junior ranks who have to be anonymous. Thanks to John bloody Major, the rest of us can't.'

'I know,' he sympathised, as they stepped into a lift. 'The Don

Sturgeons of this world have to be protected, but you and Hubert can walk around with targets on your backs.'

'Who on earth is Don Sturgeon?' she remarked, but did not wait for an answer. 'As for Hubert, why do you want to see me? He's the director, not me.'

'He's also a prat, a Home Office toady dropped in here because the Prime Minister of the day decided the place needed some new blood, after that wee scandal you and I uncovered a couple of years back. He may have been the transfusion, but you're still the heartbeat.'

The elevator stopped and they stepped out, then along a corridor. Mrs Dennis unlocked her office door and followed them into the room. It was oak-panelled and grandly furnished, in contrast to the utilitarian style of the reception area.

'Welcome,' she said. 'We'll use the conference table, but before we start, Bob, I assume you'd like coffee.'

He held up a hand. 'No thanks, Amanda, I've signed the coffee pledge, and Lowell here had a Starbucks on the way up from Victoria. By the way,' he added, 'he was propositioned by a whore, sorry, that's non-PC, by a sex worker in his hotel last night. Very English, could even have been public school. Three hundred quid. Isn't that right, Lowell?'

'Yes indeed, Chief. She said it was her way of paying off her mortgage.'

'Unluckily for her, he's a Jock, and a tight-fisted bastard like all of us. She wasn't one of yours, was she?'

'She could have been,' the deputy director replied. 'About a third of the women in this place fit that description. But if she was, she wasn't on duty. We tend to use Russian girls, or Polish. That's what our targets expect, and let's face it, chaps,' she winked, 'have you ever met a posh English girl who really knew how to fuck?'

Skinner laughed out loud. 'As a matter if fact I have, but you probably know about her. Likely she's on my file.'

'Come on, Bob,' she chided him. 'We don't keep files on senior police officers.'

'Of course you bloody do, Amanda. You keep files on everyone, apart from the odd militant Islamist who slips through the net and blows up a London bus. For example, you kept a file on Beram Cohen. I know that, because you sent my young friend Clyde Houseman through to see me last Saturday, to tell me who he was. What I didn't understand at the time was why MI5 should know about Cohen. He wasn't Islamic, he was Jewish. He wasn't an internal security threat to us. No, he was an Israeli secret service operative who got compromised and had to vanish.'

'Yes,' she agreed, 'and we helped, as you know by now. We did a favour via our friends in MI6, for their friends in Mossad, and took him on board.'

'You turned him into Byron Millbank?'

She frowned and the change seemed to add a couple of years to her age in the time it took. 'What a bloody stupid name! I was livid when I heard about it, but when it was done I wasn't involved. I was running our serious crime division then.'

'I imagine it flagged up with you as soon as my people ran a DVLA check on him.'

'Yes, that's how it happened.'

'And as soon as it did, you broke into the Rondar offices and removed his computer.'

'We did, as a precaution, although it turned out to be unnecessary. He seems to have kept his two identities absolutely separate.'

'But you knew he still functioned as Beram?'

'I did, and a very few others. Six advised us of a couple of operations he had undertaken for them and for the Americans. There was the one in Somalia, for example; that's how we knew of the connection between him, Smit and Botha. As soon as you came looking for him, trying to identify his body, I knew that something was up.'

'And you knew who the target was, but you didn't tell me,' Skinner said. 'Because MI5 wanted her dead.'

She stared back at him. 'Of course not,' she protested. 'Why the hell are you saying that?'

Lowell Payne had been following the exchange, fascinated; he had sat in on, or led, hundreds of interviews during his career, and he realised what Skinner was doing. As Dennis spoke, he detected a very subtle shift in her posture, as if she had slipped, very slightly, on to the defensive.

'Because I believe it's true,' the chief replied. 'Twenty-four hours ago, I was simply curious about the chain of events, mostly because of Basil "Bazza" Brown. As you said earlier, Mandy, you used to run the serious crimes operation in this place. Inevitably that would involve you in suborning criminals up and down the country and turning them into informants, either through blackmail or bribery.

'When we found Bazza's body in the boot of Smit and Botha's supposed getaway car . . . rented by Byron Millbank . . . and we checked him out through NCIS, they'd never heard of him. Now, Bazza might not quite have been one half of the Kray Twins, but he was a person of significant interest to Strathclyde CID and the Scottish Serious Crimes and Drugs Agency. So it just wasn't feasible that he wouldn't be on the national criminal database, unless he had been taken off it, and the only organisation I can think of with the clout to do that, is yours. Come on, he was an MI5 asset, wasn't he? Give me that much.'

She sighed, then smiled. 'I should have known,' she murmured. 'Yes, he was. I turned him myself.'

'Thought so. By the way, was Michael Thomas involved in any way, my ACC?'

'Yes, I had to involve him at one point, on pain of disgrace if he breathed a word. Why?'

'It answers a question, that's all. And gets him off a nasty hook.' He paused, straightening in his seat. 'Okay,' he went on, 'so you must see where I'm coming from. I've uncovered an operation in Scotland, planned by a man who is known to MI5. Then right in the middle, I find a key equipment supplier, eliminated to keep him quiet, and I discover that he was also known to you. At the very least that was going to start me wondering. You've got to concede that, chum.'

'Yes, okay, I do. But answer me this. If we were behind it, why did I send Clyde Houseman through to see you, to tell you who Cohen was? Surely I'd have kept quiet about it all.'

'No,' Skinner murmured. 'You wouldn't have taken that chance. If you had you'd have been betting that I wouldn't have found out about the operation on my own, without your help, and you know me too well for that. So you sent Clyde with his order, and with his personal connection to me to cloud my judgement.

'I bought into him, but now I've come to believe that his job was to make sure that the hit went ahead; not to help me, but to get in my way, and to keep me from getting to the concert hall on time, by any means necessary.'

'And I gave him orders to shoot you if he had to? Come on, old love,' she protested.

'No,' he conceded, 'just to fuck me about, to make sure we were chasing the wrong hare. It worked too. We didn't find out that the target was female until it was too late. Even then, when we did, I still assumed that it was political, as Clyde had said, and that meant that it had to be Aileen, my wife.'

'Bob,' Dennis murmured. 'This is all very flight of fancy. What on earth has brought it about?'

'Two things. First, you told me that official MI5 policy has been to steer clear of cooperation with the Strathclyde Counter-Terrorism Intelligence Section because you didn't trust Toni Field. But in fact I find out that you've had her under very close supervision, through Clyde Houseman, or Don Sturgeon, the identity he used to . . . how to say it . . . penetrate her.'

Amanda smiled and raised an eyebrow.

'Second,' Skinner continued, 'I've solved a mystery.'

'It seems to me that you've created one, but go on.'

'Toni Field's secret child, Lucille.'

'Her what?' Dennis exclaimed.

'Come on, Mandy, Clyde must have told you she had a kid. The scar was a clear giveaway, as we found at her autopsy. As soon as I heard about it, I found myself wondering why. Why did she have to hide the fact, take a sabbatical and fuck off to Mauritius to have the baby under her old name?

'A child wouldn't have been a roadblock in her career, not these days, and not even as a single parent, for Toni's mother's hale and hearty and still young enough to help raise her, as she is doing.

'So I started wondering who Daddy was, and I started to consider five people that Marina, her sister, told me about, five men in her life before they came to Scotland. The only problem was, Marina didn't know them by name, only nickname.'

'How inconvenient.' Her tone was teasing, but Payne, the shrewd observer, detected tension beneath it.

'Yeah. But somebody must have known one of them, somebody with the resources to hack into the Mauritian general registry and remove all records of the birth. If it hadn't been for the hospital patient log, we'd never have been able to prove it happened at all. Nice one, my dear. Tell me, did you have to send someone to Mauritius or were you able to do it without leaving this building?' He looked at her, inquiring, but she was silent.

'Yup,' he chuckled. 'This week, it's been a whole series of dead ends, until I found out about Mr Sturgeon and until a specialist thief of my acquaintance finally managed to get into Toni's safe, in what's now my office.' He picked up his attaché case and opened it. 'When I did, I found these.' He removed two envelopes and placed them on the table.

Amanda Dennis frowned and pulled her chair in a little. She reached out for the envelopes, but Skinner drew them back. 'All in good time,' he said. 'There were three others, but their subjects were of no relevance to this, so I've destroyed them. These two, though, they tell a story.'

He removed the contents of the envelope marked 'Bullshit' and passed them across.

As the deputy director studied them, her eyebrows rose and her eyes widened. 'Bloody hell!' she murmured.

'I wondered if you knew about him,' Skinner remarked. 'Now, I gather that you didn't. I expect you'll find that when Toni was appointed to both West Midlands and Strathclyde, Sir Brian Storey gave her glowing testimonials, both times. I don't like the man, so if you use these to bring him down, it won't bother me.'

He picked up 'Howling Mad' and reached inside. 'These, on the other hand, are a whole different matter.' He withdrew several photographs. 'I didn't know who this bloke was at first,' he said, as he handed them across, 'the one she's fucking, but I do now. Once he was Murdoch Lawton, QC, a real star of the English Bar. In fact he was such a big name that the Prime Minister gave him a title, Lord

Forgrave, and brought him into the Cabinet as Justice Secretary.

'There he sits at the table alongside his wife, Emily Repton, MP, the Home Secretary, the woman who controls this organisation, and to whom you and Hubert Lowery answer.'

She stared at the images. Even to Payne, that most skilled reader of expressions, she was inscrutable.

'Those are bad enough,' the chief constable told her, 'even without this.' He took Lucille Deschamps' birth certificate from the envelope and laid it down. 'You knew about it of course, since MI5 removed the original registration. Lawton knocked her up, fathered her child.' He sighed, with real regret.

'So now you see, my friend, how I'm drawn to the possibility that Toni Field was murdered by this organisation, to prevent her from advancing herself even further than she had already by blackmailing the woman at its head, and her husband.

'Amanda, I don't actually believe that you'd be party to that, which is why I've brought this to you and not to Lowery, who'd probably have the Queen shot if he was ordered to.'

Amanda Dennis leaned back, linked her fingers behind her head and looked up at the ceiling. 'Oh dear, Bob,' she sighed. 'If only you hadn't.'

As she spoke, a door at the far end of the room swung open and two people came into the room, one large, the other small, almost petite. Skinner had met the man before, at a secret security conference the previous autumn, not long after his appointment as Director of MI5, but not the woman. Nonetheless, he knew who she was, from television and the press.

Dennis stood; Payne followed her lead instinctively, but Skinner stayed in his seat. 'Home Secretary,' he exclaimed, 'Hubert. Been eavesdropping, have we?'

'No!' the director snapped. 'We've been monitoring a conversation that borders on seditious. To accuse us of organising a murder . . .'

'Go back and listen to the recording that you've undoubtedly made,' the chief constable said. 'You'll find no such accusation. I'm investigating a crime, and my line of inquiry has led me here. You people may think you're off limits, but not to me.'

As Sir Hubert Lowery's massive frame leaned over him, the chief re-called a day when, as a very new uniformed constable, he had policed a Calcutta Cup rugby international at Murrayfield Stadium, in which the man had played in the second row of the scrum, for England.

'Skinner,' the former lock hissed, 'you're notorious as a close-to-the-wind sailor, but this time you've hit the rocks.'

He pushed himself to his feet. 'Get your bad analogies and your bad breath out of my face, you fat bastard,' he murmured, 'or you will need some serious dental work.'

Lowery leaned away, but only a little. Skinner put a hand on his chest and pushed, hard enough to send him staggering back a pace or two. 'You were never any use on your own,' he said. 'You always needed the rest of the pack to back you up.'

'Bob!' Dennis exclaimed.

He grinned. 'No worries, Amanda. He doesn't have the balls.'

'Probably not,' the Home Secretary said, 'but I do. Let me see these.' She snatched up the photographs. 'The idiot!' she snapped as she examined them. 'Bad enough to get involved with that scheming little bitch, but to let himself be photographed on the job, it's beyond belief, it really is. Are these the only copies?'

'I'd say so,' Skinner replied, sitting once again. 'Toni was too smart to leave unnecessary prints lying around. Plus, she thought she was untouchable.' He took a memory card from the breast pocket of his jacket and tossed it on to the table. 'I found that among the envelopes. The originals are on it.'

Emily Repton picked it up, and the birth certificate. She walked across to the deputy director's desk and fed the photographs into the shredder that stood beside it. The memory card followed it. She was about to insert the birth certificate when Payne called out, 'Hey, don't do that! The child's going to need it.'

The Home Secretary gave him a long look. 'What child?' she murmured. The shredder hummed once again. 'Why did you give those up so easily?' she asked the chief constable.

'Because I'm a realist. I've been in this building before. I know what it's about, and I know that there are certain things that are best kept below decks, as Barnacle Hubert the Sailor here might say. But they're kept in my head too, and in DCI Payne's.'

'Sometimes it can be a lot harder to get out of here than to get in,' Repton pointed out.

'Not in this case,' Skinner told her. 'We're being collected in about half an hour from the front of Thames House by Chief Superintendent McIlhenney, of the Met. If we're any more than five minutes late, he will leave, and will come back, with friends.'

She smiled. 'See, Sir Hubert. I said you were underestimating this man. What's your price, our friend from the north?'

He pointed at Lowery. 'He goes. Amanda becomes Director General, as she should have been all along. Then you go.'

'What about my husband? Do you want his head too?'

'Nah. I imagine you'll cut his balls off as soon as you get him home for landing you in all this. I wouldn't wish any more on the guy.'

'I see.' She frowned and pursed her lips, calling up an image from the past as she stood in her pale blue suit, with every blonde hair in place. 'The first of those is doable, because you're right: Sir Hubert

344

isn't up to the job, and Mrs Dennis is. The second, no, not a chance.'

'No? You don't think I'd bring you down?'

'I don't think you can. Okay, my husband had an affair with someone he met in the course of his work at the Bar and, unknown to him, fathered her child. I'll survive that . . . and it's all you have on me.'

Her mirthless smile was that of an approaching shark, and all of a sudden Skinner felt that the ground beneath his feet was a little less solid.

'Explain, Amanda,' she said.

'We didn't do it, Bob.' His friend looked at him with sympathy in her eyes, and he found himself hating it. 'When you asked to see me, I was afraid this was how it would develop. The thing is, we knew about the child, and we knew of Toni Field's ambitions, which were, granted, without limits, but we felt they were pretty much contained.

'We knew what the sabbatical had been about, even before she went on it. After we deleted the Mauritian birth record, we felt she had nothing to use against us, or against the Home Secretary, so we simply parked her in Scotland, with Brian Storey's assistance. I can see now why he was so keen to help.' She grinned, but only for a second.

'We made her your problem, Bob, not ours. No, we didn't know about the photos, but if we had, I'd have been relying on you or someone like you to find them, as you did. As for the birth certificate, well, we thought that had been dealt with.

'Oh sure, she still had her career planned in her head, Scotland, and then the Met as Storey's successor, but in reality, she'd never have got another job in England. Toni Field was a boil, that was all, and we thought we had lanced her, so there was no need to bump her off.'

'So why did you plant Clyde with her?' he asked. 'To check whether she had any more damaging secrets?'

'Bob, we never did! There was no liaison, there was no Don Sturgeon. Clyde never met the woman, I promise you.'

Skinner gaped at her as he experienced something for the first time in his life: the feeling of being a complete fool, dupe, idiot.

'This is bluff,' he exclaimed. 'Repton's laid down the party line for you.' But as he did, he thought of his own ruse with Houseman, and knew that she was right.

'I'm afraid not.' She rose, walked across to her desk, and produced a paper, from a drawer. 'This is a printout of the data we removed from the Mauritian files. It shows, along with everything else, the name and nationality of the person who registered the birth, and it even carries her signature.'

She handed it to him.

'Marina Deschamps,' he read, his voice sounding dry and strange.

'Exactly. She's how we came to know about the child, and who her father was. The same Marina who told you she didn't know any of her sister's lovers by name. Marina, who invented Toni's relationship with Clyde Houseman. Marina, who it is now clear to me had her half-sister killed.' She smiled at him once more, but with sadness in her eyes. 'My dear, I'm sorry, but you've been played. The scenario you have in your head, about the Home Secretary having Toni assassinated, to keep her husband's dark secret and to spare the government from possible collapse in the ensuing scandal, it's plausible, I'll admit, but it seems that Marina put it there. But don't feel too bad about it,' she added. 'She was an expert. She used to be one of us.'

'She what?' he spluttered.

'She worked here for five years, in MI5, with a pretty high security clearance. When she applied, she was with the Met, and Brian Storey recommended her for the job.'

'Doesn't that tell you something?' he challenged her. 'Given that Toni had Storey by the balls?'

'With hindsight it does. But he may have done it to get himself a little protection from her. Marina left here when Toni took the job in Birmingham. That was our idea originally; we wanted to keep a continuing eye on her and she agreed to do it. She sold it to her sister, so well that she thought it was her own wheeze. Marina's been keeping an eye on her all along.'

'Did Toni ever know she was a spook?' Payne asked, as his boss sat silent, contemplating what he had been told.

'No, never.' Dennis gave a soft chuckle. 'Believe it or not, she also thought Marina worked in a flower shop, of sorts, after she left the Met. I can and will check, but I'm certain that while she was here she would have been in a position to know about Beram Cohen, and his second identity, and that she'd have known about poor old Bazza too.'

She looked at Skinner. 'You do believe me, Bob, don't you? If you don't, there's an easy way to test me. Call her, at home. Send a car to pick her up, under some pretext or other. She won't be there, I promise you.'

He glared back at her. 'Then tell me why,' he demanded. 'Tell me why she did it.'

'If I knew,' Amanda replied, 'I would tell you, without hesitation. But I don't. I don't have a clue. All I can suggest is that you find her and ask her. However, if you do, and knowing you I imagine that you might, you must hand her over to us. None of the stuff that we've talked about here could ever come out in open court.'

'Don't you worry about that,' he growled. 'It won't.' He started to rise, Payne following.

'Hold on just a moment,' the Home Secretary said. 'We're not done yet, not quite. There is still the matter of your continuing silence on this business. I'm not letting you leave without that being secured.'

'How are you going to do that? I've got nothing to gain, personally, by going public, but if you knew anything about Scots law and procedures, you'd realise that having begun the investigation I'm bound to report its findings to the procurator fiscal.'

'Then it will have to be edited, otherwise . . .'

He looked at her, and realised that she was a rarity, a politician who should not, rather than could not, be underestimated. He had read a description of Emily Repton as 'a prime minister in waiting, but not for much longer'. Feeling the force of the certainty that radiated from her, he understood that assessment.

'Otherwise?' he repeated.

'Show him, Sir Hubert,' she murmured.

'No,' Skinner countered, 'I don't listen to him. You tell me.'

'Very well.' She reached out a hand; Lowery took a plastic folder from his pocket and passed it to her.

She selected a photograph and held it up. 'You seem to have recovered well from the public break-up of your marriage, Chief Constable. This was taken early this morning, as you left the home of your former wife.'

'So what?' he laughed. 'Our children are with her just now, and I wanted to see them.'

'But you have joint custody; you'll see them at the weekend.'

He snatched the image from her, crumpled it, and threw it on the floor. 'Go on, then,' he challenged her. 'Leak it and see what follows. I'll tell the Scottish media that it's a Tory plot to discredit me. See those two words "Tory plot"? In Scotland they're a flame to the touch paper. They'll be on you like piranha. You've got to do better than that.'

'I can. Your ex-wife is an American citizen. Now that you and she are no longer married, she's here because she's been given right to remain. That can be revoked.'

'We'd see you in court if you tried that.'

'It would have to be an American court; we'd have her removed inside twenty-four hours.'

'And twenty-four hours after that I'm on a plane to New York and we remarry. Come on, Home Secretary, up your game. You still need to do better.' And yet, as he spoke, he sensed that she could, and that her first two shots had been mere range-finders.

'If you insist,' she replied, and her voice told him that he had been right. 'It might come as a surprise to you to learn that your present wife's liaison with Mr Joey Morocco has been going on for years. It began before you met and it continued during your marriage.'

She took a series of photographs from the folder and handed them to him. He glanced through them; they showed Aileen and the actor at various locations: in a garden with Loch Lomond stretched out below them, on the balcony of her Glasgow flat, leaving a hotel in a street he did not recognise. None of them were explicit, but they displayed intimacy clearly enough.

He handed them back, and shrugged. 'Sorry, no surprise,' he said. 'Nor is it my business any more either. By the way, after the *Daily News* photos you might be able to sell those to *Hello!* or *OK!* but nobody else is going to buy them.'

'Probably not,' Repton conceded, 'but every newspaper in the country would run this, front page. The trouble with our modern celebrity culture is that it's so damn predictable. Where there are actors, there are the inevitable parties, with the same inevitable temptations. Most politicians have the sense to steer clear of them, but not, it seems, Ms de Marco.'

She took the last two items from the folder and gave them to him. The photographs had been taken in a ladies' toilet. There were three washbasins set into a flat surface, with a mirrored wall above.

The first picture showed two women, expensively clad, watching while a third, her face part-hidden by her hair, bent over a line of white powder, with a tube held to her nose. In the second, all three women were standing, their laughter, and their faces, reflected in the mirror.

He stared at it, then at Emily Repton with pure hatred in his eyes.

'The original is in a place of safety,' Sir Hubert Lowery barked. 'Not here, though, just in case Mrs Dennis feels obliged to do a favour for an old friend. I don't have to tell you . . .'

Skinner moved with remarkable speed for a man in his early fifties. He moved half a pace forward and hit the Director General with a thunderous, hooking, left-handed punch that caught him on the right temple. The man's legs turned to spaghetti and he was unconscious before he hit the floor.

'I've wanted to do that,' he murmured, 'ever since I saw him blindside our outside half at Murrayfield.'

'I did warn him,' Amanda Dennis remarked. 'I told him you'd want to hit somebody, and since he'd be the only man in the room . . .'

'He'll be all right,' the chief growled. 'His skull's too thick and his brain's too small for there to be any lasting damage.'

He turned to Emily Repton. Her eyes told him she had enjoyed the show. 'Spell it out,' he told her.

She nodded. 'Hard man, soft centre,' she said. 'Your marriage may be over, but I don't believe you would wish to cause Ms de Marco the damage, the distress and the disgrace that would follow publication of those images. The fact that it was a one-off doesn't matter. Her career would be gone, way beyond the U-bend, and so would her employable life. As indeed it will, if one single line in one single newspaper, or blog, should ever link my husband to Antonia Field and her child.

'You can write your report to the procurer physical or whatever he's called. It will say that your investigation has reached the conclusion that the balance of probability is that Chief Constable Field's killing was ordered and funded by Mexican or Colombian drug cartels that she compromised during her time with the Serious and Organised Crime Agency. There will be not the slightest hint of impropriety by the Security Service.'

She frowned. 'I'm not going to ask if you agree. There is no alternative on the table; you will do what you're told. Go back to Scotland, Mr Skinner, and be the big provincial copper in your little provincial pond. This is London; the power will always lie here. If you can't live with that truth, you could always resign.'

Skinner stared down at her, unblinking, until the coldness in his eyes made her shiver and look away.

'You really don't know me, Home Secretary,' he told her. 'My report's already dictated and that is more or less what it says. Even if my suspicions had been one hundred per cent right, there would have been no mileage for me in pulling this building down.'

He nodded towards Lowery, who was beginning to stir on the floor. 'Getting rid of him will do nicely thanks, and I've shown you why that has to happen.'

'Agreed,' Repton said.

'But you are right,' he continued, 'that I won't see Aileen broken by you. Hell, woman, I know you and Lowery set her up. Any idiot, even me, could see that. She can't hold her booze at the best of times, and I can tell from the photo she was rat-arsed when that all went off. I'm sure that if I could identify the two other women, I'd find that at least one was on Five's payroll.

'But that's by the by; I'll go along with your deal. Your husband's safe. If you're prepared to tolerate his adultery, that's your business. I've never met the man, so he really means nothing to me. Plus, I have no practical need to remove him, since he isn't in my sphere of influence.'

'That's pragmatic of you,' she mocked, her tone heavy with sarcasm.

'But you are,' he snapped, as he picked up his case. 'And you disgust me. You're the embodiment of everything I loathe about politics and politicians. Frankly, I don't want to be any part of any world in which someone like you operates, and there are only two things I can do about that. So I'll go back to my provincial, sub-national pond, and I will work out which one it's going to be.'

Fifty-Six

'No thanks, Amanda, I'll pass on that one personally. Maybe I'll send Lowell Payne instead. I was impressed by the way he handled himself the other day, and it's persuaded me that he's the man to take over what was a vacancy as head of CTIS.

'He's in post already. It wouldn't be right of me to come, when I might not be a police officer for much longer. You take care now, and watch your back as long as that woman's standing behind you.'

He ended the call and slipped his mobile into the big canvas bag that lay by his side.

'What was that about?' Sarah asked. They were sitting on a travelling rug on the beach at Gullane, watching their two sons trying to persuade Seonaid that the seawater was as warm as they said.

'Amanda Dennis,' he said. 'She's having a two-day review of the Field fiasco in London, on Monday and Tuesday. It's a natural response: what went wrong and how to prevent any recurrence. She said she's ordered Houseman and his entire Glasgow team down there, and asked if I wanted to attend.'

'Were you serious in what you said to her?'

'About Lowell? Sure. He never wavered in there and he turned out to be very good at reading people. He's a natural for the job, and it gives me grounds to give him an acting promotion, without anyone calling it nepotism. Mind you,' he chuckled, 'Jean wouldn't be too pleased if I send him off to London again so soon, so I don't think I'll pass on the invite.'

She shook her head. 'I didn't mean were you sure about Lowell. I was talking about the last part. Do you really mean that?'

'I think I do,' he said. 'I am edging myself towards walking away from the Strathclyde job and leaving the police service altogether, as soon as I can. All the way back from London I argued the toss with myself, and I still am arguing. It's doing my head in. I never wanted to destroy the Security Service itself, only to sort any people that might have crossed the line. I'm a realist, I understand how the world has to work at times. But given what I knew, or thought I knew, I had some questions that needed answers.

'As it was, I got it wrong, although not all of it: the Home Secretary did misuse her position by having Lowery delete the Mauritian birth record. Now I'm being blackmailed by Emily Repton herself, to save her husband's reputation and both their careers. You should have heard her, and seen her. That woman is fucking evil.'

'She threatened me? Really?'

'Yes, but we both knew that was crap; that was just her way of telling me how far she could reach into my life. I've taken legal advice since. Your passport may be American, but your children are British. There isn't a judge in Scotland who'd allow your deportation.'

'But her threat against Aileen? Is that for real?'

Bob nodded. 'Oh yes. She went with Morocco to a party in Glasgow, after the premiere of a movie he was in. They'd been watching the pair of them for long enough to be fairly sure she would go, especially since I was at a security conference that MI5 had set up.

'While Joey was away schmoozing the press, Hubert Lowery's two women got her shit-faced, possibly with a little chemical assistance, then set up the cocaine scene in the toilets. I know all this because Amanda made Lowery tell her as he was clearing his desk.'

'How did she make him cough that up?'

He gave a bitter laugh. 'She threatened to tell me where he lives. That was enough.'

'Can Amanda do anything about it, now she's in the top job?'

'Not with Emily Reptile as Home Secretary.'

'If you had been right, and Toni Field had been killed on Repton's orders, what would you have done?'

'As much as I could, although that might not have been a lot, since so many of the players are dead and so much of it is deniable.'

'Are you really satisfied that isn't what happened?'

He nodded. 'Yes, I'm sure. I got taken. As Mandy suggested, I did send a car to pick up Marina, as soon as I got out of there. She'd gone, right enough. Sofia thought she was just shopping . . . or so she said . . . but she hasn't been seen since. Amanda was right. The woman made me look like an idiot. Hell, I am an idiot! She fed me little hints to steer me in the direction she wanted, towards them and away from her.

'That last scene, her identifying Clyde Houseman as Toni's mystery lover, that was the final piece of the con. I bought it, like an absolute sucker, and went charging off down to London, to commit professional suicide.'

'It wasn't suicide,' Sarah insisted. 'You don't need to do anything so drastic as quit.' She paused. 'Don't go off on me for asking this, but could this depression from which speaking as a doctor, you are clearly suffering, be related to the fact that you feel humiliated, embarrassed, and maybe even a little unmanned by what this Marina woman did to you?'

'Why should I take the hump?' he asked. 'It's a fair question. But the answer's no. At the time, sure, I had a red face. Now, I see it the same as a golf game. Marina was good, and so was I. But where I shot a birdie, she had an eagle. When that happens out there on Gullane Number One, you don't give up the game. You say to the other guy, "Good shot," and then you stuff him at the next hole. If I leave the force, it'll be because I can't go after Repton from within it. But whatever happens, I'm going to find Marina Deschamps.'

She looked at him, a little afraid of the answer to the question she was about to pose. 'When you find her, what will you do?'

'I could eliminate her,' he told her. 'As long as I don't do it in the middle of Piccadilly Circus at rush hour, I really don't believe anyone would want to know. Too many guilty secrets.' He stopped, then laughed at the alarm on her face. 'I could,' he repeated, 'but don't worry, I won't. There is an alternative.'

He jumped up from the rug. 'Come on, let's go and paddle with the kids. The water can't be that cold.'

'Okay.' She took his hand and let him pull her to her feet, then laughed, as his phone sounded. 'I thought you were going to leave that at home,' she said.

'Force of habit. I'll ignore it.'

'Hell no,' she retorted, fishing it out of their beach bag. 'You'll fret if you do that.' She handed it to him. 'It's Mario.'

'Ah, that's different.' He took it from her and accepted the call. 'What is it?' he asked. 'Has Paula had the baby?'

'She has indeed,' the new father replied. 'Wee Eamon put in an appearance about half an hour ago. Like shelling peas, the midwife said, although not within Paula's hearing.'

'Big fella, that is absolutely great, I am so pleased for you both.'

'In that case, you're going to be even more pleased. About two hours ago a bloke walked into the St Leonards office with a bag that he found when he was sorting old clothes from one of those public recycling points. It was mixed up among them all, and there was a laptop inside it, wrapped in a shirt with a Selfridges label on it. The battery was flat, but the desk staff found a charger and plugged it in. When they switched it on, it said "Byron's MacBook". I reckon we've found your man Cohen's missing computer.'

Looking at Bob, Sarah saw his face light up, saw all his gloom and pessimism evaporate, and she knew that whatever he had been told, it had been a tipping point in his life.

'Mario,' she heard him exclaim, 'that's brilliant. It means the show's back on the road. I'd like it in Glasgow in my office, by Monday morning.' She thought he was about to end the call, but he went on, as if an afterthought had come to him just in time.

'One other thing,' he added. 'I want to see wee Ramsey again, but not in my office. Find him and tell him I'll be shopping in Fort Kinnaird at noon tomorrow and that I'll fancy a hot dog from the stall by the crossing. There'll be one in it for him as well if he turns up.'

Fifty-Seven

'Welcome back, Detective Inspector,' Skinner said, with feeling. He jerked his thumb in Provan's direction. 'This little bugger's been intolerable since you've been away.'

'Tell me about it,' Lottie chuckled. 'He's never been off the bloody phone. He'll be wanting to adopt me next.'

'Everything's all right at home, is it?' Her eyes went somewhere else for a second. 'Sorry,' he exclaimed. 'It's none of my business and if you don't want to talk about it, that's fine by me.'

'Not at all, Chief, not at all,' she replied. 'I had a tough couple of days, but I'm okay now. Scott's living with his brother out in Airdrie . . . at least that was the address they gave when he made his court appearance this morning. He turned up at the house again on Saturday, but he was sober, and it was only to collect his clothes.'

'Did you know that Sergeant . . .'

Her nod stopped him in mid-sentence. 'Yes, I was told. Her husband got himself arrested for thumping her. I'd have put in a word for him if he'd battered Scott, but he must have decided that hitting her was less risky. Maybe she's with him now. I don't know and I don't want to. Jakey's come to terms with the fact that his dad won't be back, and that's all I'm worried about.'

'Of course,' Skinner agreed. 'He's the most important person involved. Right,' he exclaimed, 'if we're all ready, let me explain to you what this is about.' He smiled. 'They thought it was all over . . .' he chuckled. 'But no, thanks to a large slice of luck, the game may still be on . . .' He rose, stepped over to his desk, and returned holding a laptop, which he laid on the table. '. . . and those who don't believe in miracles may like to have a rethink. That, lady and gentleman, is Byron Millbank's missing MacBook, the place where his wife told Detective Superintendent Payne that he kept his whole life. Normally,' he continued, 'there would have been a team of experts huddled over it for a week, trying to work out the password. In this case Byron gave us an unwitting clue, when he said to Mrs Millbank that the chances of getting into it were the same as winning the Lottery.

'So we had her rummage about among his personal things, and guess what she found? Yup, a payslip for a lottery season ticket.' He opened the computer to reveal a slip of paper, with six twin-digit numbers noted on it. 'There you are,' he said, and slid the slim computer across to Mann.

'Has anyone looked at it?' she asked.

'No, it's all yours. I want you and that bright young lad Paterson to get into it, and see if you can find anything that doesn't relate to the dull and fairly uneventful life of Mr Byron Millbank but to the rather more colourful world of Beram Cohen.'

'What about me, Chief?' Provan asked, with a hint of a rumble. 'Am Ah too old for that shite?'

Skinner threw him a sharp look. 'Almost certainly,' he said. 'But as it happens I've got something else in mind for you. I want you to get back on to your friends in Mauritius, and find the birth registration of Marina Deschamps. She's thirty-two years old, so the probability is that it will be a paper record. Birth date, April the ninth, so you'll know exactly where to look.'

'Marina Day Champs? The last chief's sister?'

'Not quite,' Skinner corrected him. 'The last chief's missing half-sister. There are things I don't know about that lady, and I want to.'

'Can Ah no' just ask her mother?'

'No chance. You do not go near her mother. Leave that to CTIS, Superintendent Payne's new team. She says she doesn't know where her daughter's gone, but we're tapping her phone, just in case. Like mother like daughters? You never know.'

Fifty-Eight

'The chief seems in better form today,' Dan Provan remarked, as they stepped back into the suite in Pitt Street that he had left the week before. 'When Ah saw him on Thursday, when Ah wis closing this place up, he wis like a panda that discovered he'd slept in and missed his big date wi' Mrs Panda.'

'Why's he interested in Marina Deschamps all of a sudden?' Lottie Mann pondered.

'How come you can say that and Ah cannae? Day Champs.'

'Possibly because I have a wider outlook on life than you, and expose myself to other cultures,' she suggested. 'You've got no interest in anything that doesn't involve crime, real or imaginary.'

'Maybe no,' but Ah'm shit hot at that. Ah've thought about puttin' ma name up for *Mastermind*.'

Beside him Banjo Paterson spluttered.

'You can laugh, son, but tell me, how many murders was Peter Manuel convicted of?'

'Eight.'

'No, seven. One charge wis dropped for lack of evidence. What was Baby Face Nelson's real name?'

'Who was Baby Face Nelson?

'Eedjit. Lester Gillis. What was Taggart's first sergeant called?'

'Mike?'

'Naw, he wis the second. It was Peter, Peter Livingstone.'

'Enough!' Lottie Mann laughed. 'If they ever have a "Brain of Cambuslang" contest you might be in with a shout, but until then stop showboating for the lad. All these things happened before he was born.'

'So did Christmas,' Provan retorted, 'but he knows all about that.'

He shuffled off to the desk he had adopted, and dug out the old-fashioned notebook that was still his chosen style of database. He opened it at the most recent entries and found the number of the Mauritian government. He keyed it in and waited.

'Mr Bachoo, please, Registry Department,' he asked. 'Tell him it's DS Provan again, Strathclyde Police in Glasgow, Scotland.'

Paterson grinned across at him. 'You didn't have any problem with that name,' he said.

'It sounds like a sneeze. Yes, Mr Bachoo,' he carried on, without a pause, 'it's me again. Ah've got another request for ye, another registration Ah'm trying to trace. This one goes back thirty-two years, but Ah've got a birth date this time: April the ninth. The name of the wean . . . Ah mean the child, is Marina Day Champs. Could ye do that for me?'

'Without difficulty,' the official replied. 'That period has not been computerised yet, and the records are kept on this floor. This time, could you hold on, please. Last week I was reprimanded for making a foreign call without permission.'

'Aye sure. Sorry about that; your bean counters must be worse than ours.'

'I beg your pardon?'

'Nothin', nothin'. Ah'll hold on.'

He leaned back in his chair, the phone pressed loosely to his ear, expecting more Bollywood music but hearing instead only the background chatter of an open-plan office. He glanced across at Paterson's desk but saw that it was empty, and guessed that the DC and DI were pressing on with their task.

He passed the time by listing, mentally and chronologically, the fictional officers who had been Jim Taggart's colleagues and successors, and the names of the actors who had played them. He was wondering, not for the first time, about the real relationship between Mike and Jackie, when he heard the phone in Mauritius being picked up.

'I have it,' Mr Bachoo announced, sounding pleased with himself. 'The child Marina Shelby Deschamps, Mauritian citizen, was born in Port Louis on the day you mentioned and registered on the following day. The mother was Sofia Deschamps, Mauritian citizen, and the father, who registered the birth, is named as Hillary, with two ls, Shelby, Australian citizen. I could fax this document to you; my superior has given me permission.'

'If ye would, Ah'd appreciate that.' He scrambled through the papers on the desk, and found the Pitt Street fax number, which he read out, digit by digit. 'Thanks, Mr Bachoo. Ah'm pretty sure that'll be all.'

'It was a pleasure, Detective Sergeant. As I believe you say, no worries.'

Provan smiled as he hung up, then added the name he had been given to his notebook. 'Hillary Shelby,' he murmured. 'Hillary Shelby.' And then he frowned, as another potential *Mastermind* answer popped out of his mental treasure chest.

'Hillary Shelby,' he repeated as he booted up his computer. 'Now that name definitely rings a bell.'

Fifty-Nine

'So what have we got here?' Banjo Paterson asked himself, with his DI looking over his shoulder. 'Standard MacBook screen layout. Let's see where he keeps his email. Mmm, he's got Google Chrome loaded up as well as Safari. Probably means he used that as his search engine. Let's see.'

He clicked on a multicoloured icon at the foot of the screen. 'Yes,' he murmured with satisfaction as a window opened. 'Big surprise, I don't think; the Rondar mail order site is his home page. Let's see what else he's bookmarked. Okay, he's got a Google account for his email.'

He clicked on a red envelope, with a two-word description alongside. 'Byron mail.'

'Auto sign-in,' he murmured. 'Lucky us, otherwise we'd have had to go back to the IT technicians to crack his password. His email address is Byron at Rondar dot co dot UK. Here we go.'

He inspected the second window. 'That's his inbox. He's got three unopened messages . . . What the hell?' He opened one headed 'National Lottery'. 'Oh dear.' It was half sigh, half laugh. 'The poor bastard's lottery ticket came up last Wednesday; he matched four balls and won ninety-nine quid.'

He hovered the cursor over an arrow and the next message opened.

It was from someone called Mike, confirming a squash court booking on the following Thursday for a semi-final tie in the club knock-out competition.

'Lucky boy, Mike,' Mann muttered. A wicked grin crossed her face. 'Let me in,' she told Paterson, leaned across him and keyed in a reply. *'Can't make it, have to scratch; good luck in the final.'* She hit the send button.

'Should you have done that, boss?' the DC asked, as she backed off.

'Maybe not, but the guy deserved to know. Go on.'

He moved on to the last unopened message. The sender was identified as 'Jocelyn' also using the Rondar mail system. 'The mother-in-law, as I understand it,' the DI told him.

'Mother-in-law from hell, in that case,' Paterson replied. 'Look at this.'

Mann peered at the screen, and read:

I have just received the latest quarterly management accounts. These show an operating loss of just under seventy-seven thousand pounds and make this the seventh successive quarter in which this company has lost money. Our auditors estimate that at this rate we will be insolvent by the end of the next financial year.

I have analysed the situation and have reached the inescapable conclusion that we have been on the slide since your father-in-law passed away. He and I always knew that the key to this business is not only what we sell but, as importantly, what we buy. We have to offer our customers attractive products at attractive prices while maintaining our profit margins. When Jesse was our buyer, we were able to do so very successfully. He was sure that when you took over from him, this would be maintained, but it is now clear to me that this confidence was misplaced.

I cannot allow this situation to continue, simply to sit on my hands and watch my company go out of existence. Son-in-law or not, I am going to have to relieve you of your duties and to declare you redundant. You and I both know that you are not suited to this line of work and never have been. So does Golda but she is too loyal to admit it. I intend to handle the buying function myself, with the assistance of my niece Bathsheba. When we are back in profit, Golda can expect to receive dividend income, but until then you are on your own.

'Lovely,' the DI said. 'Byron Millbank doesn't seem to have had a hell of a lot of luck.'

'Neither did Beram Cohen,' Paterson pointed out, 'culminating in them both being in a cool box in the mortuary.'

'Aye, but we're not so lucky ourselves. This doesn't tell us anything about Cohen, and that's what we're after. How about old emails? Could there be anything there?'

'I'm checking that, but I don't see anything. There's nothing filed or archived, not that I can see. I've checked the bin and even that's empty. He must have done that manually, the sign of a careful man.'

'What about the rest of it, other than his correspondence?'

'Gimme a few minutes. Please, gaffer.' He looked up at her. 'I don't really work best with somebody looking over my shoulder.' He smiled. 'A mug of tea wouldn't go amiss, though.'

'You cheeky bastard,' she exclaimed. 'I'm the DI, you're the DC; you're the bloody tea boy around here. However, in this situation . . . how many sugars do you take?'

'Me? None, thanks. Just milk.'

She left him in her room and crossed the main office. She glanced across at Provan, but he had his back to her and a phone to his ear.

366

She shook the kettle to check that it was full, then switched it on. And watched. And waited.

As she did, her mind wandered to her shattered family. Scott had been remanded on bail to a future court hearing, and to its inevitable conclusion. He had shown some contrition when he had come for his clothes, but she had smelled stale alcohol on his breath, and that had been enough to maintain her resolve. There would be no way back for him, no way, Jose.

And for her? There would be nothing other than her career, and bringing up her son. *I will not be making that mistake again*, she told herself. *There are no happy endings; sooner or later fate will always kick you in the teeth . . . and very much sooner if your husband is an alcoholic gambler who was shagging another woman within the first year of your marriage.*

The forgotten kettle broke into her thoughts by boiling. She made the tea, three mugs, one for Provan, stewed, as he liked it, distributed them and sat at her desk, waiting patiently for Banjo to finish his exploration of the dead man's double life.

Eventually he did, and turned towards her. 'Byron Millbank,' he announced, 'liked Celine Dion, Dusty Springfield, Black Sabbath, Alan Jackson, and Counting Crows, at least that's what his iTunes library indicates. He loved his wife and child, respected his late father-in-law but had no time for his mother-in-law. That's obvious from a study of his iPhoto albums. There's only one photograph of her on it, it's as unflattering as you can get and it's captioned "Parah", which I've just discovered is Hebrew for "Cow".

'He was a fan of Arsenal Football Club, not unnaturally, given where he lived. He had an American Express Platinum card, personal, not through the company. He had an Amazon Kindle account and his library included the complete works of Dickens and Shakespeare, the biography of Ronald Reagan and a dozen crime novels by Mark Billingham, Michael Jecks and Val McDermid.

'He had an Xbox and liked war games, big time. His most visited websites were Wikipedia, Sky News, the BBC and ITV players, the CIA World Factbook, and a charity called Problem Solvers.'

'Wow!' Mann exclaimed, with irony. 'How much more typical could this man have been? You're just described Mr Average Thirty-something.'

The DC nodded. 'Agreed. There is nothing out of the ordinary about him at all . . . apart from one thing. The charity: it doesn't exist. And that's where he does get interesting.'

Sixty

'It's not a charity at all, sir,' Paterson ventured. 'If you ask me, it's more of a doorway.'

'Explain,' Skinner said.

'It's the website, sir. It's called www dot problemsolvers dot org. Dot org domains used to be just for charities, but these days that's not necessarily so. To be sure I checked with the Charities Commission; they've never heard of it.

'On top of that,' the DC continued, 'it's weird in another way. It's password protected. I only got in because Millbank was careless in one respect: he saved his passwords on his computer, thinking, I suppose, that nobody else would ever use it.'

'When you did get in there, what did you find?' the chief constable asked.

'Nothing much; it's very simple. I'm sure he set it up himself. There's just the two pages. The home page has only six words: "Personnel problems? Discreet and permanent solutions." Then there's a message board. But there's no history on the site at all. He's wiped it all. However, there is one message still up on the board. It's possible that he left it there because the reply will go automatically to the sender, without Millbank ever needing to know who he was.'

'Not Millbank, Cohen,' Skinner countered. 'This is definitely

Beram Cohen. You've found him. What did the message say?'

'Confirm payment made as agreed, to sort code eighty-one forty twenty-two, account number zero six nine five two one five one.'

'Have you followed it up?'

'Not yet, sir.'

'Then do so, tomorrow morning. Wherever the bank is it'll have knocked off for the day by now. When you find it, trace the source of the payment and find out if any withdrawals have been made from it lately. Lottie, Banjo, that's good work.' He turned to Provan. 'Now, Sergeant, you're clearly bursting your braces to tell me something. It's your turn, so out with it.'

Sixty-One

'Is this not a real bore for you, Davie?' Skinner asked his driver, as they passed the clubhouse that welcomed golfing visitors to Gullane, and picked up speed. 'Same round trip every day, sometimes twice a day.'

'Absolutely not, Chief,' Constable Cole replied. 'I love driving, especially nice big motors like this one. I've done all the advanced courses there are, too. When I get moved out of this job, as I will, 'cos nothing's for ever, I'm going to try to get a spot as an instructor.'

'Good for you. But don't you ever miss the company? Most cops work in pairs. Most cops meet people through their work . . . even if some of those are rank bad yins.' He laughed at his own words. 'Listen to me,' he exclaimed. 'Second week in post and I'm lapsing into Weegie-speak already. I'm spending too much time with that wee bugger Provan, that's what it is. Maybe being a lone wolf isn't such a bad thing.'

'Maybe not,' Cole agreed.

'No, but seriously, does this never get to you? Don't you ever get the urge to see some action?'

The constable tilted his head back slightly, to help his voice carry into the back seat. 'The last action I saw, Chief, was over two years ago. We got a call to a cesspit of a housing scheme they'd used as accommodation for asylum seekers. Some of the neighbourhood Neds had given one of their kids a going-over and the dads went after them, mob-handed. It went into a full-blooded riot. My crew was sent in there with shields, batons and helmets, to re-establish order, we were told.' He chuckled. 'There hadn't been any proper order in that place for about five years, so they were asking quite a lot of us.

'Anyway, we waded in, and got the two sides separated. Just as well, because the local hooligans had turned out in force. They were winning the battle and there would have been fatalities if we hadn't stopped it. What we done, in effect, was protect the immigrants, but they never seen it that way. We had tearaways coming at us with swords and machetes, and behind us the foreigners were chucking bottles, rocks, all sorts of shit at us.'

Skinner glanced at the rear-view mirror as he paused, and saw him frown.

'Those riot helmets, sir,' he continued, 'they're pretty good, but if somebody drops a television set on you from the balcony of a third-floor flat, there's only so much protection they can give. It probably saved my life, but I still had a skull fracture, three displaced vertebrae in my neck and a broken shoulder. I was off work for nearly a year. When I came back they sent me on an advanced driving course. I did well at it. When Chief Constable Field arrived she wanted a full-time driver, and I got picked.'

'I see,' Skinner said. 'In that case, as long as I'm here, you'll be in the driving seat. Besides,' he continued, 'this is good for me too. Having you lets me get through shedloads of paperwork that I couldn't do if I drove myself, or if I took the train, for that would be too public. And the more of that I do while I'm travelling, the more time I have to put myself about, to see people, and, as important, to let them see me.

So,' he said, pulling his case across the seat towards him, 'time to shift some of it.'

He worked steadily for fifteen minutes until the car was half a mile from the slip road that joined the Edinburgh bypass.

'Davie,' he called, 'I want to make a detour, if you would. Go straight on, then take the next exit and head left, until you come to the second roundabout. You'll see a hot food and coffee stall. I'd like you to wait in the shopping centre car park, while I pick up a couple of bacon rolls. It's a lot less fuss to buy my breakfast than to make it myself.'

'I'm lucky, sir. I get mine made for me.'

'I'm lucky too. Looking out for yourself can be a price worth paying.' He grinned as he saw the driver's expression in the mirror. 'Don't mind me,' he said. 'I'm not always that cynical. The fact is, when we are together as a family, I enjoy making it for everybody.'

His directions were clear and accurate. PC Cole spotted the stall as he passed the first exit from the second roundabout, did a complete circuit and parked in the road facing the way he had come.

'Want anything?' the chief asked him.

'No thanks, sir, I'm fine.'

He relaxed in his seat as his passenger stepped out. He watched him in the nearside wing mirror as he sprinted towards the pedestrian crossing to catch the green light. Davie had never seen a senior cop who would go to work in a light tan cotton jacket; even the CID people usually wore suits, or expensive leather jackets in the case of some of the young, newly blooded DCs.

The stallholder must have known Skinner, he reckoned, for the boss smiled at him as he gave him his order. Or maybe he was only in a chatty mood, for he seemed to strike up a conversation with the scruffy wee man who was the only other punter there.

Whatever they were talking about, it must have been serious, for the other guy never cracked a smile, not even when the chief, his back half turned towards the car, slipped him something.

Christ, Cole thought, *the wee sod's on the scrounge. Not a bad guy, my boss. He likes getting the breakfast for everybody, even for a wee panhandler like that.*

Sixty-Two

It took almost no time at all to track down the bank account of Problem Solvers, once Banjo Paterson had opened the resource site that would take him there. He keyed in the sort code and number and clicked 'Validate', then leaned back with a smile on his face that broke all previous office records for smugness.

'There you are,' he announced. 'The account's held in the Bank of Lincoln, in an office in Grantham. There's no street address, only a PO box number, but there's a phone number.' He scribbled it in a pad and passed it to his DI.

'Thanks,' she said.

'Son,' Provan grunted, 'you better get a safe deposit box for a' these gold stars ye've been gettin', otherwise you might find yersel' bein' mugged on the way home.'

Mann took the note into her small office and dialled the number. 'Bank of Lincoln,' a cheery female voice answered. 'How can I be of service?'

'You can phone me back.'

'Pardon?'

'This is Detective Inspector Charlotte Mann, Strathclyde CID, Glasgow. I need to speak to your manager, urgently. If you call me back through my main switchboard number which I'll give you now,' she read it out, 'he'll know I am who I say I am. When you ring back, ask for extension one forty-eight.'

'Yes, madam. I won't be a minute.'

She was over-optimistic, by just under ten minutes, but did have the grace to apologise. 'I'm sorry to have kept you waiting, madam, but Mr Harrison, the branch manager, has only just become available. I'll put you through to him now.'

Mann had time to growl a curt 'Thank you' before the line clicked and a man spoke.

'Inspector, is it?'

'Detective Inspector.'

'I see. My name is Nigel Harrison, how can I help you?' There was a wariness in his voice. She had heard its like often enough in her career to know that assistance was not at the top of his agenda.

'I want to talk to you about an account that's held at your branch.' She recited the number. 'We believe that it's in the name of an entity calling itself Problem Solvers.'

'Let me check that,' the manager murmured. She waited, anticipating another long interlude, but he came back on the line after less than a minute. 'Yes, I have it on screen now. Problem Solvers; it's a charity.'

'So it says,' Mann retorted. 'I'd like to know about money moving in and out recently, within the last few weeks.'

'Ahh. I was afraid this conversation might take such a turn. I don't think I can help you there. I took the precaution of consulting my general manager before I returned your call, and was reminded that it's our head office policy to afford our clients confidentiality.'

'It's my policy,' she retorted, 'to get tough with people when I believe they're obstructing my investigation.'

She was sure she heard him sniff before he replied. 'If your questions are well founded,' he said, 'I'm sure the court will furnish you with the appropriate warrant.'

'I'm in no doubt about that,' she agreed, 'but I was hoping you'd be more cooperative. You're not, and that's too bad, because my questions are now going to move up a notch. You say this client of yours is a charity, yes?'

'Yes. We have a special account category for charities.'

'So it will be registered with the Charities Commission, yes?'

'Of course.'

'Sorry, Mr Harrison; it isn't.'

'But Mr Cohen assured me . . .'

'This would be Mr Beram Cohen, yes? The late Mr Beram Cohen?'

'The late . . .' the banker spluttered. 'Oh my! What happened?'

'He died. People do. So you see, he's got no confidentiality left to protect.'

'But Problem Solvers has.'

'A bogus charity? Tell me, sir, do the words "proceeds of crime" and possibly also "money laundering", which I'll throw into the mix just for fun, have any meaning for you?'

'What are you saying?'

'I'm saying that unless you cooperate with me, my next conversation will be with my colleagues in Lincolnshire Police. No more than an hour after that, they'll descend on you with that warrant you're insisting on, and they won't do it quietly. In fact, I'll ask them to make as much noise as they can. How will that go down with head office and your general manager?'

'Well . . .'

She had been bluffing, but his hesitancy told her that she was winning. 'I don't want to bully you, Mr Harrison, but this is urgent, and you'll be doing us a great service if you talk to me.'

She heard an intake of breath as he weighed up his options and made his decision. 'All right,' he sighed. 'Recent traffic through the account, you said?'

'Yes. Go back three months for starters.'

'Can do. I have it on screen, in fact. Two months ago, the charity received a donation of three hundred thousand pounds. One month later, two money transfers of fifty thousand pounds each were made, one to a bank in New Zealand, the other to Australia. Both of these were private accounts; that means I can't see the owner's name. That was followed by a third, for thirty thousand pounds, to a company in Andorra called Holyhead.

'The most recent transaction took place just under three weeks ago. Ahh,' he exclaimed, 'I remember that one. Mr Cohen called into the branch and made a withdrawal of fifteen thousand pounds in cash. It was potentially embarrassing, as my chief teller had let us get rather low on cash, and there had been a bit of a run that morning. We were forced to pay Mr Cohen his money in new fifties. Some customers would have been unhappy about that, but he said it was no problem.'

'I don't suppose you have a record of the serial numbers, do you?' she asked.

Harrison surprised her. 'As a matter of fact I do. Those notes were brand new; we were the first recipients. I can send that information to you.'

'Thanks. It would let us tick some boxes.'

'Anything else?'

'Oh yes,' Mann replied, 'the most important of all. Who made the payment of three hundred thousand?'

'That came from a bank in Jersey, from an account in the name of an investment company registered in Jersey. It's called Pam Limited.'

Mann felt her eyebrows rise halfway up her forehead, but she said nothing.

'Is that all?' Harrison asked her.

'Yes. Thank you . . . eventually.'

'Come on, Inspector. You must understand my caution.'

'I suppose.'

'What about the Problem Solvers account? Mr Cohen was the only contact we have with the organisation, whatever it is.'

'I'd suggest that you freeze it,' the DI told him. 'I have no idea what its legal status is, although Cohen's widow might fancy laying claim to it. Whatever, it's not my problem. I'll be reporting this; I'm sure someone will be in touch.'

'Your investigation,' Harrison ventured. 'You didn't say what it's about, but am I right in guessing that it's into Mr Cohen's death rather than this Problem Solver business?'

'No, you're not; it's into someone else's murder. You see, Mr Harrison, Mr Cohen's business was making people dead. Those were the sort of problems that he solved.'

Sixty-Three

'P am Limited,' Skinner repeated.

'Yes,' Mann confirmed. 'I checked with the company registration office in Jersey. According to the articles, it stands for Personal Asset Management. Its most recent accounts show that it's worth over two hundred and fifty million.'

'Who owns it?'

'According to the public record, its only shareholder is a man called Peter Friedman.'

'And who the hell's he?' the chief asked, frowning, then muttering, 'Although there's something familiar about that name.'

'Banjo ran a search on people called Friedman,' she told him. 'He came up with two singers, a journalist and an economist, although he's dead. The only references he got to anyone called Peter Friedman were a few press stories. He showed them to me; they all related to donations to good causes, charities and the like.'

'What, like Problem Solvers?' Skinner retorted.

'No, sir. Real ones, like Chest Heart and Stroke, Cancer UK, Children First, and Shelter. Only one of them gave any detail on him beyond his name and that was the *Saltire*, in a report on a charity fund-raiser dinner in the Royal Scottish Museum, in Edinburgh, six months ago. It described him as "a reclusive philanthropist"; nothing beyond that. If a wealthy man has that low a profile on the internet, then he really is reclusive.'

'Sounds like it. Friedman, Friedman, Friedman,' he repeated. 'Where the fu—' He slammed the palm of his hand on the table. 'Got it!' he shouted. 'It was . . .' He stopped in mid-sentence as he remembered who were in which loop, and who were not.

'I'll take the mystery man from here, thanks,' he told the DI. 'I've got another task for you, Lottie, for you and you alone. Thanks to Dan, we have Sofia Deschamps' address in Mauritius, but we don't know exactly where she lives in London, beyond that it's in Muswell Hill. She moved there very soon after Toni came back from her so-called sabbatical, to look after the child. Marina told me that Lucille's grandfather, Toni's dad, bought it for her. I took her word for that, like I swallowed everything else she fed me. She lied to me about other stuff, so maybe she lied about that too.

'I want you to dig deep, get the address and look into the purchase transaction. When it was bought, and if it was indeed an outright purchase, no mortgage, then I want to know exactly where the cash came from. And while you're at it, just for the hell of it, look into Toni's house in Bothwell, asking the same questions. Remember, don't involve the guys in this and report to me alone, as soon as you get a result. Use my mobile if you have to.' He gave her a card, with the number.

'I understand, sir,' Mann said. 'What do you expect to find?'

He smiled. 'Who knows? Maybe it's something to do with living at the seaside but I like flying kites.'

'Maybe you can show me how,' she replied. 'I'm going to have to find new ways to amuse my Jakey, with his dad out the picture.'

As soon as she had gone, he picked up the phone and made a direct call.

'*Sal-tire,*' a male telephonist announced, the confident public voice of a confident newspaper.

'June Crampsey, please. Tell her it's Bob. She'll know which one.'

'There may be other men called Bob in my life,' the editor said as she came on line.

'But you still knew which one this is.'

'It's my phone; it goes all moist when you call. Why didn't you use my direct line, or my mobile?'

'Because my head's full of stuff and I couldn't remember either number.'

'I thought you had slaves to get those for you.'

'That's Edinburgh. In Glasgow they're all lashed to the oars and rowing like shit to keep the great ship off the rocks.'

'Do I detect a continuing ambivalence towards Strathclyde?' she teased.

'It's a lousy job, kid, but somebody's got to do it. For now that's me. June, I need your help.'

'Shoot. You still have a credit balance in the favour ledger.'

'Six months or so back, you ran a story about some charity dinner in the RSM. It mentioned a man named Peter Friedman, a recluse, your story called him.'

'I remember that one.'

'How much do you know about him?'

'No more than was in the paper. He's a very rich bloke who keeps himself to himself. We ran that dinner to honour people who gave decent sized bucks to good causes last year. The guests were all nominated by the charities and we sent the formal invitations. His address was a PO box in Tobermory.'

'Tobermory?' he repeated.

'That's what I said. He lives on the Isle of Mull. That qualifies as reclusive, doesn't it?'

'Hey, I'm from Motherwell. Everything north and west of Perth's reclusive in my book. Your story: was there a photo with it?'

'Yes,' she replied. 'That's why I remember it so well. I had a photographer in the hall, snapping groups; real dull stuff, but I felt we had to do it since it was our gig. Your man Friedman was in one of them and he made a fuss about it. First he tried to bribe the photographer, then he threatened him. When neither of those worked he sought me out and asked me, more politely, not to use it. I said I'd see what I could do, then I made bloody sure that it went in.'

'Did you hear from him afterwards?'

'No. Fact is, I doubt if he even saw it. The next day was the Saturday edition; most people just read that for the sport and the weekend section.'

'Do you still have the photo in your library?'

'Of course, everything's in the bloody library. I'll have somebody dig it out, crop him out of the group and email it to you. What's your Strathclyde address?'

'Thanks, but use my private address. I don't want it on this network.'

'Okay, but what's this about, Bob? Why are you interested in him?'

'His name came up in connection with another charity donation,' Skinner replied, content that he was telling the truth. 'I like to know about people with deep pockets; maybe our dependants' support group can put the bite on him in the future. Thanks, June, you're a pal. You and that other Bob must come to dinner some night.'

'I'll take you up on that, only his name's Adrian. Now I'm wondering who the hostess will be. Cheers.'

He hung up, leaned back in his chair, his fingers steepled in front of his face, gathering his thoughts and seeing images flow past his mind's eye. He sat there until a trumpet sound on his phone told him that he had a personal email, and a glance confirmed that it was from June. He opened it, then viewed the attachment. As he did, possibilities became certainties.

The chief constable rose from his desk, left his office and his command floor, taking the stair down one level and walking round to a suite that overlooked Holland Street, and the group of buildings that once had housed one of Scotland's oldest and most famous schools.

He keyed a number into a pad, then pushed open a door bearing a plaque that read 'Counter-Terrorism Intelligence Section'. As he entered the long open room, a female officer looked up at him, first with a frown, then in surprise. She started to rise, but he waved her back down, and headed to the far end of the room.

A red light above Lowell Payne's door said that he was in a meeting. Skinner knocked on it nonetheless, then waited, until it was opened by a glaring man with a moustache.

'Aye?' he snapped.

'Intelligence section?' he murmured, as Payne appeared behind the officer.

'Chief.'

'Sorry to interrupt, Detective Superintendent, but you know me. Everything I do has "urgent" stamped on it.'

'Indeed. That'll be all for now, DS Mavor,' he said, almost pushing the other officer out of the room.

'Sorry about that,' he murmured once he and Skinner were alone. 'He was somebody's mistake, from the days when a guy might get dumped into Special Branch and forgotten about, because he was too rough-edged for the mainstream, or because he'd done somebody higher up a big favour in the witness box, and an SB job was his reward.'

'Where do you want him sent?'

'Anywhere that being rough-edged will be an advantage.'

'I'll ask Bridie. She'll have an idea. Now, I have a question, best put to somebody who was here six months ago and who'd know pretty much everything that went on then.'

'That would be DI Bulloch,' Payne replied at once. 'Sandra. You probably passed her on your way along here.'

'I did. At least she knows who I am, which is a good start.'

'I'll get her in.'

'Fine, but before you do, let me set the scene. When I got into Toni Field's safe finally, and found those envelopes, there was another. It was marked "P. Friedman" and it was empty. It was stuck on to the back of another, and I reckon that was a mistake on Marina's part.'

'Marina's?'

'Oh yes. Marina knew that stuff would be there for me to find, in time, once I'd got past her stalling me by giving me the wrong code for the safe. But she didn't intend me to find the Friedman envelope. She destroyed what was in it, but failed to notice that she'd left it in there. Now, let's talk to the DI.'

Sandra Bulloch was a cool one, neither too pretty nor too plain to be memorable, but with legs that few men would fail to notice, and that she probably covered up, Skinner guessed, when she went operational.

'Peter Friedman,' she repeated. 'Yes, sir, I remember him. It was Chief Constable Field's second week here; she called Superintendent Johnson and me up to her office, and told us that there was a man she wanted put under full surveillance. His name, she said, was Peter Friedman and he lived on Mull.

'I handled the job myself, with DS Mavor.' A small flicker of distaste crossed her face, then vanished. 'We found that he owned a big estate house up behind Tobermory, set in about forty acres of land. We photographed him from as close as we could get, we hacked his emails and we tapped his phones.

'He lived alone, but he had a driver, a personal assistant type, who also flew the helicopter that appeared to be his means of getting off the island. He left the estate once a day, that was all, to go down to Tobermory, in his white Range Rover Evoque, to collect his mail from the post office, and to have a coffee and a scone in the old church building next door that somebody's made into a shop and a café.

'He had no visitors and he never took or made a phone call that wasn't about his investments. Nor did he file any emails; they were all deleted after study. I assume that if he wanted to keep something he'd print it.

'The only thing we intercepted that was of any interest,' Bulloch said, 'was an email from a consultant oncologist, with a report attached. It didn't make good reading. It confirmed that Friedman had a squamous cell lung carcinoma, in other words lung cancer, that it was inoperable, and that no form of therapy was going to do him any good. It gave him somewhere between nine months and two years to live.'

'Ouch,' Skinner whispered. 'Did you report all of this back to Toni, to Chief Constable Field?'

'Of course, sir. We gave her a file with everything in it. She kept it and she ordered us to destroy any copies.'

'Which you did?'

Bulloch stared at him, as if outraged. 'Absolutely,' she insisted.

'Did she ever tell you why she wanted this man targeted?'

'No, and we didn't ask. Sometimes the chief constable knows things that we don't need to. For example, why you're here now, asking questions about the same man.'

He laughed. 'Nice one, Sandra. You're right; I'm not going to tell you either.'

His mobile sounded as she was leaving the room. The caller was Lottie Mann, with not one result, but two. He listened carefully to her, said, 'Thanks. I'll be in touch,' then ended the call.

'Lowell,' he asked, 'has our tap on Sofia Deschamps produced anything?'

'Nothing, Chief. Only a call from Mauritius, a bloke we think was Chief Constable Field's dad, going by his distress if nothing else. Nothing from Marina, though. In fact, when she was talking to the man, she said, "Now I've lost both my daughters, and I won't get either one back." I suppose that doesn't rule out her knowing where the other one is, but from the tone of her voice on the recording, I don't believe she does.'

'That's all right, I do. Pretty soon, I expect that everything will become clear. I'm tired of this business, Lowell,' Skinner sighed, 'tired of the entire Deschamps family and their devious lives. Tomorrow, the two of us will go on a trip. I'd like to meet this guy Friedman. Can you put me up at your place tonight? Otherwise it'll be an even earlier start for Davie.'

Sixty-Four

'Sailing is not something I do very often,' Bob remarked. 'In fact, the last time I was on a boat on this side of the country was when Ali Higgins took Alex and me for a weekend on her rich brother's schooner. It was a cathartic experience in an emotional sense.'

He was leaning on the rail of the Oban car ferry as it made a slow turn towards the jetty at Craignure, landing point for visitors to the island of Mull. Their driver, PC Davie Cole, was in the car, asleep.

'Funnily enough,' Lowell Payne said, 'I remember that; on your way there, the three of you were at Jean's dad's funeral. It was the first time you and I met.'

'You're right, it was. I think about that trip often, whenever I'm feeling low. I loved it. By the end of the voyage, I was talking seriously about jacking it all in and buying a boat of my own, doing the odd charter, that sort of stuff. Then the fucking phone rang, didn't it, and it all went up in smoke.'

'What if you had?' Lowell asked. 'Maybe you and Alison would be off in the Caribbean or the Med right now. Jean had hopes for the pair of you.'

'I know she had, but they were misplaced. We didn't last, remember; Ali was more career driven than me.' He sighed, and his eyes went somewhere else. 'But if we had bought our tall ship and made it work, she would still be alive. If I'd taken her away from the fucking police force,' he muttered, with sudden savagery, 'she wouldn't have been turned into crispy bits by a fucking car bomb.'

'You both made the same choice,' Lowell pointed out. 'And it could as easily have been you that got killed. A couple of times, from what I hear.'

'Yes I know that, but still. This fucking job, man, what it does to people, on the inside. Ali and I, we spent a couple of years banging each other's brains out, yet by the time she died, it was all gone and she was calling me "sir" with the rest of them.'

He was silent for a while, until he had worked off his anger and his guilt, and his mood changed. 'By the way,' he said quietly, 'I enjoyed last night. You and Jean, you're such a normal down-to-earth couple.' He gave a soft, sad laugh. 'As a matter of fact, you're just about the only normal down-to-earth couple that I know. And that lass of yours, young Myra, she's blooming. What is she now, thirteen? She reminds me a lot of Alex when she was that age. Prepare to be wound round her little finger, my friend.'

'There is a difference, though. You had to bring Alexis up on your own. Yes, I might be a soft touch, I'll admit, but Jean's there as a buffer; she takes no nonsense . . . not that Myra gets up to much, mind. She's a good kid. That is, she has been up to now. I suppose it all changes the further into their teens they get.'

'It does, and the trick is to accept that. There comes a time in every young person's growing up when they're entitled to a private life, in every respect. When it's a daughter, that can be difficult for dads, because we all inevitably remember the hormonal volcanoes we were at that age. I was no exception, and I'll always be grateful to Jean for being a really good aunt to Alex during that couple of years.'

'From what she said, and indeed from what I saw for myself, you were a great dad.'

'Ach, we all are to our girls, or should be. I'm beginning to learn that boys take much more managing.'

'Do you think that's what went wrong with Toni and Marina? The absence of a father's influence?'

He pursed his lips. 'In Toni's case, nah; I reckon she was just a bad bitch. As for Marina, maybe it was the opposite. The jury's still out on that.'

'What do you mean?' Payne paused. 'You realise I'm completely in the dark about this trip. You've hardly told me anything. Now it turns out we're going to see some recluse in Tobermory, and I still don't know why.'

'You will.' He pushed himself off the rail. 'Come on, let's go and see if Davie's awake yet. We'll be ready to offload soon.'

Twenty minutes later they were seated in the back of the chief constable's car, as PC Cole eased it carefully down the ramp then on to the roadway.

'I thought the terminal was in Tobermory itself,' Payne observed as he read a road sign outside the Caledonian MacBrayne building. 'Twenty-one miles away: I never realised Mull was so big.'

'I'd forgotten myself,' Skinner confessed, 'until I looked it up on Google Earth. I didn't think it would have street view for a place this size, but it does. Now I know exactly where we're going.'

'The post office?'

'No, the café place next door that DI Bulloch mentioned. The Gallery, it's called. We'll have a cup of something there and wait for Mr Friedman to arrive. It's a nice morning, and they've got tables outside.'

'What if he's already been for his mail?'

'There's no chance of that. This is the first ferry of the day, and the Royal Mail van was six behind us in the queue to get off. We'll be there before it.'

The Gallery was exactly as DI Bulloch had described it. A classic old Scottish church building, with a paved area in front with half a dozen tables, four of them unoccupied. It offered a clear view across Tobermory Bay and, more important, of anyone arriving at the post office, next door.

Cole dropped them off outside, then, on Skinner's instruction, reversed into a parking bay, thirty yards further along on the seaward side of the road, half hidden by a tree and a telephone box.

They took the table nearest the street, and the chief produced a ten-pound note. 'I'm not pulling rank,' he said, 'but since I actually know who we're waiting for, it's better you get the teas in. I'll have a scone too, if they look okay. They should be; you'd expect home baking in a place like this.'

As he took the banknote, Payne sensed the excitement of anticipation underlying Skinner's good humour. There was no queue in the café. He bought two mugs of tea and two scones, which looked better than okay, and was carrying them outside on a tray when he saw the Royal Mail van drive past, slowing to park.

There was no conversation as they sat, sipping and eating. The chief was relaxed in his chair, but his colleague noticed that it was drawn clear of the table, so that if necessary he had a clear route to the street.

And then, after ten minutes, a large white vehicle came into view, approaching from their left. It was halfway in shape between a coupé and an estate car. 'How many white Range Rover Evoques would you expect in Mull?' the chief murmured.

The car swung into an empty bay on the other side of the road. Its day lights dimmed as the driver switched off, then stepped out: not a man, Payne saw, but a woman, tall, in shorts and a light cotton top, with a blue and yellow motif.

Her hair was jet black, cut short and spiky. Although a third of her face was hidden behind wrap-round sunglasses, Oakley, he guessed, by the shape of them, the lovely honey-coloured tone of her skin was still apparent, and striking.

She was halfway across the road, heading for the post office, when Skinner put his right thumb and index finger in his mouth and gave a loud, shrill whistle. The woman, and everyone else in earshot, looked in his direction. But she alone froze in mid-stride.

She made a small move, as if to abort her errand and go back to the Range Rover, but the chief shook his head, then beckoned her towards them. She seemed to sag a little, then she obeyed, as if she was on an invisible lead and he was winding it in.

He stood as she drew near, reaching out with his right foot, gathering in a spare chair and pulling it to the table. 'Have a seat,' he said. He inclined his head towards Payne, never taking his eyes from hers. 'Lowell, you didn't get up to the command floor in the last chief's time, so you probably don't know her sister, Marina Deschamps, or Day Champs, as wee Dan Provan would say. Mind you,' he added, 'even if you did, you'd have had bother recognising her with the radical new hair and the designer shades. I probably wouldn't have been sure myself if she hadn't been driving her dad's car.'

'Her what?' Payne exclaimed.

'Her dad,' he repeated. 'Peter Friedman's her father. There's been a consistent feature in this investigation. Most of the players in it have had two names, making them hard to pin down. Byron Millbank was Beram Cohen, and vice versa when he had to be, Antonia Deschamps became Toni Field, in the cause of advancing her career like

392

everything else she ever did, and even Basil Brown, gangster and MI5 grass, had to be called Bazza.'

'So what about Peter Friedman?' Marina asked, as she sat. 'What was he?'

'He used to be Harry Shelby.'

She removed the sunglasses, as if she was peeling them off her face, and stared at him, with eyes that were colder than he had ever imagined they could be. 'How did you find out?'

'MI5 erased the records of wee Lucille's birth,' he replied, 'but they had no reason to wipe out yours. It wouldn't have been that easy anyway, you being born before the computer era. When you steered me towards your conspiracy scenario, and I was stupid enough to embarrass myself, even endanger myself, by falling for it, you may have thought that I wouldn't survive professionally, maybe even personally. You certainly didn't envisage me coming after you, nor Five either, not after I'd handed them all Toni's blackmail leverage. For that's what your sister was, wasn't she? Inside Supercop, there was a nasty little blackmailer . . . as you well knew, for you were put alongside her to spy on her, and you found the evidence.'

'I . . .' she began, protesting, but he raised a hand, to stop her.

'I know you were, because Amanda Dennis told me so, and I know you did, because you left it for me, after you'd doctored it a wee bit. So come on, just nod your head, and admit it.'

She did.

'God knows what Toni got out of the civil servant,' Skinner continued, 'or the TV guy, or the other cop, but she got advancement from Storey, and I know now that she got a house out of the Home Secretary and her husband, the one your mother lives in in London. Her father didn't buy it, they did; they paid her off, and if that was known, the scandal would be compounded. That house was bought and paid for by Repton Industries, Emily Repton's family business. You knew that, Marina, and you didn't care a toss about it.

'But when she pulled the same stroke on your father, that was different. Lottie Mann traced both transactions right to the source of the money. She found out that the house in Bothwell was paid for by Pam Limited, Peter Friedman's investment company. Thanks to one single, unfortunate newspaper photo, Toni found out who Friedman really was. She contacted him and she sold him her silence, for five hundred and seventy-five thousand pounds, the cost of a nice big villa.' Skinner frowned. 'Or her silence for a while: and that was something you couldn't tolerate, the idea that she could unmask him any time she chose, so . . . you had your sister killed!'

'Half-sister,' she murmured. 'So prove it.'

He shrugged. 'I can't, not to court standards. Anyway, not only did your fiction add up, that Repton had her removed, it still does, for you could claim that everything you did was on their orders.'

'Do you really know it wasn't?' she challenged.

'Oh yes, I do. And I can prove that.'

'How?'

'It was your old man that paid Cohen to do the job, not them.'

'My God,' she said, 'you have been busy. You know that much?'

He nodded. 'Yes, I do.'

'In that case, tell me, Mr Skinner . . . I can see you're desperate to, you're so pleased with yourself . . . how did you find out who my father was?'

'I'm not pleased with myself,' he contradicted her. 'But I'm dead chuffed for Dan Provan, the guy I mentioned earlier. He's a walking anachronism of a detective sergeant, who's been hiding in Strathclyde CID for years. You probably never saw him when you were there, just as your path and Lowell's never crossed, but even if you had you wouldn't have noticed him. That's one of his strengths. The other is that he never forgets a criminal, if the crime is big enough to get his attention.'

He picked up his ever-present attaché case and spun the combination wheels to open it.

'I was never just going to forget about you, Marina,' he told her as he flicked the catches. 'I don't like being made to feel like an idiot. I take it personally. The first thing I did when I got back to Glasgow was send Provan to dig out your birth records from Mauritius. I wanted to build a complete picture of you and obviously I couldn't rely on the things you had told me, or the hints you had dropped, since you're as consummate a deceiver as your sister was.'

A flicker of a smile suggested she took that as a compliment.

'Provan discovered that your father was listed as Hillary Shelby,' he continued, taking a document from the Zero Halliburton and handing it to her. 'See? Hillary not Harry, and there's an Australian passport number. However, that surname niggled him, and the itch wouldn't go away. And that's where his special skills came into play. "Shelby," he told himself. "I know that name from somewhere." Dan isn't of the IT generation,' Skinner said, 'but he went to the computer and ran a Google search.' He grinned. 'He called it "that Bugle thing" when he told me about it. He did try the full name first off, but got zilch, so then he entered simply Shelby, on its own. He came up with a car designer, an actor, and three different towns in America, then at the foot of the page, he got Harry Shelby, and it all came back to him, and that pub quiz mind of his.

'Harry Shelby was an Australian financier, a real tycoon . . . or typhoon, as Dan called him. He built a business empire of considerable size in Australia, South Africa and in Hong Kong from the early seventies on. He started in minerals, then moved into currency trading, and pretty soon he had become a national business icon, stand-out even in an era in Australian history when there were quite a few of those around.

'In nineteen ninety-six, he was awarded a knighthood, in the Birthday Honours list. He was scheduled to be invested in Canberra, by the High Commissioner. Everything was set up, but the day before, Harry Shelby vanished, off the face of the earth. He was never seen again, and he never left a penny behind him, or rather a cent.'

'I remember that,' Payne exclaimed. 'It was big news for a week or so, internationally.'

'I confess that it passed me by,' the chief said. 'But nineteen ninety-six was a busy year for me; my mind was full of other stuff, on my own doorstep. Anyway,' he carried on, 'you can imagine that after Shelby disappeared, his whole life was dug up. It didn't take the investigators long to find out that in fact he ran out of business steam in the mid-eighties, after a series of bad currency deals that he managed to cover up. Everything he'd done after that had been a huge Ponzi scheme, paying investors with their own money, as he drew more and more in with the promise of attractive profits that were evidently being delivered. If Harry Shelby hadn't had such a big reputation, chances are he'd have been caught, but because he was such a hero he got away with it.'

He stopped to sip his tea, only to find that it had gone cold.

'Why did he run?' he asked, then answered. 'It may have been because he knew that all Ponzi fraudsters are caught eventually, unless they shut up shop before it's too late.' He paused. 'However, Provan happened upon another theory, one that the Australian authorities . . . Dan checked this with the Australian Embassy . . . believe to this day, possibly because it suits them so to do. They think, indeed they're pretty well sure, that a couple of his biggest investors were Americans,

Mafia figures, using his investment scheme to launder money. The scenario is, they caught on to the swindle, so they dealt with it the old-fashioned way. They made Shelby and his money disappear at the same time. On the day that he did, Australian air traffic control traced an unregistered flight out of Canberra heading for Tasmania. The investigators had a tip that Shelby was on it, until they dropped him out halfway there over the ocean.' He gazed at Marina. 'But we know that's not true, don't we?'

She stared back at him, silent. He took a photograph from the case, held it up for Payne to see, then passed it to her.

'That's Harry Shelby, aged about forty.'

He produced a second. 'That's Peter Friedman, photographed, to his annoyance, at a charity dinner last winter. He's over thirty years older, but I've had the images run through a recognition program, and it confirms they're one and the same man.'

He went back into the attaché and took out a third image. 'And that's you,' he said, 'from your HR file in Pitt Street. You can't hide from it, Marina. You are your father's double.'

She picked up his mug, and drank his cold tea in a single gulp. 'And proud of it,' she whispered.

'It was the newspaper photograph that did it, wasn't it?'

'Yes,' she agreed. 'Antonia was in her first month in Glasgow when it appeared. She read every newspaper, every day, to familiarise herself with the place, and she saw that. She used CTIS to trace him, then one day, just as you have, she turned up here, alone. When he got over the shock, he assumed that she had come to arrest him, but no. I mean, why would she have done that? There would have been nothing in it for her.

'Your assumption was correct; she did to him what she had done to Lawton and his wife. She showed him the brochure for the house and told him that she wanted it. She told him to forget about trying to vanish again, as she would know about it the moment his helicopter took off, or he boarded the ferry. But in truth she knew that there was no point in him running. He was dying, and even then the house was being turned into a hospice, a place for him to be as peaceful as he could be in his last days. So he bought the Bothwell place for her.' Her eyes flashed. 'He told me she should have chosen a bigger one.'

'Why did he go to the damn dinner? That doesn't sound like typical behaviour.'

'He was in Edinburgh, seeing an oncologist for tests,' she explained. 'It was that day, and he had a feeling the news wasn't going to be the best, so he went, in the hope it might cheer him up. As it turned out it did the opposite.'

'Does your mother know any of this?' Skinner asked.

'None,' Marina insisted. 'Maman is not a stupid woman. She had a good job in the civil service, but she was looked after by men for much of her life, first Anil, and then Papa. She's naive in some ways, so when Antonia told her that she had done well in property in Britain, she believed her.'

'How did Sofia meet your father?'

'He was part of an Australian business delegation to the island, in nineteen eighty, after her thing with Anil was over. Maman was in charge of official government hospitality. That's when it began.

'I was born two years later, and for all my childhood he spent as much time as he could with us. He was as good to Antonia as he was to me. That's what made her behaviour all the more despicable. You were right. She was just a nasty little blackmailer.'

'When did you get back in touch with him?'

'I was never out of touch. Gifts would arrive, and letters, never traceable, only ever signed "Papa". The theory is wrong, incidentally, about the Mafia. They were his partners in the Ponzi business, not his victims. They all made lots of money and when the time came to close it down, they helped him get away, and they planted the idea that they had killed him. In fact he lived in the West Indies for six years, as Peter Friedman. He moved to Mull ten years ago, around the same time as I came to Britain. It was then he told me his new name.'

'Whose idea was it for you to join MI5?' Skinner asked.

'A shrewd question, because I think you know the answer. Papa suggested it. The idea was that if the Australians started looking for him again, in Millbank I would be well placed to hear about it. By that time I was in a security department within the Met, so when I applied, it seemed a natural step, and I was accepted. Brian Storey was my boss then, and he endorsed me. Antonia never knew, though, not ever. The service, as it does, gave me a front as an importer for a chain of florists.'

'That sounds like an Amanda Dennis touch.'

'It was. She's a good teacher.'

'You were a good student, Marina. You could have been Amanda yourself, if you'd stayed the course, instead of letting them move you out to spy on your sister.'

'But if I had stayed, I wouldn't have been able to deal with her when the need arose.'

'By telling your father how to get rid of her? No, I don't suppose you would.'

'Papa never knew,' she said.

Both police officers stared at her.

'It's true, I swear,' she exclaimed. 'If I had told him he would have forbidden it, absolutely. All he ever did was make a donation of three hundred thousand pounds to a charity I told him about. He was a sucker for charities, especially those involved with cancer research; I told him it helped patients with difficult personal circumstances. I approached Cohen, using a contact email address I'd picked up in the service. I gave him the commission and he named his price. No conscience, that man, only a cash register. I also gave him Brown as a resource on the ground in Glasgow. I'm sorry they had to kill him, but not too sorry, as he was a traitor to his own kind. No, the decision was mine, and the orders were mine. Knowing what Antonia was, and what she might have become, I don't regret them. I'm sorry for Maman, and for Anil, and for Lucille, of course, but they will bring her up as if she was their own. Maman is still young and fit enough to see it through.'

'But what about Papa?' Skinner murmured. 'He isn't, is he?'

'Yes, Papa,' she sighed. 'I suppose you have come to take him away, as Antonia did not.'

'We haven't come to ask for a raffle prize for the policeman's ball, that's for sure. As for taking him away, we'll see about that. But I would like to meet him.'

'Then come with me, Chief Constable, and you shall.' She stood; Skinner and Payne followed suit. 'In your car? You have a car, I take it.'

'Yes, but Superintendent Payne can take that. I'll come with you, just in case the minder panics at the sight of strange vehicles. By the way, no nonsense up there, Marina. There are firearms in my car; that's a practice your sister introduced.'

'He isn't that sort of minder, I promise. Rudolf is a driver and a pilot, that's all.' As she spoke, they heard the heavy engine sound of an aircraft. She looked up and pointed, towards a helicopter above them, gaining height. 'In fact, that's him.'

'Hey!' Skinner exclaimed. 'Are you . . .'

'No. Papa is not with him. He's still at the house. Come and meet him.'

The chief frowned, still cautious, weighing her up, not anxious to be taken twice. 'Okay,' he said at last. 'Don't you want to collect your mail?'

'It can wait. Come on.' She led him across the road to the waiting Range Rover.

With the police car following close behind, they drove out of Tobermory, taking a narrower road from the one they had used earlier, passing a campsite on the edge of the small town, then climbing for two or possibly three miles, although its twists and turns made it difficult to judge distance travelled.

She slowed as they approached a gate on the right, with an unequivocal sign beside it: 'Private'. It was shut, but Marina pressed a button on a remote control and the barrier slid aside.

The surface of the estate road was gravel, but better than the one they had left. Their tyres crunched beneath them, early warning, Skinner thought, for anyone waiting.

The house itself was a grey mansion, large but not ostentatious. It reminded him of some of his neighbours on Gullane Hill, although the stone was different. She drew up at the front door, then waited until the second car stopped alongside and Payne climbed out to join them.

He was holding a pistol, in the manner of a man for whom it was a new experience. Skinner frowned and shook his head; he handed it back to Davie Cole.

'This way,' she said, leading them inside, walking briskly through a chandelier-lit hallway, and, ignoring a wide mahogany stairway, into a room on the far side of the house.

It was large, decorated with old-fashioned flock wallpaper. A bay window faced south over a sunlit garden, laid out in shrubs and fruit trees, with stone statuary among them. Soft music was playing, a female singer with a gentle voice; the chief guessed at Stacey Kent.

There was a smell about the room, a smell of disinfectant, a hospital smell, one that seemed fitting given the metal-framed bed that was positioned facing the window. Skinner saw an oxygen cylinder on the far side as they approached, and beside it, in a stand, a vital signs monitor.

All the lines on it were flat.

The man on the bed was old, but his face was unlined. He looked peaceful, with his eyes closed.

'Papa died just over two hours ago,' Marina murmured. 'Rudolf has gone to Oban to fetch an undertaker, and to take Sister Evans to the station. She's been with us for the last month. She did a great job; he was pain-free all the way to the end. The doctor from Oban was with him at the end. He was kind enough to stay overnight. He caught the first ferry back this morning.'

'I suppose I should say I'm sorry for your loss,' Skinner told her. 'And I am, honestly, even if he was a billion-dollar fraudster, and you're a sororicide . . . if that's a word. You are a first, Marina. I've come across plenty of conmen in my career . . . although not on your dad's scale, I admit . . . but I've never met someone who's killed her own sister.'

'What are you going to do with me?' she asked. Payne, standing on the other side of the bed, saw a hint of trepidation in her eyes, for the first time since their encounter in the café.

'What do you think?' the chief retorted. 'I'm duty bound to arrest you and charge you with murder. You've admitted it, and even if you recant that, I know enough now to put a case together.' And then he sighed. 'That's my duty, but the judge would be bound to knock out so much of my evidence on national security grounds that you would walk. Your problem would then be that you wouldn't walk very far, before you were hit by a runaway lorry, or killed in a random mugging, or died of a peanut allergy that nobody knew you had, or just plain disappeared.'

Her trepidation turned to undisguised fear as she acknowledged the truth in what he said.

'Who are you now?'

His question took her by surprise. 'My new identity, you mean?'

'Yes.'

'I have a Jamaican passport, in the name of Marina Friedman. My father obtained it for me, in case we both needed to move on in a hurry.'

'What was your next move? Your plan for life after Papa?'

'His will is with his lawyer in Jersey. It names me as his sole heir. He told me to go there, with the death certificate and my passport, to claim my inheritance.'

'That won't be happening now,' Skinner said.

'No, I realise that. So, what will you do with me? Will you save the expense of your abortive prosecution by handing me straight over to Amanda Dennis?'

He took a breath and blew out his cheeks. 'Like she would thank me for that,' he exclaimed. 'It would be better all round if I just shot you myself and buried you somewhere on this big island.'

She backed away, staring at him in sudden naked terror.

'Hey!' he exclaimed. 'Calm down. Better all round, but I'm not one of them, Marina. Besides,' he added, with a half smile and a nod in Payne's direction, 'there are witnesses, and your man Rudolf will be back from Oban soon. So,' he told her, 'here's what you do. You take whatever you can pack quickly, and as much as you can in the way of cash and valuables, you get in that car and you drive it straight on to the ferry. When you get to Oban, keep on driving, in any direction you can and in any direction as long as it is out of the jurisdiction of any Scottish police force.'

'But not Jersey, I take it.'

'No; there'll be nothing there by the time you get there. Whatever fortune your father's left isn't for you, it's for the people he swindled, even if some of them will be dead themselves by now.' He gazed at her. 'This is what's happened,' he said. 'Lowell and I arrived to arrest him, following my discovery of some papers in Toni's safe. Sadly, we were too late. You were never here. When Rudolf gets back and asks, "Where's Marina?" I will say, "Marina who?" That's the outcome. We get Papa, you get lost. We will be fucking heroes, Lowell and me, in Australia most of all. As for you, you will be alive.'

She looked at him, still doubting, until he nodded, to reassure her.

'You're a resourceful lady. You'll get by for a couple of years, and after that you can probably go back to Mauritius and become yourself again, because nobody will be looking for you. But don't ever show up here again, for I will know about it. You're getting away with murder, because that's what suits everybody best. But don't you ever forget it.'

PostScript

'Why did you decide to quit as leader? Were there knives out for you because of the Joey incident?'

Aileen snorted across the lunch table in a restaurant next to Edinburgh Castle. They had gone there after finalising their divorce, in the Court of Session, further down the Royal Mile.

'They wouldn't have been nearly sharp enough. No, to be frank I resigned because we are going to get absolutely slaughtered at the next Holyrood election and I don't want that on my CV. That twerp Felix Brahms will inherit it, now that I've endorsed him.'

'Foresighted as ever,' Bob chuckled.

'Of course, and there's this. I won't be a candidate in Scotland next time. One of our guys in a safe seat on Tyneside is about to retire early on health grounds. I've called in some favours; it's mine.'

'The divorce won't be a problem for you, will it?'

'I don't see it. We've settled on unreasonable behaviour as the grounds, not adultery. As for the *Daily News* pictures, they're old, cold news by now. Besides, it's a safe seat, like I said. The Lib Dems don't count there and as for the Tories, they're really too nice to use those sort of tactics.'

'Will Joey put in an appearance for you?'

'As if I'd ask him. Look, Joey and me, it's a thing from way back. I suppose I can confess now, there were other times while we were married, not just that one. Sorry if it dents your male ego, but there were.'

'I know,' he admitted. 'Toni Field had a file on you. It's long since gone into the shredder. Mind you, she did hint that there was somebody else, apart from Joey.'

Aileen's eyes widened. 'She did what? Any name mentioned?'

'No, and I'm sure I don't want to know.'

'Oh but you do. Who knows? It might come in useful to you one day. The US government ran a big hospitality shindig a couple of years back in the Turnberry Hotel. All the party leaders were there, and the champagne was fairly flowing. As usual, I had a wee bit too much, and God knows how it happened, but I woke up next morning with Clive Graham. So there you are. My deep dark secret, and Clive's, except . . . somewhere there may be CCTV footage of the two of us going into his room, and probably of me leaving. Find it and it could buy you a lot of influence.'

He sighed. 'My predecessor did that sort of thing, and it got her fucking killed.'

'What? She tried to blackmail Colombian drug lords?'

'Not quite. That was the official version. The true story's a lot different, but I'm not sharing, as the spooks say.'

She shrugged. 'Be like that. Here,' she went on, 'the way you said "My predecessor" there, it sounded as if you've made a decision.'

'I have. I've decided that I can't go back to Edinburgh. Mario and Maggie are getting on fine without me. They don't need me any more; if I went back I'd be a spare wheel. So my application for Strathclyde, permanently, is in the hat with the rest.'

'And you will get it, especially after all those headlines you got when you found that Australian fraudster.'

Bob laughed. 'You ain't kidding. The day I moved into Pitt Street, I inherited an invitation to address an Australian Police Federation conference. Since then I've had twenty-two more, from other organisations down under. Yes, I know I'll probably be confirmed in post. If not, I'll do something else. I might even retire and buy a boat.'

'And sail away, with Sarah and the kids?'

'They're all too young, and she's not ready.'

'It's cool, though? You and her?'

'Honestly? It is, for the first time really. We've discovered that being nice to each other, all the time, is all it takes.'

'Maybe I'll try that, next time.'

'Some chance of that,' he scoffed. 'You're a politician. By the way,' he added, 'the Turnberry tape did exist, kept carelessly by Toni in a plain envelope that I found deep in the desk that is currently mine. It does not exist any longer.'

'Thank you,' she whispered. 'To be honest, I was really worried about that, and not for Mrs Graham's sake.'

'It's nothing to be concerned about any more,' he replied, 'but this is.' He took an envelope from a slim document case that he had brought with him.

She took it from him and her face paled, as she studied its contents: two photographs of her, with two other women, in a ladies' toilet.

'What are . . . Bob, I think I know when those were taken, but . . .'

'You have to give up the booze, Aileen,' he said. 'You must. I didn't realise you had a problem, maybe because whenever we had a drink at home, you went straight to sleep, or else you got amorous and I put it down to my fatal attraction. But that's twice you've courted potential disaster, not counting the Morocco fiasco.'

'How did you get these?'

He smiled. 'The strangest thing happened a few weeks back.

407

Amanda Dennis called all her Scottish team down to London for a two-day performance review. While they were gone, somebody broke into their office, and opened the safe. I don't think they even know it happened, not yet. All that was taken were those photos, and the master tape. It's in there too. Somehow they found their way into my possession.'

She gazed at him. 'You know, I could fall in love with you.'

'Nah, you didn't before, so how could you now?'

She laughed. 'Okay. Then how about a farewell shag? We could get a room.'

He shook his head. 'I'm sworn to be faithful. You should try it too. Besides, someone would be bound to photograph us. For example . . .'

He took another, larger envelope from the document case. 'These are my parting gifts to you, Aileen, and my greatest. Where you're going to be after your by-election, these will represent your ticket straight to the front bench, and a fast track to the shadow Cabinet. In this package you will see Toni Field doing what she did best. You'll also recognise the bloke she's doing it to, and I think you will find that you know his wife too. The stupid bloody woman actually believed I wouldn't make copies! That same lady had you set up by those two scrubbers, who are, incidentally, no longer Security Service staff, and tried to use your moment of weakness to club me into submission and silence.'

He lifted his glass and drank a toast, to her, to them, to their past, and to their separate futures.

'Use them wisely, choose your moment, and when you do, make certain sure that the damage to Emily Repton is terminal. "Provincial copper" indeed. Doesn't she bloody know that we're a nation?'

23.